THE
ORCHID
TREE

THE ORCHID TREE

VIRGINIA COFFMAN

F

Coff

THORNDIKE PRESS • THORNDIKE, MAINE

Library of Congress Cataloging in Publication Data:

Coffman, Virginia.
   The orchid tree.

   1. Large type books. I. Title.
   [PS3553.041507 1987]   813'.54   87-1890
   ISBN 0-89621-787-6 (lg. print : alk. paper)

Large Print edition available in North America by arrangement
with Arbor House Publishing Co.

Large Print edition available in the British Commonwealth by
arrangment with Abner Stein.

Cover design by Armen Kojoyian.

*For
Paul and Peggy Wigg,
with deep gratitude.
Along with my family's memories,
the true touches of the
Hawaiian Territory in 1935
are due to these good friends.
Any errors are my own.*

1

Late in the afternoon Tracie Berenson reached the searchers who had been on the tortuous climb since dawn.

They were led by their employer, Victor Berenson, thought of as "boss man" by his enemies and rivals. They had worked their way past the terraced patches of taro soaking on the slopes above Valley House, the Berenson home, and were on the mountain itself. By sunset, when Tracie caught glimpses of her father's big straw planter hat up ahead of her, the searchers were nearing the third highest peak in the Territory of Hawaii, called Mauna Pā-ele by the locals.

The Dark Mountain, though majestically beautiful with its awesome view of four islands and its dense coat of jungle vegetation, was no place on which to be caught alone. Only those born to the island, like Tracie herself, could find their way through the forests of ohia trees, the interlacing of ferns and thick brush, the slippery, moss-covered stones and the pervasive mudholes from springs and waterfalls.

After identifying her father's hat she saw him waving as he gave orders. It wasn't difficult to separate out his sunburned, craggy Scandinavian face from the deep olive and bronze of his Hawaiian and Oriental workers.

Tracie took after him in many ways. In her childhood she had resented the tomboy nicknames given her by her father's *haole*, white friends. She wanted to have dark mahogany flesh like the Hawaiians, who helped raise her after her mother's early death. Instead, Tracie's fair skin was forever peeling and she never could get a deep tan like the children of the field hands with whom she went to Plantation school. There was little color barrier in 1935 in the small, compact world which included the great Chinese lady of the Manchu court who had married and been widowed by Victor Berenson's brother and now lived with her two children in Valley House.

When Tracie's lanky form filled out slightly and her towhead became a free-flowing sandy mop the color of the island's few beaches, she discovered to her surprise and pleasure that her fellow students at college in Honolulu found her intriguing, even sexy. It did a lot to

8

build her self-esteem, and no one could ever accuse her now of shyness or an inferiority complex.

She was level-headed enough to know she would never be as beautiful as her petite, dark-eyed cousin Liliha, but she was generally better liked. The fact that most boys and not a few men were in awe of her didn't bother Tracie too much. They were easier to handle that way and always ended up doing what she wanted them to do.

Her fondest wish had been that Victor, her father, would marry her good friend Ilima Mako, Victor's secretary. Ilima had been both companion and second mother to Tracie, and with her gentle ways she had a calming influence on the volatile Victor. It was a mystery to Tracie that Ilima Mako should disappear only the night before her wedding to Victor.

It wasn't like her at all. Ilima, who was half Hawaiian, was never foolish, never impulsive. Even this marriage to one of the most powerful partners in the Territory hadn't made her move in haste. She clearly was not an ambitious woman. Tracie was positive that Ilima had agreed to marry Victor out of love and admiration, knowing also that he genuinely needed her. What endeared Ilima even more to Tracie was the knowledge that she was not unlike

9

Tracie's own mother, who had also been quiet, sweet and subservient to Victor, yet competent in her gentle way. Her death of pneumonia on Tracie's fourth birthday had deprived the headstrong little girl of much-needed control.

Victor needed that quiet restraint as well. He always had an eye for a pretty girl, but family came first with him. Until Ilima joined his household he had never given much thought to remarriage. Now, so many years later, there was a possibility that on the eve of her wedding, Ilima Mako was deserting Tracie and Victor as Tracie's mother had "deserted" them nineteen years ago. It just wasn't like Ilima. Except for her passionate and almost religious devotion to things Hawaiian, such as the beautiful orchid tree that grew outside her bedroom window, Ilima had always been too sensible to carry out such an absurd notion as calling off the wedding at the last minute.

Yet Ilima had sneaked out of the Berenson house the night before and had been seen before dawn on Mauna Pā-ele by two cane-field workers who were gathering strawberry guavas. She appeared to be weeping, but why? What could have drawn her away from those who loved her?

Tracie threaded her way between the clinging, tickling branches of tree ferns. She tried to

10

tell herself that Ilima Mako, a small woman, might be hidden within all this jungle growth. Maybe she had slipped, hit her head. There were waterfalls, thin as a thread, that plunged down the north and east faces of Mauna Pā-ele. Poor Ilima might be lying in a rainpool amid the jungle growth at the top of those falls.

Tracie called to her father as she hurried to catch up with him. "Any sign?"

"That you, Trace?" Impatient as always, he pushed aside the fern barrier and raised his arms, as if despairing of her. "What the devil are you doing up here alone? You could have slipped, broke your neck. Anything."

"Oh, dad! I'm not an infant. I know Pā-ele as well as you do."

His arm, still reasonably lean but a lot bonier at sixty, closed around her until he gave her backside a hard slap. "Don't brag to your pappy. You never saw the day you could scale Pā-ele alone. No, we haven't found any sign of her. Frankly, I can't figure Ilima out at all. Maybe she's just playing some idiotic game with me. Trying to be cute."

Tracie shivered, feeling cold suddenly. "No. You know she wouldn't. Ilima isn't that . . . Has anyone gone down the east face yet?" She bit her tongue, remembering Victor's recent heart trouble, which he disparagingly referred to as "that little flareup I had." She was now sorry to have mentioned the dangerous area on the windward side of the mountain.

Mauna Pā-ele's sheer vertical surface was marked by jungle growth, and the deep chasm at the base appeared to be as soft as green feathers. Victor glanced at the peak only fifty feet above them where the men were gathering under the curtain of tangled ohia and ferns.

Tracie was afraid her father would insist on doing something outrageous, like lowering himself down the face of Mauna Pā-ele, so she tried to turn his thoughts to less dangerous points for the search. "Have the men followed that old trail down the south spur to the sugar mill?"

The trail had long since been overgrown by fern forests and the creeping branches of hau trees which entwined any living plant in their way. But sugar-cane workers used it occasionally during the fall cane-burning season, and the great Berenson flumes, carrying water overhead, crossed the trail on its lower level.

She might have known. Victor was ahead of her there, too. "Covered it. Leo Haupa broke his leg, by the way. Had to be carted back to the mill. That means we lost three good men for this damned search... Trace, what the hell is Ilima pulling? If she doesn't want to marry me, all she has to do is say so. What does she think I am, an ogre?"

She was touched by this slight hint of his own vulnerability and patted his arm.

"Of course not, dad. Besides, Ilima loves you." She seldom confessed to anything that would give her father more fuel for his enormous ego, but she added now, "Ilima told me only a few nights ago that she feels she has loved you all her life." She made a small joke based on truth. "When you proposed she was so excited she broke out in a rash. Remember how she blushed when you told her to get a honeymoon wardrobe and charge it to her married name?"

She had tried to make the comment light but he was too worried to smile. He looked back at his men busy beating the thickets and calling Ilima's name.

"Well, I'm already getting looks from a few of the *kanakas*...like they thought the girl was running away from me. My God! She wouldn't run off and leave me flat...make me the laughing stock of the Territory."

Of course, she thought with wry understanding, he *would* think of this whole business as a plot to hurt him, not Ilima.

"Daddy, they all know that...Have you tried the fern forest where the Ribbon Falls drop off to the north?"

"It's an idea." He started back up through the thicket.

Tracie pushed the cuffs of last year's slacks into her boots and readjusted her leather poncho. This would protect her body from the mist surrounding the series of pools at the top of the needle-thin falls. Her hair beat across her face in the breeze and she impatiently pushed the long, tawny strands as she followed her father.

She was deeply worried. In spite of the reassuring attitude that she showed her father, she suspected Ilima had been troubled for some days, perhaps even weeks, over something. At the same time there was no doubt in Tracie's mind, as she had told her father, that Ilima loved him. She was well over thirty and had never really seemed to care for any other man during the years Tracie had known her.

Coming from the nearby island of Molokai to live on Akua Island when Tracie was home from college after her sophomore year, Ilima soon fell under the spell of Akua's dominant planter. Victor had taken the young woman for granted during the next two years until she nursed him through a debilitating case of shingles. Unlike Tracie, Ilima had shown compassion and understanding when Victor exploded several times a day, demanding service from everyone, asking heaven and even the old

14

Hawaiian gods what he had done to deserve such a curse.

No one could have been happier than Ilima when she started to plan her wedding. What had happened to give her brown eyes that haunted look and to make her so jumpy the last month or so?

At the time Lili had laughed at Tracie's concern. "Why wouldn't she be nervous? Walking into all that money. She knows she's robbing the rest of us blind. And Uncle Vic most of all."

Tracie was well aware of how the rest of the Berensons felt about Ilima. They had lived their entire lives in the comfortable conviction that they and Tracie were Victor's sole heirs, and could only consider the young woman a threat.

At the age of twenty-three Tracie didn't share their fears. She was sure she could make her own way in life on whatever her father left her, plus her own initiative.

She neatly sidestepped the slippery, moss-covered rocks hidden among the ferns and made her way toward the Ribbon Falls. The trail was so close to the edge of the cliff that one turn of the ankle would send her plunging down through ferns and thickets to the swampy base of Mauna Pā-ele almost three thousand feet below. The men were ahead of her, beating the brush around the rainpool at the head of the falls. It was unlikely that she would see anything the others had missed, but she stopped and looked straight down. It was a dizzying experience even now.

Ten years earlier Lili and her brother Theo, always a sly, mischievous boy, had secretly enticed Tracie up to this spot and threatened to throw her puppy over the cliff. To ransom him she had been forced to promise Lili her best eight-by-ten glossy of Rudolph Valentino, the reigning sex idol of 1925. Theo's reward for aiding his sister was the ten dollars Tracie had received for her birthday.

But that wasn't all her enterprising cousins received...When the puppy was safe Tracie had bitten Theo in the palm, knocked him down and kicked one of his teeth loose. Lili received the coveted photograph — but torn in two. Tracie's revenge earned her a certain local notoriety, along with a healthy respect from her cousins. Tracie thrived on it.

Today when she looked down she remembered the big, brown eyes of her puppy and the fear she had felt at imagining him tumbling into that abyss. Now she could only imagine Ilima lying somewhere at the bottom of the mountain. Tracie blinked, angry that she could entertain the possibility of it even for a moment.

She got down on her knees. The east side of the cliff was in shadows, but she could still make out the flowers, like bursts of flame, that brightened the deep, luxuriant green of the cliff's face. She was startled by her father coming up behind her.

Tracie got halfway up and stiffened her back, with all her weight on her knees. "Daddy, where is she?"

He peered over. The first wisps of night fog curled upward from the swampy pools below. In an hour it would be impossible to see anything but the lacy white Pacific combers rolling in toward the shore. "I don't know, honey. Maybe she's back home by now."

She wanted desperately to believe him. "If we could just be sure! But dad—" She hardly dared to mention her new fear. "Suppose one of those spots down there isn't a lehua flower?"

Victor dropped to his knees on the pad of ferns and grass and looked down the face of the pali. "Can't you be a little more cheerful, girl? Those puffballs are lehuas. They've always grown here. Besides, Ilima would never wear red. It isn't her style."

"No. You're right. She wouldn't." But relief was only momentary. The bright bundle of color on a dripping ledge halfway down the face of the cliff was too vivid for a single flower. "Dad...the raincoat I bought last time we were in San Francisco is bright red."

"Sometimes I wonder where you get your imagination. Not from my side of the family, I can tell you."

Nevertheless, the appalling idea had taken hold of Victor. He waved to his foreman, the big Hawaiian, Sam Kahana, broad-faced, with copper skin and brown eyes so deep that when Tracie was a child she thought God must look like Sam. His heavy lips framed a smile that told her all was right with the world. He was the only man who could throw Victor in the wrestling matches they used to wage when both men were younger and stronger. At one time Victor had offered Sam a spread of his own, but the two men had been friends from birth and Sam preferred to run Orchid Tree, the corporate name of the great Berenson properties on the "Dark Island."

Sam weighed just under three hundred pounds, of which very little was fat. He was the only person besides Tracie who could, and often did, contradict Victor. He rumbled over to the edge of the pali, spread his sandaled feet and looked down.

"We need more light. All shadows down there."

18

It was ominous to Tracie that he didn't seem surprised.

"Well, get a light, for Christ's sake! Do I have to think of everything?"

"Not so's you'd notice."

Victor gave him a look but Sam only returned it and went off to find a light. The flashlight produced by the manager of the sugar mill was far from adequate, and while Tracie leaned farther over the edge, trying to convince herself that she had merely seen a clump of lehua flowers, several flaring lights appeared behind her. She realized some of the field hands had lighted kukui torches.

This gave a better view of the area about a quarter of the way down, but the breeze off the ocean only a few hundred feet from the base of the cliff sent the flames from the torches slanting backward into the lush growth around the searchers.

"Somebody get me ropes," Sam Kahana said calmly.

"Now see here," Victor began. "With that blubber of yours you'll snap the rope like twigs. You hold on up here. I'm going down."

"Daddy, for heaven's sake!" Tracie caught herself before she added, Act your age, but nothing would have been more likely to send him over the pali to prove a point.

19

To Tracie's intense relief several men volunteered and a wiry young Filipino, nicknamed Rudi after the late film star, was chosen. Rudi Arguello had begun life, like so many of his countrymen, as a hardworking hand in the cane fields, but he was ambitious and pleasant. Slender and good-looking with a profile often compared to that of Rudolph Valentino, Rudi had broken quite a few hearts among the girls at South Harbor, where the Akua sugar mill was one of the island's major enterprises. But he managed to keep his personal life carefully separated from his job as Victor's chauffeur and aide at the house.

Victor grumbled that no rope would reach far enough, while Tracie kept hoping the young Filipino would be able to manage the tricky descent and get back safely without having found anything.

She knelt with arms stretched, trying to help steady the rope, but Sam Kahana held it firm. Behind him two of the men had tied the end around the roots of an ohia tree. Her father gripped another rope, dangling it beside Rudi Arguello as a safety measure.

With a coil of rope over his shoulder Rudi flashed his best smile for Tracie as he slipped down the cliff, gradually disappearing into the shadows below the flaring torchlight. Tracie was terrified for fear the rope would break or Rudi would lose his grip, but the men now gathered at the top of the cliff urged Rudi on, as if this were a demonstration of the young man's athletic prowess.

He got a foothold on a ledge-cave near the end of his rope, unwound the auxiliary rope and tied it securely to a tough ohia root and around solid rock. Then he descended again, below the torchlight. Above him the tense searchers waited.

Tracie felt her father beside her, stiff and apprehensive. She didn't look at him, knowing he must have come to share her fears, and she didn't want that confirmation.

Rudi was swallowed up by darkness for what seemed like endless minutes. Then he became visible again, scrambling up to the first ledge. He left the second rope dangling and tugged on the original rope. Tracie realized the significance of that. There was something below the ledge that would require another trip down. She gulped down a half-audible cry.

Speechless and looking pale in the torchlight, Victor gave Rudi a hand as he regained his footing on the ledge. The youth shuddered and someone threw a jacket over his shoulders. He was wet to the skin from the perennial moisture that dripped over the brink of the pali.

21

Sam Kahana's deep voice asked the question. "Is she there?"

Rudi's dark eyes welled up with tears. Like most of the Berenson people, he had admired and respected Ilima Mako.

He slowly nodded.

2

Ilima Mako's funeral attracted an unexpectedly large group of mourners, in part due to the prominence of her fiancé. Ilima herself had always been reserved, even secretive about her family and background; so there were no personal acquaintances to be notified. But from every island in the Territory the boats began pulling in to the little bay called Akua City.

The five-day voyage from California made it impossible for Victor's mainland friends to arrive before the funeral, though Tracie replied to cables and letters of sympathy from as far away as the White House and even Buckingham Palace. The dashing and popular Prince of Wales had met Victor Berenson in India, where both men had enjoyed the hospitality of the viceroy.

One cable from Bill Dempster, Victor's fiercest business rival, provoked Tracie to anger because it cut close to the bone. It simply read, "Why?"

The inconsiderate nerve of him, Tracie thought...as if she hadn't asked herself that same question a thousand times since Ilima's broken body was raised and brought to Valley House by Sam Kahana, Rudi Arguello and two of the cane workers. The death was ruled a suicide, and the testimony of several of the house servants confirmed it when they reported to the coroner from Honolulu that Ilima had been despondent and acting strangely for the last few weeks. It was generally assumed that the gentle woman couldn't bring herself to marry Victor and hadn't wished to hurt him by telling him so. Suicide hardly seemed the answer to that, but no one could contradict her actions now.

Following a brief service Ilima's coffin had been dropped into the glistening blue waters of the channel between Akua and Molokai. That night Victor found Tracie in the den of the plantation house, finishing the last thank-you notes for the many letters and flowers received, while her cousin Lili stamped envelopes and Theo sat with them, absently fingering his uncle's various athletic awards and trophies that were displayed in the room.

Victor quietly walked over to his daughter and sat in a large chair next to the desk where she was working. "She loved me, you know.

24

I could never doubt that. When I kissed her goodnight that last—" He cleared his throat. "Don't anyone ever doubt she loved me." For the first time, Tracie thought, Victor looked old — his shock of gray hair showed new streaks of white.

"I know, dad. It was something else. Maybe some day we'll know. Don't think about it yet... Why don't you go on down to the cove where Sam and the boys are spear-fishing? You'll get good and tired and sleep like a baby."

"I always sleep like a baby," Victor said gruffly. He got up and stalked out of the room, and as Tracie watched him she couldn't help noticing how his shoulders had slumped, his walk was slower than usual. His reaction to Ilima's suicide was Tracie's greatest worry now. She was certain that what he had called a bad case of heartburn two months ago had actually been a minor heart attack, but nobody could get Victor Berenson to a hospital while he was still on his feet.

Lili had watched her uncle speculatively, then turned her attention to Theo. "Those awards aren't your sort, brother dear. Why don't you come over and make yourself useful? Stick out your tongue to lick and I'll stamp."

Theo wrinkled his nose and made a face at her. Slim and good-looking, though without his sister's dark beauty, he had a certain impudent charm that got him over a lot of rough spots. There was a distinct resemblance between Theo, who was twenty-four, and his twenty-one-year-old sister. With the Berenson confidence and the dark good looks of their mother, Tracie's Aunt Jade, who had been a beauty in her day, they were used to the comforts that came to them at Valley House. It came as a shock when Tracie reached maturity and they realized that the gawky towhead had inherited more than just the legitimate blood of Victor Berenson — one day she was expected to take over his territorial empire.

Lili and Theo, whose easygoing father had furnished the capital and land for his brother's first ventures, reaped a reasonable reward over the years following his death. Although they lived in style without the necessity of working, they had no power. While the two cousins would have welcomed a more favored position with their uncle, their mother, Jade Wong Berenson, clearly resented her lack of involvement in the running of the Berenson empire more than they did. Tracie often suspected that Aunt Jade, for all her aristocratic Chinese reserve, had loved Victor through the years after her husband's death. Perhaps even before.

But no one, not even Jade's children, ever

knew what Jade really thought; so Lili continued to use her undoubted good looks in her effort to overcome Tracie's natural advantages, and Theo practiced the belief that charm would get him practically everywhere, even with Uncle Victor.

Tracie looked up from the stack of condolence messages and studied her cousins.

"You two got awfully chummy with Ilima this last month or two. I was surprised."

Brother and sister exchanged glances. Theo flashed Tracie his most winning smile. "You know what they say — if you can't lick 'em, join 'em."

Lili backed him up quickly. "It's just that Ilima is — was — such as generous character. We just figured she might put in a good word for us with Uncle Victor after they got married. Maybe raise my allowance. And put Theo in charge of the Honolulu inter-island traffic. It's easy for you — you run the bookkeeping side of Orchid Tree. But you've been so damned snooty about giving Theo a break."

"I believe in getting my money's worth. Theo may be nearly twenty-five but he has as much business sense as a jellyfish."

Theo stopped fingering the trophies and tossed a paper clip at her. "Some jellyfish carry a sting," he said, teasing her. He flipped over the condolence messages until one caught his eye — the cable from Reno, Nevada, with the single-word message. "Hey, what's this?" he said, holding it up. "Is that all Bill Dempster sent? I thought he was a friend of Ilima's."

"He ordered a pikake lei and a maile-leaf wreath." Tracie crumpled up the cable. "Obviously he wants to know why she died. But he's not the only one. I mean to find out for myself."

There was an uncomfortable silence until Lili finally spoke. "Half the funeral guests were saying Ilima did it because she couldn't face marrying a man old enough to be her father," she said, her tone holding the hint of a challenge.

"If she had a father," Theo added.

Tracie waved him away. "You can forget the nasty comments. Ilima was an orphan."

Theo persisted. "I'd say he's lost his touch, uncle has. Couldn't hold a woman. Even a *hapa-haole* like Ilima."

Tracie got up, shoving her chair back. It made a scratchy, irritating noise across the lauhala mat. The sound matched her mood.

"If there is one thing the Berensons have never done, it's make remarks like that. I don't know of any old *kamaaina* family like ours that does. We all have half-whites in the family tree. You ought to know better than anyone. Why

28

don't you ask your mother?"

Lili muttered something but Theo merely laughed. "Wounded where I live. Okay, I'll go...Lili, are you through licking and stamping?"

Lili ignored him and he finally left the den. She watched the door close before she got up, set the envelopes on Tracie's desk and held one up between a dainty thumb and forefinger.

"I'm glad you're sending a thank-you to Bill Dempster. He may be uncle's rival but we meet him everywhere in Honolulu. I happen to like him."

"The thank-you is for the lei and the wreath. Ilima loved pikake flowers. But I guess he knew it. He seemed to know her better than any of us did." Curious at her cousin's interest in Bill Dempster, she looked at Lili.

Bill Dempster wasn't hard to take. Tracie admitted to herself that his looks appealed to her, and he was certainly more exciting than his nephew Wayne Croyde, the University of Hawaii football star whom Tracie was dating. But Bill Dempster seemed much too aggressive, too opinionated to be really attractive, Tracie thought. And he had a way of saying things that led Tracie to suspect he was making fun of her — not something she was accustomed to. And she still hadn't forgiven him for calling her — according to Wayne — a spoiled young colt in need of breaking to the saddle.

"Better watch yourself," Tracie said, "Dempster has a wife, remember?"

"No, he doesn't. He's been in Reno and today's *Star-Bulletin* says he and that actress are divorced."

"Not very gallant. You mean he got the divorce?" Sounded just like him!

Lili shrugged. "He just wouldn't put up with her shenanigans, probably. Anyway, he's free." Lili winked and giggled.

Tracie was both relieved and sorry when Lili left her to go down to the spear-fishers. The two cousins often annoyed Tracie with their frivolity, though their incessant gossip sometimes gave her some valuable information.

If Bill Dempster *had* divorced his movie-star wife, Tracie thought, there had to be a division of property, and Marta would certainly want to turn her share into cash. She was an expensive luxury for anyone, even herself. Victor might make an excellent bargain with her over some of the property received in the divorce.

The day had been busy enough so that Tracie had little time to think about Ilima, but when she finally closed her leather writing case and put the fountain pen away, her friend's presence seemed everywhere. The sound of one of the servants calling to a child reminded her of Ilima's gentle voice. In the hall that was dimly lighted by the newly installed electric light, she imagined for an instant that she heard the sweep of Ilima's long Hawaiian *holoku* over the reed mats. But perhaps it was only the persistent scratching of Ilima's beloved orchid tree against her bedroom window.

Tracie didn't believe in ghosts, but she knew that Ilima had, and tonight she shivered, shaken by the unanswered questions prompted by Ilima's plunge to her death over the sheer pali.

She looked out across the east lanai toward the shrouded hulk of Pā-ele looming there. She repeated Bill Dempster's question silently.

Why, Ilima? We loved you, daddy and I. We needed you. If you didn't want to marry him, he would have understood.

In the perfumed tropic night the bright faces of the hibiscus and the tiny orchids on their long stems nodded gently as the evening breeze came up. Uncomfortably aware of all those pale, moving blossoms that seemed to follow her as she turned away, Tracie repeated the stubborn argument she clung to. Ilima had been happy, though there was always the silence about her past. She was an orphan raised by a planter and his wife on Molokai, and her foster parents were now dead. Who — or what —

could have troubled her so? Ilima was not a woman who talked about herself anyway, so if something had been bothering her, Tracie knew she would be the last to know. But she couldn't have changed her mind about Victor so suddenly – Tracie couldn't remember a time when Ilima hadn't loved him.

No. Whatever terrible impulse drove her to make the hard climb up Pā-ele, it hadn't been the prospect of marrying Victor...What then?

Tracie's eyes burned and she knew she was going to cry again.

She concentrated instead on what she should do about the old plantation house, now that it would be without a new mistress. It should be modernized a bit, she thought, but they would eventually have to get rid of all that rattan and bamboo furniture. Someday she would have to face Ilima's room, but Tracie couldn't bring herself to take care of her friend's things now...not yet.

Tracie's sleep for the next few nights was full of dreams, nightmarish visions of Ilima Mako's face. It was always blurred, as if seen through tears, but they were Ilima's own tears, and her fine Hawaiian eyes were haunted.

Tracie woke up half a dozen times during those nights. Once, stumbling across her room in the dim starlight, she locked her door. If she hoped to keep anyone out it was an exercise in futility. There were no locks on the long-louvered doors opening onto one of the two lanais that ran the length of the house, and if she thought she was locking out ghosts, her effort was even more useless.

Deeply buried in work and schemes, Victor seemed to recover from the loss of his fiancée and his self-esteem. He jumped at Tracie's idea of buying some of the Dempster holdings that they figured must have been settled on the divorced but unbowed Marta. No one knew the particulars of the divorce or why she hadn't contested it, but Marta's moral lapses, if any, didn't sway Victor when it came to getting the better of his business rival.

Tracie's family loyalty wavered somewhat during those first days when she noticed how everyone tried to avoid talk of Ilima. Before Victor showed an interest in her Theo and Lili had treated Ilima with a good-natured indifference almost amounting to contempt. While it was true that Ilima had been closest to Tracie, she *was* about to become a member of the family, Tracie reasoned, and shouldn't have been forgotten so quickly.

Aunt Jade had never been known to address a word to Ilima that didn't have something to do with the running of the household, which was Aunt Jade's province. But that wasn't surprising. Jade was almost as uncommunicative with her niece as she was with her brother-in-law. Jade Wong Berenson never forgot that her ancestors were chamberlains to the Manchu court when Victor Berenson's father, "Swede" Berenson, was fighting New Mexico's Lincoln County War beside Billy the Kid.

One hazy autumn morning after a night troubled by what sounded to Tracie like scuffling sounds in the dark — no doubt a small rodent — she got up before her usual 7 A.M. and decided to talk to Chin Loo, the family cook, who was one of the first to report Ilima's disappearance. Was it possible they had all overlooked some clue to Ilima's suicide?

She scooped out the golden pulp of a papaya half and watched as Chin Loo brought his famed pineapple waffle into the breakfast room.

"Chin, you were a friend of Miss Mako's, weren't you?"

"Sure was." He was a short Chinese man with an unperturbable air about him who had had the same youthful look for as long as Tracie could remember. Victor had bribed him away from the Moana Hotel on Waikiki Beach twelve years earlier and he was considered one of the finest chefs in the Territory.

"Well, think now, Chin. Did you notice anything about Ilima that last night? Anything... odd?"

"Odd? Maybe yes, maybe no. Miss Ilima, she was real nice. She did not please Lady Jade, but Lady Jade, she doesn't like the women around the boss. Maybe she thought Miss Ilima would take over from her."

He had long ago given Tracie's aunt a title to fit her aristocratic bearing, but his idea about Ilima was ridiculous.

Tracie smiled as she cut into the waffle. "No one could be less bossy, no matter whom she married...Did Aunt Jade ever nag her in any way?"

Chin waited expectantly for her compliment on the waffle. She gave it with enthusiasm and he bowed his acceptance before he answered her question.

"Lady Jade, she does not nag. She is silent. It is her way. But I will tell you this. Miss Ilima — she was sad. So sad. I cannot say why."

"You cannot? Or you will not?"

"She was sad for maybe a month. Maybe two. One day I saw her cry. Back there in pantry. I say can I help her and she say nobody can. I say — excuse, please — I say, Mister Vic he won't make you marry if you don't wish and she says this funny thing. She says, I wish it and he wishes it. She looked very sad, like she was thinking of something, then she just said 'Oh, my God.' That's all. Then she left." He took up the dish with the papaya rind. "I felt very sorry for her. But when they found her I thought, it is most natural. She was so sad."

"But damn it, why?"

He shook his head and went back to the kitchen.

Tracie finished her waffle and coffee thoughtfully.

Afterward, she went out across the west lanai and headed for the barn and her mare, a vivid red sorrel named Namu. The mare had been her confidante since it was shipped to her from California the day she passed her entrance exams at the College of Hawaii.

At the southwest corner of the long, two-story wooden planter's house she stopped for a moment under the big orchid tree that had given Berenson's Orchid Tree Enterprises its corporate name. In the spring season the tree bore deep lavender flowers that Aunt Jade sometimes permitted as table decorations.

The influence of the tree itself went far beyond its height and imposing spread, with half a dozen slender rooted trunks. The orchid tree topped off just under the roof of the house, and its greedy branches, with their wide leaves, shut out half the light from Victor Berenson's upstairs corner bedroom. Perhaps it was this very power of the tree that made Victor admire it so.

Others in the household were less appreciative. Its many slim trunks made the tree look top-heavy, which it was, and even Aunt Jade agreed that it seemed the slightest wind would break its back and send those high green branches toppling over the house and onto anyone standing beneath it.

Ilima Mako's bedroom was also on that corner of the house, below Victor's, and the huge leaves with its many branches must have kept her awake at night with their whispering noises against the louvered door and window of her room. But for some reason Ilima found the tree companionable.

Tracie, on the contrary, had never liked it. She studied the orchid tree now. She heard nothing but the pleasant rustle of an autumn breeze through the thick, dark leaves. Could this have been part of Ilima's trouble? Had she allowed all the island legends to prey on her imagination? Long, long ago a Hawaiian princess had leaped from the cliff of Mauna Pā-ele to appease the gods after a devastating hurricane. Perhaps Ilima, too, had convinced herself for some obscure reason that she didn't deserve happiness.

Tracie remembered her own fears recently during her sleepless nights. Out here on the island, far from San Francisco's bright lights, the old gods seemed very near. Who knew what power they still might possess to affect a mind attuned to their ancient splendor and their terror?

Victor Berenson himself was in awe of the nature that daily encroached upon Valley House from all directions. The valley was almost a thousand feet above the sea-level shanties, frame buildings and the single pier, a jetty, that made up Akua City. But even at this height the plantation house was overshadowed by the tangled jungle growth that threatened each year to weave an impenetrable net over the old building.

Tracie started to break off a leaf but her fingers pulled back suddenly. There was nothing sinister about the tree, she assured herself. Yet she knew that her father believed Orchid Tree Enterprises would last as long as the orchid tree stood — more superstition, she had to admit.

Tracie pushed her thoughts of the tree aside and walked on past the new building they used

38

as a garage and on to the barn. Rudi Arguello, originally hired away from the cane fields to chauffeur the family in Victor's elegant Packard, had found little work to do in his new position. There was only one fairly decent dirt road and it merely led down to the harbor, so he spent his extra time grooming the horses, a task he clearly loved.

He turned the sorrel over to Tracie, who was impressed as always by his care of Namu. The mare had been so named because the family claimed she spoke gibberish to them but Tracie never had the slightest difficulty understanding her snorts, tossing head and toothy smiles.

By the time Tracie got out on the trail to the sugar mill she was more confused than ever by Chin Loo's story. To make matters worse, as soon as she reached the long spur of Mauna Pā-ele that separated Valley House from the cane fields, she saw that the air was full of acrid smoke so thick the piercing blue sky to the south was blotted out. It was late autumn and they were burning over the fields to free the precious sugar cane from the brush, leaves and debris.

She hesitated, puzzling Namu, who had been given her head and was now hauled up sharp. Tracie patted her withers in apology.

"Sorry. I was thinking."

Namu swung her head, seemed to give her a side-glance as if she understood.

She gave Namu a gentler signal and the mare ambled over the spur of Pā-ele onto the path leading down across the cane fields. Berenson's Orchid Tree Enterprises owned thirty-seven percent of the sugar refinery stock. It was a majority interest, but even that didn't satisfy Victor, who felt that the success of the company threatened what he liked to think of as his unofficial sovereignty of the island. There were other landowners, including a formidable lady called "Ma" McCallister, whose fields bordered Orchid Tree to the north, but Victor persisted in thinking of himself as a kind of uncrowned king. Since Berenson paid better than most, his employees both in the field and the household were happy to think of their boss as lord of the land.

Tracie rode down the grade and onto the truck route that circled the fields. She passed a number of truckers and field hands whom she had known most of her life. She waved to them, and as was her custom, asked about their families and made mental notes about various problems. Leo Haupa, who had broken his leg during the search, was having trouble supporting his wife and their five children. His family would have to be helped until he could return to work, she noted. Two other workers had gambled away their salaries for the past month, and even while she scolded them Tracie knew she would lend them enough to keep them from starving.

It was during times like this that Tracie found herself questioning the Berenson stand against unionization. It was a preposterous idea that the Territory's five or six landowners should submit to the discipline of the mainland unions, with all their concomitant rules, raises and strikes. The unions would never get a foothold in the Territory. Everybody knew that. This was 1935 and if they hadn't gotten in yet, they never would. Still, some of the conditions in the fields resembled peonage. She rode along the seashore past the workers' little cottages whose bare utility was pleasantly masked by hibiscus, bougainvillea and some stunted rose bushes that looked almost plain in their exotic surroundings. Tracie couldn't help briefly wondering if unionization wasn't the fairest manner in which to support their workers...

Riding alongside the rough coral shoreline, she found the two Murikami brothers, who had been picking strawberry guavas the night Ilima Mako left Valley House for the last time. They were dragging their outrigger be-

41

yond the coral outcroppings.

"Sorry to bother you," she yelled. "Can I talk to you, just a minute?"

They were polite as always but made gestures to indicate they couldn't hear her. They moved out into deep water beyond the green and foamy surf, climbed into the long canoe and began to row. Feeling vaguely annoyed that she would have to wait to speak to them some other time, she headed the sorrel back onto the path, still looking back at the outrigger and its two occupants. Namu stopped suddenly as a hand reached for the reins. Startled, Tracie found herself looking into the cool eyes of Bill Dempster.

"Don't look so indignant, Miss B. I'm not on your property — yet." His amusement at her fury didn't help matters.

"You idiot! You could have broken my neck. Never take the reins like that. Namu might have bolted."

"Don't be silly. You're talking to an old hand — one of my horses won the Derby. Fleet-footed Dempster, I'm known as."

She didn't recognize the nickname and passed it off as she tried to regain her composure. Dempster couldn't possibly know how it infuriated Tracie to have anyone else, even her father, take Namu's reins from her. Namu had a delicate mouth and Tracie regarded Rudi Arguello as the only other person with a light enough touch to handle the high-strung sorrel.

He started to caress Namu's flank, and curiously enough, Namu seemed to love it. This should have pleased Tracie, and she felt the inconsistency of it when it merely annoyed her further. But she couldn't afford to let her temper get the better of her in dealing with this rival. She must be as cool as he was.

What had Ilima called him? Warm. Kindhearted. She must have been blinded by — one had to admit it — his compelling personality. Tracie admitted that he *was* rather attractive, if you liked the type.

"What are you doing on Akua, Mr. Dempster?"

He kept stroking Namu, and the mare acted as if she'd purr if she could. "Me? Just combining business with—" He gave her an odd, searching look, then shrugged. "With sympathy to your family. You know, I was fond of Ilima and felt a bit responsible for her after her foster parents died. I wanted to pay my respects. Have the Berensons put a *kapu* on the whole island? You don't own it yet, do you?"

Victor acted as if he wanted to, Tracie ruefully acknowledged to herself. But a keep-out sign wouldn't stop aggressive men like Bill

43

Dempster. His Dorado Star products had already moved in on the islands of Oahu and Molokai. What did he need with Akua?

"No *kapu* signs as far as we are concerned, even on Berenson land. We just have a slogan: 'Hawaii for the Hawaiians.' But when you do enter our property, you are welcome — as a guest." She tired quickly of this cat-and-mouse game, wanting to know the real reason behind his visit. "What are you really here for, Mr. Dempster?" she blurted out suddenly.

He strode along beside Namu with one hand still on the reins. His eyes held an amused glint in them — exactly what had always disturbed her about the man. When he spoke she realized she had left herself open to his amusement.

"I won't comment on your slogan, my Hawaiian friend. As for my visit to Akua, as I say, there were several reasons. Is there any place here that serves a decent meal?"

"Not for a *malahini* — a newcomer like you."

She could hardly send him to the tiny sashimi place near the mill. He looked as if he dined at the Royal Hawaiian Hotel on Waikiki whenever he felt the need for a snack. He might be wearing slacks and a chamois jacket, but they were obviously custom-tailored. The only polite solution was to bring him home to Valley

House. Victor would probably have a fit, forgetting all the phony friendliness he and Bill usually showed each other on visits to Honolulu when each was probably bent on outsmarting the other. But Lili would be delighted by Bill's visit, and Tracie herself found the man stimulating, whatever else he might be.

He watched her face, the corner of his mouth twitching as if he wanted to laugh but was refraining for some reason.

"I have a very moderate appetite, you know. And my table manners, while not exactly the Queen's taste, have never made anyone leave the table in disgust."

She gave in at that and laughed. "Were my thoughts that transparent?"

"Beautifully. Clear as glass. You wondered how Orchid Tree Enterprises could profit if you invited me to lunch. You also wondered if you could stand the obnoxious fellow for two hours."

"Not at all." But it was a waste of time trying to match his cool sophistication. She smiled and added, "I have a friend from college who repeated something unflattering you said about me once."

He looked surprised. "Not our Wayne Croyde. I didn't know your fiancé was such a blabbermouth."

She noticed that he hadn't denied the conversation though. "He isn't my fiancé. He's just a friend."

"I certainly hope so. He's a nice boy, but not your sort at all. Poor devil! You'd chew him up and spit him out. However, he does think he's going to marry you."

"I can't help what Wayne Croyde thinks. Are you coming to lunch or not?"

"You mean I'm really invited inside the sacred walls? I'm overcome."

She cuffed Namu lightly so that the mare increased her step from a walk to a trot and Bill Dempster let go of the reins. By the time she looked behind her on the sugar mill trail to Valley House she saw Dempster striding along well behind her. He stopped to study the high flume that crossed over his head. When it came to business, he was certainly persistent. She laughed when spray from the flume spattered and startled him. He brushed the water away, then took off his jacket and slung it over one shoulder. Tracie could see why Lili was so infatuated with him. She had to admit he carried himself with a certain athletic grace that a rangy halfback like Wayne could never equal.

But of course, he had none of Wayne's dear, amiable good nature and clumsy helplessness. And if she *were* to marry him, Wayne would never interfere in her life, thank heaven! Maybe some day, after she'd tried everything she ever wanted to, she just might do it. If nothing else, it would certainly please her father.

When Namu crossed the rise marking the boundary of the Akua cane fields and the beginning of the Berenson plantation, Tracie pulled up and waited for Bill Dempster, who was taking his time. Namu snorted impatiently, anxious to get back to the comfort and tidbits awaiting her in her stall.

Watching Dempster's casual approach, Tracie realized she still didn't know why he had come to Akua. She recalled that she had encountered him only a minute or two after the Murikami brothers pushed off in their outrigger. The proximity was too much of a coincidence; he must have read their testimony in the *Star-Bulletin* and sought them out, knowing they were the last to have seen Ilima before her suicide. That must have been why the brothers had avoided her... They must have discussed Ilima's death with Bill Dempster.

Could it be, Tracie thought, that in spite of his flirtatious, friendly manner, he was there for some sinister reason — could he actually believe that Victor, or any of the Berensons, for that matter, could be responsible for Ilima's death?

3

Tracie expected an explosion when her father walked into the dining room and saw his main competitor being wined and dined by his daughter. At least such a reaction would provide a suitable contrast – Dempster was sure to be frozen out by Aunt Jade.

Tracie's first surprise, which was something of a letdown, was the way Jade thawed in Bill Dempster's presence. Tracie first found her in the pantry with Chin Loo, discussing in some dialect the next order from Honolulu. She came out of the pantry still talking to Chin, and looked at both Tracie and Bill Dempster with an impassive stare.

Tracie introduced Bill to her; she inclined her head briefly. As usual, she was wearing one of her *paké* robes. The long Chinese brocaded silk surcoat with the narrow standing collar only accentuated the signified manner in which she carried herself. Though Victor and

Tracie ran the plantation and its associated enterprises, on the rare occasions when Jade Wong Berenson opened her mouth, the world of Valley House came to attention.

To Tracie's astonishment Bill started to speak in what sounded like the same Chinese dialect from around Peking that Jade and Chin Loo used with each other. Judging from Aunt Jade's expression, it certainly worked in his favor. For as long as Tracie could remember, Aunt Jade's cool dignity was enhanced by the way she crossed her wrists and concealed her hands in her sleeves. Today, however, she removed her hands and placed them on her thighs as she inclined her head slightly in a regal nod, adding a few words in her own parents' language and almost, if not quite, smiling. Since she evidently had no intention of explaining to Tracie, Bill did so.

"I mentioned to Lady Jade that my father was a great admirer of her parents, who served the dowager empress of China. Her father once presented my father to Her Imperial Majesty."

"Isn't that...something." There seemed to be no other comment possible. Tracie figured it would hardly be appropriate to remind Bill Dempster that the dowager empress had been considered something of an international villainess when Tracie went to school. Only thirty years ago the empress had tacitly supported the Boxer Rebellion against all those Western nations that made economic claims to parts of China. Such blindness to the advantages of "Western progress" had shocked the world and eventually toppled the Manchus.

Aunt Jade addressed herself to Tracie reproachfully: "If I had known my father's friend would share our wretched meal, I might have offered something more suitable."

Bill Dempster had not been her father's friend, but no one ever contradicted Aunt Jade — not even Theo, who was her favorite. She stayed behind now in the kitchen to supervise the making of the delicious little hors d'oeuvres that she called dim sum. Islanders were more likely to serve either Hawaiian or Japanese food. Dim sum, along with many other Chinese delicacies, was seldom prepared for *haoles*.

Tracie was maliciously amused to find that Liliha and Theo had gone off to Lahaina, Maui, on one of the Berenson inter-island cargo boats, and in spite of Lili's passion for Bill Dempster, she would miss the visit.

Tracie had to admit it: there was something appealing about him, and like it or not, she found herself attracted to him. If he treated her with indifference, she might have been indifferent to his charms, but as it was, she realized he was looking at her very much as Wayne and her ex-classmates at the university did, with a glint that seemed to consider what she would be like to kiss, to caress. She was far from insulted.

On the other hand she couldn't help wishing she had combed her hair or at least worn a nicer blouse than the brightly printed cotton one tucked into her slacks. She didn't want him to regard Victor Berenson's daughter as a simple little thing, used to nothing but the plantation.

She showed Bill around the lower floor of the house, and assumed he would take one of the wicker chairs on the west lanai until lunch was ready. Instead, he pointed to the orchid tree. Its wide, spreading branches had worked their way across a corner of the lanai, and he picked off a leaf, examining the dark twin lobes thoughtfully.

"This is the tree Ilima liked so much."

"It's beautiful around April," Tracie said. "The flowers aren't real orchids, or course, but they make lovely table decorations." Then the impact of his remark struck her. "When did you last see Ilima?"

He didn't seem surprised by her question.

"She was in Honolulu for a dentist appointment. She called to say hi, and I came by and took her to dinner."

"I remember. In June. She stayed overnight at the Moana." She added on a more urgent note, "Did she seem happy?"

"Perfectly. We talked about her father and the family that adopted her."

"You seem to know everyone's father."

Was it her imagination or had his mood become more serious, even constrained?

"You forget. I worked a couple of summers at a ranch on Molokai and out of Hilo on the Big Island. Anyway, she was obviously in love with old Vic." He grinned as she frowned. "Sorry, I mean Victor. That's the puzzling thing about her death. It doesn't make sense." He threw the leaf away.

"No, it doesn't," she said, watching it fall. "The tree branches and these big leaves flutter in the night. They used to keep Ilima awake. She seemed to think — well, it sounds silly, but she thought of it as her friend."

He looked out at the spreading, tentlike trees. "She was superstitious, I know...But what happened to affect her so suddenly? What led her to suicide when she was so obviously looking forward to her future with your father?"

Trees with spirits and unsolved mysteries all seemed far away at this moment, in the warm, smoky October air when Tracie heard a slamming door and her father's boots as he crossed the long, shadowy parlor floor between the lauhala mats. Her muscles tightened. Aunt Jade had stopped him near one of the louvered doors, spoke to him quietly. There was no mistaking Victor's ringing demand, "Well, what the hell is he doing here?"

Aunt Jade murmured something else to which Victor bellowed, "I don't care if he knows the king of Siam. What I want to know is — what's he want from me?"

Tracie glanced at Dempster and saw that he was silently amused. He seemed to enjoy Victor's crude display and would probably make a big story out of it all over Waikiki.

She waited uneasily for Victor's appearance, aware that Dempster was watching her, not the doorway. The next couple of minutes seemed like an eternity. She couldn't imagine what Victor was up to. But apparently he spent the time getting control of himself, for when he strolled out on the lanai he was in perfect command, standing straight, shoulders level and looking every inch the gracious master of Valley House. He extended a hand that Dempster gripped in a friendly fashion.

"Sorry, Dempster. I guess you heard my bellyaching. It's been a long morning — a little trouble in the papaya groves. That storm last month didn't do a hell of a lot of good. Cut down a full half of my crop."

Dempster reacted properly, though his competitor's crop failures could hardly arouse any genuine sympathy. "I know what you mean. They tell me my papayas on Oahu failed me entirely this year. Maybe I'll have to get a few pointers form Orchid Tree."

The two men chuckled at the absurdity of the notion of getting help from a rival. At the same time they did share common problems, and Tracie realized that men like this understood each other perhaps better than they understood trusted friends. The pause in their hostilities gave her a chance to excuse herself to freshen up, and she left the two men to each other.

To Tracie it was a relief to discover that Bill Dempster had come to Akua with no ulterior motive except to ask about the circumstances of Ilima's death and to offer his sympathy to the family. Maybe he wasn't such an unpleasant, scheming fellow...

She gave her wardrobe a quick run-through but all her nice, sexy clothes were formal wear, a toe-length satin cut on the bias and several slinky crepe de chine gowns. Her day-to-day affairs usually revolved around business, mostly keeping Victor's books and accounts. In her entire closet there was nothing even remotely alluring that could be worn in the daytime.

"I'll have to do something about you," she told her rack of clothes, and ended by brushing her hair, moistening her lips with her tongue and dabbing on a Caron perfume called Nuit de Noël that her father had brought her from San Francisco. She remembered how she'd dabbed it behind her ears and in the hollow between her breasts on the night she and Wayne made love in the back seat of his father's Chandler. She had felt very modern and daring that night but afterwards, when she realized she didn't love him with a blinding, all-consuming passion, she had been ashamed of giving in to his clumsy persistence.

They had driven up to the Nuuanu Pali above Honolulu on the night of her graduation from college, and parked on the dirt edge of that great cleft in the mountains. Before them, the dark green Koolau Range seemed to burst upward, its heights razor-sharp against the moonlit sky. One thing led to another and Wayne and Tracie made love, at best a fumbling, amateurish adventure since it was the first time for each of them.

The whole thing saddened her. As time went on Wayne seemed to fill her thoughts less and less, and she found it impossible to recapture that initial attraction. Maybe it hadn't been love, only the heady thought of belonging to the university's number-one football player. She was disgusted with her behavior... she had always detested her cousin Lili's teasing antics, and here she was doing the same thing.

She tried to tell herself and Wayne that they must not continue to make love so carelessly. The last thing she needed was to become pregnant! And while he may have been frustrated, he told her he respected her for her good sense.

Dear Wayne! He was so easy to deal with... But now there was this new entanglement. Wayne thought he was engaged to her. That would have to be set right in a way that wouldn't hurt him.

Coming downstairs Tracie wondered briefly if Ilima had been pregnant, but that problem would have been solved the next day when she married Victor. And it was absurd to think she may have had an affair with another man... She was totally devoted to Victor; if anything, she loved him too much. Lili had accused her more than once of "spoiling Uncle Victor rotten."

By the time Tracie reached the lower floor hall with its big new fan humming overhead, everyone had adjourned to the dining room.

This was a dark Victorian room with expensive but depressing ebony display cases of china and a black mahogany table and chairs that Tracie had lived with since Aunt Jade brought them into the house years ago. The long windows framed an ever-growing goldenrain tree and Tracie's favorite deep pink plumeria flowers, which sent their exquisite if overpowering scent throughout the lower floor of Valley House.

Victor and Aunt Jade sat at the two ends of the table, with Dempster on Jade's right and Tracie across from him. Ilima Mako was not mentioned during lunch, the conversation centering on bad crops and the possibility of unionizing the fields. All the same, Tracie had the distinct feeling that Dempster was thinking about Ilima when he glanced around the room, and that he was studying both Victor and Aunt Jade with those speculative blue eyes.

Tracie began to wonder...had Dempster and Ilima been more than good friends? Maybe he had been in love with her. She seemed mature to Tracie, but she was near Dempster's age which, according to Lili, was thirty-five. She quickly discarded the notion of a romantic relationship between them. Even if Dempster had loved her, it hadn't been the other way around.

"Unionize my boys? Never!" Victor insisted, punctuating this by rapping the handle of his butter knife on Aunt Jade's embroidered tablecloth. "My boys belong to Orchid Tree. As long as that tree out there stands, Berenson will look out for its own."

Dempster ignored the remark; instead he praised Aunt Jade's dim sum, obviously enjoying each tiny roll of shrimp, pork, chicken or deliciously seasoned fish served to him in his own miniature basket. He wasn't like most *malahinis*. Mainlanders were always so squeamish about "different" food, squid, poi and Tracie's own favorite, lomi-lomi salmon, the raw fish that was massaged under water, marinated and, in Tracie's opinion, heaven to eat.

Eventually, Victor got onto the subject of his powerful mainland bugbear, a certain longshoreman's union leader. Tracie knew that once launched, Victor could go on for hours.

"Dad," she interrupted, "Bill was an old friend of Ilima's family."

It took Victor a few seconds to switch from talk of a catastrophic strike in the San Francisco Bay area last year to the suicide of his fiancée, and he gave Tracie a reproachful glance. She knew the subject was still painful for him, having lost a woman he genuinely cared for, and Ilima's act had resulted in a great deal of gossip about him. People were still asking each other what he had done to make her kill herself, and for him the implication that she did so to avoid marrying him was embarrassing and painful.

Dempster seemed to recognize Victor's feelings as well as Tracie's motive in changing the subject.

"One of my first jobs in the Territory was for Ilima's adoptive parents, the Murtreys. They had a spread near Kaunakakai. Nice little property."

"Which you promptly gobbled up."

"Dad!"

But Dempster took it well. He said quietly, "On the contrary, sir. When the old gentleman died shortly before the crash of 'twenty-nine, Mrs. Murtrey asked me to take it off her hands."

"Pretty handy getting the widow's permission."

Dempster ignored him, now addressing Tracie and Jade.

"Anna Murtrey needed sizable loans to keep afloat. Dorado Star made them. When she died in 'thirty-one, her nephew took over. I believe he is still running it."

"And the loans?" Tracie asked. "Were they paid back by the nephew?"

Dempster must have understood that her question was sincere, not sarcastic. He shrugged.

"The loans were personal, out of friendship. Anna was a proud woman. She had insisted, so we went through the technicality. But it had nothing to do with her heir. The books closed at her death."

"That was very generous of you."

Victor raised his head sharply. "There's a fly in the ointment somewhere."

Jade interfered for the first time. "Victor, you have no manners. This man is our guest."

Tracie opened her mouth to agree, but Dempster neatly passed over the matter. "I wonder if one of your men would be good enough to show me where Ilima died. I thought I'd like to − I suppose you'd say − pay my respects, since there is no grave."

"I can show you," Tracie said quickly.

Dempster looked at her appreciatively and said, "Why, if it's not too much trouble, I'd appreciate that."

"Of course." She was pleased, even though he might have his own reasons for checking on the stories he had heard. She couldn't blame him for that. "But we'd better hurry. It's quite a climb."

Victor turned on her. "I forbid you! You know how difficult that trail is."

Tracie reached over and patted his shoulder.

"Dad, we'll be back before dark. You needn't worry. I'm not your daughter for nothing."

"If it's dangerous," Dempster broke in, "maybe one of your hands had better show me the way."

Tracie said this was an insult, and she was only half joking. The luncheon over, she excused herself and went to get raincoats, though he refused the poncho she offered. A few minutes later they started out together, past the terraced hillside of taro patches, into the tightly woven jungle growth of Mauna Pā-ele.

She had expected that he would tire easily on the climb, and told herself she might have guessed from his firm mouth and that light of amusement in his eyes that he was no tenderfoot. To her embarrassment she slipped on the soaking boards of a narrow plank bridge halfway up the mountain, and it was Dempster who grabbed her arm and kept her from sliding down into a morass of decayed vegetation twenty feet below.

"Noble fellow," she joked, trying to play the moment lightly. "You saved my life."

He looked down at the sodden mass below and grinned. "Only if you were very clumsy. You could have slid down there on your — well, all those leaves would have cushioned you."

They climbed on in silence for a while until he tapped her arm to stop her. "Tell me, do you do this sort of thing often? I mean, is this what you want out of life?" He gestured toward the direction from which they had come.

She was proud of her contribution to the family business, her wiry strength, her ability to do many things well, and it annoyed her to have to remind him that there *were* men who found her charming.

She laughed. "How would you know what I get out of life? You never met a real woman before."

He said nothing for a moment, but she didn't back down. "You sure as hell have a good opinion of yourself."

"Doesn't everyone?" she said, returning his stare. "Don't you?"

His cool, arched eyebrows went higher and she wondered if any woman had ever said that to him before. He glanced at the thicket of tree ferns ahead, then started on up again, slipping and sliding over the wet fronds underfoot. He almost vanished among the ferns ahead of her before Tracie climbed up after him. She was soon at his side and able to warn him, "That's not a trail on the right. An ohia tree fell a long time ago. When they finally cleared it it left a huge space there. Take off to the left."

But he refused to follow her direction...for some reason he wanted to prove her wrong. He turned to the right and, losing the trail, had to retract his steps to catch up with her. He found himself behind her now, pushing ferns out of his face impatiently, taking long strides so that he almost stepped on her heels. She guessed that for a man like Bill Dempster, no woman could ever walk beside him. He liked them squaw-fashion, two feet behind.

Well, too bad, she thought as they continued their climb upward. The branches and dark-leaved canopies overhead were so thick they didn't realize for another few minutes that the sun had vanished behind dark clouds and it was beginning to rain. By the time the shower came pelting down they were nearing the pali of Mauna Pā-ele. Neither Dempster nor Tracie said a word to each other.

Soon they were drenched, going from a brisk climb in clothing moist with sweat to a downpour that left them dripping wet. He stopped abruptly, wiping his face with the sleeve of his jacket. His voice rose above the noisy spatter of raindrops on the leaves.

"She came up here? At night?"

"It must have been midnight at least. The Murikami brothers saw her. They asked if they could help her but she only ran away. They were loaded down with guavas so they let her go."

"I know. They told me." He turned and got slapped across the face by ferns. He brushed the fronds aside and strode on.

She was right . . . he *had* checked the Berenson story with the Murikami brothers. She resented it for a minute, but it was understandable. Meanwhile, she wondered if he would catch his death of cold due to his stubborn refusal to borrow one of Victor's ponchos.

By the time they forded the rivulet leading to the basin above Ribbon Falls, the shower was over and the sun shone once again. The air was heavy with smoke from the burning cane fields.

Tracie turned away, avoiding the catchpool at the head of the falls. She started toward the cliff's edge where Ilima had leaped to her death. Seconds later she realized that Bill Dempster was splashing on toward the slippery basin and she quickly called to him. Between the sighing of the wind through the heavy greenery and the splash of water against rock before it dropped in the falls, he failed to hear her.

"No! This way!" She shouted and started toward him. He swung around, one foot slipping on a wet, moss-covered rock, and started to fall toward the edge. She didn't dare scream —

64

any sound from her might further upset his balance. He reached out and caught the rough, prickly branch of an ohia tree. She waded through the stream toward him. He was pulling himself up onto the muddy bank when the branch snapped.

She caught his sleeve, heard the chamois rip, but he had somehow kept his balance and pulled himself back up onto the bank. He managed to grin at her before he gave the broken tree limb a rueful glance. It floated over the edge and plunged down toward the basin three thousand feet below.

"That was a close one," Tracie said lightly, trying to control her panic.

He looked at her for a long moment. She wondered if he thought her hard and indifferent to his danger. Apparently not. As she examined the torn sleeve his wet, chilled fingers caught her wrist.

"You're quite a woman." He laughed shortly. "But I'm sure you know that."

She made no effort to free herself. He pulled her to him and they kissed, tasting the rain and the faint acrid touch of the fern fronds on each other's lips. She felt his mouth begin to explore hers all too briefly before the warm, moisture-laden wind whipped around them and they parted.

She could see that the kiss had been a spontaneous impulse, and although it ignited something deep within her, she accepted it for what it was. Still, she had to admit to herself that even his casual kiss could give her male friends a few lessons. She had been aroused more than she ever dreamed she could be.

"Now, then," he said, dropping her hand and shaking himself like a wet dog, "just where is that cliff the papers mentioned?"

Her pulse quickened as she noted his trim, muscular body outlined by those dripping clothes that clung to him like a second skin. But she doubted if he would approve of being put on display, so she pointed southward.

"Right this way. Beyond the thicket, where it levels off."

This time he made no objection to following her. They reached the spot where the boots of searchers and the police had torn up the ground and left it bare. But rain and the lush tropical climate had already covered the bare patches with new growth. Several flame-colored lehua blossoms lay where they had been blown by the wind. The sight of them troubled Tracie as she remembered seeing the form of that broken body in the scarlet raincoat.

Dempster studied the area for a long time. He said finally, "Did she talk about dying? Did she ever mention the legends about these places?"

"We once talked about some Hawaiian princess who leaped into a volcano to appease Pelé, the fire goddess. It's an old story."

He nodded. "Did she sympathize?"

"I suppose so. I thought it was silly myself."

"You would."

"Look here, Mr. Dempster—"

He smiled. "I think you can safely call me Bill by this time."

"Anyway, I don't dare let my imagination get the better of me." She took a deep breath. She seldom confessed to the weaknesses of superstition. "A long time ago, before Kamehameha the First conquered these islands, Akua was the Accursed Place. The name itself scared the Hawaiians off."

"Akua? Doesn't that mean 'goddess'?"

"That isn't its full name. It was originally called *Akua-lapu* — a 'ghostly apparition.'"

She was surprised and pleased that he didn't laugh at her. Instead, he frowned and got down on his knees to stare at the thick green face of the pali.

"She fell to that ledge?"

"Further. Below it."

"And she said nothing to you or anyone before she left that last night?"

67

"The cook told me something," she said, recalling what Chin Loo had told her. "When he saw her crying one day he reminded her that she needn't marry my father if she didn't love him. She said, 'I love him and he loves me.' It was true, too. Ilima was so excited when dad asked her to marry him that she practically broke out in a rash. Oh, she loved him, all right."

"What else did the cook say?"

Tracie thought back to Chin Loo as he wrung his hands, trying to imitate the anguish in Ilima's voice.

"She said, 'Oh, my God.' "

"That was it?"

"That is what Chin Loo said."

He stood up, not bothering to brush off the mud crusting the knees of his slacks. He appeared to be looking through her, seeing something far away. In the smoky afternoon light his face looked gray. It seemed that he had begun to understand something and closed his eyes in the face of it.

In a strained, anxious voice she asked finally, "Do you know what happened?"

He sensed how much she cared and his mood changed. He was unexpectedly gentle.

"She's gone now. It's too late to know, one way or the other. Shall we start down again?"

They took the cane-field path and were dried out, their wrinkled clothes smelling of smoke, by the time they came to the spur of Mauna Pā-ele.

They parted there, somewhat unsatisfactorily, in Tracie's opinion, when he merely shook her hand. He didn't mention Ilima again, and his manner, though pleasant, was carefully impersonal.

"Thanks again," he called as she began to walk away.

"For what?"

"For saving my life."

"Oh, that. It was nothing."

He laughed. "I know. But I'm still attached to it."

She had to settle for that. On the way back home she wondered how he would make love. Forcefully, she thought, remembering how lean and muscular his body had looked in the wet clothes.

It was late in the day by the time she reached home. Not unexpectedly, she heard her father's voice raised in anger. It was directed against Sam Kahana, whose huge figure was silhouetted against the far wall by the bright orange and red colors of sunset. Sam stood silently in the midst of her father's tirade. Knowing that Victor would be lost if he ever drove Sam away with his irascibility, she hurried inside to try and smooth any ruffled feathers.

The minute she entered the long, old-fashioned living room, its worn wicker furniture mixed with priceless chinoiserie, she discovered that it was she whom he was railing about.

"So there you are, young lady! Did you enjoy your little fling? A fine how-do-you-do when a man's own daughter betrays him."

Sam Kahana's chocolate-brown eyes were on her. Her cousins too had returned from Maui. Lili looked peeved, obviously because Tracie had spent time with Bill Dempster. Theo was merely amused. Only Aunt Jade had the good taste to remain seated, carefully working an exquisite red satin-crested bird into a strip of black velvet. She looked up long enough to remind Tracie, "Supper will be ready in ten minutes." Then she returned to her work.

"What's this all about?" Tracie said, angered at the accusation.

Victor threw up his hands. "You tell her," he ordered Sam, who remained undisturbed.

"Seems like that Dempster, he's been busy over at Akua Sugar."

Slowly she began to understand. The disappointment at Bill Dempster's perfidy struck her deeper than she had thought it would. "He's been making trouble with the field hands,

70

I suppose. What is it? Unionizing them?"

"Worse," Victor burst out. "He's bought in."

"How much?"

"God knows how he did it. Must have bribed anyone with five shares of Akua Sugar. Thirty percent he's got at last report."

Tracie dropped down abruptly in the nearest fanback chair. This explained Dempster's charm, his apparent concern about Ilima's death. It had all been a camouflage for his real business here, even that kiss up there on the pali of Mauna Pā-ele. She didn't need Lili's little gibe to tell her that. But the girl stuck the needle in all the same.

"I hope you didn't fall for him, Trace."

"Don't be ridiculous. That's your department."

"*My* department? Look at who's talking. You hoped—"

"Shut up, both of you!" Victor yelled. "Jade, is that damned supper of yours ready yet?"

"Certainly," Aunt Jade answered calmly without looking up from her work. "In a few minutes."

No one ever got the better of Aunt Jade.

Tracie normally looked forward to their family meals together but tonight, especially after the way he'd led her on, all she could concentrate on was how to get even with Bill Dempster.

4

The next morning, after he'd calmed down considerably, Tracie met with her father in the den.

"The first step," Tracie suggested, "is to find out what properties Marta Dempster got in the divorce settlement and if they would make a foothold for us. Let's not tackle his biggest holdings. We don't have the cash to take over right now. Work on the small, sure things, like his experimental papayas."

"Nothing sure about them," Victor said. "Too damned hard to refrigerate for shipment to the Coast. Not to mention training those mainlanders to appreciate them."

"Well..." She considered doubtfully. "Then there's shipping. Everybody uses Dempster's steamship line, even you. You wouldn't dream of getting to San Francisco on any ship but the *Lorelei*. We might burrow in and contact some of the other stockholders. Maybe pledge our ranch land on the Big Island...But I think Marta Dempster is our best bet."

He lit another cigarette and considered the lighted end, then looked up suddenly. He was thinking of quite a different woman. "Why did she destroy herself, Trace? And in that terrible way? I swear to God, I wasn't mean to her, or nasty or brutal. I'm not like that."

Her heart felt squeezed with pity for him. She knew him better than anyone; any mean streak he had was superficial, contained in his harmless bellowing, his boisterous assertiveness. Nothing else.

"You do scare people sometimes with your yelling, dad."

He looked stricken. "But not Ilima. She was too gentle. I never once raised my voice to her."

"Except when you had the shingles."

"Hell! Who wouldn't, then? But once I asked her to marry me I treated her like cut glass. You know how I was." He puffed in silence, coughed, and changed the subject, though she was sure it lay heavy on his mind. "About this Dempster woman. Is she still in the Islands? Who took care of her divorce? Can we get a handle on the law firm in some way?"

Tracie stacked the letters, financial reports and blue-covered legal papers, clipped on the pile of telephone messages and offered the entire file to him.

"Mrs. Dempster's lawyers didn't handle the divorce," she said. "He got the decree in Reno, Nevada. Grounds: incompatibility."

"Then she got a fat settlement. Maybe she won't need money. That's not so good. We can't reach her."

We also have to dig up the money ourselves, Tracie thought, but didn't remind him. They might own a good-sized chunk of Hawaii, but it took a little time to raise coin of the realm. She pointed to the telephone messages.

"Wayne called last night. He hinted that Marta had been pretty promiscuous. Not that Wayne would come out and say it, but I've heard rumors, too."

"Rumors? They can be damned cruel." He must be thinking about the whispers against him after Ilima's death...

Tracie followed Victor's gaze at the piercing blue sky and the tiny village nestled two miles down over green slopes to the leeward coast. Beyond the stone jetty where the Berenson inter-island cargo boat was tied up she could see Victor's outrigger canoe, its bright vermilion sail gently stirring in the breeze. Theo must be using it.

Returning his attention to the matters at hand he began to thumb through the sheaf of papers in front of him.

"I could swear we had a great time that last day. We went sailing — we got to laughing and carrying on...kissing like school kids. The outrigger was rolling. We kidded about drowning. She said — I swear this, Trace — she said, 'I'd die before I'd hurt you.' I said, 'Me too. Only vice versa,' and she got to giggling." He slammed the papers down, making Tracie jump. "Does that sound like she wanted to be free of me?"

No, she thought, it didn't. It only made the whole affair more mysterious. She had to help him get his mind off the tragedy, since there *were* no answers.

"Daddy, the Dempster file."

His concentration returned as he began to read and soon he was discussing ideas with her.

"It says here she gets some healthy dividends and stock options on that Dorado Star canning factory outside Honolulu. We could use that as a wedge into Dempster's holdings — if she needs the money."

Tracie, who had seen Marta Dempster dining and dancing at the Royal Hawaiian Hotel, remembered the woman's jewels, her gorgeous Paris clothes. "She does have expensive tastes," Tracie acknowledged. "Don't forget...Bill Dempster is no longer paying all the bills. And old habits are hard to break."

Victor looked at her gratefully. "You're mighty loyal, honey. Helping your old man out like this. It isn't as if it was your fight. Not yet, anyhow."

"Thank heaven for that." She smiled, but she was very much aware of her own guilt. After all, her motive in this underhanded battle with Dempster was personal. She suspected again that he had come to Akua with one object, to get control of Berenson property, and in a few months, maybe even weeks, he might have the majority control of Akua Sugar – a big stepping-stone to control of the island industries. He must have known that Victor Berenson was cash-poor.

But cash-poor or not, Victor had to buy into Dempster properties. It was the only way to get leverage that would keep that damned malahini from gobbling up the Territory.

Liliha stuck her dark head around the open door at the same moment that she knocked. "Uncle, Sam Kahana wants to see you."

"What now?" Victor grumbled, "More trouble?"

The big foreman filled the doorway with his bulk. "Not this time, Boss. I know where you can get a couple hundred shares of Akua Sugar preferred. Some common, too."

Victor jumped up, shoved the Dempster file across the old, scratched walnut desk at Tracie. "I'm on my way, Sam. Tell me more."

Tracie and Lili exchanged glances and Lili rolled her eyes. After long experience they both knew that Victor was going to scrape the bottom of the barrel again, buying in all directions and raising the Berenson indebtedness to both the Bank of Hawaii and California's Bank of America. When it came to land, lumber, food products and power itself, Berenson ranked very close to the huge companies founded in missionary times. As Theo was apt to occasionally point out, "There are times when I swear Uncle Vic doesn't have a nickel for a cup of coffee."

True enough. But right now, the important thing was to get some ammunition from Dempster's ex-wife. That would more quickly needle him, and it might even move him back out of Akua to protect his investments elsewhere.

Three days later, in pursuit of Marta Dempster's divorce settlement, all the Berensons except Jade arrived in the busy Honolulu harbor aboard the company's inter-island cargo steamer, *Akua Orchid.*

Tracie was inclined to agree with her cousin Lili about one thing — she much preferred entering the harbor from the windward side, like the Coast passenger liners, watching the green darkness of Makapuu Point, Koko Head and Diamond Head come alive in the sunrise. Instead, the battered old steamer slid into its berth in the Ewa-way from the Aloha Tower, exactly the opposite direction from Lili's beloved Waikiki.

"It's so dingy around here," Lili complained. "You'd think the richest family in the Territory could afford something a little classier."

But there was worse to come. While the family was in a loading shed being decorated with flower leis by various Berenson underlings, Victor suggested to one of them, "Tanaka, you can drive us out to the Moana, if you don't mind."

"The Moana! Oh, uncle!" Lili moaned. "Everybody who is anybody will be at the Royal Hawaiian."

"Good reason for us to avoid it, then." Victor turned to her, as if a splendid idea had occurred to him. "Unless, of course, you'd rather be on your own, you and your brother. Then I'd say by all means, that pink wedding cake is the place for you."

Mr. Tanaka ventured, "Both hotels are most elegant, Mr. Berenson. You inquired about the lady who used to be in the movies—"

"Marta Dempster."

"The lady is at the Royal. The Kamehameha Suite."

"Ah!" Theo perked up. He had an undoubted taste for rich, sexy ladies.

"How about her ex-husband?" Lili asked anxiously. She clearly had her own priorities.

Tracie had started out of the shed, then stopped to hear the answer.

"I believe Mr. Dempster has a room on the *mauka* side of the Royal. Very odd man. Prefers it to the sea view."

Victor was triumphant. "You see? The man is no fool. Saves his money, like me. Now, let's be on our way, shall we?"

Led by Victor, the Berensons filed into the dazzling white light of the Honolulu afternoon. Mr. Tanaka drove them out Kalakaua Avenue, past the tropic greenery and miniature jungle of Fort DeRussy to the Waikiki area, lined with coconut palms and dominated by two deluxe hotels overlooking the famed beach. Lili was upset again at the sight of the Royal Hawaiian Hotel, a spreading pink palace set far back from the street in its grassy enclave.

"And to think we could have stayed there," Lili murmured to Tracie. Despite the newer hotel's obvious appeal, Tracie was still sentimentally attached to the old, white Moana Hotel that had stood there, solid and welcoming, since 1901.

Laden down with leis "like any *malahini* tourist," Victor dismissed Mr. Tanaka and marched under the old-fashioned marquee and into the cool, dark lobby of the Moana. As always, the air seemed to be filled with the moist, sweet odor of the flower leis.

While Victor carefully signed them all in at the lobby desk, Tracie glanced at the sailing card on its rack beside the elevators. Having been born in the islands, Tracie always felt that travel out of the Territory was an exotic adventure. Today the sailing card read:

ARRIVING OCTOBER 25, 1935, 9 A.M., S.S. *Lorelei*, from San Francisco. DEPARTING OCTOBER 29, 1935, 4 P.M., S.S. *Sonora*, for the Antipodes.

The Antipodes... how much more exotic it sounded than plain "Australia"!

"As soon as I get settled, I'm off to the Royal. Going to see if Marta Lang might enjoy a cocktail with a man her own age," Theo said.

"Lang?" Lili said. "She was born Marta Langerhans. It said so in *Photoplay* magazine. The important thing is, are she and Bill sharing her suite?"

Tracie had reached for her key. She stopped,

listening while the key dangled from the clerk's hand. Theo laughed at his sister's comment. "He's too busy trying to buy out Uncle Vic."

Victor overheard this but ignored it. "Stop chattering, you two. Here's the elevator."

He accepted the Berenson mail from the desk clerk and made a wry joke about Tracie's popularity. "How do you like that? My kid's getting more mail than I am. Anything good, Trace?"

In the elevator Tracie skimmed through the envelopes. Most of the return addresses she recognized as friends from college. She quickly spotted Wayne Croyde's large, careful writing among them. Wayne, who was twenty-three, had entered the university a year after Tracie since, according to his father, he would then have a better chance on the first string of the football team. No one had guessed four years ago just how spectacular Wayne could be. Unfortunately, his considerable talents didn't extend to the classroom, and no one even hinted at a small problem that went along with his athletic achievements. . . he was embarrassingly accident-prone.

Lili, who had her own collection of notes from lovesick male friends, peeked over Tracie's shoulder and gasped.

"That gray envelope with the black engraving — see the initials? W.D. Look, Uncle Vic. That's got to be you-know-who. Tracie's corresponding with Bill Dempster. Selling out to the enemy, Tracie?"

W.D. So it was. Lili should know. Since developing a crush on Dempster she had become something of an authority on the subject. He, on the other hand, never seemed to pay her much heed, except in the casual way a man of thirty-five might tease a young beauty of twenty-one. And although Lili was disgruntled that their acquaintance went no further, she was dogged about her pursuit.

No matter. Tracie was dying of curiosity to know what he had to say. Some threadbare apology, no doubt. She tapped the envelope against her thumbnail and managed what she hoped was a show of indifference.

"The enemy may be hauling down his colors," she said.

Victor grinned as he looked through his own business correspondence. "Good for you, honey. Lead him on a merry chase. Make the bastard pay." Luckily he seemed to expect that any correspondence between his daughter and Dempster would be about business.

The family bustled out of the elevator, then they separated and went to their respective rooms.

Tracie left her father in the living room of the suite they shared and closed the door of the small, bright room with its fabulous *makai* view of the Banyan Court and the many-shaded sea beyond. As always, busy Waikiki Beach surprised her by its diminutive size. The huge banyan tree below her window provided an umbrella for many tables during the dining hours. That tree was like Victor, she thought; the many roots like Victor's many interests, the branches like the many people who depended on him, including Tracie herself.

In spite of her self-confidence she was aware that if she hadn't been Victor's daughter she would be working now as somebody's receptionist or stenographer. Maybe Bill Dempster's lackey, God forbid!

She turned from the window, kicked off her shoes, and laid her mail and handbag on the night stand. Raising the many flower leis from her shoulders where their dampness had spotted her beige silk blouse, she turned her thoughts to Dempster's letter. Typed, so it couldn't be very personal. She went into the bathroom to remove the leis, one at a time, the cinnamon carnation, the pink plumeria, the two baby orchid leis, the white plumeria with vivid yellow hearts, and the elegant pikake. She hung each of them around the edge of the tub, but hesitated over the last white plumeria and kept it on, partly to hide the moist spots. The room radiated the grassy perfume of the flowers, a scent that would always make her homesick for Hawaii.

She considered that she had provided her indifference to Bill Dempster by this time and could afford to open his letter. Settling comfortably against the headboard of the bed, she slit the envelope crookedly with her forefinger and read the neatly typed enclosure. Strictly business, in its way.

Dear Tracie,
Sorry our last meeting ended so abruptly. What about a drink tonight in the Banyan Court? Or, if you want to live daringly, I have okolehao connections with the man who was my bootlegger until Repeal.
Eightish?

Bill Dempster

"Eightish?" she mimicked. "No, indeed, my friend. Seven-thirty-ish. I'll have a dinner date at eight if it kills me." She realized that Dempster might have made a date at that hour with the idea of dinner to follow, seeming to presume she would be delighted to accept.

It never occurred to Tracie to ignore the invitation entirely. She called the Royal Hawaiian and left a hyphenated reply to his letter. "Just say 'seven-thirty.' Mr. Dempster will understand."

"Yes, madam. And your name, please?"

"Berenson, Tracie Berenson."

The clerk's voice was perceptibly warmer.

The next thing to do was to be sure she had a dinner date, and Wayne Croyde seemed the most likely prospect. She rummaged through the mail and found Wayne's note. Dear Wayne!

Tracie Sweety,

I sure hoped you'd get to Honolulu in time to see me wearing the old colors for the last time. But my uncle Bill came to celebrate with my folks after our big victory and he said he'd seen you last week and you were pretty busy.

She scowled. *Thanks, Dempster! I don't need you to make my excuses for me.* She read on.

I pulled a calf muscle during the game, but I can't complain. It was some last quarter; I could almost say it was worth it! Bill told Dad I was a cinch for the All-Star charity game in San Francisco, New Year's. How about planning on going over to give me a boost?

Anyway, mom and dad told me to be sure and invite you to dinner while you're here. Naturally, that goes for your family, but we know how busy your father is.

I guess you know why mom and dad are so anxious for us to have a little talk with them.

Tracie smiled grimly. *You're so subtle, Wayne. Of course, they want to know when you and I are going to be officially engaged.*

And what a mess that was! She had never once told Wayne she would marry him.

I'll contact you after you get to the Moana. Hope to take you to dinner. By the way, the Queen's House at Diamond Head has organized a luau for Saturday night. I'm putting in my bid now. It can be mighty dark and romantic out here by the time we eat our way to the coconut pie.

Love you,

Wayne

She sighed and slipped the letter back into its envelope. "I really don't deserve you, Wayne."

She wished the idea of seeing him were more exciting...

The leis had made her feel sticky. The Honolulu weather was muggy and moist, typical of October. At home on Akua when the Kona winds blew from the south across the lower elevations of the island, Tracie always hiked up onto the slopes of Mauna Pā-ele with a waterproof sleeping bag and got a few hours of cool, high winds, often thick with smoke from the burning cane fields of Akua.

In Honolulu there was no way to escape the heat but by surfing off the narrow beaches of Waikiki, and this was more a Hawaiian than a *haole* custom. Tracie had never mastered surfing like the Hawaiians around her, but at least, she thought, she could stand up on Wayne's surfboard and (with teeth clenched) ride in on a gentle wave.

Meanwhile, she had to arrange for her date with Wayne tonight. It must be timed so that he arrived about twenty minutes after her meeting began with Dempster. In the Banyan Court, of course. She reconsidered. "I'd better give myself a full half hour with Dempster. Just in case we find more to talk about."

Her first thought was to wear one of her dinner outfits...maybe the sleeveless green sheath with sexy waistline. Or should she waste time buying something new?

In the dresser mirror she studied the tailored

gold and beige of her silk blouse and sleek, hip-hugging skirt that was too short for the current ankle-length style.

In the end, knowing all the time that she should have been calling Wayne, she decided on a flattering silver-blue crepe formal and sent it down to be pressed.

The phone rang; it was Wayne's mother.

"Wayne wanted to reach you himself, dear, but he had to go meet someone at the university. He may have failed his senior thesis. Well, my dear, what does someone like our Wayne care about the English novel or some such musty old subject? Ask him who the Walter Christie choices for All-American were last year and he'd answer you just like that."

"How true! Mrs. Croyde, could you ask Wayne to meet me tonight at eight o'clock in the Banyan Court?"

"Why, of course, dear. And you must come up to dinner with us very, very soon. We'd love to have your daddy and your cousins too, but I suppose, in view of his condition..."

"His condition?" Tracie interrupted. Had the woman heard some gossip about his heart murmur or whatever it was two months ago? An appalling thought...if so, it would soon be all over the Territory.

"I meant Miss Mako's — ah — accident."

Ashamed at having forgotten Ilima so easily, Tracie tried to make up for it by enthusiasm of her acceptance.

"I'd love to come. We'll see about dad. We can get together later about the date. Shall we?"

Mrs. Croyde agreed and hung up in high spirits.

The rest of Tracie's afternoon was taken up with meetings at which Victor surprised and gratified her by soliciting her opinions where appropriate. But the subject of educating Californians to the taste of papayas did not excite her at the moment.

Why the devil hadn't she ordered a new wardrobe this fall, like Lili, who was growing even more beautiful with her dark hair, sloe-eyes and curvacious figure? Still, she managed a pretense of interest in Victor's problems until he finally asked her how she would handle her cocktail date.

"For God's sake, Trace, don't overwhelm the guy."

"Who? Me?"

"You know. Just let him think you're all sugar and cream."

"What a revolting thought! I'd rather be thought of as chili peppers and curry, something with zip."

He grinned. "You know. And I know. But

you can get more flies with sugar than with vinegar. So use the sugar."

Nothing like having her father's permission to throw herself at Bill Dempster — up to a point. She drew the line at anything — or anyone — that threatened Orchid Tree.

"Okay. But what are you going to do about Marta?"

His smug look made her smile. "Your old man will spread a little of his well-known charm. I've got first bid on the beauteous Marta for dinner tonight. I'll talk her into selling the cannery stock. I can be pretty persuasive when I want to be," he said with a wink. "Here we are. If I don't see you before tomorrow, good luck, honey."

"You too, dad."

They hugged and went their separate ways.

By evening Tracie had gone through several moods and come out on top of them all. She wouldn't give Bill Dempster the satisfaction of changing her character *or* her wardrobe just for him. She gave herself a last once-over before leaving her room.

Tall and slim, wrapped in the simple blue-gray crepe that set off in muted contrast her tawny hair and hazel eyes, she felt that she would be entirely dependent upon herself, not these silly wrappings. Anyway, the dress showed off her figure, which was as good as Marta Dempster's any day. At the last minute she got out her diamond chandelier earrings and fastened them on. She swung her head, enjoying the flash and sparkle of the jewels within the cloud of pale hair.

She addressed her reflection with some slight pleasure.

"Not bad, Trace, if I do say so myself!"

She could read the young elevator operator's admiration in the way he looked her up and down. Thus armed with male approval, something she usually found unnecessary, she stepped from the elevator and started out to the Banyan Court. She heard a buzz of voices around her in the lobby. Her name was mentioned. It was a commonplace reaction when she appeared in Honolulu and she took care not to look as if she noticed. The comments were usually critical and at best they expressed curiosity: "So that's the Berenson girl."

Outside in the blue dark of the Waikiki evening, with the surf humming up the beach only yards beyond the court, the usual crowd was scattered among the tables under the dark banyan tree. It was difficult to make out faces, but the wardrobes were varied as always. There were flowered beach pajamas here and there, dominated by crepe, satin and chiffon evening gowns and the stately *holokus* with trains, which gave enormous dignity to several two-hundred-pound Hawaiian women. The men were less picturesque, some in tropic whites, though many preferred the open-necked Hawaiian shirts.

The scent of gardenias was everywhere. Corsages gleamed white on the shoulders of many women. Only the newcomer *haoles* were swathed in leis. And Bill Dempster was nowhere to be seen. She glanced at her watch; she was two minutes early...damn!

She was often caught like this waiting for her father and had taught herself to handle the matter with aplomb. She signaled to the waiter. Luckily, he knew her. "I am to meet Mr. Dempster for cocktails. Can you give us a nice little table?"

The young waiter smiled knowingly. "Sounds like a merger, Miss Berenson."

She laughed. He knew his island politics. "Who knows? Has he reserved a table?"

"Oh, yes. Mr. and Mrs. Dempster are there in the center."

They certainly were! Marta Dempster, ex-actress but still fancying herself the movie star, sat facing Tracie, her golden blonde hair in ringed curls around her heavily made-up face. She was leaning forward, one hand on Bill's, her dark lips pursed, as Bill lit her cigarette.

Tracie considered it a sickeningly intimate scene. She told herself severely that her sole interest lay in buying up Marta's shares in a Dempster corporation. This domestic scene seemed to put that idea out of the running. To Tracie, the woman's full-skirted chiffon gown made her look like a cloud of pink cotton candy, but there was no getting around it, Marta Dempster was a beauty.

Tracie hesitated, but she was much too proud to let anyone, especially Bill Dempster, guess her real feelings. She strode forward with head high and an almost arrogant self-confidence.

5

Something in his ex-wife's face warned Dempster. He looked over his shoulder and, as did other diners, gave Tracie a long, wide-eyed stare as she approached his table. He seemed fascinated as she made her way between the tables with a nice swinging of the hips. Recalled to manners, he stood up so suddenly he knocked over his chair.

Dempster's unexpected awkwardness, compounded by waiters hurrying to right the chair, gave Tracie a slight edge for the moment. She held out her hand which he took, still looking her over. She reserved her best smile for Marta Dempster, who was also giving her the once-over.

"Mrs. Dempster. Or should I say Miss Lang? How nice to see you like this!"

Marta too was charming. "How nice of you to say so! We've met before. A luau at the Croydes, but what a madhouse that was... hundreds, I'm sure. And I remember you were surrounded by some of those young stallions in a celebration at the Royal last year."

"A graduation party," Dempster put in, adding with malicious humor, "Makes us feel old and decrepit, doesn't it, Marta? This girl just graduating from college, while you and I—"

This was a mortal insult to a woman in her late twenties.

"Speak for yourself, darling. I remember my graduation as if it were yesterday." It was well known that Marta had been discovered in a Sunset Boulevard hash house at fifteen, but no one was rude enough to mention it. Marta got to her feet. "I mustn't dally here any longer. I do have a date. I hope you'll both forgive me if I run."

"What a shame, Miss Lang!" Tracie said with polite exaggeration.

Dempster gave Tracie a satirical look but she reserved all her attention for the actress who stood on tiptoe to give her ex-husband a peck on the cheek, then floated past the diners with chiffon trailing in a cloud around her.

Dempster reached over to pull out Tracie's chair but she beat him by a second or two and they both sat down. He was still watching her quizzically.

"Don't you think you overdid the adoring fan bit?"

Tracie laughed. "I read once that it's impossible for an actor or actress to receive too much attention."

"You may be right, in her case. What are you drinking?"

She shrugged and saw that the gesture had attracted his attention to her bare shoulders beneath the narrow straps. She wished she knew what he was thinking. Maybe it was because of the twilight and the faint, romantic shadows, but he looked better than ever to her. He wore his sophistication like a perfectly fitted suit, even though he was casually dressed in a blue shirt open at the neck, and a gray sport jacket.

"Make mine a dry martini."

"Afraid to try oke, I see."

She never refused a dare. "Can you get it? I thought it was illegal."

"As I said, I have friends."

"All right. Make mine okolehao." She thought it typical of a *haole* newcomer to make a big thing out of the strong alcoholic drink the old-timers and Hawaiians had drunk for generations.

She hoped Marta Dempster was meeting her father for dinner. Meanwhile, Tracie was left in command of the field, and an attractive field he was. So much so that she thought she'd better watch herself...She still didn't know why he had invited her to cocktails...possibly he was suspicious of why the Berensons had come to Honolulu.

She looked around, returning the waves and the blown kisses of friends whose faces gradually faded away in the first starlight. Somewhere, a Hawaiian trio was playing "The Cockeyed Mayor of Kaunakakai," and under the buzz of conversation at the other tables Tracie hummed the tune. Aware that Bill Dempster's sometimes forbidding blue eyes were studying her, she smiled, flipped one hand over and waved it in an expressive hula gesture. "Do you hula?" she asked, feeling playful.

That broke his train of thought, whatever it had been. "Lord, no. What do you take me for?"

"Wayne does a fair hula. So does dad when he's swacked. His favorite is 'Cockeyed Mayor.'"

He chuckled. "Was it named for him?" His hand caught her moving fingers, so unexpectedly she almost forgot his question. She made no effort to release them but gave him a sassy, insulted look.

"You have long fingers," he said.

"I have long bones."

He didn't seem amused. His thumb followed

the joints of her middle finger. She wondered if he was deliberately trying to arouse her. If so, he succeeded.

"So you have," he said, and just as suddenly released her fingers. She felt briefly let down by it and reverted to trivialities.

"The song was named for a movie star who shall be nameless. You said you worked at Kaunakakai once."

"In my younger days. I was hot out of college and planning to own the world. I started there. A beautiful island, Molokai."

Whatever arrangements he had made with the waiter, he hadn't mentioned the drink but the okolehao arrived nonetheless. He raised his glass, touching hers in salute. "Here's to us, partner."

"Partner?" she said, startled.

"In the Akua Sugar Company," he explained innocently.

She wanted to hit him, but it was important to keep his good will and not let him suspect what she and her father were up to. She sipped her drink with deliberation. This was no time to lose control, to let him get her drunk. It would be just like him to try so that he could worm some business secrets out of her. It seemed unlikely that he would have a more flattering motive. There was something very self-contained, a cold streak about him. In a way it attracted her. She always liked a challenge...things that came easily weren't worth having.

She swirled her drink around in her glass. "It's silly, but it's usually hard to persuade people about the beauty of Molokai. Because of the leper colony. Weren't you afraid?"

"Don't be ridiculous. This is nineteen thirty-five, hardly the dark ages. Even a *malahini* like me knows better than that. Anyway, that was across the island from where I lived. I delivered supplies down the cliff to the peninsula a couple of times. But you don't see me running around with bells on screaming, 'Unclean.' "

She gave him a genuine smile. "Bravo. Here's to you." She clicked her glass against his and then sipped again, watching him over the edge of her glass. "You still haven't told me what this little drinking session is all about. Is it a peace offering?"

"What for?" He seemed genuinely puzzled.

"For cutting in on Berenson ground."

"Has Old Vic staked a claim on the whole of Akua? It's still part of the States. No, I asked you here to thank you for saving my life. It was the least I could do. And don't say again that it was nothing."

That made her laugh. She was feeling the

effects of the oke and enjoying the heady sensation of flirting with him when she became aware of the long, lean figure that had emerged from the far side of the banyan tree.

His rough, sunburned features were lighted briefly and then blurred like the other shadowy faces around the court. Taking a closer look, she realized that it was her father. As usual, he had his eyes on two pretty girls passing him on their way into the Banyan Court. Victor had sense enough not to fool around with the young ones, but he enjoyed looking.

Tracie panicked, afraid Bill Dempster would suspect Victor was looking for Marta Dempster, which he probably was. Tracie raised her hand, fooled with her hair, stretched a long, pale strand to its fullest extent, and pointed toward the exit with her forefinger, hoping her father would understand the message.

Bill raised his head, confused by the gesture.

"Had my hair done only an hour ago," she explained, "I can't do a thing with it."

By the time Bill turned Victor had taken the hint and melted in behind two mainland tourists heavy with leis.

"Thought it was my dinner date," she said.

He accepted this lame explanation without any sign of disappointment. Apparently, nothing would break him down. She looked at her watch. "Now I really do have to run. It's been nice, Mr. Dempster."

He made no effort to stop her but got up with her. "Eventually, it may even be 'Bill' and 'Tracie.'"

"Or Tracie and Bill." But she smiled when she said it.

"I'll walk you out to meet him. Wayne, I suppose."

She let him take her arm but resented his easy assumption.

"Why on earth must it be Wayne? I do know a few other men."

"I never doubted it. Who is he?"

She laughed at the absurdity of this. "Wayne."

Beyond the court the waves broke and rolled up the beach, then retreated slowly like distant echoes. She felt they echoed her own puzzlement with Bill Dempster...

Why this brief cocktail date with no effort to hold her for a second drink? She didn't believe for a minute that line about having saved his life. She had an unpleasant feeling that she was being used for some reason, yet sensed that he was attracted to her. It worked both ways. She couldn't be wrong about that. But he seemed to be drawn to her in spite of himself. Why the reluctance? Maybe he still loved his ex-wife, she reasoned. But he had treated

Marta cavalierly tonight, with no sign of affection. Maybe he just didn't trust Victor Berenson's daughter.

Well, he had reason for this mistrust. All the same, she hoped her father had taken Marta somewhere else for dinner. Their scheme would be doomed if Dempster saw them together before Victor could make an offer for some of her stock.

They reached the lobby just as Wayne Croyde's six-foot-four figure loomed over the other evening guests and he loped toward Tracie. "Do you pick them by the pound or the yard?" Bill muttered.

"Does your trusting nephew know you talk about him like this?"

"Certainly, I wouldn't say anything to his face that I couldn't say behind his back."

Amused at his way of expressing it, she tried to remember her own loyalty to Wayne. It was easier to do so when she realized that others in the lobby were also watching the tall athlete, but he seemed oblivious to the stares. Spotting her, he made a grab for Tracie and in doing so accidentally pushed one of the straps of her dress off her shoulder as he bent to kiss her.

She hugged him and returned his kiss.

"I'm ravenous," she said. "Where are we going?"

Wayne was surprised. "I thought you wanted to eat here, honey. You always liked the Moana. We had the greatest night of my life, starting from Waikiki. Remember?"

She blushed, afraid Bill Dempster would understand. For a moment she couldn't think of anything to say to distract the older man from Wayne's babblings. Then she felt gentle fingers on her back, putting her shoulder strap back in place. Glancing behind her she saw that those fingers brushing her shoulder belonged to Bill Dempster. He was too damned appealing. And he had certainly ruined poor Wayne for her.

She started herself by saying abruptly, "Your uncle was just leaving. Shall we be on our way?"

Wayne shifted nervously, trying to cover her rude behavior by his own apology. "She doesn't mean that the way it sounds, Bill. Tracie's always playful."

Bill Dempster refused to take the hint.

"The truth is, Wayne, I tried to get you at the house an hour or so ago. I just heard the news."

Wayne looked at him blankly, though clearly Dempster's remark had a special meaning for him.

"I was just on campus," Wayne said. "You heard? Bill, what's the story? Yes or no?"

"You made it!"

To her own amusement Tracie found herself shunted aside while the two men shared a piece of news that was apparently cataclysmic. Wayne threw his long arms around Bill, who returned the embrace with a few cuffs between Wayne's shoulders.

Tracie began to suspect the reason for this glee. "Is it true? You made the Walter Christie list?"

Wayne was speechless, so Dempster explained.

"All-American. One of the year's best. Halfback position. Nudged out Pittsburgh's Ken Davis, I'm told. I knew he'd do it."

Tracie was genuinely pleased for him. She knew her father would be delighted too. "Wayne, that's wonderful. Then you're a cinch for the San Francisco All-Star game."

Dempster agreed. "I got the managing director on the overseas line immediately. And I needn't tell you, every scout in the country, except the Rose Bowl rooters, will be in San Francisco New Year's Day."

"I only wish there were as many pro teams as there are college teams," Wayne complained. "As it is, there will be forty-four players in San Francisco and only half a dozen good openings afterward. I've got to have a job to fall back on, just in case."

"Negative thinking. None of that allowed," Bill said firmly.

The two men began to argue over other likely choices for All-Americans, completely forgetting Tracie, who took her gold compact out from her evening bag to pass the time. She was used to football talk.

Before she opened her compact a bellman passed her, furtively slipping a piece of paper to her. She turned away from the two men and unfolded the sheet of Moana Hotel stationery.

Victor had scrawled, "Say you're going to the toilet." Crude, but to the point.

She pinched the sleeve of Wayne's neat new dinner jacket. "Back in a minute."

"Sure, honey. Sure. Bill, you're dead wrong about Finegold. Andy Kerr will pick him for the East team. Andy's no fool, and the East needs a slippery quarterback. He's mighty good."

Obviously, Tracie would not be missed. She strolled across the lobby toward the ladies' room. Near the entrance to the Court she saw Victor and walked over to him quickly.

"Where is she?"

"In the head. Broke the buckle off her shoe. They're glueing it back on. She wants to keep her damn cannery stock. Dempster settled money on her. No other corporate interests.

Nothing we can buy into except the cannery."

"Oh, damn!"

He glanced back, lowered his voice to a hoarse whisper. "That guy wants something, Trace." She didn't have to ask who. "He's even been questioning your buddy Wayne."

Disillusioning; yet it fitted her own suspicion of Bill Dempster's real interest in her.

"What can I do about it, dad?"

While he spoke, he had his eyes on the two men across the lobby. Both were waving their arms in heated talk. Obviously, they were arguing about somebody's forward pass. Tracie tried to keep her mind on her father's problem but she couldn't help being pleased by Dempster's interest in something as normal as football. It made him less steely, more human.

"Trace, it's up to you. Find out what Dempster is trying to use against this family."

That startled her back to reality.

"Use against us? Dad, what could he have? I know more than you do about our taxes, our accounts, our books. We're legal."

"Not that. It's something he's even mentioned to Croyde. Marta asked me what the mystery was. He's trying to get at us through Ilima."

"Ilima? In what way?"

"Who knows? He suspects something. I'm

damned if I know what. But the idea that any of us led her to..." His voice trailed off. "You know I loved Ilima almost as much as I love you. And a hell of a lot more than I love your cousins."

"Dad, it can't be."

"Well, it is." He looked around uneasily. "Marta's coming back. Check with me later."

She patted her father's hand. It trembled as she'd noticed it did occasionally, a painful reminder to Tracie of his mortality. She watched him stroll off with his still-powerful stride. He maneuvered Marta out under the marquee and into a taxi. He seemed pleased to be with her as she looked up into his eyes with the melting expression that had won her so many parts at MGM. Doing a double-take, Tracie suddenly realized that Marta Dempster just might be trying to add Victor to her long list of suitors...what then?

Tracie shook the unpleasant thought from her mind and returned to Wayne and Bill.

"Gentlemen, you're penalized for too many times out. It's back into the game for both of you."

"Sorry, honey." Wayne kissed her on the top of her head and she was annoyed to catch a glimpse of Bill Dempster's grin, as if he saw through her and knew that Wayne's kisses only annoyed her.

"Let's go," she said, deliberately turning her back on Dempster. "I can't wait any longer. I'm starved."

With pride and a little embarrassment Wayne dismissed his uncle. "Sorry, old man. Talk to you tomorrow."

Dempster patted his back in what Tracie regarded as a most patronizing manner. "Sure thing, Wayne. My, my! It does my heart good to see you youngsters out on the town. Have fun...and think of me."

Tracie could have sworn that last remark was for her, but she gave no indication of having understood it.

Wayne was in such good spirits she felt bound to share his mood and during the drive toward town through the warm tropic darkness she filled in each of his breathless pauses with a perfunctory remark:

"That's wonderful."

"Really terrific."

"Great."

"You'll be the best."

She sensed she was repeating herself but he didn't seem to notice. Finally she broke into his proud reverie.

"You're quite fond of your uncle, aren't you?"

"He's the best."

"I'll bet! And he just loves the Berensons."

"Well, now, honey..."

"He has a terrific imagination. I suppose you believe everything he tells you."

"Aw, Trace, it's just that he felt sorry for Miss Mako. He knew her family and all."

Then Dempster *was* after something. What did he know or suspect?

Her quick, short laugh sounded strained even to her own ears.

"For heaven's sake, what does he think happened? Father and I would really like to know."

He was looking ahead, his eyes fixed on the road. His new graduation gift, a white Cadillac, rolled smoothly up into the Nuuana Valley. They were headed up between dark, primeval walls of jungle vegetation toward the Nuuanu Pali, a high crack in the Koolau range that looked out north and east to the windward coast.

Tracie sat up, suddenly realizing what he had in mind. She was in no mood to repeat the mistake she had made with Wayne months ago.

"Now, Wayne, we aren't going to do any smooching up at the pali. Or anything else."

"Why not?"

She avoided the truth, giving him the most obvious reason. "Because it's going to be cold. The wind is sure to be blowing across the pali. It always does."

He reached out for her with one arm but she avoided him, pressing against the door and looking back through the rear window.

"Honolulu looks beautiful tonight. Let's go back. There's a big passenger liner at the Aloha Tower. All lighted from stem to stern. Isn't it beautiful?"

He wasn't interested. "The *President Taft*. She's sailing at midnight for Yokohama with a gaggle of San Francisco Shriners aboard. Dad and mom are down seeing some friends off. You wouldn't like it. Everyone on board must be over thirty. Maybe forty."

"All the same, please turn around. You promised me dinner and I'm still waiting."

He was disappointed but began to watch for a place to turn the Cadillac around.

They had passed a trickling waterfall minutes before. The rising moonlight made the spray glitter against the dark walls. The bird and insect life within that jungle growth was muted at this hour but it existed, as it existed on another pali, where Ilima Mako's body had lain for hours after her death plunge.

Would they ever know why she had taken her life? Tracie had a sudden, vivid memory of those moments when her friend's body was raised to the cliff's edge, the flesh pale and waxy in the flaring torchlight.

"Why?" Tracie sighed, staring down at her fingers, wondering.

Wayne hadn't heard her. He swung around a curve with screeching tires and pulled onto a stretch of level ground smoothed by long years of tourist visits to the pali lookout. Except for the car lights the rising moon gave the only faint illumination to the view before them, the sheer walls of the mountain range plunging down to the jungle floor that extended to the far highway on the coast. There was a lush beauty about this unexploited section of Oahu that Tracie had never failed to appreciate.

Wayne reached for her, trying to draw her resistant body to him. "Honey, don't be like this. I promise we'll get married — I told my folks. They're all for it. It'll be all right." His big hands were busy below her breasts. He seemed to be trying to get her long skirt up around her knees. She used her elbows hard against his chest.

"No, I said!"

His massive strength could easily have overcome her, but he didn't want to hurt her and they only wrestled briefly. With a sudden, miscalculated move he caught her against him, intending to kiss her throat. She pulled back, then screamed. One of her chandelier earrings was caught against the collar of his dinner jacket. She remained trapped to him briefly until she managed to free herself without losing an earlobe.

"Must you be so...clumsy?" she muttered as she refastened her earring.

Wayne was desperately apologetic.

"I didn't mean it, honey. I swear to God I didn't. Does it still hurt? I'll kiss it and make it better."

"No!" His brown eyes looked so stricken she tried quickly to soothe him. "I'm fine," she said, stroking his arm. "Please don't worry. Let's just go back and eat."

Much shaken by the encounter, and especially by her scream, Wayne said, "Sure. Any place you say."

Their faces were suddenly lighted by a car coming up to park at the pali beside them. Wayne made his turn and left the two in the blue Buick to make love without witnesses.

"Hope they have better luck than we did," he said as he headed back down to Honolulu. After a few minutes of silence he said, "You don't really love me at all, do you?"

"I like you. A lot."

He looked straight ahead. "Bill Dempster says your father ruined you."

Her spine stiffened. "Oh, he does, does he?"

"He didn't mean that like it sounds," Wayne

added quickly. "He meant that if your mother hadn't died when you were a kid, you wouldn't have to work so hard, trying to run Orchid Tree. She'd have taught you that's a man's work."

She gritted her teeth. She had loved her mother and had never really gotten over the feeling of abandonment when she died. In some ways Ilima Mako had replaced some of the love and security she longed for from her own mother. But did it ever occur to Bill Dempster that Tracie might enjoy her work for Orchid Tree? Obviously not.

Wayne's free hand crept toward hers. She took it and they held hands in what she hoped was a friendly way. "I don't suppose you'll want to see me play the All-Star game in San Francisco now," he said after another long silence.

"Of course I will. I know dad will want to go. We'll be rooting madly for you."

He seemed genuinely pleased and she was relieved to have soothed him until he dropped another bomb. "My folks expect us to announce our engagement pretty soon. What can I tell them?"

"Just put them off. Say we don't want to rush into anything."

"What about—" He licked his full lips nervously. "What about when we — you know — made love?"

"We were discovering our real feelings — or trying to. Weren't we?"

He gave her a sudden, unexpectedly penetrating look. "Someday I won't be so easy to get rid of."

She felt at a loss to answer him.

"Wayne, I'm sorry. Really."

The sincerity of her remark seemed to have some effect and his mood softened. "Okay, Trace, whatever you say. But if I'm not picked by the pros, and they always stick to mainlanders, I'll have to get a job. Maybe something in sports. Keep your fingers crossed about that." He looked at her. "There's no one else, is there?"

"Of course not!"

He considered this and found a new hope in her easy dismissal of the idea. "Then I've still got as good a chance as the next guy."

She liked him too much to hurt him again. Besides, he was right. She compromised by smiling and squeezing his hand. During the rest of the drive to the Alexander Young Hotel in downtown Honolulu, Wayne was in excellent spirits. As he talked ebulliently about the upcoming game Tracie couldn't shake the many questions in her mind, especially those about her own feelings.

6

Victor was much too busy during the next couple of days to check in with Tracie. Lili had hinted that Theo was seeing something of Dempster's ex-wife, but until there were complaints from Victor, Tracie decided not to worry about it.

Late one afternoon they were out on the narrow beach between the Moana and the exclusive Surfer Club. Tracie was trying with indifferent success to stand on Wayne's surfboard while Lili stretched and preened herself on the warm sand. She hadn't gone unnoticed by three attractive young Hawaiians who were working on their outrigger canoe several yards away.

Putting her weight on her knees, Tracie scrambled up on the surfboard as Wayne held it. The board itself bobbed gently on the green waters. This should be simple, she thought, especially with Wayne holding the board more or less level, letting it sway rhythmically with the tide.

She held her breath. "All right. Now!"

As she shifted her weight, Tracie became aware that the skintight trunks of her two-piece white bathing suit were about to reveal her navel. She lowered her arms, pulled up the white belt that outlined her slender waist, and lost her balance so that she almost slid off the board. She couldn't help thinking of the amusement Bill Dempster would have found in her predicament, not to mention her father. But Wayne's good-looking, slightly heavy features were set in his effort to concentrate on helping her.

She found her legs trembling but she managed to stand up, stretching her arms out to balance herself until she stood precariously on the board. A wave rolled in and she found herself riding it, poised forward like a figurehead, with arms stiffly outstretched.

But she didn't ride far...Wayne had lost control of the board and it swerved and tilted, mounting the wave's foamy crest and she quickly lost her balance. Still scrambling and clutching the air, she hurtled over to the left and went under. When she came up, furious at herself for failing, she was so close to the shore that she had to wade the rest of the way in, hearing laughter from her audience on the beach.

Blinking water out of her eyes, she saw that a man in a plain beige sport shirt, slacks and Japanese sandals had joined Lili. Bill Dempster. As she expected, he found Tracie's fall from lofty heights amusing and Lili, anxious to please him, filled the sultry air with her carefully orchestrated laughter.

Wayne hurried out of the water behind her, hoisting the massive board onto his shoulder, "You all right, Trace?"

Not wanting to sound like a poor sport, Tracie transformed her scowl to a grin. "Sure. Don't I look it?"

"You certainly do," Bill told her, though she hadn't addressed him. "That was nicely done. When are you going to demonstrate for us, Liliha?"

Lili gave him her tight, catlike smile. "I wouldn't dare. You've got to have big muscles to get away with stunts like that."

Bill deliberately looked over Lili's petite curvaceous figure in its new black one-piece maillot. "Your muscles all seem to be in the right place..."

She smiled and stretched like a black kitten at his compliment.

Tracie's long legs covered considerable sandy

territory as she passed Bill Dempster, ignoring him. She sank down on a beach towel beside her sunburn cream and the wrap-around skirt specially blocked to match her favorite *Tapa* cloth pattern. She threw the skirt over her shoulders and took off the rubber slippers she usually wore to prevent coral cuts.

Wayne loomed over her, cutting off the sunlight briefly with the surfboard. "Got to get rid of this, honey. Be back in a jif."

"Sure thing." She unscrewed the black lid of the cream jar without looking toward Lili and Bill Dempster, but she could hear them. Lili was squealing, squirming and in every way appearing to enjoy herself while Bill applied sunburn lotion to her exposed golden flesh.

Feeling that her little cousin had outmaneuvered her, Tracie made a pretense of enjoying her solitude. She allowed her fingers to move over her own legs, from the long, trim thighs to the knees, with only a quick, furtive glimpse in Lili's direction. Lili had propped herself up with her elbows buried in sand behind her. Her black hair, worn close like a waved cap against her piquant face, was in vivid contrast to Bill Dempster's breeze-blown sandy hair as she tilted her head against his.

The activity between them continued but Tracie made it a point not to look or listen.

She had almost succeeded in blocking them out when Lili let out a shriek, startling several other sunbathers. Tracie looked over. Lili was all in a twitter, but Bill was strangely calm. Lili had pulled away from his touch with shrill indignation. "I don't. I don't. Maybe Tracie does. She's blonde and everybody knows they get freckles. But not brunettes."

"It really doesn't look bad," Bill insisted, tracing something between Lili's shoulder blades where she couldn't see it. "Very small. Is this another?"

What the devil was he doing?

Whatever it was Lili got up, shaking off sand, and made a bolt for the hotel. Bill Dempster had gotten up with her but he lingered, moving slowly while he refolded a towel and packed up a bottle of sunburn lotion.

As he slowly passed Tracie, she called to him. "What was all that about?"

He gave her a mischievous look but said innocently, "I believe your cousin is allergic to freckles."

"Lili doesn't freckle."

"Really?" Again the innocence.

She laughed.

He looked over her body with deliberation. "Now you, on the other hand, could really freckle. Better let me finish you off with that lotion."

She was already savoring the prospect of his hands caressing her body with the cream but she reminded him, "Wayne is coming back any minute. He'll do it."

"Can't. He's too busy with the press." Bill dropped the towel, taking up her own jar.

"The press! How do you know?"

"I'm psychic."

His skillful fingers began working the cream from her shoulders down to the small of her back, and then from the curve of her hip over the firm flesh to her knees, which he slapped smartly before he began the same systematic massage of her right leg.

"Why isn't Wayne coming back? What did you do?"

"Me?" he said, withdrawing his hand from her thigh. "I merely told the *Star-Bulletin* and the Honolulu *Advertiser* that Wayne was chosen for the New Year's All-Star game."

She was pleased for Wayne's sake. "Was he really? How wonderful! Did you have something to do with it?" She looked at Dempster with new respect, but something about his eyes warned her that her respect was wasted. "Or am I giving you more credit than you deserve?"

"You are."

"Should I be flattered?"

"If you like." He tapped her thigh and she jumped. "Get dressed. I'm taking you to a native feast. A real live luau. And I'm – we're invited. Out near Diamond Head. The Queen's House, or something."

She was still tingling from his touch, and the thought of spending an entire evening with him excited her. On the other hand she had more or less promised Wayne to visit the Queen's House with him. She hesitated. "Sounds like fun. But I think Wayne has it in mind."

Bill was his usual confident self. "Not tonight. He has a meeting and dinner with several local Shriners about the San Francisco All-Star game."

"In that case . . ." She got up so quickly she almost, but not quite, missed the hand he offered. They walked across the sand toward the hotel. They were silent, which surprised Tracie, who thought Bill Dempster had a line of patter for all occasions. Was he sorry she had accepted his date, puzzled or just speechless with delight? That idea made her smile.

She was still smiling when they met the little group in the Moana bar – two newsmen, a photographer and Wayne's football coach, all huddled around Wayne, punching out questions.

"I'm off to the Queen's House," she called

out to him. "See you later."

They all turned with varying degrees of interest or annoyance at her interruption. Wayne was apologetic but obviously pleased that she found him receiving so much attention.

"Okay, honey. I'll be there soon as I can get away."

So much for her ridiculous loyalty to Wayne!

For some reason Bill Dempster followed her to her room. When she started to open the door she found it unlocked, and as Dempster pushed it open for her he got a clear view of Victor Berenson standing across the room, looking out the window at the Waikiki surf.

"That you, Trace?" he called. "Look at that water. Must be a hundred shades of green. Not blue like our Akua waters at all."

Afraid he would mention Marta Dempster, she spoke up quickly. "Just a minute, dad. We have a visitor."

Bill appeared much too pleased to see Victor. He almost pushed past Tracie to reach her father. They shook hands and greeted each other like the best of friends while Tracie eyed them both suspiciously. She fingered the tie to her skirt as a hint that she wanted to change for the evening, but the two men were still exchanging amenities. What hypocrites businessmen were!

"I hear tell you're buying into Akua Sugar,"

Victor said like a true ranchero welcoming the pushy, inexperienced gringo. "Welcome to the island, and all that."

"Good of you to say so. I've got a lot to learn about sugar."

"Oh, you'll catch on quick. We've got a great climate there. Miss some of Kauai's bad hurricanes and the Big Island's volcanic spewing. What do you think of Wayne making All-American?"

"A credit to the Territory. How are you getting along with Marta?"

The sudden change of direction caught Victor unprepared. "Getting along with who?" Victor asked dumbly.

Tracie knew there was no use in letting Dempster scare them off.

"Dad, Bill and Marta are divorced, after all. I'm sure he doesn't care whom his ex-wife keeps company with."

"Far from it." Bill was all sweetness and light. "Marta was just telling me at breakfast — we met for breakfast—" he interpolated, seeing their exchange of glances. "Marta said you'd treated her to a great time. Especially last night, at that navy fellow's house up on Mount Tantalus, Marta loved it."

Victor recovered. "So she said. Mighty pretty, she is."

"Seems to be the common view."

They didn't know what to say to that and Tracie was disconcerted when Bill added, "Nothing like your daughter's looks, though. Or, at least, that's this *malahini*'s opinion."

Tracie felt the heat suffuse her face. Was she actually blushing? But the compliment had been unexpected.

Victor agreed complacently. "I always thought so myself. Still and all, Marta strikes me as a fine figure of a woman. The same sweet spirit of my late fiancée."

That staggered Tracie, but she wasn't alone in her reaction. Surely no one would fall for that remark, least of all Marta's ex-husband. Bill looked at her, opened his mouth to say something but she beat him to it. "You can't mean that, dad. Nobody could be less like our Ilima." She would have enumerated the differences, but with Bill present it was awkward.

Bill showed no such reluctance. "Marta is a treasure to all her friends, I'm sure. But I'm afraid they find her an expensive trinket. Miss Mako was never that." He moved to the door, then stopped and turned. "Luckily, I only settled cash on my ex-wife. God knows what she'd have done if she got her pretty little claws on any of my companies. See you downstairs in half an hour, Tracie?"

"Make it an hour."

Victor hardly let him close the door before he assured Tracie. "He's lying, you know. Marta admitted she has those ten thousand shares in the cannery here on Oahu."

It was interesting that Dempster should lie about it. Evidently, he was genuinely afraid Victor might persuade Marta to sell it.

Tracie rustled around getting ready to bathe and change for the luau. As she hung her new silk beach pajamas on the bathroom door she said to her father, "Better sign her up before he talks her out of dealing with you."

Victor frowned. "My kid giving me orders now? Pretty soon you'll be taking over Orchid Tree, if I'm not careful." But he grinned as she closed her door. She could well imagine his bitterness and resentment if she really tried to take over, and he knew she wouldn't do it.

While she bathed in the luxurious suds, using long, vigorous strokes on her body, she wondered if her father really *was* jealous of her own work. Surely, he understood it was all done in his name.

She ran her hands along her thighs and remembered Bill Dempster's touch. Too bad he'd placed himself in competition with Orchid Tree...being with him was a lot more exciting than Wayne's company. But he always managed

125

to arouse her suspicions. What was he after tonight?

She was even less sure when they drove out along the moonlit road among coco-palms, flaming poinciana and bougainvillea to the Queen's House, an estate planted at the dark foot of Diamond Head, a section of the island that seemed untouched in its lush and rugged splendor.

Unlike Tracie's younger dates who tried to draw her close as they drove, Bill Dempster made no attempt as he maneuvered his smooth Chrysler roadster, a six-cylinder Imperial she would like to have owned herself — even if it was more than five years old. The palm fronds, swaying in the quiet air as the car passed, cast curious shadows across his face that made him seem even more mysterious. He spoke so seldom she wondered if she'd done something to make him angry. If so, she refused to feed his vanity by asking what it was.

They turned off the highway into the grounds of Queen's House, newly transformed from a home to a restaurant. They were immediately engulfed by hibiscus hedges and, in the darkness, the scent of flowers still warm from the day's hot sun. Tracie smoothed the wide legs of her outfit and began to pull back her hair when Bill put out a hand, stopping her.

"What—?"

"Leave it," he said. "I like it loose."

She was pleased, though surprised. She began to think that maybe he had driven her all the way out here just because he liked her. It was a good feeling.

The evening crowd had already gathered on the grass in a long double line. Most of them sat cross-legged on Japanese mats. Less limber patrons were furnished with folding chairs that didn't look any more comfortable to Tracie. She said as much and got a rueful response from Dempster as they found places on the grass.

"Ah, youth! Now, when you get to my age..."

She laughed, stuck one finger into her tiny Japanese rice bowl and came up with a thick covering of poi. She licked her finger while he watched each of her moves, not taking his eyes off her. His close attention made her a little nervous, especially her own reaction... Why must she be so anxious that he see her at her best?

"Three-finger poi is as far as I've gotten," he told her. "Even that takes a bit of doing."

"Hard to take up on your fingers?"

"Hard to get down. You know what it tastes like? Wallpaper—"

"That cliché is so tiresome. Tell me, honestly, how many times in your life have you tasted wallpaper?"

Two Hawaiian boys under the direction of the chef, a huge man formerly of the Royal Hawaiian, lifted a steaming bundle of ti leaves from the pile of white-hot stones in the *emu*. They dropped the container poles on the grass. Delicious odors of roast pig drew appreciative sounds from the prospective diners. Tracie hugged her own shoulders in anticipation. Bill was amused by her enthusiasm.

"I'd rather have a thick steak and a stein of beer at Original Joe's in San Francisco."

"A mere commonplace," she teased him. "You *malahinis* don't know what real taste is."

He frowned at the remark. "How long do I have to conduct my business here in the Islands before I'm accepted as one of you?"

His maddening attitude toward her, either praise verging on adoration or total suspicion, made her anxious to shake him into some straightforward emotion without the extremes.

"I accept you," she said patting the crown of his head. "I hereby dub thee *kamaaina*. Old-timer, islander and one of us."

He reached across her plate, took a finger of poi from her bowl, licked it off his finger, watching her all the time.

"Now we are one."

He sounded serious, almost too serious, and she wasn't sure what to say...could he have really meant it? She suspected a double entendre but thought it better not to pursue it now in this crowd of people.

When they had worked their way through the pork, the lomi-lomi, the squid, the endless packets of food steamed in taro leaves, to the coconut pudding, washing it all down with beer, tea, or, less obviously, okolehao, couples began to get up to walk off their meal in the landscaped Japanese gardens while Hawaiian musicians played beneath one of the flowering trees.

The paths wandered over little humped bridges beside miniature streams that surrounded an old, Victorian two-and-a-half-story house. The large dining room of the house itself was used as a restaurant during bad weather, but tonight the long windows were empty and the house looked desolate. Tracie continued to enthuse over the luau, but Bill remained silent; his thoughts seemed to be elsewhere. She was about to take the path around the front of the house toward the hibiscus drive but he took her by the elbow and directed her toward one of the Japanese bridges over the meandering stream. The great abundance of island foliage growing everywhere made the area dark in spite of the moonlight. She started up the humped bridge with Dempster but caught the high, curved heel of her pump in a knothole and was stuck for a minute. She stepped out of the shoe.

"Serves me right, wearing pumps with pajamas." But she knew she'd only worn them because she thought they would show off her figure better.

Dempster laughed at the mishap and knelt to free the leather-covered heel. Limping on a few steps she suddenly felt hands tightly clasp her shoulders from behind and a familiar male voice. "Beware, me fair beauty! One push and I can send you to the bottom of the sea." The "sea" was a stream about four inches deep, but in this perfumed dark she was nonetheless startled by her "attacker."

To cover her reaction she swung around impatiently. As she had known he would be, Theo stood there, his slanting black eyes shining with laughter.

"Scared you, didn't I?"

"Don't be so juvenile. Anybody would think you were a five-year-old."

"All the same," Theo reminded Bill Dempster, who arrived with Tracie's shoe, "I scared the daylights out of her. You saw her."

"I certainly saw Tracie. And you." Bill's voice was mild, but his eyes were hard.

He gave Tracie her shoe without bothering

to slip her foot into it. He was looking at Theo with an expression that seemed to Tracie more than questioning — it was a speculative look. Knowing Bill's interest in Ilima's death, she was chilled by an idea...was he perhaps thinking that Theo had used that slick tongue of his and his disarming ways to send Ilima Mako into a depression that resulted in her suicide?

Tracie said quickly, "Theo, what are you doing here anyway?"

"Looking for you. Old Wayne drove me out here. He's scouting around over by the *emu* looking for you. I promised to drag you back to him if I found you."

Bill waved him away. "Easier said than done. Run along, Theo. I'll attend to Wayne."

"All right, if you say so. Just don't blame me if he feeds you to one of those Portuguese men-of-war. A nasty sting there."

Bill didn't look impressed by the meaningless threat. He grinned, gave Theo a friendly push and sent him on his way.

"Don't say you haven't been warned, Trace," Theo called over his shoulder as he left. "He's after something. How's your virtue holding out, cousin?"

"Oh, shut up!" she shouted back at him but he'd already disappeared behind a huge spreading poinciana flame tree whose heavy-laden branches were brushed aside at his passing.

When they were alone again she turned to Bill, her tone frank. "Is he right? Are you after something?"

She watched as his hands, pale in the moonlight, reached for her and she eluded him, stepping back, then aware that one more step would land her in the stream.

"Of course I'm after something. We both know that." His fingers held her now, maneuvering her closer to him, though she tried to stand her ground. Whatever he might say, she knew that beneath all this sexual sparring his real interest in her family was threatening. He still suspected they had somehow been partially responsible for Ilima's death. It was maddening to know this and still passionately desire the feel of his mouth crushing hers, his body warm against her flesh. They kissed and her arms instinctively went around his shoulders, urging him closer, harder, but a part of her knew that his passion was merely a means to an end. And that end was decidedly not romantic.

Her fingers caressed his neck and shoulders beneath the loose open collar of his shirt while their mouths explored each other's and she felt him press hard against her. His own fingers worked under the low scoop neck of her blouse, sending shimmers of excitement through her body.

But the bridge could not remain deserted for long. The path approaching the bridge wound along the opposite side of the little stream to lose itself in various flowering shrubs, a convenient cover for any other lovers who reached the area. After Tracie and Bill were interrupted a second time she freed herself, proud to have done so before he let her go. "This isn't going to work, you know."

"Come along then." He would have headed for the spreading poinciana across the stream but she stood firm.

"Let's be honest, Bill. Your only interest in me is in the hopes that you'll discover something evil about the Berensons...am I right?"

She had caught him unaware. He looked upset, not at all guilty, certainly not ready to confess she was right.

After a moment's silence he said, "Don't you give yourself credit for arousing my – ah, shall we say – my passion for you?" He recovered his cool, ironic manner. "I do want you, you know. And I'm beginning to dislike my noble nephew more every hour."

This was more like the real Bill Dempster, she thought. He was the business rival she could joke with and tease.

"You needn't, on my account. I've no intention of marrying him. Or anyone else, for that matter."

He laughed abruptly. "Another thing you and I have in common. But that needn't keep us from enjoying ourselves."

"Certainly not. Providing you get rid of that odd notion you seem to have, that the Berensons are a band of murderers."

"I didn't think that for a minute."

"We aren't, you know. Ilima committed suicide. All the evidence says so. She wanted to die and she chose her own way. Why she did it, we'll never know."

"And that interesting *why* is what I wish I knew."

She stepped away from him and walked off the bridge, back toward the Japanese lanterns where a Hawaiian troupe, three girls and three men, were entertaining tourists with a graceful hula.

Now it's too late, Tracie thought. Bill Dempster had spoiled the soft, perfumed night with his suspicions. Though he walked beside her, she felt they were miles apart. Until he got over his ridiculous ideas about the Berensons, he would have to remain a man not to be trusted. Nor was her mood lightened when they finally bumped into Wayne.

"Hey, Bill, I'm beginning to worry about you," he said after kissing Tracie. "I know you've done a lot for me, but I don't intend to trade off my girl in return . . . By the way, guess who I saw having dinner with your ex-wife before I left the hotel tonight? Tracie's daddy. Better hotfoot it back to Waikiki and rescue one of them."

Bill shrugged, excused himself, and left. Was he rushing back to intercept Victor and Marta? Or had he known about their meeting all along? In spite of everything, Tracie found herself passionately hoping that his interest in his ex-wife was not personal.

7

Tracie felt that at least one of the enterprising Berensons, herself included, should be able to persuade Marta Dempster to sell her interest in the Oahu cannery. With that in mind, the actress was invited to Akua Island for a week as a guest at Orchid House. Tracie reasoned that this would work out especially well since there were no hotels on the Outer Islands, and it gave them access to her without the interference of her ex-husband.

In spite of their motives for inviting her, all of the Berensons but one found her a lively and entertaining guest with her gossip, her vivacious personality and her surprisingly good nature. Only Jade, whose opinions and beliefs were usually expressed by eloquent silence, remarked to Tracie, "The lady is not an easy guest. I hope she is not to be the next mistress of the house."

Tracie laughed. "Strictly business. Dad doesn't

take to women with bigger egos than his own. Marta is too stuck on herself."

She was less certain when Theo and Victor took Marta down to the *Akua Orchid,* anchored off the Berenson jetty in the bay. There the two men quarreled because Theo refused to leave the boat. Theo eventually escorted the movie star back to Honolulu.

"Escorted and God knows what else," Victor complained as the rest of the family returned to the plantation house.

Whatever went on between Theo and Marta Dempster, it cost Theo his chance of a free trip to San Francisco for the All-Star football game. Lili would be cramming in Honolulu, hoping to pass her final exams. Theo was perfectly willing to remain in Honolulu as well until he discovered that Marta Dempster was about to sail – alone – for the Coast and a "B" film in Hollywood.

Tracie and her father sailed for San Francisco soon after, seeing for the first time the skeletal pilings at either side of the Golden Gate that would mark the rise of the new bridge across that turbulent rush of water.

On New Year's Eve day father and daughter finally arrived at San Francisco's elegant old St. Francis Hotel. The crossing had been rough, but Victor appeared unshaken.

"Theo and Lili are lucky after all," Tracie remarked. "Right now I'd rather be back on Kalakaua Avenue...at least the sidewalks don't keep rolling and weaving like the deck did." After being shaken about on the seas, Tracie felt that even the stately pillars that lined the hotel lobby seemed to be swaying.

But Victor was never very sympathetic about anyone else's weaknesses. "That's enough of that," he said firmly. "Any Berenson who gets seasick is a disgrace to our name."

"Sure, sure, pop. But you looked green around the gills yourself last night when that little tub keeled over about ninety degrees."

"Never felt a thing. And it wasn't ninety degrees. Anyway, we'll be going home on the *Lorelei*. She's a real beauty. Not a little tub."

"You'll make Bill Dempster crow over you. He's mighty proud of his flagship."

Having absently acknowledged the greeting of the hotel manager, Victor began to riffle through his mail. A telegram from Los Angeles interested him. He ripped open the envelope and tossed it on the immaculate floor, scanned the telegram and waved it before Tracie's eyes.

"Let Dempster crow. We've got Marta's ten thousand shares of Dorado Star Pineapple. And two dollars below the market. I'm starting to bore into that guy's holdings. All you have

138

to do is send her the check. I'll sign it."

"Well, there goes my sable coat," she joked.

He had given her the sable sport jacket for Christmas, and she knew at the time she shouldn't take it. In the end, the price would come out of Orchid Tree earnings. But she had yielded to her own desire for a fur that would compete with those of the wives of her father's mainland business associates. Besides, she thought, Lili was well into her third fur and never asked where the money came from. The only problem for Lili was selecting a night in Honolulu cold enough to wear it.

Luckily, Tracie found San Francisco's seasonal weather just right for the fur, with the morning fog just burning off under the cool winter sunlight. She would have the chance to wear her Christmas gift.

In spite of her new jacket and the prospect of the fun they would have in San Francisco, known all over the Pacific as The City, she couldn't shake off an uneasiness, a sense of foreboding. Try as she could to put her finger on it, she didn't know why. She sensed that something, some ill-luck, hung over the family. Could it be the unsolved mystery of Ilima Mako's death?

But it was absurd. Tracie might be superstitious at home, surrounded by legends and the tropical, sometimes violent nature of Akua, but this was practical, modern San Francisco. What harm could premonitions do here?

All the same, she wondered if Bill Dempster was possibly leading Victor to overextend himself. Maybe he wanted Victor to buy into companies like Dorado Star Pineapple. It was a painful suspicion for two reasons. She didn't want her father's lifetime of work destroyed. But the other reason overshadowed the first, to her chagrin. She didn't want Bill to put up an insurmountable barrier between them.

As she waited at the registration desk, her mind wandering, Victor and the hotel manager were discussing the prospects of the West team in the New Year's game. Victor immediately covered a bet before being escorted out of the great high-domed lobby to the elevators. He flirted, as usual, with the elevator operator, a petite beauty, and scowled when Tracie reminded him that they were only here for three days and that he had promised to go with her when she picked out a gown and peignoir for Lili. Lili had decided that the popular style of wearing pajamas to bed had run its course and extracted a promise from Tracie that she would buy the peignoir for her as a belated Christmas gift.

Victor argued about having to accompany

Tracie as he was being shown around their sixth-floor corner suite. "You don't need me to help you pick something out for her," he insisted. "Good God! What do I know about women's nightgowns?"

"Plenty. You've bought enough of them."

He grinned suddenly, his rugged face relaxing and his pale gray eyes alive with memories. "I do seem to have the knack, don't I? Well, we'll go out now and get it over with."

"Give me at least time to wash and change, for heaven's sake!"

"Well, hurry. Chances are these stores will be closing for New Year's Eve before long."

"Okay, okay!"

When they met half an hour later, Victor was surprised by her changed appearance. "What's this? Trying to impress Wayne? Not like you." Victor's eyes were thoughtful. "Or is it his parents you want to impress?"

She had changed to a sleek black Schiaparelli suit with wide shoulders and a peek-a-boo blouse of moss-green chiffon, then tucked her hair under a newly fashionable green brocade turban. Her father was clearly startled with the result.

The minute he began to quiz her she realized what she hadn't considered before. All her sudden, uncharacteristic concern for feminine furbelows was very real, and she had to admit it was all for the benefit of Bill Dempster. It would be just like him not to show up, after all her fussing around to attract him.

"Who you expecting? King George? Or the mikado of Japan?"

She smoothed on her long kid gloves. "Just thought I'd try and do you credit. This is a dressy town." She took his arm. "Let's go."

"Do me credit? You're as big a liar as your old man."

"Sure. It's what you respect about me... hold on."

She went back to her room, pulled her new fur jacket off its padded hanger and dangled it over one shoulder.

"Now I'm ready to impress the natives."

They left the suite in excellent spirits, exhilarated as always by the invigorating weather and the clang-clang of a passing cable car on Powell Street.

Tracie's new jacket attracted little attention in this cosmopolitan city, but it made her feel more festive, as if she were playing one of the madcap heiress roles so popular in comedy this year.

Victor debated whether to go to the City of Paris, Magnin's or one of the specialty shops, all of which he had glimpsed from the Union

Square windows of his hotel suite. They ended up at the White House department store because a window display had caught his eye. In the lingerie department the saleswoman proved haughty, as if she couldn't be bothered.

"Never mind," Tracie whispered. "Let's pick out something. I'll handle her."

Either he wanted the woman to suffer or he had been disconcerted by her manner. Whatever the reason, he couldn't make up his mind about anything Tracie showed him.

"If it was for a lady friend I could decide in a minute. But for a niece — and the kid's small, not long-legged like you. The sizes seem all wrong."

The saleswoman gave Tracie a long, contemptuous look, obviously imagining she was Victor's current — or about to be ex-mistress. So much for the impression made by Tracie's new jacket. While her father shook his head over pink satin and a peignoir trimmed in white rabbit fur, Tracie looked around the lingerie department.

Across the room a heavy-set woman, stifling in a mink coat of an incredibly rich ebony shade, was giving a salesgirl trouble. She kept examining silk stockings, running them through gloved hands. The butter-soft leather gloves must be at least elbow-length, Tracie thought.

Soft as they were, they still caught on the delicate silk, causing snags that made the patient young saleswoman wince, though she made no objections.

The furred customer complained loudly. "You're still a teeny bit off. I told you a flesh color. I mean *my* flesh."

Tracie caught the young saleswoman's eye and smiled at her sympathetically. The girl brightened, smiled back. When she did so Tracie couldn't help noticing how lovely she was, her tight cap of dark hair framing a heart-shaped face with a tender mouth and big, heavily fringed brown eyes. She was small and, like Lili, seemed to be well-curved without being plump. Tracie looked her over from another vantage point and nudged Victor. "Dad, ask that saleswoman about the size. Her figure is rather like Lili's."

Victor gave the girl an indifferent glance, then looked again. In his dictatorial way he took up Tracie's suggestion as if it were his own.

"Send that girl over here. And miss — maybe you can take over the heavyweight customer."

"Well, I — we do have our rules. But –" The saleswoman seemed impressed in spite of, or perhaps because of, his rudeness. "Excuse me."

Seconds later, the pretty young saleswoman

with doe eyes was walking shyly around the salon, holding various silk, satin and chiffon nightgowns up before her. Victor questioned her about her own taste but it turned out that she was a "cotton and batiste" girl.

"Whatever that means," Victor remarked.

She confessed, "I adore these things, but they aren't — well, as you can see, I wouldn't do them justice. They need women who are used to silk."

"Don't be silly," Tracie cut in, indignant that the girl should run herself down. "You'd look marvelous in them. Believe me, it's quite easy to get used to luxury."

The salesgirl smiled. Her shyness, or maybe her looks, impressed Victor, and something about her reminded Tracie of Ilima. It was that quiet humility, Tracie decided.

Victor began to make conversation by asking the girl her name. Diane Thorpe. To Tracie's embarrassment he began to quiz her in a more personal manner...Was she married?

"I was married. I'm divorced." She hesitated as if she found the word shameful.

"Couldn't have been your fault," Victor said bluntly. Subtlety was not his forte.

Sensing his genuine interest, Diane Thorpe offered more. "Ray — gambled. But all this must sound very sordid to a gentleman like you. . .I do think your niece ought to love this blue silk gown and the robe. Anyone would."

"Would you?"

She flushed and raised her small chin. There was pride in the movement.

"I hope you aren't making fun of me. I shouldn't chatter so much, I know." She bit her lip, as if ashamed for having been so forthcoming. "I'm sorry," she said.

Tracie suspected Victor was more touched by her looks than by her situation. "Your — chatter, as you call it, is delightful, isn't it, Trace?"

"Mrs. Thorpe!" The senior saleswoman returned with what, to Tracie, was a measured tread. "There are other customers. You really must not dawdle. This gentleman's time is valuable."

Flustered, Diane Thorpe dropped the gown and Tracie knelt to help her pick it up. Diane confessed in a low voice, "I'm only here during the holiday rush. I'm actually a stenographer, but these days you take what comes along."

"I know what you mean. It doesn't look as though this Depression will ever end," Tracie said. "Where I live, over in the islands, everything is much higher than on the Coast, and the wages are lower too, I'm sorry to say."

"You mean the Hawaiian Islands? Oh, how romantic it must be!"

Tracie agreed. "Unless you work in the fields," she added ironically.

But Diane Thorpe's face was alight with the picture conjured up by the word "Hawaii." "All the same, if times are hard everywhere, it must be easier to enjoy them there. I think I'd give my soul to work there."

"Mrs. Thorpe?" her superior called again. "This gentleman is still waiting."

Victor contradicted the woman in a genial way. "Not at all. Mrs. — Miss Thorpe, shall we settle on the blue? And the white one with the blue ribbons?"

"And the black set," Tracie put in. She knew Lili's tastes.

Diane Thorpe began closing the sale, folding the sets carefully in the elegant White House boxes. "If you're going to be doing more shopping, sir, I could deliver them to your home. Or your hotel."

"The St. Francis. But that won't be necessary. Anyway, no need in putting you out. I'm not spending any more time shopping. I'll tell you that."

"I wouldn't mind, really."

The girl had an enchanting smile; even Tracie was taken by it. Her lack of pretension was appealing and to Tracie she seemed so... for lack of a better word, nice.

Evidently Diane Thorpe had made an impression on Victor as well. Later in the hotel suite, Tracie caught him looking up the girl's address in the telephone book.

"How do you think she spells that name Thorpe? With or without an *e?*"

"What on earth do you want with that? Are you going to call her?"

He seemed in excellent spirits as he hummed the new hit tune, "I'm in the Mood for Love."

"Just checking. Want to see where she lives. You know. If she lives alone."

"Whatever for? She looks like a decent young woman, but for heaven's sake, Dad. . .you don't intend to call her, do you?" Tracie couldn't believe he could be so taken with the young woman he'd only spoken to for a few minutes.

"Why not? Besides, the girl liked me. I could sense it. Maybe I reminded her of her — well, her father."

"Just so long as you don't remind her of a cash register."

She knew it was a catty thing to say, but the conceit of men! She closed the door of her room to get ready for the evening. A few minutes later the phone rang. "Yes?" she answered automatically.

She heard a breathy little gasp and a vaguely familiar voice on the other end of the line.

"I'm so sorry to bother you, but I have the sash."

"The sash?"

Suddenly Victor was on the extension in his own suite. "What sash? Who is this?" he barked.

"Oh, Mr. Berenson. I'm awfully sorry. You see, I found the satin sash to the black gown. It had fallen behind the counter. I wanted to be sure you got it."

Victor's normally gruff tone suddenly became warm and avuncular. "Well now, this isn't the Dinah Thorpe who just waited on us, is it?"

The girl was obviously delighted that he hadn't forgotten her name — or at least part of it. "Why, yes it is, sir! I didn't think you would remember. I'm Diane Thorpe."

"Don't call me 'sir'...makes me feel old as Methuselah. Are you calling from the store?"

"No, I'm downstairs at a lobby phone. Near the desk."

"I'll be right down to get it," Victor said. "A belt, did you say?"

Diane Thorpe explained again.

"You just hold on," he said. "I'll be right down. It's the least I can do after you came all this way to deliver the doo-dad."

He hung up. Tracie stood staring at the phone. After she heard her father leave the suite she finally put it back on the dainty,

149

carved night stand. She felt like an eavesdropper and was vaguely troubled by what she'd heard. Could her father actually be interested in the young woman? Possibly he, too, found a similarity to Ilima in her...Although Victor had outwardly resumed life as usual since his fiancée's death, she knew that inside he was still troubled by it.

Curiosity warred with her common sense when her father hadn't returned half an hour later. Obviously they had found more to talk about than the sash of Lili's nightgown.

Still, she was surprised that her father would take a liking to such a young woman — certainly she was several years younger than Ilima, who had been in her mid-thirties. She reminded herself that this Mrs. Thorpe *was* rather pretty, so she shouldn't be surprised if her father was attracted to her.

Her curiosity was satisfied when Victor ushered Diane Thorpe into the Louis Quinze salon of her suite. He rattled the doorknob to her room and called to her. "Trace, come out here and play chaperone for this very proper young lady."

Tracie opened the door and found Victor directing a timid Diane Thorpe into one of the stiff satin chairs. Mrs. Thorpe jumped when she saw Tracie. She sat on the very edge of her chair, seemingly ready to leave at a moment's notice.

"Miss Berenson, it was a belt. Sash, that is. It was accidentally left out of your package. Well, your father and I got to talking. He was telling me about your island of Hawaii."

"Not Hawaii, honey," Victor patiently corrected her. "Hawaii is the Big Island. You know — active volcanoes, the Parker Ranch. Remember last fall when the lava flowed all over the place?" Mrs. Thorpe looked blank but interested nonetheless. "And Oahu is where Honolulu is. But we live on Akua. Smaller, but mighty pretty."

"It sounds heavenly." The young woman relaxed a bit, seemed excited just hearing about it. Her brown eyes shone. Then the tissue-wrapped sash fell out of her lap, reminding her of why she was there. She picked it up and handed it to Tracie, who thanked her.

Diane started to get up. "Really, I don't want to take up your time. I know you've got a million things to do." She raised her head in that small, proud way that Tracie had first noticed in the store. "I have a few things of my own to do. Happy New Year, Miss Berenson. Mr. Berenson."

"No, no. Wait." Tracie stopped her, for some reason not wanting her to leave yet. "Please.

The least we can do is offer you a toast to the new year. Father?"

Victor beamed. "Coming right up." He went over to the elegant sidetable, started elaborately mixing a jugful of martinis. Belatedly, he remembered to ask Diane, "What'll you have? Dry martini? Or maybe a manhattan? Not bourbon, by any chance?"

The girl refused awkwardly. "I'm afraid I don't drink very much. Ray seemed to feel it gave him some kind of control over the world, but in my experience it just makes people cruel." She saw Victor stare uncomprehendingly and added, "I beg your pardon. I shouldn't have said that."

Tracie was indignant at her father's manner and pulled up a chair, waving Diane back to her seat.

"You're perfectly right, Mrs. Thorpe. I couldn't agree with you more. Tell me, what is your life like? Are you a native San Franciscan?"

Diane smiled. "Funny. Mother always used to say that's the first question a San Franciscan asks. I was born in Oakland."

Victor chuckled at that as he handed Tracie the little martini glass. Accepting it, Tracie snapped, "There is nothing funny about Oakland." But her father, like so many other Territorial citizens, had close links to the Bay City and inherited its extreme chauvinistic attitude.

While Tracie sipped her drink she tried to make Diane Thorpe feel comfortable. It wasn't easy. While the young woman lacked Ilima Mako's quiet elegance, it was obvious that she was trying hard to be agreeable in an awkward situation and Tracie felt compelled to help her.

"You're single now, Dinah... Diana?" Victor said, oblivious to the young woman's uneasiness.

"It's Diane," Tracie said.

He waved this aside as a technicality, and since Mrs. Thorpe actually flushed with pleasure, no harm was done.

"I'm divorced, Mr. Berenson. I had to, although my folks never approved of it — but I had to."

Victor patted her hand. "Don't think about it. You're free of this fellow now."

But Tracie sensed that there might be more problems than her father guessed. "Does he still bother you?"

"Oh, no." Diane Thorpe said firmly, but then glanced nervously at the door. It was an embarrassing betrayal of her fear. "Not for months, anyway. I don't think he knows where I live. And even if the store tells him, it won't matter. I won't be working there after the first of the year. I live at a rooming house out in the Mission District. He'd never think to look for me there."

Diane saw that Victor was finishing his drink. One of the things that pleased Tracie about the shy, proud young woman was her quick sense that she shouldn't overstay her visit. She got up and before either Tracie or Victor could stop her she was on her way to the door. She paused and turned.

"I really can say good-bye in your way... *Aloha*, Miss Berenson. Mr. Berenson."

They were both touched by the thoughtful gesture. "I'll see you to a cab, Miss Dinah," Victor said, starting after her.

Tracie shook hands with her and watched her go out into the wide corridor with her father.

When Tracie returned to her own suite she had to hurry through her bath. The New Year's Eve banquet was a formal one and she knew she would need time to prepare if she wanted to compete with the San Francisco party-goers.

She didn't hear her father return to his suite. When the phone rang she was sure it must be him, reporting some excuse for his delay. She was caught in a wisp of a bra, her satin panties and silk stockings, about to wriggle into the smooth, bias-cut white satin evening gown she'd selected for the evening's festivities. With her hair tangled in the halter neck of the gown she reached for the phone, trying to free herself.

The voice she heard filled her with a pleasant tension.

"Tracie? Glad I reached you. This is Bill Dempster."

She found it hard to keep her voice calm. "Hello. So you made it into port."

"Barely...rough crossing. Look, Tracie, I've wangled an invitation to the New Year's Eve banquet tonight for the big shots organizing the game."

"Yes, at the Palace Hotel."

"I figured Wayne couldn't take you. I certainly hope he's in training."

"Right."

"Well?" After a pause, he added, "Getting a date out of you is like swimming the Golden Gate. Takes a little out of a fellow. What do you say?"

"I'd love to. But dad and I will be leaving for the Palace any minute."

There was a distinct pause.

"But I just saw Victor leaving the hotel with—" He amended, "—leaving by the Geary Street entrance."

That explained why Victor hadn't returned to the suite.

She was surprised by the news, but recovered rapidly. "With that pretty Mrs. Thorpe, of course. I'm meeting them later." She could hardly believe her father had gone off with a comparative stranger. But she had to admit he might have done worse. Diane Thorpe was very much in the tradition of the other women Victor had genuinely cared for, and she appeared to be a decent, respectable young woman.

Bill must have seen through Tracie's lie, but he had the good manners to accept her explanation.

"In that case, let me pick you up here. You can catch up with your father and his date at the Palace."

She forgot her coyness in that instant. She felt reckless and excited by the prospect of spending a few hours with Bill Dempster.

"I'd love it, Bill. Pick me up at seven-thirty. You really are a darling."

He laughed. "I've been called a lot of things. I'll accept that."

She untangled her hair from the glistening satin gown and felt it drop over her shoulders, enjoying the feel of the material as it hugged her breasts, her waist and hips. She smoothed the skirt down over her legs and looked critically at the mirrored results...not bad.

She was suddenly grateful to her father for having freed her for the evening.

8

Bill Dempster waited for her in the long, luxurious cross-corridor of the lobby floor. By this time the early New Year's Eve crowd was gathering in the St. Francis lobby, and Tracie had to elbow her way over to him.

He spotted her, first with a blink of surprise, then deliberately studied her, from the unfashionable flowing hair, held back from her face by pearl-studded combs that had belonged to her mother, to the high-heeled white brocade pumps. He was impressed.

"By God, you are something!" He held his arm out to her and she grasped it lightly. "Shall we go?"

"Why not?" But she softened the impudent question with a happy smile.

A mob milled up and down Powell Street, some of them jamming into the crowded cable cars for the steep climb to Nob Hill, then over and down to Fisherman's Wharf to end the celebration. Cabs pulled up in front of the St. Francis and zoomed off, stripping gears noisily. Holding onto Tracie, Bill elbowed his way past a line of guests waiting for cabs. He must have infuriated all those waiting their turn, and as he helped Tracie into the cab she overheard the angry remarks of those cheated out of their turn.

Inside the cab Bill let her go reluctantly. He sat looking at her, then one hand reached out, fingered her diamond eardrops.

"Real, I suppose?"

She shrugged. "I didn't buy them. They could be glass, for all I know."

She had never thought much about jewelry until now, when she wanted to impress Bill Dempster with the Berenson financial power. With her cool, confident smile pasted on, she waited tensely for his fingers to continue their exploration, moving down to her throat. The necklace was not ostentatious, the diamonds small but almost perfectly matched, leading to the teardrop stone between her breasts. Though she tried not to appear affected by his touch it was impossible to prevent a pleasurable shiver when his fingers examined the teardrop diamond, his knuckles grazing her breastbone.

"They certainly aren't glass," he remarked.

In her confusion at his touch she lost the

train of conversation. "What aren't glass?" she said.

"The diamonds, of course," he said innocently, though his gaze was directed at the cleavage revealed by her fur jacket.

The cab made its way into the Market Street traffic. Though it was still early in the evening the air was filled with honking horns, noisemakers and shouting. The cab driver half-turned to them.

"How about lettin' you folks off along here on Market? I'll never get through New Montgomery. Everybody and his brother unloading. Must be big doings. Probably the clearing weather brought them out. Been sprinklin' all week."

Bill glanced at Tracie and got her nod.

"This will be fine. Let us out here."

It was just as well. Making their way to the side entrance of the famed Palace Hotel, they caught glimpses of the limousine and cab lineup at the carriage entrance. Half the gentry of San Francisco seemed to be pouring into the hotel, formal gowns sweeping the sidewalk below full-length furs, with escorts suitably stuffed into white tie and tails and, in some cases, collapsible opera hats.

"I've never been in San Francisco on New Year's Eve before," Tracie confessed. "I love it."

"I'm beginning to myself," Bill said, again with that studied expression.

Many in the crowd were bound for the All-Star Dinner Ball in a dining room overlooking the interior Palm Court a story below. When she had been parted from her sable jacket she let Bill show her through the reception salon, which was already crowded. Guests stood around in little groups with either a martini or a manhattan in one hand and an hors d'oeuvre in the other. None of them seemed aware of the room itself with its lofty ceiling, delicate wainscoting and beautiful framed panels all gold and creamy-rich.

Bill nodded and waved to various acquaintances, but didn't stop. Tracie suspected he was merely showing her off to his friends, but she decided to take this as a compliment. They finally inched their way to the dining room, whose long table with two wings had already been set. Its famed gold plates, double-damask napery and heavy silverware impressed her, though she wouldn't have admitted it to him.

"Reminds me of stories about the last queen of Hawaii," she remarked. "Liliuokalani would have felt perfectly at home here."

The crystal chandeliers and wall brackets suddenly blazed with light and Bill said, "Stand right where you are."

Startled, she obeyed. He pulled open the crimson velvet portieres that lined one side of the room, and she swung around to gaze at the interior of the Palm Court before her. The other floors, up to the high dome, were closed off. But a number of early arrivals in the Palm Court stared at her where she stood a floor above them.

"You're attracting a crowd," Bill commented. "It'll be bedlam down there by midnight and we'll have a clear view."

She pretended to preen for his benefit. "Marta Dempster has nothing on me." She stopped, chastising herself. "Sorry. Is she a sore subject?"

"Sorely expensive. Shall we join that herd at the bar?"

"I don't need a drink. I'm drunk on—" She threw her arms out jubilantly, "—on New Year's Eve."

Tracie swung around and accepted his arm, and they returned to the reception salon in high spirits.

Tracie and Bill caused no stir as they joined the party, particularly as they were eclipsed by Victor Berenson's arrival with a quiet, uncertain, somewhat dowdily dressed young woman in an ankle-length street dress with huge puffed sleeves and a tan raincoat that Victor was removing.

Tracie gasped.

"Where the devil did he find that child?" Bill said. "Oh, it's the young lady I saw at the hotel," he said after looking at her more closely.

Tracie tried to play along but she wanted to choke her insensitive father. Apparently he had simply invited Diane Thorpe to the banquet without giving her time to change. It was cruel and thoughtless — and typical of him.

"What a rotten trick to play on her!" Tracie muttered. "Let's go and show her she's among friends anyhow."

Bill agreed, but as they walked the length of the room he asked quietly, "Who is she? Has he known her long?"

Tracie was about to blurt out that Victor had only met her that afternoon but she knew it would only make matters worse. "Not too long," she said casually. "I know her. She works here in the city. She's very nice."

The two couples met and introductions were made. Diane was even more reserved than earlier that afternoon, no doubt because she knew she wasn't dressed appropriately. Victor was his usual expansive self.

"Isn't she lovely? Name's Dinah Thorpe. This is my friendly young rival who thinks he's going to run me out of business, William Dempster. What say, Dempster? You'd never guess I met this pretty little creature behind a counter in a department store this afternoon."

Before Dempster could think of a suitable reply Tracie held out her hand, still in its sleek opera glove, and shook Diane's shrinking fingers.

"How nice to see you again, Mrs. Thorpe! You're just in time. These gentlemen have nothing better to do, so why don't we let them get us something to drink, shall we?"

The men started to walk off obediently until Diane stopped them in her shy, breathy voice. "Could I — I don't mean to cause any trouble, but I'd like a glass of water, if I might."

"Oh, come now," Victor coaxed. "It's New Year's Eve. Surely you'll have one little drink. Say a manhattan. You'll like it. I'll have them water it down with cherry juice or something."

But Tracie noticed that Bill had already signaled one of the waiters who was pouring a champagne glass full of water from a miniature pitcher. This annoyed Victor but he let the incident pass and took two glasses off the tray, a martini for his daughter and a manhattan for himself. Like Tracie, Bill Dempster took a martini and proposed a toast.

"They say it's bad luck to drink to a happy

new year before midnight, so — here's to good friends." He clinked the rim of Diane's glass. "And new friends."

Tracie refused to let him know she was piqued because he drank to Diane Thorpe before he drank to her. She gaily added, "Amen to that. And here's to us. May we all live a thousand years."

Diane gave an embarrassed little laugh. "Good heavens!" But she joined the toast. This time Bill's glass touched Tracie's and she caught his penetrating gaze over the glass. This time she was unafraid to return it — his suspicions about her family were suddenly the farthest thing from her mind.

Soon they were joined by other guests, who appeared to want to welcome Victor's daughter to San Francisco, a voyage she hadn't made in more than a year. Victor and Bill as old football fans were always welcome, but Tracie was sure their friends' real interest lay in the identity of Diane Thorpe and her connection with Victor Berenson. Neither Tracie nor her father offered any explanation.

A waiter came along with hot hors d'oeuvres and Bill offered her a curled up bit of meat on a toothpick. It smelled of garlic. She refused it and took a caviar and salmon canapé, but when Victor offered Diane the toothpick she accepted with her attractive smile and ate the meat off the stick. Victor did the same.

"Good, aren't they?"

Diane hesitated. "It was odd. What was it?"

Victor beamed. "Snails."

The young woman choked, coughed and turned pale. Bill quickly offered her a canapé. "Try this. Not quite so exotic."

"If you were closer," Tracie told her father, "I'd give you a good swift kick where it would do the most good."

Unperturbed, Victor grinned in return, but Tracie's remark had shocked Diane. "Please, it wasn't his fault. I should have known. I thought it was an anchovy."

Everyone smiled and murmured understandably, giving Victor a chance for a private word with his daughter.

"You notice how she fits in? She's really a find."

"What does that mean?"

"Did you know she takes shorthand and can type?"

"Yes. She told me so in the store today."

"And that she's being let go come January second?"

"I knew it was a temporary job. Now see here, dad, she's a decent young woman. Respectable."

"A divorcée."

"Just because she's pretty and young doesn't mean you can — well — just watch yourself. She seems very inexperienced."

"If I had a mustache I'd twirl it," he teased her. "Ah, here she is. Dinah, we're going in to dinner now, so you can stop giving Dempster the benefit of those soulful eyes."

Bill and Tracie walked in behind them.

"She seems like a nice kid," he remarked.

"She older than I am."

"You'd never know — I mean," he corrected himself in a hurry, "she isn't used to all this. She's quite unsophisticated. But not stupid."

"I hope dad doesn't try to take advantage of her."

"I doubt if he could," Bill said, chuckling. "As I say, she's no fool."

They searched for their places and finally found them. "Here we are," Bill said. "We didn't make it to the head table, you notice. Unlike your father."

Unlike Diane Thorpe as well, Tracie thought. She felt a slight twinge of jealousy. She and Bill were seated far down a side wing of the table while Victor and Diane sat not far from the managing director of the charity game.

"I'm every bit as naive as Diane Thorpe is," Tracie insisted as she picked up the gold plate set before her and examined it. "I haven't eaten on a gold plate since I was a girl. Dad took my cousins and me to a banquet for some descendant of King Lunalilo, but we couldn't eat off the gold plate. They put down our china plates on top of the gold...Well, I'll be damned!"

A waiter was doing the same thing as she spoke.

Bill laughed, and Tracie noticed an unexpected tenderness in it. "Someday, the way you Berensons are going, you'll have an entire gold service, if that's what you want."

Banishing her own childhood dreams of splendor, Tracie took up her cocktail fork (definitely silver) and began to eat the oysters on the half-shell.

The long dinner was interrupted by toasts, good-natured betting on East versus West in the next day's game, and especially by the rising sounds of celebration in the Palm Court below them.

It was nearing twelve before most of the guests began to drift off to further celebrations. The heavy portieres had been opened by this time and those remaining at the banquet could watch the dancers below circling to the strains of "Cheek to Cheek."

"Shall we?" Bill asked, standing close behind Tracie, his mouth tickling her ear.

"That depends. Shall we what?"

"Join the crowd down there."

"I don't like to leave dad with Mrs. Thorpe. He's liable to make things rough for her if he takes her home."

"If so, he's already done it. They're gone."

She looked around. A dozen people shared their vantage point, watching the dancers in the court below, but Victor and Diane Thorpe were not among them. She was slightly troubled but reminded herself that the young woman was old enough to take care of herself.

"And God knows my father is old enough."

The remark stopped Bill for a minute. "How's that?"

"Nothing. They're beginning to throw serpentine and confetti. Let's get down there before the new year begins."

They pushed their way out to the elevator and in a few minutes were gyrating through a rhumba among the dancers in the Palm Court. Varicolored lights played over them. The cacophony of music, voices and echoes bouncing from wall to wall grew louder.

"Can't hear yourself think," Bill complained. "Do you mind?"

"Well, it's to be expected. It was always called The City That Knows How. That covers about everything."

She laughed. The noise, and especially the

music, got into her blood. She had never danced so well, her hips and shoulders swaying provocatively to the music. Her pulse pounded and she knew she could have gone on like this forever. She felt the same passion in Bill. His cool, clever blue eyes were hot with excitement, and when they came together in the dance his arms held her firmly.

They were still close in each other's arms when the music broke off and the crowd began to count off the seconds while the drum rolled: "Twenty-three...twenty-two...twenty-one..."

Holding her, Bill joined the call: "Twenty... nineteen... Come on, sweetheart... seventeen..."

She echoed him, "Sixteen...fifteen..."

Noisemakers snapped in their faces. Toy horns began to blow, almost but not quite drowning out the cries: "Five...four..."

"Happy new year!"

They were entangled by more confetti and streamers while the colored spotlights turned, giving the figures around them a ghostly effect, like phantoms − first green, then blue, then crimson.

"Happy nineteen thirty-six!"

Bill's face neared her to kiss her but he stopped when he felt her suddenly become tense.

"What is it?"

She smiled lamely. "That's weird. I suddenly felt — I don't know, scared." She laughed, pushing the feeling aside. "I should never have eaten those oysters. Happy nineteen thirty-six, pal. Let's start in where we left off."

They kissed, and a good deal of her apprehension was banished in their embrace. She adored the way he held her and demanded a response from her tremulous mouth...tremulous only in the aftermath of her fear. But fear of what? She had no idea.

Breathing hard, they parted briefly with their arms still interlocked.

"How's the weird feeling?" Bill said, still concerned.

"Gone. Evaporated. You are a genie."

"Genius? Tell it to your father."

"No. A — never mind." She began to laugh, her spirits reviving. "We must look like we were caught in a snowstorm. You've got confetti all over your head."

"You too."

They began to shake their heads while moving out of the Palm Court together.

"By merest chance," he said, "I just happen to have a suite upstairs. Nice view. Like to see it and have a nightcap before I take you back to the St. Francis?"

She marveled at his smoothness — at the

170

casual ease of his invitation. Perhaps he was used to nightcaps in his room with single young ladies. After all, these weren't the prewar days of innocence. This was 1935...make that 1936...

"Why not?" she answered gaily. "I think I have room for just one more very small drink. About so big." She gestured with her thumb and forefinger.

They walked to the elevators arm in arm in what seemed to be an excellent understanding. "I feel heady, as if I'd drunk too much champagne," she murmured, her head now resting on his shoulder.

"But you didn't. I ought to know."

"It's New Year's Eve, that's all...last year we celebrated at home on Akua. We were all together and Ilima was there, really enjoying herself. We had a wonderful time, all of us."

She thought he might have lost interest in Ilima by now, but when they left the elevator on the seventh floor Bill pursued the matter. "That was a long time before this past fall. I imagine Victor must have been getting a little tired of her by the time their wedding came around."

"What?"

"Well, he always has been kind of fickle. According to everything I hear." She was beginning to react with indignation when he back-tracked. "Okay. Maybe he loved Ilima. But I'll bet the rest of your family wasn't as enthusiastic about the marriage. You've got to remember that after he married her, their share of the estate would shrink considerably."

"Are you saying one of us pushed Ilima over that pali?"

He sighed. He must realize by now that this conversation was not conducive to lovemaking.

"No. Everything points to the fact that she died alone." He started to unlock the door to his suite but stopped briefly with his hand on the key. "The truth is, I believe someone said something and drove her to do it."

"But what would anyone hold over Ilima? She never did an underhanded thing in her life."

"It might not have been something she did. Damn this key! Stuck again."

Once again Tracie was torn by the easily rekindled sadness at the loss of her friend and hurt by Bill's suspicions. She put her gloved hand over his on the key. "Ilima was the sister I never had."

For the first time he reassured her in what appeared to be an honest way.

"I know."

She had to be content with that.

They moved into the elegant, high-ceilinged foyer and then into the living room itself, all gold and grass-green with copies of French pastoral watercolors and delicate chalks, surely not to the taste of a practical businessman like Bill Dempster. The furniture was even more stiffly uncomfortable than that in the Berensons' suite. The couch, armchair and credenza seemed to be one Louis earlier. Louis Quatorze.

But the view of San Francisco across Market Street and toward the lighted Ferry Building was especially exciting on this night. The world screamed and swirled and shrieked past those windows. Tracie pushed aside the thick lace curtains and looked out.

"Hello, nineteen thirty-six," she called, getting back into the mood.

Bill busied himself rattling fat, rectangular crystal decanters, pouring brandy into snifters and bringing one to Tracie. She took the glass and stared into his eyes, trying to find some tiny indication that this was more than his standard prelude to lovemaking. It was hard to tell. His eyes, too, searched her face. Was he looking for assurance as well?

"What fools we mortals be," she whispered with a smile, and the tense, searching look vanished. The amused and cynical Bill Dempster had been there beneath the surface all the time.

He was smiling now but she was unsure what it meant. When he took his own glass and began to sip the brandy she wondered what was going through his mind. She sensed that he still wanted her, and God knew she wanted him. But what would it lead to?

Behind Bill she saw the open door to the bedroom of his suite. Somehow the whole situation, now that they were there, seemed tawdry, but she had contributed to it — she certainly couldn't blame it on Bill Dempster.

Her lips were still moist with the French brandy when he drew her to him. She bit her lips nervously, and felt the glass in his hands pressing into her bare back just above the low cut of her satin gown. She shivered. He smiled and set the glass down.

"Want to go home?"

She said nothing, torn between her desire for him and an uncertainty that was based on a strong sense that he was using her in some way that had nothing to do with sex.

"You are a darling," she said finally and kissed him, intending it to be no more than an "I've had a lovely time" kiss. But almost as if it were against her will she felt her arms go around his neck, holding him prisoner, and he responded as she knew he would, with the same passion that burned in her.

There was the taste of him and the pressure of his thighs against her as he insistently pushed her back toward the bedroom, holding her against him so close she could feel the pearl studs on his shirtfront through her clothing. He dropped her on the lavish bed in the semi-darkness of the bedroom and she lay there momentarily, white satin and gold flesh faintly gleaming in the lights from the street outside the long, elegant windows.

Her pulse was racing as he dropped down on her. He was dark and shadowy in the faint illumination from the street. He bent down to kiss her hungrily, moving from her lips to her throat. He was used to getting what he wanted, she thought, and was certainly adept at mixing business with pleasure. She started to struggle beneath him.

"I always knew you were a hellcat," he muttered, twisting and holding her arms beside her while his body crushed hers.

"No!" she pushed hard, then gathered her strength to throw him off. She could not trust him. Maybe she *had* begun to love him, but he was only using her. He had made no commitments to her. He invited and took what he wanted. Afterward, she would be committed because she would want him again. And again.

She breathed long and hard, seemed to yield.

Then she pushed him with a suddenness that astonished him. She slipped out from under his body, feeling his fingers drag across her disheveled gown, trying vainly to hold her slippery body.

She caught a glimpse of his face, stormy and furious.

Trying to calm him she spoke as honestly as she ever had in her life.

"If I loved anyone, it would be you."

Uneasily, she watched him ball his fist. He brought it down hard on the smooth surface of the little night stand.

"You really are a bitch!"

She knew that she'd led him on and that it was true, but how could he possibly understand the confusion of her feelings? "I don't mean to be."

Perhaps he read something of her real feelings, or guessed that she doubted the depth of his own involvement, because the scowl gradually vanished and his expression seemed kind, almost warm. Maybe he was seeing her in a different light. He shrugged and said lightly, "Oh, well, better luck next time."

The remark once more put her on her guard, though it in no way reduced her hunger for him. Someday, she knew, she would forget her suspicions, her fears, and love him and be loved, even if for him it was only a passing affair.

The sounds of New Year's revelry had died down somewhat by the time Tracie had pulled herself together. It was surprising how few wrinkles there were in the satin evening gown, and her hair, though disheveled, still looked attractive. She took up one of his silver brushes from the dresser and repaired the damage until her hair gleamed sandy gold. Bill watched her as he got into his dinner jacket again.

She wrinkled her nose at him in the mirror. "Do you realize I may have to return to the St. Francis without a wrap? That checkroom is bound to be closed by now."

But Bill Dempster appeared equal to anything. He produced her sable jacket from his closet. "I bribed the girl to bring it up here right after the banquet."

"You dog!" But she smiled when she said it.

His hands did not linger on her shoulders as she had expected when he wrapped the jacket around her. But then his eyes studied her face again as if he were trying to read her true feelings. It was an impossible task, since she didn't know herself what her feelings were. She felt passion for him, but judging by her father and her cousins, passion could be brief and shallow. Was there anything else about Bill Dempster that could make him the one man in her life?

As they left his suite she hoped and prayed that they would someday know the ecstasy they had almost had tonight, that they would share more than a brief evening of love together.

9

Hugging her arms against the cool night and recalling another recent, more muscular embrace, Tracie let herself into the St. Francis suite as quietly as possible. She didn't want to awaken her father. It was almost two A..M. and the football game would begin all too soon.

By the time she had bathed and gotten to bed it was a quarter to three. Shortly afterward, she heard her father moving around in the living room between their two bedrooms. A small object, probably a brass cigarette box, fell off the cabinet near her bedroom door. This was followed by a gentle knock — gentle, in any case, for Victor, who usually banged when he wanted to announce himself.

"Go to bed, for heaven's sake!" she muttered to herself.

He tried again, knocking a bit louder. He wasn't going to go away. Yawning, she got out of bed, stepped into her satin travel slippers and slipped on her heavy satin dressing gown as she stumbled over to the door.

"What is it?" she said sleepily.

"Just a word, honey. Little question."

She threw open the heavy door. "Have you any idea what time it is? Good Lord!...Have you been with Mrs. Thorpe all this time?"

He was feeling good but far from drunk. "Lord, no! That's a decent young woman, I'll have you know. Just met a couple of sports-writers in the Southpaw Grill across the street. We had a few. I laid a couple more bets on the West team tomorrow."

"Today."

His eyes opened wider. "Right. Today. Anyway, I wanted to ask you what you thought about Dinah. Competent girl, wouldn't you say?"

His question surprised her. "Competent? Who knows? Don't tell me that's what attracted you."

"Well — you do need a secretary, and all. What with Ilima gone. And she says she takes shorthand. Types, too."

Tracie leaned against the wall. "If she didn't work out we'd have to pay her way back, see that she gets home to the Coast."

"Sure. Sure."

"And — dad?"

He began to look apprehensive. He knew that tone.

"You said she's a decent young woman. No midnight seductions under the coco-palms. You know what I mean?"

He began to remove his overcoat. As he did so his fringed white silk scarf fell out of a pocket along with a small, worn, black kid glove. He let the scarf go and smoothed out the dainty glove.

"I wouldn't hurt her," he said, looking up. "She's kind of like a scared little bird. Looks at you so trusting..."

Tracie studied him as his voice trailed off. It was a god-awful hour, but she thought he was sincere.

"Okay. We'll check, see if she's who she says—" She broke off. "I'll call her after the game and talk to her. I'll also see how she feels about a temporary job."

"Temporary? Now, just a—"

"To start with. Lots of people can't cope with our climate. We'll just wait and see. *Goodnight, dad.*"

She closed the door, leaving him there with the small black glove in his hand.

If Tracie was not in quite her usual fine mood at one o'clock New Year's afternoon, she didn't show it as she climbed the stairs to the Kezar Stadium press box in the company of Wayne Croyde's parents. Several men from the various wire services were already seated next to battered typewriters, eagle-eyed spotters and piles of paper cigarette packs. Thermoses were likewise handy, "against the chill" as Arla Croyde explained, ordering her stout, purple-faced husband Leopold Croyde to "Get organized, my love. I'm freezing."

It was Leopold's job to mix the contents of the steaming thermoses with those in his set of three silver flasks.

"Yes, dear. Coming right along." He reminded her in a lower voice, "Though they always serve coffee and sandwiches in the half."

Arla paid no attention to this. A good-looking redhead who was similar to her brother Bill, only in the deep blue of her eyes, she enjoyed her "little nip" and was apt to be cranky without it.

"Where are the programs? Oh, thank you, Tracie."

She riffled through the pages. "Doesn't my boy photograph well? He really could be a movie star." She folded back the first few pages of the program and Tracie glanced at the page that was handed to her.

"Awfully good."

"Quite the Adonis," a male voice offered over Tracie's shoulder. "Now, if he can lead the West to victory, he'll do my wallet a big favor."

Tracie felt the quick excitement of Bill Dempster's voice.

Mrs. Croyde turned around and smiled. "Dear Bill! I knew you'd show up to cheer our boy on. Didn't I say so, Leopold?"

"Er — so you did, my love."

As for Bill, he kissed the cheek Arla Croyde presented and then, feeling he was on a roll, kissed Tracie's cheek as well. She grinned and took the brandy-laced hot coffee he offered in a paper cup. Mrs. Croyde missed none of this.

"You know, Bill, it's not official yet, but Wayne is going to marry this gorgeous creature."

Bill was all innocence. "Is that a fact?" He gazed intently into Tracie's eyes with an expression in which she caught glimmer of amusement. "When?"

Flaming with embarrassment, Tracie stammered, "N-nothing's been decided. I mean — we don't really have any plans."

"My dear!" Mrs. Croyde gasped.

Leopold Croyde fumbled to smooth over the exchange. "Now, love, we must let the children handle these things for themselves. It really isn't our affair."

Others had begun to edge into the press box along the aisles and sideways and the Croydes turned to speak to the new arrivals. Bill took this opportunity to murmur in Tracie's ear, "Affairs are more fun, my dear."

She considered it wise not to hear him.

Tracie joined in greeting the newcomers. There were hugs all around while the red-jerseyed East team ran out onto the field for a pregame warm-up. The rest of the stadium, now packed, cheered.

There was a stir in the press box at the arrival of the popular Victor Berenson, accompanied by a neatly dressed young woman in a belted raincoat and a smart blue tam. Tracie felt rather than saw Bill Dempster's surprised reaction beside her. At least the presence of Diane Thorpe told her where Victor had gone this morning when Tracie would have liked to have him escort her to the stadium. She greeted Diane in a friendly way, shaking the young woman's hand.

"Diane! You're here at last. Mr. and Mrs. Croyde, may I introduce you to our good friend, Mrs. Thorpe? Diane Thorpe."

While the Croydes welcomed Victor and his attractive companion, Bill Dempster commented to Tracie, "Your father looks a bit winded."

Tracie studied her father. He had stopped at the top of the steps and was breathing heavily, his hands on his hips. He looked gray, his features strained. His grin didn't fool Tracie.

"Touch of asthma," he said, catching his daughter's look.

She knew he would be furious if she fussed over his health in front of all these people, but she was worried. "Dad, come and sit down. You're blocking everybody's view."

He understood that and sat down abruptly in the seat assigned to United Press, whose occupant had gotten up with his glasses focused on the field. Victor had to rise again and find his own seat. It was obviously an effort, and Tracie exchanged a quick, worried glance with Bill. While Victor eased down onto the hard bench, Bill murmured, "Shall I get a doctor?"

She knew that if he did so there would be a scene. Relieved, she noticed that her father had started to regain color and was letting Mrs. Thorpe fuss over him without a murmur.

Tracie looked at the two with a hard smile. "Well, I'll be damned! He gave her my seat."

Bill was amused. "Don't be jealous. You're lucky. You get to sit by me."

"Thanks. Not that I'm jealous. But I don't like people giving away my property."

His glance at Victor was enough. She explained crossly, "I'm referring to my seat."

The West team, in blue jerseys, came running out of the tunnel and spread across the field to the roar of the partisan crowd. With Bill's glasses Tracie made out Wayne, whose parents, wildly excited, were nudging neighbors and pointing him out.

By kickoff time Tracie could see that her father was very much himself as she watched him explain the technical aspects of the game to Diane Thorpe. She picked up the game quickly but cut in to ask about the Shriner's Crippled Children's Hospital for whom the game was played.

"She certainly knows how to get around my father," Tracie said, and accepted in her cup a few more drops of the brandy Bill offered.

"Maybe she really likes him," Bill said.

"Don't be silly. She's trying to please him. She wants that job."

"What job?" For some reason his voice was sharp, catching her unaware.

"Why — the secretarial job. We need a secretary at Orchid Tree. Ever since Ilima died we've been fumbling along." She looked at him. "Dorado Star does have secretaries, doesn't it?"

"Certainly. But it's not quite the same, is it?"

She hated it when her own doubts and questions were voiced by him. He sat there rubbing his coffee cup between his palms and staring at Victor and Diane Thorpe, who had their heads together while Victor explained why a field goal try by the West went wide.

Tracie tried to ignore them. "Wayne seems to be bottled up. He was counting on today's game to show the scouts."

"He'll show them."

Bill was right. In the second quarter Wayne surprised everyone by intercepting a pass and zig-zagging to the East fifteen-yard line before being brought down. The Croydes went wild. Bill used this celebration to embrace Tracie, who returned the hug and kiss with enthusiasm. Diane Thorpe was watching them. Catching Tracie's eye she smiled. Tracie wondered if there wasn't a wistful note in that smile. Perhaps she was thinking of her own lost love...

Victor and Leopold Croyde were on their feet, waving arms, yelling, "Go for broke!" It was far too much activity for her father, Tracie thought. She leaned forward and tugged at her father's topcoat, but he waved her away impatiently.

Unfortunately for Wayne and his team, they failed to make good on his run. At halftime the score was still even at zero. Victor complained as he began to look around for food while the working press nearby toted up statistics. Tracie had always heard about the fabulous Shriner pageantry between the halves and watched wide-eyed as bands played while marching the length of the field. They were dressed in splendid satin and velvet costumes, scarlet and green, blue and gold, purple, an Arabian Nights in color, and Tracie couldn't take her eyes off the field for a moment.

"Mrs. Thorpe has taken your father out," Bill said as the halftime entertainment ended.

She looked around in a panic. There were many reasons why Victor might have left the press box. The simplest was a trip to the toilets below. But he would hardly ask a new acquaintance, a woman, to accompany him. Maybe they intended to visit the guest box, not quite so hard to get into as the press box, but many of his friends were there.

Tracie got up quickly. "How did he look?"

"Hard to say. You've got to handle this with care. He isn't going to thank you for embarrassing him in front of this crowd."

She had to admit Bill knew her father's nature. "I'll be careful."

"Shall I go along?"

"I can handle it."

All the same, she was glad when he followed her down the steep stairs to the rest rooms. Bill started in to check but Tracie saw Victor down on the grounds inside the stadium where the VIPs parked their cars. He and Diane Thorpe were headed toward the Berenson limousine.

Tracie remarked wryly, "Do you suppose we've interrupted a little smooching in the back seat of the limousine?"

Bill disagreed. "Not while there's a game on. Your father is a sportsman. There may be a little groove in his life later for Mrs. Thorpe, but this isn't the time for it."

Tracie wasn't comforted and looked around furtively.

"Where the devil is the chauffeur? We may need him to get a doctor."

"If you need one, I'll get him. Don't worry."

He was being awfully considerate. If this kept on she would have to stop thinking of him as dangerous. Remembering the night before and their interrupted lovemaking, she was relieved to be able to rely on him.

The chauffeur was standing near one of the tunnels, watching the third quarter, and judging from the roar of the crowd, there was quite a bit of action on the field. But Tracie no longer had any interest in the game. She reached the big black limousine and found Victor slouching in the back seat while Diane Thorpe held a silver whiskey flask to his lips. She looked over her shoulder in obvious relief as they approached.

"Oh, thank heaven it's you, Miss Berenson! Your father seems tuckered out. It was all those stairs. He asked for a little whiskey. Here. Would you like to—?"

Victor waved his daughter away impatiently. "Asthma. That's all. Give me that flask again, Dinah." He sat up a little straighter, pointing out to Tracie, "She's first-rate in an emergency. You stay right here, Dinah."

"Diane," Tracie reminded him, but it was a small matter and useless anyway. A minute later it was "Dinah" again and the young woman smiled at Tracie.

Victor leaned forward. "I'll be right as rain. That you, Dempster? Bet you got your fingers crossed hoping I'll kick the bucket and leave room for you. Well, don't you believe it. I haven't run out my string yet. Dinah, tell Dempster to scout what's doing on the field. I've got three thousand riding on the West today."

Dempster went off as an enormous swell of sound rose above the stadium walls.

"Evidently somebody's scored," Tracie remarked before turning to her father again. "Father, do you have any pain? Your chest? Your arm?"

She started to get into the car but Diane Thorpe was in the way. The young woman tried to draw back to give her room but Victor was growing more vigorous by the minute.

"I'm fine. Perfect. I told you, I couldn't breathe. It was asthma. You know how I get it in spring."

"This is winter."

Despite Tracie's concerned remarks it was clear he didn't welcome his daughter's interference. His new secretary appeared to be more than an adequate substitute.

Giving up with trying to find the source of his trouble Tracie started back to the stands, reaching them just in time to hear another stunning explosion from the football field. She met Bill Dempster coming out to relay the score.

"How is he feeling? Ready for a shock?"

She guessed that Victor's bet might be endangered.

"East scored?"

"In spades. Three touchdowns, one conversion. West has one field goal."

"And Wayne?"

"Poor devil. It was his intercepted pass that set up the East's second touchdown."

"Oh, lord! It'll be a sorry trip home."

They decided to wait a few minutes before

telling Victor the bad news, just in case the West made a comeback. But it wasn't to happen. By the time Tracie and Bill reached Victor the crowd was pouring out of the stadium and Victor had already heard the bad news: East — 19, West — 3.

Victor was glum as they rode back downtown but he pleased Tracie by giving Bill a ride and dropping him off at the Palace Hotel before heading up Geary to the St. Francis. Tracie would have liked to accept the date Bill offered her that evening but she knew Wayne and his family would need comforting.

It wasn't until she reached the Berenson suite with Victor and Diane that she realized her refusal of Bill's invitation might have saved bloodshed.

A cable was waiting for her from Theo in Honolulu.

PINEAPPLE CANNERY DEAL ARRANGED BY FORMER OWNER WD STOP HE KNEW COMPANY DEEP IN TROUBLE WHEN HE SETTLED IT ON HER DAY BEFORE DEPARTURE STOP INTENDED IT FOR PRESENT OWNER LOVE THEO

Tracie's recent gratitude to Bill turned to disgust and anger. Bill had put his ex-wife up to selling Victor her stock. In doing so he had cost

Victor all his ready cash and much of the money Orchid Tree needed if it was to hire the seasonal spring workers.

And to think he'd almost lulled Tracie's suspicions by trying to make love to her! She looked at her father, who was showing Diane around the suite. He didn't need this shock on top of his bad spell today.

Maybe Diane Thorpe *could* help. The quiet little woman with her big brown eyes seemed to be a calming influence on Victor. In that respect, she truly was like Tracie's lost friend.

10

It was Bill Dempster who provided Victor Berenson with a physician in spite of the holiday. Dr. Kenji Tokuda was about thirty-five, personable and had only one handicap as far as Tracie was concerned; he was a classmate and close friend of Dempster's from Stanford. He talked Victor into going for a proper hospital checkup, which, once completed, only vindicated the cantankerous patient.

"I told you I'm strong as a horse," Victor announced as he supervised Tracie and Diane Thorpe while they packed.

Tracie disagreed. "You're not strong as a horse. Dr. Tokuda said you have an irregular heartbeat and a heart murmur besides."

"It never murmurs a damn word to me. Dinah, you look mighty pretty in those polka dots. Trace, whyn't you dress more like Dinah here, instead of like you just stepped out of a slick magazine?"

Tracie refused to be ruffled. "Because my bones would look pretty funny in dots. I don't have Diane's petite figure."

"Curvy, you mean."

Diane blushed and explained to Tracie, "I thought voile would be appropriate in a warm climate like the Islands."

Victor was feeling good enough to tease her. "Don't forget to get your money changed before we sail. And how about your passport?"

Diane, reacting as Victor expected, got flustered.

"But I thought – oh! I've never had a passport."

"Ignore him," Tracie advised Diane on her way out of the room. She had been headed out to see Wayne, who had pulled a ligament in his leg during the final minutes of play. "He has the sense of humor of a two-year-old! Hawaii is still part of the U.S.A."

Victor grinned, pleased with the success of his joke. Diane finally joined in with his laughter, despite her embarrassment at being fooled.

Fortunately Dr. Tokuda, who lived in the Islands and had a practice on the Big Island, was sailing on the same ship with the Berensons, the *President Hoover*. Victor's checkup and three-day stay in the hospital had caused the family to miss the deluxe passenger liner,

Lorelei, for which Tracie was grateful. She knew she couldn't trust herself with Bill Dempster, who most likely would have prepared an excuse for his nefarious stock dealings.

He might even agree with Victor's astonishing view of the trick that caused him to spend money on stock Bill Dempster wanted to unload. "All's fair in love and you-know-what," Victor had said easily when Tracie told him that Dempster had put Marta up to selling the pineapple cannery stock. All the same, Victor's craggy face hadn't quite concealed the speculative narrowing of his gray eyes. He would come up with some sort of revenge against Dempster.

Meanwhile, Wayne and his parents were delighted to see Tracie, even though it was a brief visit to say good-bye. This made her feel guilty as well as angry at herself. Why was it so impossible to appreciate Wayne's sterling qualities? He was worth a dozen of Bill Dempster, and he needed her now. His injury had occurred in front of every scout in the stadium, probably lessening his chances to be drafted into the pros. But she had to go back to Akua City, especially now...her father needed her to keep the plantation running smoothly.

The *President Hoover* was a fine, sturdy ship but Honolulu was only one of its ports. Its real destination was Yokohama, and the luxury cruise ship amenities were played down. Worse, Diane Thorpe proved to be seasick for most of the voyage, though she made a valiant effort to fight this scourge.

With his usual compassion, Victor remarked to Tracie as he sat down to a thick steak garnished with lobster, "If I'd known she was going to spend all her time in her bunk I'd have thought twice before bringing her along."

"You didn't 'bring her along.' You hired her," Tracie snapped. "We don't all have cast-iron stomachs."

But the voyage had been smooth. It was just Diane's misfortune to have gotten seasickness.

Victor's carping finally ended on the beautiful morning just after dawn when they caught their first glimpse of Molokai, a dark smudge on the port bow. Off to starboard he proudly pointed it out to Diane, who stood eagerly at his side. "That's Makapuu Point. Then comes Koko Head, and pretty soon, old Diamond head itself. And we're nearly home."

Diane clapped her hands in delight, a habit that Victor found charming. "And that is your island?"

"Lord, no! That's Oahu, where Honolulu is. We're on Akua. That's off to the southwest. Behind Molokai and Maui."

"I'll never learn all the names," she moaned. "I really have tried but it's so confusing."

Victor patted her on the back as she leaned over the rail, looking out over the clear water. "It'll come to you. Don't worry."

"But it's so wonderful. Honolulu and Waikiki Beach and the South Seas right at our doorstep."

"We're not in the South Seas, Dinah. And we're not staying in Honolulu. That's just a big, ugly city. We're headed right home for Akua the minute we shake off this old tub."

Tracie tried to argue that Honolulu was not an ugly city, but when she sensed Diane's disappointment at not being able to see it she dropped the matter, instead focusing on the beauty of their own land. "You'll like Akua much better, Diane. It's a real tropical island. You've never seen so many varieties of flowers...and the trees. I'm sure you'll like it."

"I'm sure I will," Diane said, not wanting to seem disagreeable.

"That's a good girl," Victor said, glad her mind was off Honolulu at least for the moment.

The big liner had dropped anchor in quarantine off Diamond Head, and it seemed unfair to Tracie that with all the romantic fantasies of glamorous Waikiki that Victor and she had filled Diane full of, they should be so close to it and yet so far away. Victor only rubbed the salt in by pointing out the narrow white strip of sand and the sprawling pink beauty of the Royal Hawaiian Hotel.

"And on the horizon there," he gestured, "that's the Koolau mountain range. The city is beginning to crawl right up all those canyons. My girl here says they're rainy, dark and spooky but that's mighty valuable real estate. And down to the harbor — the fleet, that's Ewa-way. Beyond the city, around Pearl Harbor. Greatest fleet in the world."

Tracie suggested, "Can't we spend the night on Oahu and then leave bright and early tomorrow?"

Victor would have none of that.

"Nope. Got to get home. Whole place has probably fallen apart with no one but Sam Kahana to oversee things."

Tracie rolled her eyes disgustedly in full view of her father but he only chuckled.

Of course she could appreciate his anxiety to get home. She was anxious to study the books, see how they could outsmart Bill Dempster and keep their own affairs in the black. Bill still didn't know why she had turned down his invitations during the two days before he sailed. There were moments when she wondered what his next step would be. And she had to wonder: would she have found him so attractive if she and her father had been able to walk all over him?

It must be a love-hate relationship, she decided — she loved to hate him.

Later, when the ship was steaming slowly into harbor in the shadow of the Aloha Tower, Diane Thorpe whispered plaintively, "If only I could have seen Waikiki just once!"

"You will. We come over to Oahu every few weeks."

"Really?" Her mood lightened. "Oh, I love this job. I do hope I can make it permanent."

Tracie pretended not to hear her as she waved to Theo on the dock below. How odd, Tracie thought, that Lili was nowhere in sight.

Dr. Tokuda stood at the rail a few yards away and Tracie moved along the rail to thank him again. His presence had been reassuring on the voyage. He was a lean man, slightly above average height. His intelligence and reserve were obvious on first acquaintance, and his lively sense of humor came as a delightful surprise — altogether an appealing man, Tracie thought. But she knew he was happily married, she even knew his wife, Michi, who had been a couple of years ahead of her in college. After exchanging news of mutual acquaintances, Dr. Tokuda became quite friendly with the Berensons and Diane Thorpe, and together they passed several hours of the voyage dancing to the music of the ship's swing band.

"Home again, home again," he quoted. "God shed His grace on thee. I think I have two quotes a little mixed."

She laughed. "I want to thank you for everything, not least of which was your dancing. Tell Michi she taught you well."

"Matter of fact, I taught her," he boasted. Then his gaze drifted to the mountains that hovered over Honolulu on three sides.

"Homesick?" she asked.

He nodded. "Although I never feel at home on Oahu. But when I see that little town of Hilo tomorrow I will know my odyssey is over. I managed to combine my medical convention with the All-Star game which, incidentally, I lost fifty dollars on."

"Will Michi be angry?"

"She'll be delighted. I lost the fifty to her. She bet me the East would win."

Tracie laughed.

As they were docking Victor came along and made an offer that indicated he, too, thought of Dr. Tokuda as a friend as well as his physician.

"You anxious to get home, doctor?"

"I am, sir."

"Okay. Come along with my gang here. My

cargo ship is taking us home in an hour. The *Akua Orchid* goes on from Akua to Hilo harbor. How about it?"

Dr. Tokuda was delighted. He would be home more than twenty-four hours early. He shook hands with Victor, adding, "If you or your family should ever need my services, you may count on me, Mr. Berenson."

"Unlikely, doc. But I'll sure keep you in mind. Well, gangplank's down. If you have any more bags, put 'em with ours on the dock and my men will load them on the *Akua Orchid.*"

Minutes later, Tracie and Victor were greeting Theo in the shed beyond the dock. Victor shook his hand, clapped him on the back, said he looked fine "after loafing for two weeks" and accepted the orchid lei his nephew dropped over his head. Tracie showed Theo more affection as he bubbled with his usual enthusiasm and gave her a kiss with each of the remaining three leis as he dropped them around her shoulders — one orchid, one of ginger and one of plumeria, her favorite.

She then introduced him to Diane Thorpe and Dr. Tokuda. Theo quickly noticed the undoubted familiarity between his uncle and the pretty new secretary, but he gave her his most charming welcome, nonetheless. Theo had barely turned to shake hands with Dr. Tokuda

202

before Victor was anxious to leave.

"Where the hell is your sister?" he asked Theo. "We're sailing as soon as the *Orchid* is ready. If she doesn't have time to get down to the dock, we may as well find out right now."

"She had breakfast with Bill Dempster," Theo explained, with a side-glance at Tracie, hoping for a reaction. "He got in two days ago on the *Lorelei*. But she'll be at the dock in time to leave with us."

Knowing how her cousin thought, Tracie knew he'd deliberately phrased his remark so that she couldn't tell who had invited whom. There was a world of difference.

On the way through the wharf area to the dock Theo kept searching for lei vendors. Across the street from the Matson docks he located one, a heavy, majectic-looking Hawaiian woman, stringing vanda orchids while seated on a folding chair behind her board counter.

Theo turned to Diane Thorpe, who was staring at all the sights, pointing at the high, waving coco-palms, gasping at a distant flowering bush.

"Mrs. Thorpe, you look naked."

"What?" Tracie said, by this time exasperated with him. "Theo, stop trying to be funny."

"I'm not." He grinned, gestured toward the

lei vendor. "You need dressing up, Hawaiian-style."

"He's right for once, Dinah," Victor said, not to be outdone by his nephew.

Diane was obviously excited by being the cause of rivalry between the two. Her brown eyes shown in anticipation of the lovely blossoms.

"Is it true? Can I wear all those flowers too, even if I'm not — you know — one of them?"

She was soon assured on this point when Victor came back to drape her dress with half a dozen flower leis. She was so overcome by the gesture that she threw her arms around him, hugging and kissing him.

"What a wonderful, *wonderful* man you are! I'll never forget you."

By the time Theo reached her she had recovered her careful reserve and with a sheepish glance at Victor she merely gave Theo a smile and ducked her head to receive the leis.

Walking beside Tracie, she apologized all the way to the *Akua Orchid*'s gangplank for her behavior. Tracie began to find her exceedingly humble gratitude just a bit boring. She was ashamed of herself, but there it was.

"I really am so sorry," Diane repeated. "I don't know what came over me. I never behave like that. But Victor — Mr. Berenson — has been so kind to me. From the very first."

"And you seem to have dazzled Theo."

"A sweet boy."

Tracie thought of her roguish cousin as many things, but a "sweet boy" wasn't one of them.

Lili Berenson stood at the gangplank of the cargo liner with the man who had driven her there, Bill Dempster. After hugging her uncle and asking what he had brought her from the Coast, Lili met Dr. Tokuda and Mrs. Thorpe with descending notes of interest.

Standing to the side of this activity, Bill remarked dryly to Tracie, "Your cousin has a touching interest in members of her own sex. You can see how fond she is of Mrs. Thorpe."

Though Tracie was amused by Bill's candid remark she tried to play down his cynicism.

"Lili is okay. You seem to enjoy her company."

"Yes." He smiled at her, and said lightly, "In case you're wondering, she came over to me this morning while I was having breakfast in the Royal's dining room. Satisfied?"

"It's none of my business."

"Perfectly true...but getting back to your friend Mrs. Thorpe, Lili is going to be a problem. She thinks the woman is a threat."

Startled, she said, "What on earth do you mean?"

"If your father marries her, it may cut down Liliha's inheritance considerably."

"I can't believe you would suggest something as crude as that again. Besides, it could cut Theo's inheritance too, and he's fawning all over—" She realized what he was saying and added indignantly, "Father has hired a secretary. Not a wife. As a matter of fact, she's more my secretary than my father's. And I seriously doubt that he's interested in marriage again. He's not going to repeat that tragedy."

Bill's eyes were hard. "I certainly hope not." He hesitated, glanced at the little group at the foot of the gangplank before he returned his attention to Tracie. His voice had taken on a warmer tone now as he reached for her hand. She suddenly withdrew from him, busying herself with her vanity case and handbag.

"You did your best to avoid me those last few days in San Francisco. What happened?"

"Nothing at all," she said coolly. "Let's just say that dad and I owe you something for that trick you pulled with Marta's stocks."

His hand fell back; he seemed puzzled. "Don't tell me you're sore about that. I thought we understood each other. You and your father tried to bore into my interests when you finagled that stock from Marta. What do you call that?"

There was no use arguing over it, Tracie

reasoned. She and Victor were only trying to get even after Dempster pushed his way into Akua Sugar and on the very island the Berensons had staked out as their own.

"No one's angry about it," Tracie said, her voice still calm. "We just have to find a way to keep you out of Orchid Tree Enterprises."

He took a deep breath and then turned away with a shrug. She couldn't see his face, but his tone was as light as her own. "You must admit my ploys at least have succeeded in throwing us together."

She agreed just as easily. "One of the stock dividends, you might say."

She thought he just might have been sincere. He did seem to seek her company, to want her. It couldn't all be put on, that scene the other night in the Palace Hotel, or at least so she wanted to believe. Still, she wasn't naive enough to think she was a major factor in his plans.

Tracie turned abruptly when she heard her father calling to her.

"I admire the way you snap to attention," Bill said, teasing her.

She wrinkled her nose at him and walked away. Bill followed, striding along to reach her side. "Don't forget what I said."

"What's that? — all's fair in love and war?"

"No. Don't encourage that young woman to stick her neck out. There could be trouble."

"For heaven's sake, will you drop that foolish idea?" Tracie said, beginning to lose patience.

Bill didn't answer. He saluted Victor, then called, "Hi, Kenji! See you made it across the Pacific without the Dempster Lines. Lili, thanks for your company at breakfast." With that he turned and walked away from the wharves. Tracie steeled herself not to give him the satisfaction of looking back.

True to Victor's promise, the *Akua Orchid* pulled out half an hour later. They had fair seas for January under blue skies, and when they steamed into Akua's U-shaped leeward harbor after noon Diane Thorpe kept saying it was the most romantic sight she had ever seen.

"Inside the harbor the water is every shade of blue and green you can imagine. Mr. Berenson—"

"Victor."

"It's just the way you described it. You've created a paradise."

Theo and Lili exchanged faintly contemptuous glances. Even Tracie found the comment a bit much. "He didn't exactly create it himself, Diane. He did have a little help from higher powers."

"I'm the biggest landowner, and that makes me the highest power on Akua and don't you forget it," Victor announced in his blustery way that was only half joking.

"Of course. But it took a man like you, Mr. — I mean Victor — to know what to do with it."

Lili sidled up to Tracie. "Where did you pick *that* up? Did you ever hear such syrup? I swear, she's enough to give us all diabetes."

Tracie had a certain sympathy for her cousin's viewpoint but thought it unwise to say so. Lili was the last person in the world to whom you could confide a secret. "She took some dictation while we were at sea. She's reasonably competent."

"Oh, great!" Lili hit the rail with the flat of her hand. "We no sooner get out of Ilima's clutches than we fall into this mess."

Chilled by Lili's bitter dismissal of Ilima Mako, Tracie demanded, "What do you mean by that?"

Lili knew that tone, and since she didn't feel at all secure with her powerful uncle she retreated quickly. "Nothing. It's just that this awful woman is a lot worse than Ilima ever was, and you know it."

"Did you talk to Ilima alone the night she died?"

Lili backed away slightly; she looked pale. Was she frightened or just shocked at the implied accusation?

"Not a word. She wasn't much on small talk. She never wanted to talk about anything interesting. Like men...or clothes."

No, Tracie thought. Ilima wasn't likely to be driven to suicide by anything that someone as shallow-minded as Lili could say.

Tracie moved toward the sailors who were throwing the gangplank across from the ship's waist to the jetty dock. It would be uneasy footing without a handhold for a landlubber like Diane Thorpe. Tracie tried to reassure her. "Dad will wait right here on the deck. I'll go across to the jetty. We'll both have our arms out. You can reach either of us."

"Let me do that," Theo interrupted. He made a graceful, sweeping gesture and then leaped nimbly across the plank, landing on the jetty with a graceful spring.

Dr. Tokuda laughed softly. "I may have some unexpected patients if this keeps up," he said to Tracie.

"Don't worry about me," Theo called back to him. "I can take care of myself and little Diane too."

Tracie could see that her father was unpleasantly aware of the difference between his sixty years and her twenty-eight, especially since Theo's leap had impressed the young woman. There were too many currents here,

Tracie thought, and crosscurrents could produce riptides.

Anxious and trembling, Diane Thorpe made the crossing, a distance of five feet. She would have fallen into Theo's waiting arms but she was still swaying by the time Victor reached her and caught her around her waist and shoulders. She hid her face against his shoulder, apologizing in a muffled voice. "It's vertigo — when I look down. I'm so ashamed."

"Nothing to be ashamed of. You poor little thing."

"This from pitiless Victor?" Tracie murmured, but only Dr. Tokuda heard her. He smiled with understanding.

"Come on," Victor urged them. "Car's waiting. It had better be." He walked Diane along the stone jetty toward the sleepy little village. He seemed totally oblivious to stares from the Hawaiians and Japanese lingering around Mr. Nakazawa's Mercantile Center, a clapboard, two-story shop with a rotting porch. Victor waved to his favorite beachcomber, Albie Wimble, who was too drunk to see him and went on snoring from where he was propped up against the barrels and nets he used for fishing.

As Victor and the others moved ahead Tracie and Dr. Tokuda exchanged good-byes. Tracie then followed the others ashore where, flanked by her cousins, she followed her father and Mrs. Thorpe into the village itself. It must have seemed microscopic to a woman used to San Francisco. The main street, unpaved, ran a hundred yards or so around the waterfront, then tapered off into what was little more than a trail, though trucks lumbered over it. A ship chandler's store, a saloon and a broken-down, two-story hotel (now closed) were the landmarks of Akua City, along with the Mercantile Center, which stocked staples and some fresh produce. This area was bisected by one other road, coming down from the plantations in the interior, including the Berenson property.

There were a number of shacks built around the harbor, half-hidden behind bougainvillea and coco-palms. These belonged to field workers or owners of the small papaya and taro patches that dotted the island. Rising steeply behind the village and the harbor was the first range of mountains, their rigid backbone broken by passes leading to hanging valleys and still higher ranges.

A sailing schooner had anchored near the southwest tip of the harbor with blue sails in the process of being furled. Small fishing boats, a single catamaran and several sampans dotted the harbor. There were no other signs of activity.

"How odd, like a deserted paradise," Diane murmured as she surveyed the scene.

"You wouldn't call Akua deserted if you could see all the goings on in South Harbor, over that ridge," Victor boasted. "That's the Akua Sugar Company, one of my projects."

"Thirty-seven percent yours," Tracie reminded him.

Waving aside trivialities, he added, "Anyway, I'm the guy who made it pay. You've got to admit that. Where the hell — where in thunder is Rudi with the car?"

With perfect timing Victor's heavy old black Packard rumbled toward the jetty.

Tracie caught Diane's stare at the handsome driver and smiled. "Looks like Valentino, doesn't he?"

"Oh, no!" Diane breathed ecstatically. "Like George Raft...those eyes!"

When Diane saw that Victor wasn't too pleased at the comparison she took his arm impulsively. "How generous you were, Victor, to think I might be of use to you in this paradise. And I will be, I promise you."

Tracie gave her the benefit of the doubt. She probably meant it. But it was unlikely that Lili would think so. And Theo? It was hard to say. Was he really taken with Diane Thorpe, or was he merely trying to prevent any relationship from developing between her and his uncle? Theo had certainly worked overtime breaking up Victor and Marta Dempster — and succeeded at that.

"Looks like I'm stuck walking," Theo grumbled, noting that the car would be full. "Tell mother to hold lunch until I hike in."

Victor paid no attention, but Diane Thorpe gave him a friendly, grateful glance as she was boosted into the back seat of the Packard. Victor was about to get in after her but remembered his manners and took the front seat beside Rudi, who carefully refrained from staring at the newcomer.

The girls waved at Theo as the big Packard chugged up the steep dirt road and around through a narrow mountain defile choked with giant ferns and wild keawe. They traveled a thousand feet up to the hanging valley presided over by the long, weathered, two-story plantation house with its vine and flower-covered lanais that ran the length of both east and west facades of the house.

"From the west lanai," Tracie pointed out, "you can see the entire harbor."

"And from the east lanai you see Mauna Pā-ele," Lili put in. "Not that you'd want to, for heaven's sake. Not with its history."

"Lili..." Tracie nudged her while Diane

looked from one spot to the other with signs of interest.

"It has a history? Victor told me about some of the things that have happened here, but—"

"Here we are," Victor announced, and seconds later Rudi pulled up in front of the three wooden steps that led to the long lanai. The house looked green and shadowy in the sunlight that filtered through the plants that surrounded the house.

Victor first helped Diane, then Lili out of the car as Theo trotted up to the house, almost beating them on foot. On the other side Tracie stepped onto the running board and down to the ground. She was halfway up the steps when Diane's eyes widened and she reached for Victor's arm.

"How very odd! In that window by that big, bushy tree — I thought I saw someone. But she just seemed to — vanish."

Victor squinted at the southwest corner window behind the gently moving orchid tree.

"You mean Ilima's room? Impossible. You're imagining things." But sunlight drifted through the open slatted windows, filtered by the greenery everywhere, and to Tracie's uneasy gaze, a face did appear to float in the green light of the room...for one ghastly moment she thought of Ilima.

"It must be mother," Lili said with a laugh. "She pops up in the weirdest places."

Ashamed of her cowardice, Diane attempted to make amends. "It must be wonderful, actually living in a primitive jungle."

Having their beloved plantation referred to as primitive and a jungle did not sit well with either Victor or Tracie, but Lili only looked at her quizzically and shrugged.

Aunt Jade came to the door and greeted them in her usual unemotional way, allowing her children to kiss her ivory cheek, merely squeezing her daughter's hand, though she lingered longer in her son's embrace. She accepted Tracie's faintly brushed kiss without returning any outward affection. Victor was still cross with Diane over her remark about the house and seemed eager to dismiss her so that he could attend to other matters. He barely muttered her name in introduction to Jade before leaving her to the women and stamping off down the hall to his study, where he bawled to one of the young houseboys, "A drink, and make it quick, boy!"

"Aunt Jade, where have you put Mrs. Thorpe?" Tracie said, trying to get things settled.

Aunt Jade was not receptive. "The cable gave me very little information," she said curtly. "Since the young lady is to be employed in

216

Miss Mako's former position, I thought it proper to place her in Miss Mako's room."

Lili giggled as Diane opened her mouth wordlessly. She didn't want to stay in the dead woman's room and turned to Tracie, silently pleading for help.

"Not Ilima's room. Let's find somewhere else. I'm sorry, Aunt Jade. We saw you in her room a minute ago and I know you must have gone to a lot of trouble over the arrangements."

Aunt Jade's dark eyebrows raised. "I came from the kitchen. I haven't been in the corner room since this morning."

Tracie suspected she was lying. "Must be mother's little joke," Lili whispered to her in passing. Tracie only hoped so . . .

11

Before the week was out Tracie was already sick of hearing Diane's incessant, "I don't want to put you to any trouble." Because, of course, her mere presence was trouble.

It was obvious that she couldn't sleep in the room Aunt Jade had selected for her, and she could scarcely eat any of the food prepared. The delicious raw salmon repelled her, and she found the squid intolerable but only after Theo had told her what it was. His mother gave him a penetrating look but her son remained unperturbed, as if he enjoyed Diane's inability to adjust to her new surroundings.

The young woman redeemed herself, at least with Victor, when he complained of a kink in his back and she volunteered to massage him. This was performed on the rattan living room couch in full view of the family. Tracie was relieved that the woman improved her father's temper and perhaps his back as well.

Before going off to bath and bed one evening Tracie visited Chin Loo, who was polishing silver in the kitchen.

"How goes it, Chin? I'll bet you were relieved at the peace and quiet while we were gone. Was it boring with the family off gallivanting around the Coast?"

His graceful hands continued to move back and forth, stopping now and then to give an extra dig at the tiny crevices of the heavy silver handles with their pineapple design.

"Maybe alone. Not boring."

Tracie had meant the remark as a mere politeness. Something in his manner, maybe the side look he gave her, was disquieting. She knew that Chin Loo was an educated man in his own way, and chose his words with care.

"Did you have company? I hope the people from the sugar refinery haven't been wandering around here. They know this valley is off limits."

"No. Not sugar people. Sugar people, they are afraid of Lady Jade."

Tracie smiled a touch ruefully.

"You get along with Aunt Jade. She isn't too officious with you when we're gone?"

He shrugged. "Lady Jade is plenty official. But we understand each other. No trouble."

She saw no reason to pursue the matter ex-

cept that she sensed he wasn't telling her everything. She was about to leave the kitchen by
the back door and check the stall where Namu
was stabled when she noticed a light was burning in the old cookhouse across the kitchen
garden. The dilapidated, one-room cabin wasn't
used anymore, but Victor had insisted on pre-
serving it since it was the original building of
the old Orchid Tree Ranch.

"Who on earth is in the cookhouse? There's
a lantern burning."

Chin Loo didn't look at her, but continued
to lean over a knife handle, scrubbing hard.
"My lantern. I sleep there. Nice and cool. No
Kona weather in that hollow. The fern forest,
the hau tree, they protect."

Tracie was even more puzzled. "The Kona
weather has been over for weeks now."

"Not here," he persisted stubbornly. "Bad
Kona weather."

She considered the dark tropical setting with
its pervasive scent of moist, dead vegetation
and live, sweet flower perfume, probably the
ginger and the plumeria bushes scattered
through the garden. At night they all seemed
especially alive. She remembered suddenly
something Ilima Mako had once said: "On a
moonless night I can imagine each and every
one of those millions of creatures out there

220

alive, with eyes to see in the dark. Even the flowers."

"Think of them as your audience," Tracie had teased her. "You are the star. You have a soul. They haven't."

"I believe they all have souls," Ilima had answered in her quiet way. "Some of them are fond of me...like the orchid tree. It is my friend. I don't know why."

"Neither do I," Tracie had said. "It's an obstinate thing. Always in the way. In a high wind the branches make a terrible noise, rattling not only against your room but the one upstairs."

But Ilima didn't see it that way, always defending the beauty of the overgrown tree, giving it an almost mystical quality. It was one thing Tracie resigned herself never to understand about her friend.

Tracie glanced at the tree now, spreading outward and upward at the southwest corner of the house, then turned back to Chin Loo, still wondering why he preferred sleeping in a run-down room whose roof threatened to collapse, rather than in the little bedroom that was his private domain on the ground floor of the plantation house. It got southern exposure and was between the pantry-stillroom area and Ilima's old room.

Good heavens! Was it something about Ilima's old room? Tracie knew many of the Hawaiians had their superstitions, but the Chinese of her acquaintance always appeared quite the opposite. Like Tracie herself, they always searched for natural causes, and Chin Loo was extremely sensible.

She looked again at the corner of the building and the big umbrella shadow of the orchid tree, then stared at Chin. Seeing her gaze he must have guessed what she was thinking but only returned her stare blandly. He began to fold his cloth and replace the silverware in a huge, old-fashioned chest, slipping each item carefully into its satin-lined pocket.

"What about the women servants? Are they afraid of the house?" She knew Kaahumanu, the housemaid, had the small room on the second floor, above the back staircase. This strong, heavy, middle-aged woman often permitted one of the temporary female help to use the extra twin bed in her room so that the girl didn't have to return to the sugar colony late at night.

Chin shrugged. "Kaahumanu, she came back after Lady Jade talked to her."

"You mean Kaahumanu didn't want to sleep here either?" It seemed incredible. The only time such things happened was when someone spread a rumor based on the deepest Hawaiian supersititions. What had happened during their absence that made those who remained fearful of staying in the house?

Everyone, she corrected herself, but Jade Wong Berenson.

"Chin, I hope I'm not prying, but I'd like to know. Is the household afraid that Ilima Mako's spirit will come back?"

With everything now in order Chin wordlessly reached into a high cupboard, got out a kerosene lantern with a metal shield against the weather. He lighted the wick with a match and shuffled past Tracie, out the next door.

"Goodnight," he said, inclining his head to her in princely dismissal before he stepped down to the pebble walk and walked toward the cabin.

Tracie went after him. "You haven't answered my question. Are you afraid Miss Mako will come back?"

His large, unlined face turned upward to her, illuminated by the light from the kitchen. "Miss Ilima already come back. Good night, missy."

So that was the problem. But how — or why — did they seize on such a ridiculous notion? Could someone familiar with ancient Hawaiian beliefs have planted it with the intention of disrupting the entire household?

Since she was already outside, she followed the rough pebbled path to the orchid tree. A large flat leaf brushed against her nose, making her sneeze. She shook one branch and then another and smiled at her own childish taunting of the tree and its supposed spirit.

Tracie continued to walk around toward the lanai on the west front of the house. Behind her she heard the branches of the orchid tree scratching against the slatted west window of Ilima's room. The room itself was pitch dark. Tracie studied it thoughtfully. There was no haunting face floating in the green silence now...there was nothing there at all.

At the north facade she stopped to survey the house again, then walked around to the back. The taro patches and rice fields on the stepped levels of the mountain range glistened under a few scattered stars.

"And while I'm at it," she called, menacing the mountain with her fist, "I'm not scared of you either."

A male voice bellowed from the shadows of the lanai, "You talking to me?"

She was ashamed of the start he gave her.

"Is that you, dad?"

"Who'd you think it was? The tooth fairy? What the hell are you up to, sneaking around in the dark, yelling at mountains? Or was it God you were shaking your fist at?"

"Really, dad. I'm not that foolish."

"Better not be. Sometimes I feel like He's closer to us right out here on this island than anywhere else."

Tracie paused for a moment, not knowing what to say. They usually didn't talk about such things.

"Well, look at you," she said finally. "What's so fascinating about Mauna Pā-ele? How long have you been staring at it?"

He came out into the starlight, his arms folded across his chest.

"Long enough to see lights moving up there. Some of the cane workers have been having a luau. They have some women up there with them. Not bad lookers, either. Filipino and Korean, I'd say."

"And you'd like to have been there."

"You guessed right. Now, I'm going to bed and I advise you to do the same."

"Maybe I will. 'Night, dad."

She stepped up on the lanai, kissed his cheek and felt his hand briefly pat her shoulder. For Victor Berenson this was the height of paternal affection.

"That girl may just work out," Victor said as they went inside. "She's absolutely crazy about

225

me. And that's not a bad thing, in a way. Helps to keep 'em in line. No sudden demands for a raise or Sundays off."

"You have such a warm heart, dad," Tracie said sarcastically, though not in an unkind way.

He was starting up the front stairs when she said impulsively, "Have you heard? The servants believe Ilima's bedroom is haunted. I understand they all scatter to the four winds when night falls."

She waited for his deep chuckle. In the silence that followed he started up the stairs again, stopping at the landing for a brief moment. "Typical," he said, before he went on.

It was not the reaction she'd hoped for.

Because it was so late there seemed nothing else to do but go to bed. Unfortunately, the aftermath of all the fun and excitement of the San Francisco trip remained with Tracie, and the prospect of bed only reminded her of that ecstatic hour in Bill Dempster's hotel suite. How could she explain to him that she feared herself and the depth of her involvement with him? Such knowledge would only give him more power over her; so he must go on thinking she was a tease. If only he were someone else, someone whose business wasn't pitted against her family's...a man whose

226

emotions she could trust!

To work off some of the restlessness she walked through the long, darkened ground-floor hall to Ilima's room, determined to throw off the servants' superstitions once and for all. The door of the small bedroom was unlocked. She pushed it open, peering in by the dim hall light. She felt for the light switch on the wall beside her, pressed the button and the ceiling lights came on.

A cluster of globes in a china shade elaborately decorated with flowers made the room look utterly impersonal in the bold light. It might as well have been a bedroom in the Moana Hotel, excellently furnished and with no homey touches but for a vase of long, graceful stems of vanda orchids on the night table. Beside it was a big double bed with a bright brown and white kapa cloth spread on top of the white chenille spread.

A scratching, scuffling sound made her inspect the room more carefully. The branches of the orchid tree, of course. There they were reaching out against the windows, creating the sound that seemed to worry susceptible people.

"But I'm not one of them." She said it aloud, just to be sure she convinced herself.

At the same time she was aware that it was in this very room that Ilima had sat, troubled over...what? Something that had depressed her so much that she felt she had to take her own life. Tracie closed the door and crossed the room to the bed. She sat down, remaining very still.

Aside from a certain moistness in the air and on all the furniture, which was true of most rooms in this climate, she felt nothing unusual. She could hardly believe that only a few months ago there had been nights when she, too, imagined Ilima Mako's gentle presence in the house.

It had been downright wicked to suspect Ilima of doing anything so cruel as to come back and "haunt" the family. In life she had been the kindest, most understanding of women. Why would her nature change in death?

What am I talking about?

Angry that she had even permitted herself to consider the idea of Ilima as a ghostly presence, she stood up, ready to leave. The bed covers themselves still smelled faintly of Ilima's body powder, an exotic scent compounded of pikake and other flowers. The scent made her uncomfortable, making Ilima's presence seem more real. She gave the room one more look, then crossed it hurriedly. It wasn't until she closed the door behind her and went out into the hall that she admitted to herself that she was running away from that powdery perfume.

She rushed along the hall toward the front staircase. A light step in the upper hall shook her slightly, but she wasn't surprised when she saw Lili fluttering toward the staircase, all white silk and blue ribbons. "Is that you, Tracie?" she whispered.

"It's me. What on earth are you doing wandering around in your nightgown?"

"Couldn't sleep. I thought I'd heat some water and rum. That always helps."

"Maybe I will too," Tracie said.

With Lili beside her she felt safer...but against what? They silently moved down the stairs together. Before they reached the bottom Lili began to sniff the air. "That's funny."

"What is?"

"That smell. Like face powder. Not mine, though."

"Body powder."

It seemed to have followed them the entire length of the house.

12

Aunt Jade refused to accept her daughter's belief that the air in the hall outside Ilima Mako's empty room had a subtle odor of perfumed powder.

"It makes me sneeze," Lili insisted.

"You have no reason to be in that part of the house anyway," Aunt Jade reminded her, "unless you plan to assume my responsibilities."

Tracie was amused by her cousin's quick denial.

"Of course not, mother. I must be imagining it."

"Precisely. And what does my niece say?" Aunt Jade turned her dark eyes on Tracie who, like everyone else, was overwhelmed by Lady Jade Wong's regal aura.

"Me too." But she stirred herself to pursue the matter. "I just thought the room could be refurnished and used for some other purpose."

Aunt Jade vetoed this, partly, as Tracie suspected, because it wasn't her own idea.

"When my brother-in-law has company from Honolulu or the Coast he will need that room. I remind you that the Outer Islands are not Honolulu. Do you see hotels here on Akua? Or Molokai or Kauai? So, they must stay at Valley House. And every room is used."

That was clearly the last word on the subject.

Lili went away muttering to Tracie, "I just hope whoever sleeps there likes the scent of pikake."

For once, Lili was glad to be sent off to college in Honolulu. At least there, she'd told her cousin, there were some interesting men to meet.

Tracie and Diane Thorpe went down with Theo to see her off on the *Akua Orchid*. It was Diane who made excuses for Victor's absence just as Ilima Mako used to do. "He would like to have been here. He told me so. But they're threatening a strike at the sugar mill and he has to settle it."

Amused at the idea that there might be some controversy on the island, Theo whistled. "If Uncle Vic loses his temper he's liable to throw the strike leaders over Mauna Pā-ele, the way King Kamehameha tossed his enemies off the pali."

"Oh, no!" Diane blurted, shuddering at the

thought. The memory of Ilima's suicide was undoubtedly fresh in her mind and, as Theo knew, his comment wasn't tactful.

"Don't worry," Tracie said with all the confidence of one who looks to the past for answers. "There's never been a strike on Akua. The workers wouldn't dare. The mill sees to it that they're taken care of practically from birth to death. They'd never get that from a union."

Tracie was surprised when Diane persisted on the subject. "Still, they may wish to decide for themselves. Look at the general strike we had on the Coast a year ago. Everything around the Bay area came to a complete stop. It was terrible."

Tracie impatiently brushed aside such non sequiturs. What did labor affairs on the Mainland have to do with the time-tested paternalistic practices of the family companies that ruled the Territory?

They remained on the jetty, waving to Lili until the cargo ship swung around in the harbor and headed out into the blue depths of the Pacific. As they turned away Theo draped an arm around Diane's shoulders and said cheerfully, "Now let's get back to the haunted house."

"Don't say that, please." Diane's brown eyes widened with alarm. "Your sister told me about the powdery scent in the hall."

This was all the prompting Theo needed — he had succeeded in frightening someone. "That's nothing. You ought to smell it in the room itself. You can't miss it. She's there, all right."

"Theo, shut up!" In spite of her firmness, however, Tracie was relieved to reach the car and have the subject changed.

Theo took this opportunity to seat Diane beside him, with Tracie jammed against the door. At least, she reasoned, he was now showing off his knowledge of the local flora and fauna instead of talking about perfumed powder in haunted rooms.

The truth was, Tracie herself still imagined that powdery scent near Ilima's room, and like Lili, she dreaded the moment when the scent would drift elsewhere, perhaps to pervade the entire house.

In the next few days the subject was forgotten but the scent indisputably remained, despite Aunt Jade's thorough cleaning of the room. It was simply not discussed, perhaps because Victor Berenson's growing attachment to Diane had replaced it as the main topic of conversation, particularly between Theo and Tracie. Neither of them liked Victor's growing dependence on her, Theo through natural concern for

233

his inheritance and Tracie through jealousy at the loss of her own influence over her father.

It was shattering to give him a sound piece of advice only to have him turn and ask someone as inexperienced as Diane Thorpe *her* opinion. The young woman was diffident but she managed to speak up, almost in spite of herself. Aware of her own feelings, Tracie did nothing to prevent Theo's rather devious attempts to win Diane over for himself. He failed, but not for lack of trying. Either Mrs. Thorpe was too clever to be caught by his surface charm and impudence, or she genuinely cared for Victor Berenson. It was becoming clearer by the day that Victor believed this to be so.

Tracie found her suspicions confirmed one bright day in February when she rode Namu across the north end of the island under a piercingly blue sky. She intended to look over the little papaya grove in the plantation belonging to the salty widow of a sea captain. Devlin McCallister had sailed in and out of Lahaina, Maui, at one time transporting human cargo from Japan and the Philippines to work the lands of the Territory.

Tracie made the trip hoping that Belle McCallister, his widow, could advise her on how to make a profit on the delicious fruit of the papaya, when most mainlanders didn't know a papaya from a mangrove root. Tracie patted Namu's flank and the nimble-footed mare made her way over the ridge between the papaya grove and the lush, rolling knolls and meadows where Mrs. McCallister's Hawaiian *paniolos* ran a few head of white-faced cattle.

Tracie took care not to urge Namu past the line of ironwood trees that was the only barrier — fragile though it was — between the storms that rolled off the windward shores and Mrs. McCallister's lush green haven. Beyond the ironwoods' lacy barrier were the usual sheer, jungle-clad cliffs that made the shape of Akua so spectacular when viewed from the sea. Only two areas, the sugar mill harbor and the little village of Akua City, sloped gently to the water's edge.

Although it was Tracie's habit to speak to the mare, she'd never heard an answer, but this time there was a definite hiss. Tracie and Namu both raised their heads sharply. Belle McCallister, known as "Ma" on the island, tall and lean, her wild hair a vibrant red, stuck her head around the lacy brush of a tree, waving Tracie to silence. She then pointed to something about a hundred yards down the line of trees. Tracie leaned over Namu's withers and saw Diane Thorpe locked in the embrace of a rangy gray-haired man.

Tracie caught her breath, glanced again at the sharp-eyed woman who'd pointed out the couple. Knowing her tendency to gossip, Tracie decided to react casually, shrugging indifferently as if it were the most natural sight one would expect to see in this remote area. She was shocked, but determined not to let the woman guess what she felt.

The light-footed mare carefully avoided the grassy little pool formed by Akua's unusually wet winter, but the two lovers had been disturbed by Namu's movements and Diane shrank away from Victor's arms in embarrassment. "I – we – I don't know how it happened. That is –"

Victor swung around impatiently. He didn't appear flustered, but the louder he raised his voice the more he convinced Tracie that he, too, was uneasy.

"What do you mean you don't know? Lord! I kissed you and you wanted to be kissed. Stands to reason." He caught Mrs. McCallister's interested gaze and added, "Perfectly respectable. I've just asked Dinah to marry me and she's accepted."

That was enough to bring Belle running toward the lovers as fast as her long legs could carry her. She shook hands with both of them.

"Welcome to McCallister Ranch, Victor. Miss Thorpe."

"Just showing Dinah the island and part of her future empire." Ma raised her eyebrows and he amended, "Yours, that is. Parked the truck down by Menehune Pond and walked up here. She got tuckered out and we stopped to look at the sea view."

"Mr. – I mean Victor – pointed out Molokai off there and you can just see a tip of Maui, a little bit that way," Diane said eagerly, as if the old woman had never seen it before. "It was very exciting."

Tracie had dismounted and was leading Namu over the spongy ground toward her father and Diane. With a grin Mrs. McCallister took Namu's reins while Tracie hugged the bride-to-be, then her father. All in all, Tracie reflected, he could probably do a lot worse. But this was barely the end of February. Ilima had been dead less than six months.

Mrs. McCallister had no such qualms. It seemed highly appropriate to Belle, a two-fisted drinker, that they should be invited in for an engagement toast. The McCallister house was a two-story building with screened porches that would have looked equally at home beside a neat Iowa or Indiana wheat field. Mrs. McCallister herself was born in Indiana and had carried a good deal of her solid, unpretentious background to this more exotic corner of the world.

She had, over the years, acquired a few of her late husband's habits, including his taste for hard liquor; luckily she could hold it. Like many islanders during Prohibition she had stocked up on okolehao, which proved more potent than all the liquor sneaked in by rum-runners and Oriental cargo vessels. She poured an inch for Tracie, more for Victor, but hesitated over Diane's heavy ruby glass.

Diane quickly stepped in to handle the matter.

"Just a sip, please. I'm afraid I get an upset stomach over practically nothing."

"Well, nobody's perfect," Victor said. After Belle proposed a toast "to the king of Akua and his new queen," Victor drank his liquor in one long gulp, under Diane's admiring yet faintly alarmed eyes.

Tracie took hers less easily, grimacing as the hard liquor went down. "I don't see how any of us ever got used to it. So help me, it tastes like lye. No offense, Belle."

"None taken, girl." Mrs. McCallister knocked hers off with ease. "You two going to live here, I opine. Not running off to the bright lights of Honolulu or Waikiki, and all?"

Tracie saw Diane's eyes light up at the suggestion, but whatever hopes she might have had were quickly dashed by Victor's hearty response. "Surest thing you know. 'Course, we might visit Oahu now and then, but this is home sweet home. Dinah wants it that way, don't you honey?"

"Oh, indeed. Yes."

Pitying her, and understanding her self-absorbed father too well, Tracie decided to speak up.

"Surely, dad, you're going to Oahu on your honeymoon. Waikiki is getting popular nowadays too. The Royal Hawaiian was just made for honeymooners. Or the Halekulani...those bungalows on the beach. Charlie Chan country," she explained to Diane. "His first adventure took place there."

But the bride had picked up on her earlier suggestion and clung to it tenaciously. "Oh, yes. The Royal Hawaiian Hotel. I'd adore that. Could we, Victor?"

Her soulful gaze and the okolehao proved a potent combination. Victor surrendered with his usual grace. "Well, hell, why not? I might get in a little business while I'm there. I wouldn't half-mind owning some of that Kahala land that isn't under control of the Bishop estate."

"Some honeymoon," Tracie muttered to Mrs. McCallister under her breath; the doughty woman responded to the remark with a knowing grin.

Tracie left the pair a short time later. She wanted to get home before her father in order to forestall any imprudent remarks by Theo about his uncle's marriage. Any sense of opposition was sure to plunge Victor into immediate action, and Theo might find himself thrown out and forced to make his own living. Tracie suspected this would be an inconceivable fate to Theo, whom, despite his shortcomings, she genuinely cared about.

To her surprise her cousin was resigned to it when he heard the news. "I suppose the next step will be the patter of little feet," he said, opening the bar to get an early start.

"Good Lord!"

"And we'll be expected to welcome the kid as if he were a true Berenson."

It *was* a painful thought. Worse — the child might be a boy. Tracie was perfectly willing to abide by any new will her father made. She had great confidence in her ability to support herself, but she found it extremely painful to contemplate losing her position in Orchid Tree Enterprises, or to see herself superseded by a male heir who would get all the affection, the trust and responsibility that had been hers almost from birth. She reminded herself that she, like Theo, was looking too far into the future, and quickly resolved to make the best of whatever happened.

Not surprisingly, it was Jade who had the most negative reaction. To everyone's astonishment the elegant, inscrutable woman said absolutely nothing when Victor blurted the announcement. Jade retired to her two-room suite complaining of a headache, and didn't show up for dinner.

Tracie, even Theo, worried over Jade's extreme reaction, and they both talked too much and too fast, attempting to cover the awkwardness the prospective bride and groom created for the rest of them. The whole family felt Jade's absence and seemed at a loss to know what to do about it.

At the end of the evening Diane followed Tracie out to the west lanai, where she stood taking in the night air with its scent of rain-washed flowers. "She hates me, Tracie."

"Don't be silly. Nobody could hate you."

She tilted her head toward the corner of the house behind them. "She does."

Tracie looked past Diane to the house itself. "Aunt Jade?"

"No." Diane was behaving curiously. She

crushed the knuckles of both hands against her mouth. Her voice was muffled but above her tense hands her eyes looked terrified. "Her. My pre – predecessor."

"Mother?" Tracie stared at her. "Not my mother, I take it. Are you by any chance thinking of Ilima Mako?" Diane nodded. "Well, you couldn't be more wrong. Ilima Mako never hated anyone. You'd have liked her. She would have been a friend."

"I can just imagine." Diane saw Tracie's surprise at her tone and the beginnings of a frown. "I can't help it. It's not the living I'm afraid of, but the dead."

The fact that Tracie sometimes shared this absurd fear didn't make it any easier to hear it now from Diane. She grabbed Diane's arm and marched over to Ilima's deserted room. As always, the moist double leaves of the orchid tree waved against the slatted door. Tracie pushed them aside impatiently. They snapped back, sprinkling her with water, and Diane cried out. Even Tracie was slightly startled at the wetness. She caught her breath but the small incident only made her more angry. "Look in there. This minute. See anything?"

After hesitating for a moment Diane pressed her nose against a warped slat. "It's mostly dark."

Diane turned away from the window. "It's not this room that scares me." She lowered her voice uneasily. "Tracie, I keep feeling she is near me. I don't know what it is. You might call it...an aura. And there's something else... *like perfume. Or a body powder.*"

Tracie had never mentioned her own perceptions to Diane...how had the same thought occurred to this young woman who wasn't even familiar with the scent? So far as Tracie knew, only one other person had smelled the same odor of perfumed powder, a kind of sweet, dusty smell that immediately brought Ilima to mind.

It wasn't until they turned to enter the house together that Tracie spoke again. "That aura you think you felt...have you discussed it with Lili?"

Diane stopped in the front hall, gripping the big rattan chair against the wall. Her eyes looked enormous with fear. "Then she has sensed it too?"

Tracie saw she had made a serious mistake in her question, merely encouraging this talk of ghosts and auras.

"Of course not. But Lili is so flighty, and likes to scare herself about such things. Do you want me to go to your room with you?"

Diane gulped in gratitude. "If you would, I'd

appreciate it so much. I don't like to mention it to Victor. It might remind him of his — of Miss Mako."

They avoided the ground floor with its little cross-hall at the south end of the long house near Ilima's room and made their way to the second floor and Diane's bedroom, located at the back of the house. Diane had left the Tiffany lamp on the night table on, and the green and scarlet art deco designs on the glass shade gave the room a curious atmosphere. Like a brothel, Tracie thought, though her experience of brothels was limited to what she'd read.

Diane stood irresolute in the middle of the lauhala mat. Suddenly she swung around in a circle, looking at every corner of the room.

"I don't smell it now, but I did earlier. It wasn't a perfume. Not heavy like that. More like—" She broke off, waving her hands.

"Like powder."

Diane stopped with her hands in midair. "You do know!"

Tracie groped for excuses. "You must remember, Ilima was in every room. She didn't use perfume itself but her powder was perfumed. It's bound to remain in these rooms that have been closed up since she died. We haven't had many visitors."

Diane went and sat down on the neat single bed.

"Tracie, I love Victor. I do!"

"Well, of course you do." Diane's strange insistence puzzled and rather annoyed her. Women always said they loved the man — especially the rich man — they were going to marry. What else were they expected to say? Tracie started to the door.

"What I mean is that even though I love Victor, I can't marry him until I know something."

Tracie stopped impatiently. "All right. What is it?"

"Why did Miss Mako commit suicide?"

Further annoyed by the blunt question, Tracie turned the doorknob sharply. "I swear to God, I wish I knew!"

She left hurriedly, before she could decide whether or not she had noticed the faint scent of perfumed powder creeping into the room.

She felt there was only one person she could discuss these ridiculous fears with — Bill Dempster was a matter-of-fact man. No odd psychic phenomenon would bother him.

His arrival with Lili one rainy day in March was the answer to a prayer, even though it came on the eve of Victor's marriage. It appeared that Diane had decided she would marry Victor after all, even if she didn't know why her predecessor had died.

13

Tracie at first was surprised that Bill took the trouble to come to Victor's wedding. She wasn't surprised, however, when Lili confessed that she had badgered him into coming. Certainly he wouldn't have done so otherwise, and Tracie found it bothersome to have him there on those terms.

The weather on the weekend of the wedding was threatening and showery, but judging by the acceptances to Aunt Jade's elegant invitations, weather would not put a damper on the excitement. Jade herself had shown the way, rising from her bed the day after Victor told her of his plans, appearing to accept Diane as the new mistress of the Berenson plantation.

Day after day, she checked all menus and household matters with the confused Diane, who then turned to Tracie and Theo for advice. Theo's responses always seemed edged with malice, only confusing the girl more. Tracie tried to be helpful but when she began to get bogged down with Diane's questions she simply said, "You'll have to learn the way things are run gradually, the way Ilima did." She knew her words sounded a bit hard, but Tracie herself wasn't happy about the marriage. She thought both parties would be sorry before it was over.

When the old produce truck borrowed from the Akua City grocer, Mr. Nakazawa, pulled up under the orchid tree and Bill Dempster helped Lili down, Tracie didn't have time to hide her obvious delight at the sight of him. Nor did she have a chance to open her mouth while Lili babbled on. "Look who I brought. He's staying through the ceremony and for the whole weekend. We don't have to leave until the inter-island boat Monday afternoon."

"I hate to be a killjoy," her brother said as he shook hands with Bill and they started into the house, "but what about your Monday morning classes?"

Lili pushed him away, holding out her hand to Bill, who grinned indulgently but refused to take it.

"Obviously I'm cutting classes," she explained to her brother. "There's only two before lunch anyway. Philosophy — what do I need that for? And French. I'll make that up later.

Well, aren't you glad to see the prodigal return? Get out the fatted calf. Spread the glad tidings. Where's mother?"

Jade came out on the lanai with her hands concealed as usual in the sleeves of her quilted jacket.

"You should have let us know Mr. Dempster was coming," Jade said as her daughter kissed her on the cheek. "Your guest may not find the food for the wedding party to his liking. I've sent for your uncle. He took Miss Thorpe for a walk to the sugar mill."

Bill inclined his head slightly, a compromise greeting that suggested a bow. He knew her well enough not to extend his hand.

"I am quite certain my tastes run with the Berensons and their guests, Madame Berenson."

She returned the bow, removed one hand from her sleeve and gestured toward the interior of the house before she went back inside.

"Come on, Bill," Lili said when he didn't follow. "Don't stand out here all day. It's going to rain again. Let Cousin Tracie be. She likes to get soaked."

Bill glanced at Tracie, who smiled and looked away.

"Sorry," he said, slapping the wheel of the old truck. "Promised Mr. What's-His-Name I'd return his chariot."

"Oh, how silly! What do you think servants are for? Rudi will take it back to Mr. Nakazawa."

Theo snickered. "My dear, unselfish little sister."

Their mother called, "Liliha, Theo, I'm waiting."

"All right, mother, we're coming. Since you can't get rid of Ilima's old room, why not put Bill in it? He's not afraid of ghosts."

With that Lili went inside with Theo loping after her. Tracie started to follow until Bill caught her by one arm and held her. "I need someone to show me the way back here again."

She scoffed, "A likely tale. That's over a two-mile walk, uphill. You'll probably borrow poor Mr. Nakazawa's truck to return."

"Coward." He shook her arm but didn't let it go. "You're afraid to be alone with me."

She rolled her eyes and to prove it was otherwise, got into the truck before he could boost her up. He laughed and went around the truck, getting in behind the wheel.

In silence they rattled down the muddy road just as another shower swept across the island, heading for the heights of Mauna Pā-ele. It took all Bill's concentration to get the truck around innumerable switchbacks without turning over or running into a keawe thicket. The shower had quickly turned into a downpour. "I don't want to pick on Mr. Nakazawa but I wish he had some side curtains for this old wreck. Are you getting soaked?"

"Won't be the first time."

Was he, too, remembering that day on Mauna Pā-ele and their first rain-soaked embrace? He looked at her wordlessly. They hit a tree stump and the wheels churned mud briefly. He revved the engine and a minute later they were on their way again, now within sight of Akua City.

He startled her by remarking suddenly, "You have a beautiful mouth. You ought to smile more."

"Give me something to smile about and I'll oblige."

"A touch, a touch, I do confess."

"That sounds educated."

"This will surprise you, my soggy beauty, but I had to do something at Stanford between scrimmages." He pulled into the grassy lot beside the Nakazawa store and sat there for a minute or two studying Tracie while the rain pelted the roof of the truck, spattering across his shoulder and onto his legs.

"You're getting soaked, too," she reminded him.

"But it's warm rain. I just noticed."

"Of course. That's our liquid sunshine."

"Are you wet through?"

She laughed. "Practically."

"I've got something I want to show you. Further around the harbor. Some land I have an eye on."

That sounded ominous...Was he actually planning to undercut the Berensons in their own front yard? Wasn't the sugar mill enough?

"Sounds interesting. Is it a secret?"

"Secret? I'm only asking you to look at it. Want to chance it now or wait for the weather to clear?"

"Why wait? We're both soaked anyway. It isn't as if this were the first time we've been caught in a downpour."

This time her reference to the earlier day was more direct, but now she didn't care what he thought...she wanted him, and there was nothing she could do about it. Still, she hadn't forgotten that there was something behind Bill's interest in her, and she decided that while she wouldn't allow herself to trust him, she could still enjoy his company for whatever it was worth...

"Well?" He stuck his head out of the cab of the truck, squinted into the sky and then swung out of the truck. The next thing she knew he was opening the door on her side of the truck. He looked windblown and wet, but there was a glow in his eyes and she couldn't deny their attraction. Damn him!

"This is one time you are going to get out like a lady."

"Don't be ridiculous."

Her scornful tone didn't seem to have any effect on him. He reached for her, locked his hands around her body just below her rib cage, lifted her out and refused to let go. Even Wayne, who thought they should be married, wasn't this aggressive with her.

She put up the struggle he must have anticipated but she relaxed a few seconds later, seeing he was expecting that and well able to handle it. She had mixed reactions. She would like to have slipped through his hands, just to show him who was in command, but she was also delighted by his touch, his hands, feeling him against her body, the same delicious prelude to a night she remembered so well.

Instead of pretending outrage she laughed and as she'd expected, he was caught by surprise. She felt his fingers weaken their clasp but he still didn't let her go. She found herself looking into his eyes and it seemed he was searching her face for something, some assurance. She couldn't be sure and only returned his gaze, aware of the tension building between them.

Then, suddenly, his lips were on hers and they clung to each other, exploring, absorbing, passionately enjoying each other and the heat between them, while the squall overhead moved on, leaving a patch of blue sky over Akua City.

When he finally released her they were out of breath and laughing, but both aware of a serious undertow to their light-hearted mood.

"Blue skies," Bill said. "A good omen. We've worked our way out of a storm. Want to come and see the ground I told you about?" He still had his arms around her, but she could feel the tentative slackening of his grasp, as if he weren't quite sure that her mercurial nature would let her agree.

"Why not?" she said, and made no objection when he caught her around the waist again and pulled her to him. They started off down the unpaved street to the trail that followed the horseshoe curve of the harbor.

"Poor Mr. Nakazawa!" she teased him. "Doesn't he even get a thank you?"

"He got a very liberal fee for that crate. Anyway, I'll thank him on the way back. I may need to borrow that crate again to get up to your plantation house."

She shook her head but laughed at his easy assumption that he could take what he pleased, do what he wanted. He sometimes reminded her of her father in that way.

They strode along happily at a stiff pace, now and then showered with raindrops falling from the tall coco-palms or a spreading poinciana tree just beginning to turn scarlet with spring flowers. Tracie noted as they walked that he was genuinely interested in the land with its heavy jungle vegetation on gently rising ground. Finally they reached the south end of the harbor. Here the ground rose rapidly until they were thirty feet above the blue-green harbor waters with their lacy coating of foam. The heavy growth of flowering trees and palms had retreated here, leaving grassy, low vegetation and a scattering grove of jacaranda trees already showing a faint lavender suggestion of the floral haze that would appear later in the spring. They had taken root near the cliff's edge, proliferating further back until they joined the jungle growth of the valley between the Akua City harbor and the south coast of the sugar-cane field. Despite their fragile beauty they seemed to challenge the Pacific wind and weather.

Bill suddenly released Tracie when they reached the grassy area and stood with one hand on his hip. "Well, what do you think?"

It was a setting she and her cousins had looked at on their hikes a thousand times without actually seeing it.

"About what?"

"The setting...a house."

She pretended to consider the possibilities but she was sure he deliberately wanted to confuse her. Undoubtedly, he wanted to cut away the jacaranda and put up some kind of factory.

"Whose house?"

He was beginning to show a little impatience.

"Anybody's house. Yours."

"I couldn't judge for anyone else, since I have my own house. But if a person just came to live here for the first time, she — or he — would probably love it. It's not as wet as our valley. And it has a fabulous view. But I guess Valley House has spoiled me for anything else."

He turned back to her, studying the jacaranda trees with their soft fern foliage. "Yes, I guess it has spoiled daddy's girl for any other life," he said without expression.

"Daddy's girl! I don't think I like that."

"You weren't meant to. Shall we go back? Can't run the risk of letting somebody else get Mr. Nakazawa's heap before we strike another bargain." His voice had returned to the easy, sardonic tone she knew so well.

She felt the day had gone a little flat, but her relationship with Bill Dempster had always been like that, up and down.

"Sure, but we don't have to worry. Some of the crowd is arriving from the sugar mill side — the Oahu gang from Honolulu in the inter-island boat. And dad chartered a boat to pick up the Tokudas and some others from Hilo. They'll stop by Lahaina, Maui."

"Nobody from Molokai?" he asked, picking up a fallen tree limb and swiping at the earth as they walked back to Akua City.

It was puzzling, the way he always brought the subject back to Molokai. It was an island even more neglected by mainland visitors than were Kauai and Maui. Probably its unpopularity had something to do with Kalaupapa and the leper colony, a small peninsula that had its own special beauty, including its population which had managed to survive and even to enjoy life.

"Nobody was invited from Molokai for the excellent reason that we don't know anyone on Molokai," she said stiffly.

"No. I suppose not." He went right on as if they had been discussing Victor's bride all along. "Will you tell me one thing, honestly? Why is he marrying her?"

It annoyed Tracie that he was so blunt. "Because he loves her, naturally. Why else would be marry her?"

He surprised her and perhaps himself by

256

blurting out angrily, "I don't know why any man is fool enough to ask any woman to marry him. Believe me, it's easy to satisfy lust. It is damned hard to handle a marriage. Or even a proposal, when it comes to that." He laughed suddenly and unexpectedly. "But marriage isn't a very great priority with you and me, is it?"

"Heavens, no!" she said, wondering if he meant to insult her. "We've got too much to do with our lives." Probing for more details about his plans for the jacaranda hillside, she added, "For instance, I suppose you plan to put up a Dorado Star cannery in place of those lovely jacaranda trees."

"Very likely." He threw away the stick he'd been carrying to poke at the ground. He had a good pitching arm, she thought. She liked his style — but that was hardly news.

"It seems a shame. Those trees are glorious in late spring."

His voice held that same ironic edge he had used against her before. "You don't say. I had no idea you even saw the place."

Now what? Obviously, he was trying to provoke her, but she resolved to ignore the opportunity. This was the eve of her father's wedding and she wanted things to go well. She briefly thought of that last nightmarish wedding eve they'd spent searching for Ilima...but they must not let anyone think of that today.

Bill's disgruntled mood evaporated when they reached Mr. Nakazawa's store and the truck was returned. By the time they returned to the house Victor and Jade were greeting other guests who had come over from the sugar mill harbor. Victor was his usual boisterous, expansive self, a man as well liked as he was feared, but it was Aunt Jade who took care of their needs, arranging guest rooms and providing food to their many guests.

Lili had expected that her three-month absence in Honolulu would entitle her to some special treatment in the family, but she soon found that her mother was too busy to spend any time with her, and her brother had suddenly begun to follow the bride-to-be like a faithful retainer.

When Tracie arrived with Bill, Lili was so glad to see him that she forgave him for running off with her cousin. Bill made a helpless gesture to Tracie when Lili insisted he keep her company on the lanai. Tracie grinned at him and hurried off to the kitchen at Jade's summons.

There she found Aunt Jade and Chin Loo deep in discussion in their own language. The woman interrupted herself long enough to check on the matter of sleeping arrangements with Tracie while Chin Loo checked the buffet in the dining room.

"I've given Liliha's room to the Croydes. She must sleep in your room."

"We can manage."

"And the small southwest bedroom on the lower floor—" She stopped. Tracie stared at her, but her aunt only returned the look. "That, I think, will suit Mr. Dempster."

Tracie opened her mouth, thought it over and saw that it was eminently suitable, under the circumstances. Bill Dempster was forever bringing up the subject of Ilima's death. He would soon prove that her own experience with the powder scent was, like those of Lili and Diane, nonexistent, the result of too much imagination.

Tracie agreed. "He was very fond of Ilima. He knew her family."

Aunt Jade raised her dark, proud head. There was something in her gaze that made Tracie uneasy. Aunt Jade probably loved no one in the world but her two children. Tracie had never analyzed her own feelings for her aunt. The cool affection of a lifetime was based on Tracie's respect and admiration for her. But the woman's magnificent almond eyes could be frightening, and they were never readable. "He

259

was acquainted with Miss Mako's parents?" she asked.

"Foster parents. Ilima was adopted, you remember."

Her gaze shifted from Tracie's face to Chin Loo, who had come back from the dining room complaining. "Miss Tracie's big man. He eats the decorations for the cocktail buffet."

"Heavens! That will never do." Tracie went off, laughing, to lead Wayne Croyde away from the taro leaves, the manoa lettuce and the other greenery. They highlighted the flower centerpiece of early moss rose and ginger, the hardy cup-of-gold and the huge, dazzling lehua flowers that were like giant puffs of flame. Thank goodness, Tracie thought, no one had the bad taste to decorate the house with delicate ilima flowers.

Tracie found Wayne perched on the corner of Aunt Jade's long dining table, crunching macadamia nuts between nibbles of pale, curling lettuce.

Seeing him now, oddly endearing as his eyes lighted up when she called his name, Tracie wondered why she was perverse enough not to love him. She had spent an hour with a man who wasn't half so well suited to her, or she to him. Ambitious, ruthless and driven, Bill Dempster should not be the man she loved. She could manage Wayne. He would give her no trouble, and he sincerely loved her. Not to mention that he had no ulterior motives for wanting to marry her. When it came down to it, she thought, she really wasn't good enough for him — he was generous and sincere, and she was far too easily given to taking advantage of his good qualities.

Wayne got up from the table as she crossed the room to greet him. Her guilt at her lack of feelings for him and her attraction to his voice caused her to overdo it, as usual, and she kissed him exuberantly. Wayne returned the embrace, though he was more genuinely glad to see her. "Hey!" he blurted out, releasing her. "You're all wet."

"I was out in the last shower. How is your foot?"

He corrected her gently. "It's my leg."

She was embarrassed by her own apparent indifference to his injury and squeezed his heavily muscled arm. "How dumb of me! I meant your leg." She struggled for an excuse. "This marriage has us all mixed up. It was so unexpected." Thinking he might sense that she didn't approve of it she added quickly, "He swept her off her feet, you might say. It was awfully romantic."

"It's disgusting."

She was so surprised at the remark that she

almost stammered. "But why?"

His unruly hair made him look even more innocent and naive as he shook his head. "She's way too young for Mr. Berenson. And as mother says—" *Oh! All this was Mrs. Croyde's reasoning!* "—she's nice and all, but she's kind of – you know – common."

"Just inexperienced, and maybe naive. But she makes dad happy, and that's all that counts."

He ran his long fingers through his hair. "It's just like you to see the good in her. But she's going to cut you out. Wait and see."

She didn't want to discuss this very personal subject with Wayne. If she started thinking about Diane's new place in Victor's will, whatever that was, she would have to acknowledge hypocrisy on her own part. She was trying very hard to approve of the marriage, to salve her own conscience about thinking the marriage a disaster. It might well be a disaster for herself and her cousins, but her father certainly deserved another chance at happiness. Still, was Diane Thorpe really *right* for him?

There it was again...could it possibly be her own greed that made her doubt the wisdom of the marriage? Please God, she thought silently, don't let it be so. She didn't need her father's money. But she *did* need to know she was important to Orchid Tree.

Glancing toward the kitchen and pantries she wondered if these same thoughts were running through Jade's mind. Like Tracie, Aunt Jade had a position that was her whole life. Eventually, it would be usurped by Diane Thorpe Berenson.

"My father made this estate great," she said, denying Wayne's remark. "It was nothing before he took it over. My cousins' share of their father's inheritance has been ensured to them and I'm provided for by my percentage of Orchid Tree profits. If dad wants us to share in his will, it's his choice. He owes us nothing."

Wayne refused to see the cold-blooded reality of this. He caressed her damp shoulders with a tender touch that irritated her by its compassion.

"Leave it to you, sweetheart, to see the unselfish side of it. And I admire you for it. But I still think there are going to be problems."

"Please!" She stuck a luscious pink slice of guava into his mouth to end the discussion and went upstairs to change her clothes.

Lili was in Tracie's bedroom hanging up clothes in the one closet they would share. She had pushed Tracie's hangers to the back of the closet and seemed to have brought her entire wardrobe.

"Moving in for the summer?" Tracie asked,

pushing Lili's clothes to the other end, ignoring her cousin's pained outcries. Tracie knew that once she'd put her foot down she and her cousin could share the room amicably with no more territorial squabbling. Victor had never believed in squandering money on nonessentials, like added bedrooms, when they were only used a few times a year, and because of their lack of space Mrs. McCallister had agreed to take in several wedding guests. Easygoing Theo was designated to the room above Namu's stall, and the sugar mill guest house was put to use as well. In this way, twenty-four of the guests plus the seven servants who attended them were accounted for.

Lili was in great spirits, which Tracie correctly attributed to Bill Dempster's attentions. While Lili changed to a deep blue crinkle-crepe evening gown that made her piquant face appear wickedly innocent, she prattled on about him.

"I think I've broken him down. He says he's tired of locking horns with unconquerable mountains. Wonder what he was talking about?" Her little smile gave away the naive facade.

She suddenly had Tracie's attention. "He was tired of doing what with what?"

"You know. The highest mountain in the world. Locking horns with Everest, he said. I didn't pretend to understand him. He said he was mixing metaphors, too, but I didn't notice. Would you wear my sapphire pendant and earrings if you were me? Or would it be overdoing with the pearls?"

Tracie was busy undressing for her bath, trying hard not to envy the delicate beauty of her cousin or the confidence that let her pursue Bill Dempster without reserve or suspicion.

"Kitten, you'd look good in gingham and seashells, and you know it."

The compliment capped Lili's mood, and she left the bedroom on her happy conquest of Bill Dempster. She left behind her a woman highly unsatisfied with herself in many ways.

After bathing and changing, Tracie found most of the wedding guests shuffling around the spacious living room with its curious mixture of rattan, bamboo and priceless polished Chinese furniture. One man was leaning so hard against the back of a loveseat that Tracie winced for Aunt Jade, to whom the furniture belonged. Most of the guests dangled the stems of cocktail glasses between two fingers. One brandy Alexander had already been spilled on the floor and the shards of glass were being collected by Kaahumanu under Aunt Jade's supervision. Her aunt was expressionless as

265

usual, but her fingers were out of their sleeves for once and they flexed angrily.

Victor sipped Diane's cocktail, then smiled as she sipped from the opposite rim. After both were photographed by Theo with his Eastman Kodak, Victor went off to the far end of the room to discuss union organizers with two sugar-mill executives.

Mr. Croyde bellowed to anyone who happened to be passing by, "I know I'm a disgrace to good liquor, but I like ice in my martini. Any chance?"

Diane Thorpe, looking virginal and extremely nervous in her mauve dress with cap sleeves, smiled at him and offered a small crystal bowl of ice with silver tongs. "Me too. I mean, I like my drinks very light."

"That's not my trouble. I just like more to drink. Those itty-bitty glasses don't hold more'n a gap-and-a-swallow. But you put a martini in a bigger glass with ice and you've got two-three swallows."

Diane didn't reply, smiled tensely as she set the bowl down. Tracie was disturbed by her pallor and by her trembling hands. She caught Diane's wrist while Mr. Croyde filled his martini glass with ice and went away to add some gin.

"Are you all right?" Tracie asked.

Diane's smile flickered and dissolved. She swallowed hard. "Fine, thank you."

"Bridal nerves?"

"I. . .I guess so."

A shadow crossed between them. Both women looked around to see Theo standing nearby, seeming to watch Diane closely. "You don't look so good," he said. "Can I help you?"

Tracie was surprised at his concern. Unless it was a matter of life and death, Theo usually displayed what he thought of as a worldly, sophisticated indifference to illness, even his own.

"Some water. If you don't mind." Diane's soft eyes had an excellent effect upon him. He even reddened a little, pleased to be of help, and hurried across the room to the glass tea wagon with its liquors and mixes.

Tracie saw him pass Lili and Bill Dempster. Bill glanced over at Tracie, puzzled by all this sudden activity. Diane whispered a hurried excuse and left the room abruptly. Tracie followed in time to catch her around the waist as she swayed.

"What is it?"

Diane shook her head. "Just nerves. Don't make a fuss, please. Victor will be angry. Sickness makes him cross."

This was too true, as Tracie knew very well,

but it sounded brutal when spoken aloud. In spite of Diane's objections Tracie looked around for Victor, then remembered she had seen him at the far end of the room, gesticulating dramatically to Ma McCallister and Dr. Tokuda about something, probably the president. Nothing could set him off like a reference to Franklin Roosevelt. Probably Diane was right. No use in telling father anything yet. He would just show the least compassionate side of his disposition, possibly before a roomful of tongue-wagging friends.

Lili and Theo came over to them, Theo carrying the glass of water crowded with chips of ice. Diane took it and leaned heavily against his shoulder.

"You don't imagine that poor sappy creature is jinxed too!" Lili muttered to Tracie.

"What a thing to say!" Tracie said, silencing her.

Diane broke away from Theo. "I'm sick. My stomach hurts. I must get — bathroom."

Tracie hustled her to the tiny guest toilet across the hall. Seconds later Diane leaned over the wash basin and retched. Tracie motioned and Lili handed her a towel. Diane took it, trembling. Her flesh was icy with sweat.

There were footsteps in the hall and Tracie heard Bill Dempster ask, "Is something wrong?

Anything I can do?"

Tracie called out, "You can get my father. He certainly ought to—"

"No!" Diane almost shrieked. "He'd hate it. I'm fine. Really!" She raised her head, scrubbed color into her face with the rough towel and stepped out in the hall with a bright smile. "See? It was just bridal nerves. That's all."

Impressed by her vehemence Theo backed away, feeling awkward. "Sure. Sorry."

His sister gave Tracie a meaningful glance, but getting a blank look in return, she nudged Bill.

"Let's go, We're not wanted here."

Bill hesitated. "I'll be with you in a minute. You and Theo go on. Your guests are probably wondering."

They didn't like it, but they were spurred to obey by the sight of their mother watching them from one of the open doorways to the living room. "Wait for me," Diane said. "I'm fine. I don't want to go in alone."

Bill stepped aside, said nothing until she had gone back to join her guests.

"Do you really think it's bridal tension, or whatever she calls it?" he asked Tracie when she was out of earshot.

"Probably."

"But you aren't sure."

She stared at him. "If you're implying some-thing was in her glass, you're way off."

"I hope so. But how can you be so sure?"

"Because my father drank from the same glass. Theo took a picture of them."

Bill looked relieved, but Tracie was unnerved by the suggestion. While the events of the evening had been innocent, she couldn't shake off her growing uneasiness over the rapidly approaching marriage.

14

Because she wanted so desperately to believe Diane's attack had been mere nerves, Tracie felt an enormous relief when the evening was finally over. The guests drifted off early to their sleeping quarters, having been tired by the sea air sweeping across the decks of various ships that had brought them to Akua. But someone had to keep an eye on Diane, given the remote possibility that Bill Dempster was right.

Though she knew what her father's response would be, Tracie decided he had to know that his bride needed protection. She caught him just after he'd seen Diane to her room. He heard the sharp click of the lock and chuckled, though he frowned when he saw Tracie at the far end of the upstairs hall.

"How do you like that? Locking out her bridegroom. In a few hours we'll be man and wife."

"It isn't that, dad. This is a big house and

she isn't used to all these people." She hesitated, trying to word the problem diplomatically. "She's been a little nervous. She had a stomach upset earlier this evening."

He rolled his eyes. "Don't tell me she's going to be sickly, like your mother."

"Dad! Somebody ought to hang you by your thumbs."

He was astonished. "Why, for God's sake?"

"Because you have no sympathy for suffering."

He backtracked sheepishly. "Well, hell, of course I don't want her suffering. I just didn't think."

"You never do."

"Okay. I'm sorry. I really do love Dinah, you know. She suits me fine. She's a well-meaning little thing. Exactly the kind of female I approve of. Not like you modern kids."

He put his arm around her and they walked toward the back stairs. She was on her way to help Aunt Jade check on forgotten personal items or smoldering cigarettes, some of which always remained after parties that scattered throughout the lower floor.

"Be good to her, dad." She took a breath. "There is just a faint chance that she got hold of something tainted. Maybe it was the fish in the hors d'oeuvres or something."

Victor stopped and leaned against the bannister at the top of the stairs. His pale, gray eyes looked worried. "It's not something like Ilima's problem, is it?"

"No. Undoubtedly, it was all the excitement. I only meant it might be a good idea to keep an eye on her during the time you're on your honeymoon."

"Well, of course I will. What kind of a honeymoon would it be otherwise? I told you. I love the girl."

"Then that's all that's necessary. Good-night. And I know you'll be happy, dad."

"Sure. She suits me right down to the ground. 'Night, honey."

She went on down the stairs, turning before she stepped into the short rear hall that passed Ilima's room. She was already in the hall when she heard Lili's familiar giggle and reflected cynically that the girl's fear of the room seemed to dissolve under the attentions of its current occupant.

She found Aunt Jade in the dining room with Chin Loo. Her aunt was rearranging the exquisite jade display before the silk screen on the far sideboard while Chin Loo squatted near the long hem of her robe, picking at a hole in the rug.

"Smoke, smoke, smoke," Chin Loo grumbled.

"Always they got to smoke."

Aunt Jade looked at Tracie. Her hands still caressed the jade Buddha.

"The bride was not well tonight."

"A little nervous, I imagine."

The graceful fingers became still. "Her own party, and she leaves her guests...the new mistress of the household."

Tracie said, "You will always be mistress here, Aunt Jade. Diane won't interfere."

The older woman shrugged. "That would not be proper. But she will not be a true wife to your father."

"She's inexperienced, but she'll learn."

"No. She does not love him. Perhaps the other did. If so, I am sorry." She avoided Tracie's eyes before adding the explanation. "Sorry I misjudged her."

"Maybe we're wrong about Diane. I think she needs someone to look after her. Someone to give her security. That is a love, of sorts."

Aunt Jade remained her implacable self. "She is not good for this house. She will bring down disaster."

"Auntie, for heaven's sake!"

But the woman only folded her arms in her sleeves and walked out. Tracie and Chin Loo exchanged looks, feeling the apprehension between them. Aunt Jade's pronouncements always had that effect on those who knew her.

Hearing Jade's voice in the hall, Chin Loo looked suddenly fearful. "Who does she talk to now? It is late. There is no one awake. Does she talk to—" He stopped, afraid to say what he was thinking.

The horrible thing was, Tracie knew what he meant to say. She felt her body become stiff with tension. This was silly — she would simply find out whom Jade was talking to. She passed Chin, walked out through the archway into the hall with a firm stride.

It was becoming too absurd; clearly, she was letting her nerves get the best of her. Aunt Jade had come upon Bill Dempster in the hallway. She raised her voice uncharacteristically. "I do not wish her in that room. There is no more to be said."

Bill's careful politeness with the proud woman remained intact. "Lady Jade, you saw Liliha run up those stairs. She had no intention of staying in my room. Nor did I invite her. In fact, she followed me in here."

"I do not permit my daughter in that room," Jade said, disregarding his argument.

Tracie held her breath, waiting for Bill to pick up on the woman's curious concern. "It isn't me you're worried about. It's that room you object to, isn't it?"

Jade's mouth closed firmly, like a coin purse snapping shut. She passed him, turning sideways as if afraid of contamination, and went on to her room.

Tracie cleared her throat. Bill said, "I know you're there, Tracie. That was an interesting little encounter, wouldn't you say?"

She didn't want him to jeer at her own fears. "How do you mean?"

"Here. Come with me." He took her hand and she followed obediently, fully aware that she wanted to be invited to his room. The door of his room – Ilima's room – was ajar. The ceiling light was on, making the room look tawdry, far from the friendly haven it had been when Ilima lived in it.

"What happened to Lili?" she asked.

"Ran away."

"Scared her, did you?"

He grinned. "Unlike you, she doesn't appreciate the finer things in life."

She studied him shrewdly. "But that wasn't the real reason she ran away, was it?"

His fingers slid from her hand upward along her arm until he reached her throat and then her clavicle, lingering over the fair, soft flesh beneath the plunging neckline of her russet satin evening gown.

"I'm afraid I didn't offer enough inducement

to counter whatever else it was she felt in here." His head bent to Tracie's bosom and his lips moved slowly over the full curve of her breast. She wanted to tell him to wait until they were in bed, but couldn't. The sheer bliss of his lips on her breast made her knees weak; she caught her breath, unable to speak.

Then suddenly, it was over. He raised his head, looking her full in the face. "See what you're missing?" he said softly, and let her go.

A slightly teasing look on his face warned her that if she responded in kind he might rebuff her. It wasn't at all like her to be caught so defenseless that she swayed when he let her go. She didn't know what game he was playing, but she knew that she could play it as well, if only for the pleasure of it.

"Nobody says I have to miss anything," she said, but he'd turned away and began to walk around the room, as if searching for something. Suddenly he stopped. "Smell anything? Perfume? Anything at all?"

So he knew about it, too. Lili must have told him.

"Bill, is it true? Some of us feel there's a kind of presence in here and out in the hall. Once we even imagined we sensed it on the front staircase."

He shook his head. "Don't be ridiculous. I

could understand if your servants believed something so superstitious, but not you."

They were getting far away from the sensual mood of only a moment ago. "Then you don't smell the powder?"

"Absolutely not. Except yours. And very sexy it is."

"Thank you. I had no idea the effect it could have on a man." Her voice was calm but inside she was angry at herself for having let him lead her on.

She reached behind her, opened the door and moved out into the hall as if the earlier moment was of no importance. Still, she hoped he would come after her. If only he would stop playing his shrewd little games, pitting Lili against her and then pretending he wanted her again, she would have gone into his arms, gone to his bed. In the hall she looked back.

"Sleep well," he said, with that same teasing smile and closed the door almost in her face.

Now embarrassed that he'd simply let her go, she resolved that somehow she would get even with him . . .

She moved away from his door, remembering suddenly his earlier concern that someone may have attempted to poison Diane Thorpe. Apparently he'd forgotten about that, caring for little more than the pretense of seducing Tracie. He didn't even sense the nearness of Ilima's presence...or at least he said he didn't. Could it be something they were all imagining? And if it was, why did they all sense – or think they sensed – the same thing?

Tracie went upstairs. Passing the various guest rooms, she heard laughter and talking in one or two rooms, a sharp but muffled marital quarrel in another, until she finally reached her own room.

Lili was already in bed and Tracie noticed she was huddled under the covers. It was seldom cold enough on Akua for a blanket. Even after one of the rare hurricanes people didn't use more than a sheet.

Remembering Diane Thorpe's illness that evening, Tracie was worried. "Feeling all right, Lili?"

"I guess so." Her dark eyes peered out from under the silk binding of the blanket, blinking at the light. "I was in her room tonight."

"Yes, I know. He says he doesn't feel anything in there."

Lili jerked the blanket down. "Well, I do. She was there. Tracie, *what does she want?*" Lili's slight figure shivered. "And now we've got another one to worry about. What if something happens to Diane?"

"Don't talk about it. Don't even think about it."

In spite of their fears they both slept straight through until a little after seven the next morning when they were awakened by the servants bustling around with coffee trays, each containing a hibiscus flower, fresh golden papaya halves, lemon and lime to season them, and richly decorated hot cross buns, since it was the Easter season.

"Mother has probably been up for hours, along with Chin Loo," Lili said, having forgotten her fears by daylight. "I really wonder when she sleeps."

Perhaps never, Tracie thought. Her aunt was indefatigable, except on that recent night when she was told her brother-in-law was marrying again.

By nine o'clock the dining room was busy with the comings and goings of the guests who breakfasted from the two buffets set out for them. Diane had refused all offers to send for a mainland friend who would act as her bridesmaid. It suggested that in spite of her sweet, compliant nature, she had surprisingly few friends at home. Tracie was gratified to be chosen as a substitute and Victor, too, was delighted.

"You see?" he told Tracie. "She fits right

into the family like she was born to it."

Diane had wanted to wear her best wine-flowered beige gown, but Tracie and Lili had insisted she must have a new white dress for the wedding.

Diane was aghast. "I can't wear white. I'm a divorced woman," she kept repeating as they shopped for the gown in Honolulu one week-end.

"Well, don't say it like you were a scarlet woman," Lili said matter-of-factly. "Anyway, everybody will expect to see you in white."

So Diane had chosen a white wedding gown but couldn't be talked out of layered taffeta with puff sleeves and innocent little frills around the high neck. Lili sighed once the final choice was made. "We're never going to make a fashion plate out of her," she complained to Tracie. "I hope Uncle Vic doesn't expect one."

"She's a very nice person, and I think she'll make dad a perfect wife." And I certainly hope he will make a good husband, she added to herself. Everything she said about Diane Thorpe was true, but sometimes she wondered if such an even-tempered disposition might eventually pall on her mercurial father.

While Tracie, Lili and Mrs. McCallister adjusted the bride's stiffened white lace hat on top of her glossy dark hair, Theo bounded in, whistled at the sight of the four women and proposed a riddle. "Guess who just arrived with the general manager of Akua Sugar? Uncle Vic sent her an invitation, and she's already hanging onto her ex-husband."

His sister stamped her blue satin pump. "Tell us, for heaven's sake!"

"Marta Dempster, of course. In the flesh. And what flesh! Sorry, girls. She's going to outshine you all. She's wearing a red outfit cut down to here."

Diane mourned, "I knew it." She stared at her reflection in the long mirror that had belonged to Tracie's mother. A pale, uncertain image looked back at her.

Lili rolled her eyes. "Leave it to her to pull something like that." But she quickly dismissed the unexpected guest and gave Tracie a grin. "Anyway, Wayne Croyde likes me. And he's been a darling, especially since you've practically ignored him since he got here."

But Tracie wasn't paying attention to her cousin's chatter. "Red to a spring wedding. How tacky can Marta get?" she muttered. "Look, Lili, don't you think we should play up her eyes a bit more?" she said, studying Diane's face.

"And more rouge. What about lipstick?"

Lili and Tracie went to work on Diane's

makeup and when they finished they thought they had produced a very pretty bride, bringing out the loveliness of her brown eyes and the softness of her mouth which, Lili assured her, "a man might find very kissable. Don't be too shy, Diane. You have to give a little."

Tracie was watching the bride's face in the mirror, reflecting on what a remarkable change could be made when just a little makeup was judiciously applied. But something in her expression seemed puzzling as Lili complimented her. She didn't look as pleased as she might have been...she looked thoughtful, older.

Was it sadness Tracie thought she saw in her eyes? Maybe it was regret at the loss of the dashing young gambler who had been her first husband. Or was Diane sorry now to be marrying an older man? Knowing there was nothing she could have said or done about it, Tracie felt pity and again doubt that the marriage could ever work.

The ceremony started at twelve-fifteen. With Mrs. McCallister at the grand piano in the long living room, the music of Wagner took Diane Thorpe down the main staircase with Tracie going before her in green georgette over silk, Lili following behind her in blue and Theo proudly escorting the bride. He had never looked more handsome. No one would have guessed from his gallant poise that Victor had chosen him only reluctantly in an effort to please his sister-in-law. Victor was well aware of what he owed Jade for the care of the family and the house.

As Tracie passed Bill and Marta she heard the woman remark, "Now *that* would be a more suitable match. Cute, isn't he?" She was obviously referring to Theo.

Bill caught Tracie's eye as she passed and said deliberately, "Cute is just the word for him."

Tracie wanted to laugh at his tone and looked away quickly.

The altar had been set up before the fireplace, and Sam Kahana, Victor's best man, looking solid but powerful in his morning suit, stood beside the groom. Both men had been sipping bourbon for the past hour and Victor was feeling exuberant, accepting the light remarks of the guests in a lively spirit, behaving exactly as they expected him to behave — like a gentleman pirate.

The ceremony was over quickly. Everyone said afterward that the bride's replies had hardly been audible but Victor Berenson's voice rang out through the living room and the entrance hall.

Following the vows the bride and groom exchanged affectionate if brief kisses. After the groom, Theo was the first to kiss the bride. He held her in an embrace that brought whistles from the crowd. The bride blushed and gave him a warm smile. Victor reached for Marta Dempster and embraced her while Bill, too, kissed the bride. Marta made the most of her own opportunity, and the result was a series of flash shots for posterity, one of which appeared on the front page of the Honolulu *Star-Bulletin* the next day with a caption reading, "BEST MAID AT BERENSON NUPTIALS?"

The crowd trailed to the dining room where Jade's long table deserved a front-page picture itself. Diane went to her and embraced her new sister-in-law in front of all the guests.

"How good of you, dear Jade! I'll never be able to handle things like this half as well as you did. I'll have so much to live up to."

Tracie and Lili did not miss the past tense the bride used in her praise. "Don't tell me she's going to try and throw mother out. She has more nerve than I'd have," Lili whispered to Tracie.

Tracie said firmly, "She won't do it as long as I'm around." She made allowances for the bride's inexperience but this was no time for Diane to flaunt her new position in front of every Berenson friend in the Territory, and not a few enemies. Tracie knew she shouldn't interfere, but she couldn't help saying, "Oh, don't worry, Diane. Aunt Jade will be here for a long time to help you, won't you?"

Aunt Jade's closed lips smiled. Tracie became aware that Bill, who had moved next to her, was watching her thoughtfully. The others around them, too, felt uncomfortable at the remarks until Theo clapped his hands. "Cut the cake, somebody. My glass is empty again. Don't want to run out of champagne before I get my cake. Some of that pink frosting, if you don't mind. And a smidgen of white."

The relief was palpable. The photographers gave orders, directing the bridal couple. Victor's long, sinewy hand closed over Diane's fingers on the shiny new knife, and she cut into the three-tiered macadamia and coconut cake.

An hour later some of the guests were still going around the buffets for additional helpings of fresh crab, pork baked in taro leaves, the delicious dolphin called mahi-mahi, tender manoa lettuce and local vegetables, lomi-lomi salmon, endless *haole* dishes like cold prime rib slices, potato and macaroni salds, plus, of course, poi in its many disguises.

For the Oriental guests, Chinese, Japanese or Korean, there was a special, smaller buffet, and

286

through some perversity it was better attended than the polished bowls full of Hawaiian food popularized by *haoles*.

After the cake was cut and more photos taken, Wayne Croyde accompanied the younger Berensons and Mrs. McCallister down to Akua City to see the bride and groom off on the *Akua Orchid.* Wayne hung back once they reached the cargo ship, but Tracie had been softened by the ceremony and urged him on with an arm around him in a friendly fashion.

He squeezed her hard. "I like weddings. Didn't think I would. I can just picture you in one of those pretty white dresses."

She rolled her eyes skyward.

"Well, maybe not with all the ruffles Diane had on," he added, "but mom has a wedding dress that would look great on you."

She understood his feelings, the impulse she herself had briefly felt during the procession and ceremony. "I don't know, Wayne. I'm afraid I don't seem ready yet."

He bent over to whisper and she controlled a nervous giggle as his lips tickled her ear. But her mood quickly sobered at his message.

"Tracie, your dad's got a wife and partner now. Maybe you should reconsider my offer . . . you may get edged out."

"Don't be silly," she snapped. "Nobody can

take my job away. It has nothing to do with them."

But of course, he was right. She felt discouraged and depressed about her position with Orchid Tree Enterprises. She must do something...make a decision about her future...It would be easy to marry this tall, awkward, lovable man, but she knew she could never focus her life on marriage, home and children alone — an attitude that never failed to baffle her girlfriends in college. The men she knew, like Wayne and probably Bill Dempster, assumed they could change her as almost every other woman of her acquaintance was changed, given new priorities that Tracie felt were unsuited to her real nature. She wanted love, but like Bill Dempster, she wanted it on her own terms.

Impulsively she glanced up at the jacaranda heights above the southern headland of the little bay. Bill Dempster had talked about building one of his damned factories or some other monstrosity there. But then he had gotten off on the subject of a home in that location being preferable to Valley House. Trying to put down the Berensons, no doubt.

If he were only sincere and genuinely loved her for what she was, they might have been perfectly matched. But he would be the last man to want a wife who was both bedfellow and partner.

Meanwhile, Victor had gotten what he wanted – a compliant wife. He was in great spirits, claiming he felt like a boy again as Diane's head rested against his shoulder.

"Take care of yourself, dad," Tracie said as she hugged him. "You may feel like a teenager but you're not one, you know."

"Watch that."

"Dad, you know what I mean. Anyway, have a good time."

"That's better." He went on to kiss Lili on the forehead, and clapped Theo on the back. "You take care of these little beauties, or you'll hear from me."

Theo tried to look modest, unassuming and trustworthy. It was clear, however, that he put more into his farewell to the bride than the others did, hugging her tightly. She had followed her husband, giving each girl a peck on the cheek and returning Theo's embrace with the admonition, "I know you will take care of – I can say it now – my new family and my new home."

Theo only smiled in response.

The ship's engines rumbled underfoot. Mrs. McCallister blessed them all jokingly and received a big kiss from Victor in return. Then the gangplank was pulled in and the *Akua Orchid* sailed out of the blue-green waters into the main current of the turbulent Akua-lapu channel, headed for Oahu and Honolulu harbor.

The mood of those on the dock was curiously ambivalent. In one respect, as Theo put it, "It's kind of like flat champagne without them." But Lili, too, had an honest observation.

"I feel relieved. There was a lot of tension, I thought."

"Me too," Tracie confessed.

Mrs. McCallister raised her hand to shield her eyes from the sun and watched the old cargo ship round the headland.

"Seemed like a nice little thing."

Tracie winced. "Don't say that. That's how dad talks about her. I expected something a bit more romantic from him."

After they'd left the dock Theo gallantly helped Mrs. McCallister over a puddle of rainwater in front of Mr. Nakazawa's store. The woman was pleasantly surprised, having plowed through puddles without help for twenty years, but she duly noted his excellent manners.

"You're a good lad, Theodore. I hope your uncle's new will takes into consideration that you may be better than you look."

Lili and Tracie only laughed but Theo took the implication of her remark seriously. He stopped dead in his tracks and the younger women almost piled into him.

"What new will?"

The girls looked at Belle McCallister, who realized she had spoken out of turn. Not a subtle woman, she blustered, "Well, hell! That's expected. A new wife, and young and pretty, and all. It was yesterday morning he called me in and asked me to sign it. Me and that Filipino boy, the good-looking one. Victor wrote the will out in longhand. Anyway, we signed it. I know old Vic, though. He's got a strong sense of family. He's bound to give you some thought."

"*Some* thought," Lili muttered.

Even Tracie was shocked. "Then he's made a new will already? He didn't mention it or discuss it with any of us." What hurt most was the fact that he hadn't thought enough of their feelings to talk it over or explain. She had argued a dozen times that Victor owed them nothing; yet he had handled the whole thing in such a secretive way, like a coward afraid to face the family. Her father had shown this streak in other ways. It was a quality she disliked, and knowing herself to be like him, she was disturbed by flaws she might find in her own character. It was a thoughtful group that climbed back into the Packard and drove back to the plantation house.

"I wonder how long the marriage will last," Theo said, breaking the silence.

"My Lord!" Mrs. McCallister yelped. "He's barely on his honeymoon and you're divorcing him already."

Theo said, "She's too young, too pretty and fragile for him."

"We'd have been better off with Ilima Mako." Everyone looked at Lili. She added defensively, "Well, it's true."

"I never approved of mixed blood," Mrs. Mc-Callister said, considering the dead woman. "Not good for either side, I always thought." Clearly, Tracie thought, Belle wasn't aware of how her remark might offend Lili and Theo. "But frankly, the Mako girl fitted in every respect. She was sensible and obliging. A good neighbor. I don't know why she was so moody those last weeks. If you ask me, your father had nothing to do with the tragedy, Tracie. All that rubbish about not wanting to marry him! I always suspected it was something else."

Tracie took her arm quickly. "Haven't you any idea at all? Anything she said to you? Even a hint?"

Theo interrupted, slapping the wheel as he maneuvered around a switchback and barely missed a landslide of mud and the slippery palm fronds of a fallen tree. "Too late now. We've got to concentrate on the present bride. It's not her fault, you know. It's uncle's."

Lili remarked, "Too bad none of the old-time *kahunas* are still around to put a curse or something on her."

"Keep your damn mouth shut!"

They all stared at Theo, feeling that the conversation had gotten out of hand in some mysterious way.

15

Tracie wasn't at all pleased with the way Bill Dempster behaved with Lili. To Lili's delight he seemed to go out of his way to demonstrate his fondness for her. The only comfort for Tracie's anger and jealousy was Aunt Jade's surprising observation. "You need not look so, Tracie. He treats my little girl as he would treat a child. He is jovial; he is kind and teasing. But he is not serious about her. I do not think he will take advantage of her."

"That may be true, but can we trust him? He's trying to get control of Orchid Tree. I'm sure of it."

They were on the west lanai watching Bill teach Lili to toss a football. The lesson was not a success and Lili was hysterical with laughter. Bill too seemed to be enjoying himself. Aunt Jade glanced at the beautiful spreading tree that was now coming into blossom. "The orchid tree? Then may he destroy it. There is evil in it."

"Aunt Jade!" Startled by her vehemence, Tracie explained unnecessarily. "I mean the company. You know what store dad sets by that tree."

"I do know. None better." Aunt Jade's delicate oblique-shaped eyelids closed as she remembered old days, good times. "I was present when he and my husband planted it. Victor said, 'It shall stand as long as Berenson Enterprises stands.' And my husband said 'Amen to that.' Yes. I remember. But it is an evil thing."

Tracie looked at her curiously. "Why?"

"I remember the last hours of my husband's life. There was no wind, but the branches scratched and prodded at the house mercilessly. It wished to reach him, that I know. And it would have if my husband hadn't died."

"Auntie!"

Jade shrugged. "So it seems to me. And it did so again when the Mako woman agreed to marry Victor...and the night before Diane Thorpe married Victor."

With growing compassion Tracie understood some of Aunt Jade's bitterness. It was more and more evident she had loved her brother-in-law Victor all these years — an unrequited love. It must be even more painful now, when the new bride was already talking about taking over, edging her out. Tracie shifted the subject carefully. "But you believe Lili is safe with — with Bill?"

Aunt Jade looked at her, her eyes revealing something like contempt. "You are so like your father. You do not know love from hate. You are blind, both of you. Take care for what it will cost you."

It was an extraordinary thing to say. Almost like a witch uttering a curse . . . or like an oracle, veiled and unseen, without emotion.

But as it turned out that very day, Jade was wrong. Bill Dempster showed once more that he was everything Tracie suspected him of being, and she discovered it in the most innocuous way: he told her so. He had promised Lili he would be back in time to catch the interisland cargo ferry that ran between Oahu, Akua and Molokai, reminding her he would get her back to her sorority house in Honolulu safe and sound before dark.

"Do you have to?" Lili had teased, with a sly side-glance in her mother's direction.

Bill almost spoiled his standing with her by his assurance, "I never rob the cradle, sweetheart."

She made a face at him, ignoring her brother's laugh, and went into the house to make herself more seductive. Bill then explained to Jade that he would be back in no time, but right now he had to complete some business with the Akua Sugar Company.

"Of course. You *do* have a minority holding," Tracie said, as if it had only just occurred to her. She was dying of curiosity and beginning to smolder with suspicion. "Are you sure you can find your way to the factory?"

Bill was all politeness. "Well, of course, I'd get there quicker with a guide...but I guess you're too busy with your bookkeeping and all."

"I don't spend all my time huddling over the books. Besides, Namu needs the exercise."

"For Namu's sake, then. Don't hesitate to come along."

She received that with the retort it deserved. "Don't worry. I won't hesitate. Rudi Arguello will find you a mount. I don't know if you can manage Big Boy. He belongs to dad." She had hoped that would nettle him, but he only said evenly, "I'll chance it. I'll also borrow one of those big coco-straw hats too, if you don't mind. I'm prepared for every danger but sunburn."

"Every danger?" she echoed with a grin, and they started out together.

As she had found out the first time he handled reins, he knew his way around horses. Big Boy accepted him with only a brief snort and a tossing of the head to show who was boss. They cantered over the ridge between the Berenson valley and the widespread cane fields, making small talk until Bill broke through the polite insincerity.

"Why don't you ask what you're dying to ask me? What am I up to now?"

"Okay. What?"

He reached out, leaning toward her, and patted Namu's mane. "It's a way of mixing business with pleasure."

She returned the gesture, mocking him by patting Big Boy's black withers. "We'll outvote you. Thirty-seven to thirty-two percent."

That was when the jolt came, and it came quietly.

"Not thirty-two. Forty-two percent. I settled for the extra ten percent a few minutes before your father's wedding. Scraped it up from the Murikamis and others."

Her lips felt icy and stiff. She managed to equal his calm, on the surface, at least.

"Your timing is exquisite."

"So are my intentions. Your father's interest in conditions in the cane fields has been falling rapidly. We both know it." He waved down her protest. "He behaves as if he were in the nineteenth century...But I'm willing to turn the ten percent over to you whenever I can depend on you not to give it to Vic."

"Of course I'll give it to dad," she snapped.

"What do you think I am?"

"I'm sorry for that. Think it over. I'd like to see you using your initiative instead of following in Victor's shadow. If he won't encourage you, then somebody else ought to. Did it ever occur to you that his example may be corrupting you?"

She was shaken by indignation. "My father — corrupt me?"

"Please... Don't misunderstand... His ideas. His economic views. This king-of-the-island business. Think about it. The shares will be yours in the long run."

"You can wait forever."

He looked ahead at distant South Beach and the anchored cargo ship belonging to the sugar company. Storm clouds hovered above the darkening waters but the sun still shone overhead.

"In that case, I will wait. Let me know when you can think for yourself. As I said, I came here for business and pleasure." He added after a second or two, "Would you believe it if I told you the pleasure was in seeing you?"

"Ha."

"Well, I had another proposal in mind, besides the stock."

"I'll bet you did."

"But it didn't pan out. Jacarandas lost out to orchid trees."

The orchid tree! That damned tree kept coming up. She banished the rest of his glib excuses, not understanding their implication, and fastened onto that.

"Jade is afraid of our orchid tree. Do you think it's possible that Ilima let that thing frighten her in some way? She really was superstitious, you know."

"Easy, boy." He patted the big black. "No. The tree had nothing to do with her death. What killed her were hints and suggestions and lies, I believe. All based on an old fear that poor Ilima carried around with her as long as I've known her."

"But I was her best friend. If she was afraid of trees, or cliffs or marriage – whatever it was, I would have known."

"You wouldn't have known this. She didn't dare to tell you. Your family wouldn't have hired her if she had. Certainly Victor would never have married her, if he knew."

"What, for God's sake?" she cried.

Two cane-field workers loped across the road in front of them. Tracie answered their greeting automatically, though all her attention was focused on Bill Dempster. Obviously he hadn't intended to tell her this about Ilima. Had he planned to keep it a secret forever? Short of Ilima being a criminal, what could it possibly be?

"Tell me, Bill. Please. What did Ilima do?"

He pulled up short and reached out for Namu's reins.

"I don't want this to get further, though it is possible someone in your family already knows it."

It was a good thing he had gotten hold of Namu. Tracie's sudden jerk on the reins confused the gentle mare. "Knows *what?*" Tracie didn't think she could bear another moment of not knowing what Ilima was guilty of.

He took a long, deep breath. "I can't prove anything. But someone may have preyed on an old fear Ilima had. I told you I knew Ilima's father."

"Adoptive father."

"I knew her natural father as well. Her mother died about the time of Ilima's birth. Tuberculosis. But I met her father on Molokai. He was always at the foot of the mule trail when I delivered supplies down to the peninsula."

She licked her lips nervously. "The — peninsula?"

"Kalaupapa."

Comprehension had been slow. "I don't believe it," she said sharply. "Are you trying to tell me that Ilima's real father had Hansen's disease? Leprosy?"

"In an advanced stage. He was a jolly fellow.

301

I liked him a lot. But his disease took the elephantiasis form. It took some getting used to."

She recovered from the news but was still shaken. "You forget. I've known lepers. Those being shipped to Kalaupapa are sometimes on the lower deck of the inter-island steamers we use. They've traveled on the *Akua Orchid.* They are kept to themselves but some of them are people we've..." Her voice trailed off lamely, "...known." She paused for a moment. "But not Ilima. She had none of the signs."

"Of course not. But this is a woman whose girlhood was haunted by fear. Her foster parents worried over this obsession of hers. Old Mako, her natural father, didn't die until 1930. I took Ilima down to see him in his last days. She insisted and we were given permission. So far as I know, Mako was dying of a kidney failure that had nothing to do with the disease, poor devil. Naturally, we were careful. But the danger of exposure is less than one would think."

"I know that. We aren't completely medieval here in the Islands."

"Nevertheless, the progress of the disease had given Mako a frightful appearance. When I took Ilima back to Honolulu where she was working at the time, she seemed to accept her father's death. Then, this past June, when I met her at the dentist's in Honolulu, and she told me of her engagement, she seemed to be haunted by this old fear. I tried to reason with her, but I had the distinct feeling she was being hounded by someone else, someone who knew about her fears and was playing on them. Subtly, perhaps. Who knows? But it was there. She hinted as much, though I couldn't get her to talk about it. It stood to reason when you told me she broke out in a nervous rash."

"That was natural. The excitement of the wedding, and all the plans."

"Exactly. But suppose someone played on that fear, made her think the rash was something else, more serious. It would explain the suddenness of what she did."

Tracie remembered Chin Loo and what he said of Ilima's desperate unhappiness – that she loved Victor, but was unable to marry him.

Tracie whispered, "The cruelty of it. The awful, vicious cruelty." She paused for a moment, the implications of what he was saying finally sinking in. *"If* you're right," she added. "We don't know if that's what actually happened. There may have been some other reason...she could have done it on her own, without prompting from anyone."

"Maybe," Bill said, but he didn't sound convinced.

After that disclosure her intense interest in his purchase of the Akua Sugar stock seemed almost petty, unreal.

If only Ilima had confided in her...she could have reasoned with her, made her see that her fears were blown way out of proportion. Still, Victor was bound to have found out about Ilima's father. What then? Tracie knew that the young woman couldn't have stood being rejected by him, wasn't even willing to risk the possibility of it. Her death in itself was terrible, but to think that one of the Berensons could have caused it made it all the worse.

"Bill, what exactly did Ilima say that made you think we Berensons were involved?"

"Your cousin Lili had let everyone in Honolulu know, in strictest confidence, what the family thought of the marriage."

"She would."

"So when Ilima told me what was troubling her, I figured maybe your family had something to do with it. We talked about the fact that some of the Berensons were against the marriage, and I reminded her that it would make them apt to say anything to discourage her. It didn't seem to make a difference. I remember her saying that maybe this time they were right."

"*They?*"

"I don't think she meant it that way, but you know Ilima would never want to point a finger at anyone, so she just said 'they.' "

It was hard enough to think that there was even one person in her family who could behave so cruelly, but more than one? It seemed almost impossible, but it was a suspicion she couldn't easily shake off.

Seeing how upset she was, Bill moved to comfort her, closing his hand on hers. "I'm sorry, Tracie. Sorry for a lot of things, but this especially. I know that it doesn't involve you, and I hate to see you hurt this much." He squeezed her cold fingers. "Believe me, I never thought you were capable of something like this."

"Thank you." But the shadow remained between them. Her suspicions of his own motives had been reinforced. No doubt his efforts to buy into Orchid Tree Enterprises were motivated by the desire to repay them for what he thought they had done to Ilima Mako. And very little evidence there was, too!

She didn't even bother to think of trying to sabotage the Dempster deal with Akua Sugar by acquiring six percent of the minority stock elsewhere, from Belle McCallister and others, which would put Victor back as majority stockholder. For the moment she didn't care. There were more important matters at stake now — he had managed to make her entire family suspect, and a part of her hated him for it.

Meanwhile, he tried to bridge the chasm that had suddenly opened between them.

"I really have the interest of your father's company at heart, Tracie. When you aren't blinded by prejudice and complete devotion to old Victor, even when he's wrong—" She started to interrupt but he rolled over her angry protest, "—you're probably more intelligent than either he or I. At any rate, the time of the paternal slave owner is dying fast. The Civil War ended years ago. But not here. These islands have plantations, ranches, fields, and hundreds upon hundreds of *kanakas, paniolos,* field hands, all working at low wages—"

"Our people love us. They wouldn't work anywhere else. Even if they could."

"Even if they could." He repeated this without inflection but she heard the ugliness of the fact itself.

"So you're going to bring in the unions."

He tried to smile and ease the blow. "I've got nothing to do with it. They're here. Any month, now. Any week. The way we'll survive is to reorganize, accept them and cut down the paternalism."

"Just throw our people out, right? Sounds

306

like Reconstruction all over again."

"No, make it a gradual process. It's called progress."

She didn't dismount as they reached the side door leading to the factory offices. He held his arms out to her but she ignored him. With an enormous effort she managed a laugh.

"I'll let you go on in to weave your little webs. I've got to get home to protect my family and my people from what you call progress."

She turned Namu, gave the mare her head and started away.

"Tracie?"

She heard him but kept going.

"Tracie, I'm afraid you won't be getting rid of me," he called after her. "I've taken a room here on the island, near the sugar refinery." She reined in Namu long enough to hear his sardonic finish. "Not quite up to the jacaranda cliffs, but since I'm no longer in the marriage market, it can't matter."

Was he seriously trying to imply that he'd been proposing to her when he took her to the cliffs? What a fool he must think she was to believe that! He had already managed to gain control of some of the Berenson property. Nobody knew how far he was prepared to go for the rest of it, even if it meant marrying a Berenson.

16

Victor Berenson's honeymoon ended abruptly when the bride and groom returned unexpectedly to Akua Island. Victor said that Orchid Tree Enterprises needed him, while Diane added she was anxious to get back and learn to run her new household. Probably there was some truth in both excuses.

Valley House had barely settled back into the run of things, after Lili's return to Honolulu and the departure of all the wedding guests, when a phone call was received. It was Lili, who spoke at great length with her mother and brother.

Theo, as always, was not above repeating some of Lili's gossip to Tracie.

"Lili says Uncle Victor was struck by a drunk on the beach and Wayne Croyde sent the man on his way with a good kick. I doubt uncle liked that. Too many people saw him fall. Lili says he becomes livid when anyone mentions it."

"I shouldn't wonder. What on earth did they fight about?" Theo didn't answer and Aunt Jade merely shrugged. "Probably a *malahini,* some tourist who had too many mai tais."

Tracie still couldn't make sense of it, though it did explain why the honeymoon had ended so suddenly. And a good thing it ended when it did, she thought. Victor had managed to draw checks totaling over twenty-five thousand dollars for the three weeks.

When Tracie questioned him on the phone Victor made it clear that she had no business "nosing into" his affairs. He assured her that if he wanted to order new wardrobes for himself and his bride it was his right to.

"Matter of fact, Marta Dempster is back and I insisted that my wife do something about her wardrobe. That actress has nothing over my little Dinah, even though she thinks she has."

That certainly explained the large expenditures. But his testy manner on that subject warned Tracie not to bring up the incident on the beach...she would have to wait to get the whole story.

Meanwhile, Aunt jade, visibly upset, discussed with Tracie the hurried changes that Victor wanted made before the return of the honeymooners.

"He asks — no, he demands that two rooms

be made suitable on the second floor – his bedroom and the small guest room beside it. It will be weeks. There must be a door cut between them."

Tracie, who had been on the phone all afternoon trying to get a loan on the rice and taro crops to tide them over until the fall payoffs, was outraged at Victor's insensitivity.

"Fine. Tell them that until the two upstairs rooms are prepared, they will have to use the rooms on the ground floor."

"But they do not have an adjoining door," Jade said, then stopped herself and flashed one of her rare tight smiles. "But as you say, the rooms adjoin. And Victor has always been fond of the orchid tree. He should not mind sleeping in Miss Mako's room for a little while."

"But Diane will, and I'm sure dad won't force her to stay there if she doesn't want to. He'll have to be sensible and stay in his own room. He won't have a choice. After a few days he'll be satisfied with the familiarity of his own big room. And I'll bet Diane will love the room next to it."

Aunt Jade was less certain. "That is to say, Victor will do this for his wife. I do not think so."

"Well, he certainly can't let poor Diane be scared to death in Ilima's old room."

310

Aunt Jade only shrugged with a knowing look. Tracie may have known her father for twenty-three years, but Jade Wong's acquaintance with him was much longer. She seemed to understand too well what Victor was – and wasn't – capable of doing.

Tracie was of two minds about the early return of her father and new stepmother. She wanted them home. Not only did she miss her father's company, she longed for his reassuring presence. Since that terrible news from Bill Dempster, she'd been haunted by creeping suspicions she couldn't shake off whenever she passed Lili's room or looked at Theo or Aunt Jade. It would have been perfectly in character for any of them to play on Ilima's fears if they knew about them and her father's identity. Although Tracie didn't believe any of them capable of murder, she knew that a small, persistent hint was very much in their style.

And what about Diane Thorpe's illness the night before the wedding? Was that just "bridal nerves" or someone trying to scare her out of the marriage? If so, who was responsible? Certainly not her cousins. Such a direct act just wasn't in their nature. Then what about the others in the Berenson household? Chin Loo? Sam Kahana? Rudi Arguello? It was inconceivable. What about one of the wedding guests? Perhaps the Croydes, who worried so about Tracie's inheritance in their assumption that Wayne would marry her. Again, ridiculous. Diane had been nervous for the most natural of reasons. Still the suspicion would not go.

The night before Victor and Diane returned home Tracie woke up from an uneasy sleep, unable to shake these unsettling thoughts. She got up, fumbled for an old satin robe that had worn thin at the elbows, and wrapped it around her. Her nerves were on edge and at the same time she knew perfectly well there was no reason why she should be so uneasy.

For one thing, Bill Dempster had no proof of anything. Secondly, there was no reason to believe anybody but Diane Thorpe was responsible for her nervous stomach during the party.

She paced the room hugging her upper arms as the thoughts continued to tumble through her head, refusing to give her peace. It was far from cold; yet something—

She stopped and sniffed the warm, humid air. It was faintly scented. Her own Nuit de Noël perfume? No. A powdery scent. Her fingers shook as they gripped the flesh of her arms.

"Oh my God, no!" she said softly.

It was pikake.

She swung around, saw nothing but the

barred moonlight seeping through the slatted blinds. She stood for a long minute staring at the hall door. Then, mustering up a sudden spurt of courage, she crossed the room, hesitated with her hand on the doorknob long enough to take a sharp breath, and abruptly opened it.

No ghostly apparition loomed out of the darkness in the hall. Nevertheless, she was shocked to see her cousin Theo, looking unusually pale, staring at her from a short distance down the hall. He was fully dressed, at least in slacks and a flowered shirt, and wearing Japanese clogs.

She was about to ask him what he was doing tiptoeing around the halls at this hour, but something in his expression, the genuine fear in his eyes, stopped her. He licked his lips nervously. His easy smile flickered like an afterthought.

"You hear something too?"

"I don't know. I thought someone might be out here." She made up her mind suddenly. "Lili and I have noticed that somebody has been using Ilima Mako's body powder. It was unusual. Pikake. Have you noticed it?"

"So that's what it is," he said, obviously relieved. "I knew it smelled familiar. I was beginning to think it was her ghost trying to get

313

in. Whoever it is, I think you should tell them to stop. Gives me the creeps."

With that he turned and Tracie watched as he walked back to his room. He stopped once and sniffed before he went into his room and shut the door.

Tracie took little comfort in the knowledge that Theo, who was normally insensitive to anything beyond himself, shared her awareness of a ghostly presence in the Berenson house. If it *was* ghostly, she reminded herself.

She reached around into her room, turned on the lamp and studied the section of hall carpet. No sign of spilled powder or any other explanation, such as a sinister joke played by someone in the household. Worse, the scent had vanished now. Was it all her imagination? And Theo's as well?

She leaned back against the door, fully awake now. "Ilima? Are you here?" she whispered. Even the faint sound of her own voice frightened her. "Why? What is it you want?"

The hall seemed alive with papery little whispering sounds. Again Tracie stepped into the hall. Again there was nothing. No scent. No sound. She felt her way to the end of the hall, looked down the back stairs. Whatever had disturbed her and Theo was gone — if it had ever existed. But she didn't have the courage to go down to that room where the orchid tree scratched at the slatted windows.

Finally she went back to her room and fell asleep. Things would be better when her father and Diane returned. At least there would be more life in the house.

Mr. and Mrs. Victor Berenson returned to Akua the following afternoon, bringing Liliha back with them. She insisted that she wasn't going to pass her exams anyway; so why waste the time at school? The newlyweds themselves were slightly the worse for a rough crossing. Diane had been seasick, which Victor found both inconvenient and unpleasant, especially when his lively niece was spritely as ever. But seeing the effort Diane made to present a happy face to her welcoming family, Victor managed to recover a certain blustering, jolly mood and proudly pointed out that his "little Dinah" had gained two pounds. "Marriage agrees with her. Anybody can see that."

Aunt Jade, who had accepted her daughter's embrace and now held her hand, said, "Yes. One can see that. It is good to have you home again, Victor."

He kissed her with gusto, hinting, "And my little Dinah."

Diane reached out, almost planted a light kiss

315

on Jade's cool cheek but the older woman had turned slightly and the kiss met empty air. Lady Jade Wong Berenson was not a woman to be embraced by outsiders.

"And Mrs. Victor," she added while Diane tried to recover from the affront. The muscles of her face stiffened, and Tracie was glad to see this touch of pride. It wouldn't help her to fit into the family if she remained too humble, especially when Victor had a habit of taking women at their own evaluation.

Between them, Tracie and Theo managed to cover the awkward moment. Theo hugged Diane until he lifted her off the lanai floor, though he had already greeted her at the jetty. "Welcome home, Aunt Diane," he said exuberantly.

Diane blushed at Theo's attentions but they did make her feel welcome and she relaxed as Aunt Jade ushered the family inside.

Lili could hardly wait to boast to Tracie of her new conquest. "Guess who I saw a lot of in Honolulu? He came to the sorority house and picked me up. He was ever so sweet."

"What Bill Dempster does is of no interest to me," Tracie said coolly.

"Don't be silly. He's too old for me anyway. I'm talking about Wayne Croyde. We even went to the Royal one night with Diane and Uncle

Vic. He's so sweet — Wayne, I mean. At first, all he talked about was you. But I got him off that quick enough. Especially after he rescued us from that drunk on the beach." She stopped, clapped her hand over her mouth and giggled. "I wasn't supposed to mention that. Uncle Victor didn't come out too well. He got knocked down while trying to defend Diane...well, aren't you jealous?"

"Because I wasn't knocked down?"

"Because I'm stealing the love of your life."

Tracie laughed. All she felt was a curious, cool relief.

As Jade had predicted, Victor found nothing wrong with her suggestion that he and Diane use the room that had once belonged to Ilima Mako. Aunt Jade showed him the room newly arranged with his special chair, his favorite books, a pile of Amazing Stories, the edition of Jack London autographed personally by Jack and Charmian London, his Charlie Chan books, and the net with which he had made his big dolphin catch during a spear-fishing expedition with Sam Kahana.

Tracie seldom interfered with the running of the household, but she'd felt sorry for her aunt and now she felt guilty over having suggested this sleeping arrangement. The bride hadn't said a word as she stood in the doorway look-ing in. But when she dropped her vanity case Tracie couldn't help noticing that the young woman was trembling.

Tracie's own guilt made her even more angry. She had counted on her father refusing the room. "Dad, you've got a perfectly good pair of rooms upstairs, and they're better finished. This is so tacky."

"I'll thank you to mind your own affairs, young lady," he said, hitting the bed. To Jade's chagrin a spiral of dust rose. Evidently the servants were still afraid to come into the room. "And while we're on the subject, if you keep on neglecting your work, I'm going to have to get me a man who knows his way around. I should have done it in the first place, I guess." He explained to Diane, "I'm too soft-hearted for my own good. But with me, it's family first." He chucked her under the chin. "Always was. Always will be. Now, you can be happy here, honey, can't you, if it makes old Victor happy?"

Tracie had enough to think about on her own behalf, but she noticed that his wife looked pale as her lips formed an uncertain smile.

"Yes, dear." She dropped her handkerchief and waited while Jade stooped to pick it up and return it to her. The sight of the older woman's dark head bent before her evidently reminded her of an even greater problem.

"Victor, will you mind very much if I begin to – as we say – earn my keep? I want to establish my own system in the housekeeping department."

Already numbed by her father's threat to remove her from her beloved Orchid Tree Enterprises, Tracie was further shaken by Diane's announcement. It seemed to have no effect on Jade, but Tracie was certain her aunt was alarmed by it. This sounded very much like Diane's getting even with the woman she blamed for putting her and Victor into Ilima's old room.

But Victor couldn't see the significance of her remark and passed it off as irrelevant. "Of course, whatever makes you happy," he said as he tweaked her chin.

All three women were disturbed. The silence seemed pregnant with disaster. A scratching noise, like fingernails over a slate blackboard, made everyone look quickly at the west window. Victor chuckled. "Just my orchid tree. Sometimes it sounds almost human."

But Diane didn't see the humor in it. Without a word she turned and went out into the hall. Understanding her feelings, Tracie went after her. "Diane, it's ridiculous. There's no need for you to stay in that room."

The young woman sounded as if she were close to tears. "Oh, yes. I have to. If he wants it that way. I wouldn't mind if only I knew he really loved me."

Tracie was taken aback. "Of course he does. He wouldn't have married you if he didn't want — I mean, if he didn't love you."

"Never mind." Diane began to shake off her dress jacket. The new, pink-flowered voile dress beneath it lacked style, but it made her look curiously vulnerable and pretty. "Anyway, I've made up my mind. I'm going to run this house."

The situation had grown awkward once again with Diane's resolve to "run" Valley House. Tracie broached the subject cautiously.

"I know how you feel, Diane. But believe me, there are a million ways you can help dad and keep busy. They say my mother was always on the go. We have hundreds of people employed by Orchid Tree Enterprises. They all have families who need looking after. Ilima was busy from early morning until at least ten at night."

But her words seemed to have little effect as Diane walked on into the kitchen. Tracie followed her, beginning to feel alarmed at the situation.

"Diane, you really mustn't interfere with Aunt Jade just yet. Give yourself time to get used to the family — and for them to get used to you." Anything to prevent the predictable explosion.

Chin Loo had heard the women and came out of the pantry. He stood in the doorway, silent and impassive. Tracie, well aware of his deep devotion to Lady Jade, sensed more trouble ahead.

Meanwhile Diane resolutely walked to the kitchen table and took a big taro leaf out of the bundle lying there. She began to tear it as if it were lettuce. She was still shredding it when she looked directly into Tracie's eyes.

"You talk about your people as if you owned them. You and this Mako woman, and your Chinese aunt and the rest, you make me think of plantation wives before the Civil War."

Tracie reminded her quietly, "This *is* a plantation. Many of our *kanakas* can't read or write. Some of the Asians don't speak English. They have to be looked after. You are needed among them."

Diane dropped the bits of taro. For the first time she seemed to have been aroused to betray deep memories and hurts. The idea did her no harm in Tracie's eyes. The young woman would have to develop strength if she was going to remain a member of the household.

"I grew up poor, Tracie. Don't ask me to play Lady Bountiful with a bunch of ignorant foreigners. I had to fight their kind from the time I could walk." She pushed aside the green shreds. "Incidentally, when I'm running things, we won't be serving spinach."

"It's taro. We use it for practically everything. Like the laulau wrapping, and the luau food you liked so much."

Chin Loo shuffled into the room and began to collect the taro leaves. Diane stared at him for a minute, then her delicate features crumpled as she fought back tears.

"I guess I spoke out of turn," she said, groping for Tracie's arm. "And I did want to make an impression...to show I could take care of things. You know what I mean, don't you?"

"Sure I do." Much relieved, Tracie put an arm around her. "You're handling everything wonderfully. And believe me, dad needs a wife just like you; so come along and let's get your room ready. You are *not* going to sleep in Ilima's room. We'll see to that."

"Oh, thank you. You're so kind to me."

Thank God they had escaped those dangerous shoals, Tracie thought. She could only hope there would be no other trouble in the near future. She caught Chin Loo's cherubic expression as she and Diane left the kitchen. In spite of his unlined face, she suspected there was no love lost between him and the new bride.

Fortunately, Lili and Diane had struck up a reasonable friendship during the honeymoon and Lili was anxious to show off all the bathing suits, swim slippers and matching wrap-around beach outfits that she had chosen for Diane. Tracie couldn't help noticing that Lili's taste in clothing far surpassed her young aunt's, but she was careful in the compliments she made on the outfits.

Theo helped out by so deliberately praising Diane rather than the clothes that the bride reddened prettily. Her big brown eyes looked at Theo with a warmth that perhaps even Diane herself wasn't aware of. Tracie could hardly blame her, considering Victor's heavy-handed, double-edged compliments.

"How about this girl, Trace? Looks a damn sight better than she did before our Lili took her in hand, wouldn't you say?" Victor said, coming into the bedroom.

Tracie said quickly, "She always looked terrific. That color is lovely on you, Diane. You wear clothes awfully well."

Except for Victor's thoughtless remarks, the rest of the evening went well. Even Aunt Jade seemed to have recovered from the new bride's stubborn attempt to take over.

After two nights, perhaps full of honeymoon delights, Victor decided that, as he put it, his bride should be humored. Their things were moved back upstairs to Victor's big, comfortable bedroom and the room beside it which was decorated, according to Diane's taste, in ruffles and a baby-blue color scheme. Tracie was relieved to see that Diane was now happier and gradually fitting into the family. Meanwhile, Ilima Mako's room remained unoccupied.

In spite of her angry remark to Tracie, Diane began to visit the fields, sometimes rather timidly asking Rudi Arguello to drive her in the old truck used for farm produce. After several weeks of this Rudi seemed to feel that Tracie should know "what the young lady was up to."

"Mrs. Victor sure likes to look at the pineapples and papayas and the taro fields. She tries to talk to the workers. But mostly they don't know what she's saying, and she upsets the wives. She even wants to drive out now, though the rain's coming down again."

Tracie, who was balancing the books for the first quarter, sucked on the pointed wooden end of her pen and tried to figure out how to get around the problem without offending or discouraging Diane.

"She's only trying to help. Just give her a chance."

"But Miss Tracie, she is always talking to them about their conditions. I get complaints. They think she is criticizing them."

"Well, she had to struggle herself when she was young, so you can't really blame her. Besides, I told her it would be a help for her to get to know the workers and their families." Obviously her intended solution was turning into a problem – but anything to keep Diane out of Aunt Jade's kitchen! "Okay, Rudi, I'll do what I can. But our boys have a lot of sense. They'll see that she's just trying to be helpful."

"Sure, Miss Tracie. As you say, the men have a lot of sense." About to leave her study, he hesitated and added, "The Dorado Star man talks to them, too."

So Bill Dempster was already at work, undermining the Berensons on their home turf.

Tracie started to bring her fist down hard on the last quarter's (low) profit sheet, but remembering Rudi was watching her she managed to stop the gesture, thrust her fingers out flat and laughed.

"Don't worry. We can trust our boys."

"Right. We can trust the men." He gave her

his warm understanding smile before he turned and left. In his correction she thought she heard the echo of Bill Dempster's lecture on paternalism and felt embarrassed. Times had been changing all around them, and the Berensons were apparently the last to realize it.

But the realization didn't mitigate Bill Dempster's schemes. And all the lovemaking in the world wouldn't blind her to his real intentions.

"I'm going to get him," she said to herself softly.

Rudi Arguello stopped in the hall and leaned back through the doorway. "You said something, Miss Tracie?"

"No, it's nothing. Rudi, do you by any chance know whether Mr. Dempster is on the island now?"

"Sure. He's with the men at the sugar mill. They are organizing."

She gritted her teeth. "Well, there goes the sugar mill."

Even Rudi seemed to be taken in by the union talk. "But it makes them work harder. Gives them something to work for. Maybe it will be better for everyone. Mr. Victor, too."

Tracie could see it all now...Orchid Tree Enterprises would go broke, and the other great family estates would probably follow. In the end the Territory would return to its primitive, unproductive past.

"We'll see," she said, and looked back to her work.

"Mrs. Victor is calling," Rudi said, "excuse me."

A few minutes later Rudi passed the study door again with a blue raincape draped over his arm.

"What happened?" Tracie called to him.

"Mrs. Victor changed her mind," he said, looking into the study again. "Too much rain, she said. She told me to hang up the wrap."

Tracie glanced at the desk. She wasn't in the mood for more figure work anyway, and this would give her a chance to mend any damage done by Diane, unintentional though it was.

"I'll take the truck, Rudi. Maybe I can straighten things out with the men."

Rudi sounded doubtful. "Maybe." Nonetheless he gave her the cape. She threw it on, put away the books and went out to the lanai. A cloudburst was coming down, but toward the southwest there were clearing patches. She pulled the blue hood over her head and ran for the truck. Rudi had left the keys in the ignition. The motor huffed and puffed until the truck finally leaped forward.

She knew Rudi had driven out around the wet, terraced fields of taro and rice on his last two drives, following the muddy road toward Ma McCallister's fields, so Tracie took the same route. Everything looked as it always had. She was pleased to see that the overseer, a stocky little *hapa-haole* named Huber, was busy along the upper fields. This gave her a chance to speak freely with the field hands, especially the women, who were trying to repair the damage throughout the papaya grove that had been badly hit by this latest spring storm.

The road got steadily worse, with muddy ruts and submerged, spongy vegetation sucking at the wheels of the old Ford. A couple of times she spotted women in protective coconut hats, but it was impossible to recognize them as they stooped to pick up fallen or smashed fruit along the edges of the road.

During a slackening in the cloudburst one solitary worker proved to be Mrs. McCallister, who waved to her, pointing to indicate that she would meet Tracie at her house. Tracie waved back and nodded. Mrs. McCallister went on filling her apron with fruit. She spotted another woman at a distance who turned and changed direction abruptly at the sight of the chugging, plodding truck.

Suddenly, Tracie saw a man tramping toward her, dressed *haole*-fashion in a belted raincoat and a soaking felt hat. It was Bill Dempster, out doing his best to stir up trouble for the Berensons, no doubt. The rain didn't seem to bother him. His stride was brisk and certain, like everything about him. She was dismayed to find that as always, his mere appearance, even when soaking wet on a jungle path, was enough to excite her.

She debated with her baser self, which wanted to stop for him. That self had all the arguments: "You want to lay down the law to him anyway. Now's your chance."

He signaled to her as he stepped into her path and raised his hand, dripping wet. She stopped the truck, reminding herself that she couldn't very well run over him. He leaped onto the running board.

"Thanks, Mrs. Berenson. This will save me a couple of miles."

So he thought she was Diane. With her knuckle she tilted back the hood while he settled down beside her. He stared at her, frowning. Then his teasing grin appeared.

"Out checking on massa's old plantation?"

"That isn't funny. I know how you've been sowing discontent among our workers. If you're not careful, you're liable to find yourself ostracized by the islanders."

"A few years ago," he agreed cheerfully, "but not today. The Depression has begun to soak in." He looked out at the drenched pineapple field, bordered by a dark jungle of keawe thickets that were almost impenetrable. Then he understood her surly behavior. "I'm not proselytizing among Berenson workers, if that's what you're thinking. I don't play it that way. The sugar mill is a different matter. I have a majority interest there."

She said nothing, knowing inside that she was beginning to weaken. "Tracie, are you ever going to believe anything I say?"

She didn't believe him yet − she couldn't, but he did have a winning way about him. Her mouth twitched faintly with the beginnings of a smile. He leaned over and traced her lips with his wet forefinger, teasing her. "One little smile? We can go on with our feud when we get back to civilization."

She tried not to let him see what his touch did to her and tried to refocus her thoughts in the muddy road ahead. "What are you doing in this neck of the woods?" she said, trying to sound casual as the truck rumbled forward.

"You don't think I'm courting Mrs. McCallister?"

She laughed in spite of herself. "No, but you must be out here for a reason."

"I came here to make a proposition. Dorado Star wants to lease her westerly fields for an experiment in vegetables. But she wasn't home."

"She's out there somewhere, surveying her papaya groves. I passed her a little while ago. I don't think she lost as much as we did. Ma is a canny soul, and her western fields are better protected." She looked at him with her half-smile, responding as always to his warmth and the sensuous excitement in his eyes. "But that's why you want her westerly fields, naturally."

"Must we talk business in this exquisitely romantic setting? You and I do our best collaborating in the rain."

She laughed again and was still laughing when the shriek of wood tearing from pegs and nails shocked her. Before she realized what had happened Bill slapped the wheel, turning it hard, but it was too late.

A muddy stream bank had given way at the beginning of a plank bridge, and the truck plunged downward. Tracie struggled to get the door open, fighting off Bill as he struggled to pull her back and down to the floor.

17

The truck came to a halt with the front end buried in mud. The fall had been about ten feet. A stream meandered along several feet further below them. The jolt had been enough to throw Tracie at the windshield, but Bill's powerful arms held her in a vise and she got no more than a hard bump on the left temple.

They huddled on the ruptured floorboards of the truck for an endless time, hearing the two left wheels spin down to a gurgling halt in the mud. Somewhere around them timbers still cracked and rattled, the aftermath of the break in the plank bridge.

Tracie finally managed to pull herself together and rubbed her head. "Wow! That was a close one. That old bridge has been threatening to go out for years. Are you okay?"

Bill released her slowly. They had been tangled together and during those close seconds she felt the pounding of his heart which, oddly enough, reassured her. This time as he held her, she felt safe — a feeling she wasn't accustomed to with Bill Dempster. Between the rain and the stream bed around them, it was difficult to make out anything but his close presence, his eyes and something else — a drawn, tense expression that told her something was wrong.

She managed to straighten out, carefully moving so that she wouldn't hurt him.

"Are you all right?"

"Sure," he said. "How about you?"

But she could tell he was lying. Even in the murky light, shuttered by the heavy jungle growth over the bank of the stream, she could see that Bill was putting on a tremendous effort. One of his legs was jammed against the brake and he winced as he tried to move it.

"Easy. Don't move fast," he said as she tried to prop herself to help him. "Be sure nothing is broken."

"I'm fine. But your leg!" She started to touch it but he pulled back.

"Feels like a pulled muscle. Or probably a sprain." His right arm too was badly bruised against the dashboard. The raincoat sleeve and shirt sleeve were torn, the flesh of his upper arm badly skinned and bleeding. She cried out at the sight of it.

"We've got to get out of here. You need help."

He brushed aside her concern. "Don't be silly. This is nothing. You ought to have seen me after the big game. Cal and Stanford, that is."

"Football!" She rolled her eyes. "I'm going to get you some help."

She banged and pushed at her door but it was jammed against the roots of an ohia tree whose trunk had grown twisted on this rainy slope and now hung over the stream at a forty-five-degree angle, very much like the truck. Bill had finally untangled himself, and letting out a grunt or two, managed to get his door open.

"Here. Easy does it. We don't want to throw this old crate off kilter."

She slid gently after him along the seat. She was relieved when he got out and saw that he could stand without help, one foot buried in muddy fern fronds, the other propped against the running board. He held out one hand to her.

"Watch it. The thing is tilting."

She got out without putting her full weight on him and they backed away quickly along the riverbank. A minute later the truck began to give way. Its right wheels had sunk deeper into the morass and it rolled over on its right side, splashing them with mud, soggy green debris and water.

"That was a close call," Tracie said, more coolly than she felt. She looked Bill over. He grinned, took her arm and they started up the stream bed together. He was limping but otherwise seemed in excellent spirits. She felt she had a reasonable excuse as she put an arm around his waist, under the torn and mud-spattered raincoat.

He chuckled at her effort to support him. "I see I've been going at this all wrong. I should have broken my neck a long time ago. But how did I know my blood was the way to your heart?"

Behind them the truck made a gurgling, sucking noise. When they looked around it was completely on its side, right wheels and door buried, the two left wheels spinning in air again.

"I wonder how much Orchid Tree can salvage," she remarked. "It never rains but it pours."

"Apropos. But you must admit we were lucky. If it had exploded, or if we turned over in that thing—"

She looked at his arm. "Don't remind me. Right now we've got to stop that bleeding."

He looked around at their sodden surroundings. "The question is, how do we get back to civilization?"

They would have to climb up out of the stream bed first, and in spite of his easy, joking manner, he still limped. She stopped to study the situation. Overhead, between the lacy tree-tops, a patch of blue appeared. It was the first good news she had seen.

She considered the opposite bank of the stream, remembering vaguely that Ma McCal-lister's former overseer had a cottage some-where near here, built on stilts to avoid the water seepage of the low-lying fields to the east. The overseer had been fired about ten days ago after a disagreement over padded expenses on the pineapple crop, but, Tracie reasoned, maybe all his things hadn't been removed yet and they could find something there that could be used to stop the bleeding of Bill's arm.

In the meantime she tied her handkerchief around it. The handkerchief slowly reddened, though the flow of blood seemed to have less-ened. "Just let it go," Bill insisted irritably. "It'll stop."

"You're as bad as my father."

"Them's fightin' words, ma'am."

She grinned and pointed out the direction of the overseer's cottage. Bill answered her question about his condition with a pretense of indignation.

"Me walk half a mile? Nothing to it. Matter

of fact, I could carry you. Stand still. Stop struggling."

"You idiot! Look, we can cross the stream over there on those pebbles."

Though he didn't insist on carrying her, he managed to make the crossing through the slippery, soggy leaf-mold without turning his ankle. Once they had climbed the opposite bank, she was able to point out the overseer's little wooden house on stilts not quite a half mile away.

The sun was shining by the time they reached the badly rutted dirt road leading to the overseer's house. Their wet and blood-stained clothes were soon steaming in the welcome heat as they walked.

Tracie was intensely relieved to feel Bill Dempster's fingers still closed warmly around hers during their trek to the curious wooden house on stilts. His injured ankle and arm certainly hadn't slowed him, though she suspected that he was in considerable pain. She admired him for his effort to conceal his discomfort, and squeezed his hand in a show of sympathetic understanding.

To her surprise he seemed to return her admiration, as he demonstrated when they climbed the warped steps of the three-room cottage and stood leaning on the rickety little porch rail to catch their breath.

"I suppose you'd call this thing a lanai." He indicated the porch that ran completely around the little building.

"In its way, but never mind that. Have you had any experience breaking into houses?"

He put both hands on her shoulders and stood looking into her eyes in that intense, disturbing way that always made her knees feel weak.

"I don't know anybody I'd rather break in with. Did I ever tell you, you are definitely my kind of woman?"

"I don't recall, offhand."

His mouth was temptingly near. She found it inviting in spite of her suspicion about his schemes. The electricity between them was so intense that she thought they were going to make love right there on the overseer's creaking porch, but then he withdrew suddenly after studying her for a moment. Maybe he read her too well — guessed her mistrust, but recognized her desire. She tried not to let her disappointment show when his hands dropped from her shoulders and he drew her over to the door. Locked, of course, though not a very sturdy lock. She saw him wince as he tried the window beside the door, but when she moved to help him he grinned and elbowed her aside.

"This is not a case of ladies first."

"That's what you think. Come around here. The south window is broken. Even I could unlock this one."

"I don't doubt it. In fact, I'm quite sure you could do anything you set your mind to. I never underestimate Victor Berenson's daughter."

They had been getting along so well that she resolved not to be upset by his faintly derisive reference to her father. She said lightly, "If you insist on behaving like every other man I know, I suppose I'll have to pretend to be as weak and feminine as my new stepmother. Here, let me hang your coat over the rail to dry."

He let her slip his raincoat off, edging it gently over his bruised arm while he reached in through the broken pane with his good hand and pushed the window up. She saw that the handkerchief around his upper arm was now sodden but he insisted that the bleeding had stopped. She longed to care for that wounded flesh and was astonished at her own unexpected compassion.

"Here goes the second-story man." In spite of his injured leg, Bill climbed in with athletic ease. Meanwhile, Tracie spread his raincoat and her own borrowed cape over the splintering rail before she accepted his offered hand and climbed through the window after him.

The three small rooms were bare except for a triangular Delaware Punch bottle, an Eskimo Pie wrapper and a Coca-Cola bottle, evidence of a clandestine picnic, probably by two local boys. They settled down tiredly against the wall, sitting on the floor. Bill let Tracie tear and strip his shirt sleeve. She unfolded a white linen handkerchief and pressed the clean inner fold against his flesh, tied it precariously with two knotted strips of his shirt sleeve. She felt his gaze following her movements and wondered what he was thinking...She didn't have to wait long to find out.

"I knew you could handle it," he said. "Don't you know that in my day ladies fainted at the sight of blood?"

She could afford to be sardonic. "Only after they had put their brave knights back together. Now, let's examine that ankle of yours."

He made no objection and as she bent over him she felt his fingers caressing her hair lightly. Fearing that he would take his hand away, she pretended not to notice. As she worked on pulling off his soggy shoe and sock she thought it funny to find herself so aroused while in the middle of something so decidedly unromantic. She looked up at him, a slight smile playing on her lips.

"What's so funny about my feet?" he said,

pretending to be insulted.

"No calluses, no corns. Unheard of."

His sunburned face had begun to look distinctly sallow, but her unexpected compliment seemed to restore his healthy color and disposition.

"I never wear corns on a social call."

In spite of his breezy manner, his ankle looked badly swollen.

"It's nothing but a sprain," he insisted. "I know one when I see one. I've had plenty."

"What we need is a wet compress," she said, ignoring his protests. "There's certainly enough water outside. If only we had some cloth!"

"I believe the customary gesture is to use a strip of the handiest petticoat."

She wrinkled her nose at him. "Don't look at me. I seldom wear petticoats with a wraparound skirt." Her innocent suggestion was enough.

He reached down and pulled her toward him, drawing her up along the length of his body. His hands moved to her waist, unfastening the New Mexican belt buckle her father had given her years ago. He slowly unwrapped her skirt and moved his hands over her thin silk panties. She pressed her lips against his and as his hands explored her body, now unbuttoning her blouse, she reached for his belt, fumbling to undo it.

"Do you know how long I've wanted you?" he whispered, his voice slightly hoarse. Her only response was to meet his steady gaze as they finished removing their clothes, and their bodies clung together briefly before he moved himself inside her. She wrapped her long legs around his hips, pinning him tightly, urging him on. They climaxed together in a violent burst that rolled through their loins and their bodies in great waves. Exhausted, yet pleased to have satisfied each other so perfectly, they began to laugh and he kissed her gently, first her lips, then her nose and eyelids.

When they finally lay apart against the wall of the dusty, empty room he turned his head close to hers and his mouth sought hers again. They kissed while their hands explored areas they had ignored earlier in their haste, and to their mutual delight, their second coupling stirred them to the same waves of passion that had rocked their bodies the first time.

They sat up against the wall together, and held hands for a delicious, satisfying few minutes. Then she glanced at his swollen ankle, and the reality of their situation came flooding back to her.

"I've got to get you some help. You certainly can't walk clear to Ma McCallister's house."

"Try me," he said and slowly got to his feet

again, making what she suspected was a painful effort not to show any weakness. "Come on, lazybones. We're on our way."

"At least let me pull myself together. I don't want every *kanaka* in the neighborhood to know what happened."

"We don't call them *kanakas*, sweetheart. Not anymore."

"Oh, shut up!" They were back to their usual banter, but he only laughed at her.

They dressed, and she smiled ruefully at the image they presented, their clothing mud-splattered and stained with his blood.

Then they left as they had come, through the window.

As they walked down the steps to the dirt road, Tracie caught Bill looking back at the forsaken cottage. He glanced at her and grinned.

"That little bungalow has more charm than one would expect to find in it." He reached out and pulled her to him.

They made their way toward the main field road, enjoying one of the rare armistices in their battle. She tried not to walk too fast for him, but he limped along, refusing to slow his pace.

They met Ma McCallister striding along the field road and before she reached them she guessed what had happened.

"My land! You two are a mess. I opine it was you that busted my old bridge. How'd you make out? You look awful. Any bones broken?"

Tracie said, "His ankle looks bad, and he's got a bloody arm. I'm fine."

"Nothing wrong with the arm now," Bill put in, "and she's got a bump on the head." He kissed the bruise on Tracie's temple, a gesture that wasn't unnoticed by Mrs. McCallister.

"Seems to be more huggin' and kissin' going on in your family, Tracie."

Slightly embarrassed, Tracie said, "It's not much of a bump, I can hardly feel it. By the way, we'll have to call home and get another car. Mr. Dempster shouldn't walk on that ankle."

Mrs. McCallister nodded absently and waved away the problem. "Sure, sure. What I really want to know is why you tried to cross that damned bridge. Didn't you see my sign?"

"What sign?" Bill said sharply.

She pointed back along the road. "I found it at the bottom of the ravine where you crashed. Wrote it myself, 'bout two days ago. And it was still stuck up there good and hard this morning. I tried to warn little Mrs. Victor when she drove by. But I guess that was you, Tracie. Remember when I waved to you? All that pointing and all?"

Behind them Bill said quietly, "Do I understand that you thought Miss Berenson was her stepmother?"

"Sure. She was wearing Mrs. Victor's blue cape."

"What's this all about?" Tracie wanted to know.

Bill turned to her. "How many people knew you were taking the truck?"

"Nobody. Except Rudi Arguello, of course. I don't know whether he told anyone."

"Then if there was an accident at the bridge, anyone might expect Victor Berenson's wife to be in the truck."

Tracie froze, remembering all Bill's hints against the family. "Are you trying to tell us something?"

"Certainly he is," Mrs. McCallister said. "Putting it bluntly, he says someone was out to do damage to the person in that truck of yours. Could have been someone who expected your stepmother to be in it."

"That's ridiculous."

Bill asked, "Would you rather someone was trying to do *you* harm? Considering what always seems to be happening in that happy little home of yours, it seems to me that sign was removed intentionally, either for your sake or Diane's." He saw her swelling up with indignation and added, "I'm not accusing your family, Tracie. It could be anyone who works for Orchid Tree...maybe a laborer with a grudge."

Ma McCallister rubbed her chin. "Sounds possible. Been a lot of agitating lately."

"Thanks to this troublemaker here," Tracie put in.

In an even voice Bill reminded them both, "I've never agitated, as you put it, against either of you. All I've been doing is showing them at the sugar mill that fair labor conditions will improve the output."

"Poppycock!" Mrs. McCallister blurted out.

Tracie was too disappointed in Bill, too angry, and above all, too worried to express her opinion. There were a dozen ways in which Mrs. McCallister's sign could have disappeared into the creek, none of them involving a plot against Diane Berenson. It was even less likely that anyone wanted to give Tracie some broken bones, or, as was remotely possible, a broken neck.

She shifted her position, now wanting to avoid his touch and the upsetting effect it still had on her good sense.

"We'll have to get to your house and call home. Mr. Dempster shouldn't walk any further on that foot until it's properly bandaged."

"I assure you, ladies, I can outwalk both of you."

Mrs. McCallister made a wide gesture. "Don't have to. My jalopy's this side of the bridge. About fifty yards down the road. I'll get you back to Berenson's but we'll have to make it roundabout, through Akua City."

Now even Bill thought a ride was good news.

They started off again but Tracie was keenly aware that in leaving the overseer's cottage they had locked the door on a very special hour of her life. Remembering Bill's personal vendetta against her family, she wondered if there would ever be another hour filled with such joy.

Should she warn the family of his ideas? They ought to be prepared for any further accusations.

To put things in their proper perspective, she reminded Mrs. McCallister, "Your sign probably just fell into the ravine, you know."

"Sure."

"Or it was blown there by the wind. Or the rain."

"Seems like."

Bill Dempster said nothing.

18

No host could have been more gracious than Victor Berenson when he found Bill Dempster under his own roof and, as he called out with his familiar grin, "Helpless in my hands, by george!"

Tracie found it disquieting, especially when in spite of the sprained ankle, Bill rose to the occasion and behaved in an equally hypocritical manner, considering the suspicions he couldn't seem to banish.

It was painful for her to accept both his caring for her as evidenced in their passionate lovemaking and the cynical posturing now on display. Once again she found herself torn between her yearning and her doubts.

Before being driven by Rudi Arguello to his room at South Harbor, Dempster spent dinner and the evening charming not only Victor and his wife, but even Aunt Jade and Theo.

It was Lili, of all people, who pointed out

to Tracie an even more disquieting habit of Bill Dempster's.

"Have you noticed how he studies people? Even the servants. Everybody."

"I know he's putting on an act with dad and probably with the rest of us."

Lili's pretty forehead wrinkled in a heavy frown. "He does it when he thinks we aren't looking. Like he expected to catch us stealing pennies or something." She cocked her head to one side. "In a certain light he looks older than I thought."

The meaning of this non sequitur was crystal-clear to Tracie. "Older than Wayne, you mean?"

Chin Loo appeared silently in the archway opening into the hall. On seeing him Aunt Jade got up from her stiff-backed chair and went to him. As they walked together to the kitchen Lili whispered to Tracie, "Diane just came back from the kitchen a minute ago. She's meddled with the servants again. Mother is smoldering, I can tell you."

There was no doubt of that.

"Oh Lord!" Tracie glanced at the threesome seated at elbow's length from the tea wagon and its miniature bar. Diane Berenson, looking pretty and almost pathetically eager in deep pink voile, had interrupted Victor in order to give her own opinion on something. Tracie could see that her father was annoyed. Diane's fingers lingered softly over the nape of his neck, but it was disconcerting to see from Tracie's angle that Theo sat so close to Diane on the long couch.

Lili nudged Tracie. "Chin Loo is even worse than mother. He just can't stand that insipid creature."

"Chin Loo is not in a position to judge one of us," Tracie reminded her. "And Diane is far from insipid. She's trying to make a place for herself in a very difficult household."

"Tell mother. Don't tell me."

"I may do just that."

Tracie followed her aunt down the hall to the kitchen. She glanced to the right as she crossed the little rear hall that led to Ilima Mako's old room, but at this hour of the evening with a houseful of people, she felt none of the clammy fear that the room often inspired. This fact convinced her that it had all been her over-worked imagination. Judging from the voices in the kitchen, she reminded herself that it was far better to focus on real problems.

Aunt Jade stood in the middle of the room with hands crossed in her sleeves, listening to Chin Loo. The little man's expression was calm but his voice, as he spoke in their own Peking dialect, made Tracie shiver.

He was obviously furious. His pupils caught the light and seemed to burn like shiny black coals. He waved a thin pink leather belt and it required no keen understanding to guess the object of Chin Loo's anger.

Tracie cleared her throat, startling the two. Just like conspirators, she thought in dismay. Now she found herself almost believing the foul thoughts Bill Dempster had planted in her head.

"Chin Loo, I see you've found Mrs. Berenson's belt," Tracie said, trying to sound cheerful. "Aunt Jade, won't you come back and join the party? We've been missing you."

"The young woman has been advising Chin on the preparation of the meals," Aunt Jade explained. "He was over the entire island today gathering fruits and vegetables for the next week. Even the McCallister woman sold him some, at a bargain. But Mrs. Victor tells him that he buys the most expensive ones and she will hereafter place the orders with Hilo or Honolulu."

Tracie found herself speechless. Her gaze moved from her aunt to the cook. And because the poison had entered her system from Bill Dempster, she wondered just where on Mrs. McCallister's land Chin Loo had been. Could he have caused her accident in the truck? "The young woman was most animated," Jade continued. "She expressed herself in no uncertain terms. That is how she lost her sash."

Chin Loo dropped the belt on the kitchen floor, directly on the water drops that had dripped from the heads of bright, yellow-green manoa lettuce on the big worktable.

Tracie pursued the subject uppermost in her mind. "It's too bad we didn't know where you were today, Chin. You could have let Mr. Dempster and me ride back with you. Were you anywhere near the plank bridge that fell to pieces under us?"

Aunt Jade said, "He was with Mrs. McCallister this morning. It was very early."

Chin Loo said nothing.

Tracie returned to the immediate problem. "We must remember that my father's wife is in a position to make changes—"

Aunt Jade's body stiffened perceptibly.

"—to make a few changes," Tracie amended. "But if we handle her right, I'm sure she'll be agreeable. I'm afraid we've all treated her more like a second-rate guest than the lady of the—" She felt her aunt's shock, but couldn't help insisting, "Well, she *is*, after all. If she were any other woman, we'd all have been in hot water by this time." She ended weakly, "However, I'll speak to her. If we try to be reasonable, I'm sure everything will work out."

Feeling that she had at least dampened the coals of rebellion, Tracie was about to return to the living room when she was stopped by Aunt Jade's flat statement. "I do not think she will be a problem for long."

Her cold tone was like a shower of ice.

"What do you mean?"

Jade's carefully shaped black eyebrows raised. "Victor is tired of her. He does not keep what he grows tired of." She smoothed the gold embroidery of her padded sleeve and left the kitchen. Carefully avoiding Tracie, she passed with her imperial dignity and returned to the living room.

In spite of Tracie's caution in bringing up the matter the next morning, Diane was driven to tears of outrage and self-defense. "I only suggested. I never made demands on the cook or anyone."

"I know you didn't. It's just that you have to approach people very carefully when you begin to give orders."

Diane felt for a handkerchief, found the napkin on her breakfast tray and used that to dab her eyes. She was upset, but still determined to defend herself.

"I don't sleep well. That's why I let Victor

go about his business earlier this morning. He wants me to ride out with him when he sees to the fields and all. But I worry, and that makes me lie awake. I'm a good wife. Really, I am."

"I know. Please don't cry. It will all work out." This was more optimistic than Tracie felt.

Diane insisted, "I never gave orders to anyone. All I said was that I got sick when I ate pork and poi and raw fish."

Tracie admitted to herself that this kind of reaction was enough to upset the entire economy of Akua Island. She knew that somehow she would have to explain.

"Our habits in this household go back fifty years, so you have to be cautious about changing them. It has to be done gradually, Diane."

The young woman considered this advice but found it wanting.

"I thought it would be b-better after we left Honolulu, but it's almost as b-bad here." With shaking fingers she refolded the napkin. Tracie felt she had missed a page in her stepmother's sad story. She sat down abruptly on the side of the big bed.

"You weren't happy on your honeymoon?"

Diane sobbed, "I could have been. But I'm so scared."

"Scared of what?" For an instant Tracie wondered if Diane was talking about her old fears of Ilima Mako.

"Of him." Diane waved a hand aimlessly, shifting her legs so that her coffee spilled onto the bedsheet. She apologized, the terrified look still in her eyes. She tried to blot up the coffee stain but Tracie took the napkin from her and demanded firmly, "Afraid of my father?"

"Victor? Oh, no! I love Victor. He has his ways, he doesn't like to be contradicted or shown up, so I try to be careful. But I never dreamed *he* would find me here."

"For heaven's sake, who?"

"R-Ray."

"You're afraid of a man named Ray."

"My ex-husband. Raymond Thorpe."

Now they were getting somewhere. "You're afraid he'll find out you married again." This probably explained why Diane Thorpe hadn't wanted any of her mainland acquaintances to stand up with her at the wedding. Tracie wondered if Raymond Thorpe was actually dangerous and that idea led her back to Diane's earlier fear.

"Don't tell me the drunken man on Waikiki Beach was Ray Thorpe!"

Diane nodded.

"Is he dangerous?"

Diane hesitated. Then she held out her left

hand, showing Tracie her wrist. "He cut me here when I said I wanted a divorce, then told everyone that I'd cut my wrists deliberately." Two raised, threadlike scars crisscrossed her pale skin.

Tracie was indignant at the thought of her having been so abused. "Why didn't you or dad have him arrested when he attacked you at Waikiki?"

Diane leaned across the breakfast tray, clutching Tracie's sleeve in panic. "He hadn't done anything. What could they arrest him for? Victor grabbed him first. Your father was so brave. I loved him for it. But if we made trouble Ray would just get angry and lie in wait sometime. Somewhere. Maybe he wants money from me. He thinks I would ask Victor, perhaps. But I couldn't."

Several ideas whirled through Tracie's brain. An enemy making trouble for Diane and indirectly for the Berensons...She found herself almost grateful for the ideas it suggested.

"You haven't seen your ex-husband since that day on the beach?"

Diane shuddered. "No. But I know he wouldn't come this far just to cause trouble at Waikiki. Tracie, he could be anywhere."

"Even on Akua?"

Diane looked around nervously. "Is it possible?"

"It's possible, though a stranger on this island would certainly stand out. Shouldn't we tell dad and let him check on it?"

"If you think he would remain calm. But I'm terribly afraid he might go off in a fit, the way he acted on Waikiki Beach."

How true!

"What about Theo?" Diane ventured. "I'm sure he would help us. He might find out from these natives whether they've seen anyone around who looks like Ray."

Theo was hardly a strong ally but he would be delighted to act as a detective, even more so if it involved Diane's safety. Tracie didn't like to throw her stepmother and Theo together any more than necessary, but something had to be done. In spite of all these tentative plans, she knew the man who could really help her calmly, cleverly, and without getting into fist-fights.

She decided that, ultimately, she would have to get help from Bill Dempster.

"We'll need a picture of your ex-husband," she told Diane. "Can I borrow a snapshot?"

"I didn't bring any to Hawaii. I tore up most of them a long time ago. Except the early ones when we — when we were happy." She paused for a moment, then added eagerly, "But I could describe him. And Lili saw him. If I were an artist I could sketch him." She sighed for old memories. "He has changed. When I first met him he was terribly handsome. He has greenish eyes. They looked bloodshot the day on the beach, but they really were lovely once, and kind. And he's so fat now."

Impatient to get to the point, Tracie waved away the old Ray Thorpe.

"Is he tall or short? What about his features? What kind of nose does he have?" Diane began to describe him, but her description was so vague that it could have fit just about anyone.

"We're not getting anywhere," Tracie said, interrupting her. "We'll need you to identify him."

Diane drew herself up with her knees against her chest, shivering. "I can't let him see me again. He might do anything. He might even hurt Victor." She hugged her knees while Tracie rescued the tray. When Tracie turned back to Diane her brown eyes widened at a memory.

"Tracie! Last night Bill Dempster said you might have been killed when you dropped into that ravine near Mrs. McCallister's fields."

A chill ruffled the back of Tracie's neck. "It wasn't that deep. But I suppose we were lucky. We might have broken our backs in the jolt." She stared at Diane, putting two and two together. Absurd as it was, an uncomfortable suspicion took hold of her. "You expected to be in that truck with Rudi, didn't you?"

"When you came in you had on the blue rain-cape I always wear. Someone may have expected me."

"That's awfully farfetched."

Diane settled back to consider this. It was never difficult to convince her. She seemed to have a desperate need to be liked.

"I guess so. Still, if Ray was on the island somebody would have seen him."

"Not necessarily, but we're going to find out. And if we do find him, you're going to have to come forward. Meanwhile, Lili will be able to help me. She saw him."

"Thank you, Tracie. But in the meantime I wish somebody could persuade Victor to stay around the house until we're sure."

Tracie smiled. "If his bride can't, nobody can."

With that she left the room, showing a greater display of confidence that she felt.

It wasn't difficult to find Lili. Her cousin was on the phone to Honolulu, chatting away very prettily to Wayne Croyde. Tracie knew that if she interrupted Lili would be sure to think it was motivated by jealousy, but some things couldn't wait. She went downstairs to the office extension.

Lili heard the click as Tracie picked up the receiver, and snapped, "Wouldn't you know? We've got my cousin spying on us. Trace, I'm talking to Honolulu. You always tell us this costs money."

"I'll only be a minute, and it's important. Wayne, don't go away. This is for you too," Tracie said.

Wayne sounded good-natured as always. "Hi there, Tracie."

"It's about that business on the beach when that drunk knocked dad down and you sent him on his way."

Lili gave a little shriek that she suppressed quickly. "Tracie, we don't talk about that."

"Sure. I remember," Wayne said.

"Have you ever seen the man since?"

"Why?" Wayne said. "Not that I would notice the guy. It was awfully bright on the beach that day and I was squinting a lot. He was wearing blinkers. You know, a white eyeshade."

"You wouldn't know him by sight?"

"He was just another *malahini*."

"Sunburned," Lili put in. "He had on a bathing suit with a striped top. Black and white. Are you through, Tracie?"

"I am if either of you think you can identify him."

"Sunburned and sort of tall," Lili said, anxious

to get Tracie off the line. "Not as tall as Uncle Victor or Wayne. The man had a paunch. He was in his forties."

"Forties! I had the impression he was younger." Wayne's voice came over the line amid a certain amount of inter-island static. "Naturally he'd look older to Lili."

"Neither of you knows any more about him?"

Wayne asked again what it was all about, followed by Lili's urgent plea. "Do get off the line, for heaven's sake!"

Tracie ignored her cousin and continued patiently. "Wayne, do me a favor. Check with the Moana, the Royal, the Halekulani, and the Alexander Young downtown. See if they had a Ray Thorpe registered on the day you met this man on the beach."

"I can do that when I go back," Lili put in. "I remember him."

Wayne was obliging as well. "What's the name again? I'm not sure I could pinpoint the day. I'll check for two or three days around that time."

"Make it a week or so. You are a darling. Maybe I'll send Lili and Theo over to help you, if they will."

"They will," Lili said eagerly. "I'll take the first inter-island boat and we'll do it together."

Tracie laughed at her cousin's obvious eagerness before she hung up the phone and went to find Theo. Initially he didn't like the idea of going off on a wild goose chase in Honolulu until he was told "Aunt Diane" expected him to escort his little sister. "In that case I just might," he agreed. "Honolulu's always lively."

After seeing her cousins off on what they called between themselves the "leper boat," because it stopped offshore from Kalaupapa, Tracie spent the rest of the day touring Akua. She first visited Mr. Nakazawa in Akua City. He was talking with a pair of Hawaiian fishermen who worked along the waterfront. None of the men had seen any strangers disembarking from any vessel.

She left a message for her father, who was out on Mauna Pā-ele discussing the flooding problem with several other ranchers. Akua Sugar's waterfront was busier, an easier camouflage, but there would be more witnesses there as well. Now she had to approach Bill Dempster, who was at the sugar mill, about the news she'd learned from Diane.

Her ambivalent feelings for Bill were not improved when she learned he had gone off to Hilo to hire *paniolos,* Hawaiian cowboys, to run experimental beef cattle in a secluded valley of Akua. It was doubly annoying to realize that she had tried to talk her father into doing the same thing three years ago after a visit to the Big Island.

But the trip wasn't a total loss. She found Leland Tebbs, the plant manager at the Akua sugar mill, having lunch with Frank Huber, the chunky little foreman of the Berenson taro and rice terraces. Both men were curious and promised to keep a weather-eye out for strangers of Ray Thorpe's general description.

She repeated the story to the Murikami brothers, who stopped mending nets and walked with her to the broken-down Sugar Factory Hotel. The two-story wooden structure, with the ubiquitous roofed lanai and peeling wallpaper, served as the mill's guest house. Of its presently housed guests, most of them permanent, minor officials of the sugar mill, one was William Dempster.

The only newcomer to the hotel proved to be a stout, garrulous, unshaven planter from one of the outer islands of the Tuamotu Archipelago. After meeting Tracie he grinned and invited her into his stifling room. He was not Ray Thorpe. She declined the invitation with thanks and left, followed by the apologetic Murikami brothers.

Tracie spoke to everyone she saw along South Harbor, but no one had seen a stranger who was unaccounted for. Tracie knew the search wasn't over, since, as the Murikamis pointed out, there were any number of coves and a few beaches around the east and north faces of Akua. An enterprising athlete or, for that matter, anyone who hired a private boat and its skipper, could land there.

As she made her way back to the mill she thought again of the possibilities... why couldn't she simply believe the bridge collapse was an accident? And even if it was, what about the incident with Ray Thorpe on Waikiki, which was hardly a coincidence, and Diane's illness the night before the wedding? It was all *too* coincidental. Was it possible that Ray Thorpe had been on the island that long ago?

There was no way to be sure — yet.

Back at the mill, Leland Tebbs reminded Tracie that the Berensons were expected at the *hukilau* in two nights, a torch-fishing exhibition by the young locals. As usual, everyone took the opportunity to hold a night picnic on the beach. The islanders would take affront if the Berensons or any of the other plantation owners didn't make an appearance, but there were few who would want to miss it. Beyond the combination of moonlight and the flaring torches a good many romances were started, and the occasion was always entertaining, one way or another. Tracie was dying to ask if Bill Dempster would be back from the Big Island by that time, but she knew her life would be much less complicated if he didn't appear, so she bit off the question.

Meanwhile, she lingered at South Harbor among dozens of mill workers and field hands changing shifts. She had known most of them all her life and they had always been considered trusted friends, but today they seemed evasive. Maybe it was her imagination, fueled by her knowledge of Bill's meddling, but she felt that they buzzed a good deal about her and her family when she was just out of hearing.

Troubled by their unusually cool remarks, she decided to question Huber about it. He saw the workers every day and would know best what was on their minds.

"We aren't actually ogres, just because we like to take care of our people," she said, catching up with the foreman.

"Quite so," the stocky little man agreed quickly. "Anybody in the islands will tell you that, Miss B."

After their brief conversation ended she couldn't help wishing that his agreement had been based on genuine feeling rather than expediency. She asked Tebbs whether Bill Dempster's union-organizing had disturbed the running of the mill or the fields. "Not really," he said.

"I've worked on the Coast, up near Sacramento, where they're organized and they get more done in eight hours than our people here. They've got definite responsibilities... Frankly, Miss Berenson, I think it's all to the good, in the long run."

Though she knew she should have been relieved to hear that work hadn't been disrupted, the opinion he offered was unsettling.

She left South Harbor and went up the south slope of Mauna Pā-ele in the hope of catching her father. The spring afternoon was unseasonably hot. Sunlight dappled the leafy path and raised little spirals of steam as it dried the water-soaked jungle. Several harmless centipedes had claimed the main trail in one place and Tracie decided to skirt around them, letting the little creatures slither and snake their way back into their own concealed jungle habitat.

She pushed past entangled ferns as she made her way up the mountain. Her father was nowhere in sight. As she walked she began to think about Ilima and the possibility that she'd been driven to suicide by the curel suggestion of someone who knew about Ilima's family and her persistent fear. Could the recent accidents and mishaps somehow be connected with Ilima's death? If so, it seemed even less likely that

Diane's former husband was behind any of it...

Having reached the peak of Mauna Pā-ele Tracie stood staring at the shimmering sea, its foaming aquamarine current rolling out to join the heavy blue waters of the Molokai and Maui channels.

What had been Ilima's last thoughts as she stood in this very place, Tracie wondered. "If only she'd talked to me"...Surely she could have convinced her friend that she had nothing to fear in her father's true identity.

Suddenly Tracie felt very close to her dead friend and she tensed; her presence seemed to envelop her, and it seemed that if she turned around it would be the most natural thing to find Ilima standing there. But as quickly as the feeling had come it was gone, and again Tracie was aware of how alone she was, standing on the cliff's edge. She took a deep breath, her tension momentarily relieved. It was the same feeling she'd had in the house, whenever she detected the scent of Ilima's perfumed powder. If the presence was real, what did it mean? Was Ilima trying to warn her of something?

The wind always blew across the top of Mauna Pā-ele and she sniffed the familiar tropical smell of salt and earth that, curiously enough, she had loved with her earliest memories. She and her cousins used to fancy the sigh and moan of the wind carried voices and they marveled at how like human sounds they were.

Suddenly she made out the distinct sound of her father's voice, which verged on the drawl that testified to his origins in the Southwest. She recognized the other voice, heavy and deep, as that of Sam Kahana. The two men were about fifty yards north of her at the little saucer pool above Ribbon Falls, hidden by the giant fern growth and a twisted ohia tree.

"It was a mistake," Victor said. "But hell, man! I'm not too old to need a female. She's a pretty little thing. Those big brown eyes and all. It's the clinging I can't abide."

Tracie groaned. Whatever her feelings were at the announcement of his marriage the deed was done, and it would be disastrous emotionally and financially if it ended so soon.

Despite her more practical concerns Tracie had developed a certain sympathy for Diane and wondered how she could ginger the young woman up, persuade her to act more independently without completely upsetting the household.

Sam Kahana seemed to be thinking along the same lines. "Nothing's perfect, you know," he told Victor. " 'Specially marriage. Like you say, Mr. Vic, she's awfully pretty. Other guys got their eyes on her. Maybe she just needs a little more time."

Tracie started toward them, then stopped, smiling at the way her father took the foreman up on this point that flattered his ego.

"Who's got their eyes on her? Well, I suppose they would. On the whole, you have to admit my taste in women has been pretty damn good." Tracie tensed, not sure she wanted to hear anymore of her father's opinions on women. "You take Marta Dempster," he rambled on, "the movie star. There's a fine figure of a woman. Saw a lot of her in Honolulu."

"On your honeymoon?" Sam wanted to know. Tracie found his surprise natural under the circumstances.

Victor agreed flippantly. "Can't have too much of a good thing." Tracie was unable to keep silent after that remark.

"Dad, you are disgusting," she called out and made her way to the men.

"What the devil are you doing, listening in on my private conversations, girl?" her father answered, looking around for his daughter.

"Private? You bellow them to the world. I'm sure they heard you across the channel in Lahaina." Before he could give her an argument she cut in, "I have to talk to you."

"Nag, nag, nag."

"I'll be going," Sam wisely said. "We're getting things cleared away so our boys can attend the *hukilau.*"

"Coward!" Victor called after him, but the big man wordlessly started down the steep, slippery trail beside the trickling falls.

"Don't look like that, dad. I'm not going to bawl you out. Diane does cling a bit, but she may have reason. Her first husband was nothing like you." She was approaching the real subject obliquely.

"My God! I hope not. He used to hit the poor kid. Took a knife to her once. Gambled away all her money. Left her with a pile of debts."

"I know," she said as they started down the main trail together.

He looked at her oddly. Perhaps he guessed that she was working toward a subject he wouldn't like.

"What's this all about?"

"The drunken man on the beach at Waikiki..."

Suspicion hardened into certainty. "Who told you about that?"

She shaded the truth with a heavy brush. "As I understand it, this drunk got fresh with Lili or Diane and you knocked him down. Then,

370

luckily, Wayne came by and separated the two of you."

"Luckily?"

"Diane told me. Otherwise, she said, you probably would have knocked him out."

That mollified him. "So she told you, did she? Not much on secrets, that girl. Means well, though. Yes," he went on, "that's about how it was. Fellow kicked up sand. Put a hand on my wife's leg. Bare leg, you know. She was wearing a two-piece bathing suit. Well, I swung on him, knocked him flat. He got up. That's when young Croyde came along." He had been breathing heavily as they walked but calmed down as he related this as if it had just happened.

"He's Diane's ex-husband," Tracie said. "We're trying to find him."

"So that's why he got so—" Victor broke off uneasily. "No point in digging him up now. I gave him what was coming to him."

Tracie understood his reluctance too well. The truth of the incident would reflect on Victor's own conception of his manhood.

"Would you know him if you saw him again?"

"Hell, no! He had an eyeshade on. I just caught a glimpse of him. Forget about it," he said, becoming agitated again. He stumbled against her, cursed the slippery leaves underfoot as she reached to steady him.

"Got to clean this place out. All this damn debris."

She felt his heart racing as she let him go. It worried her and she decided to drop the subject of Ray Thorpe for the moment. As they walked along they chatted amiably about other, less serious matters until they finally reached the house.

An hour later Victor had his first painful attack of "heartburn." Diane, terrified, immediately assumed he had been poisoned. She ran down the hall in a panic, crying, "I knew he'd find us."

No one except Tracie understood the meaning of what she said, and the rumor began to spread among the servants that young Mrs. Victor was a little bit *pupule.* Crazy.

Although Tracie said nothing, she secretly shared Diane's fear until Dr. Tokuda came over from Hilo and diagnosed the pains as possible angina pectoris.

"He's lucky it was a light one. We should get him to Honolulu at once," he said, but the patient heard this and the resulting uproar made everyone run for cover. "Later," he promised Dr. Tokuda. "But I'm not missing the *hukilau.*"

Tracie would almost have preferred to believe it was the work of Ray Thorpe. At least that danger was concrete and could be warded off, whereas Victor's failing health ate at the core of Tracie's security.

19

Victor Berenson did not go out for torch-fishing during the *hukilau,* but it wasn't for lack of trying. Dr. Tokuda telephoned to Honolulu and arranged to have two cardiac specialists brought in on a chartered boat. Both confirmed his original diagnosis, forcing Victor to stop dismissing his problem as "heartburn." This did nothing to improve his already surly mood as the family fussed around him, Diane especially.

While the doctors examined Victor, Lili called from Honolulu to express brisk regrets that her Uncle Victor was sick and to report to Tracie on their findings.

"Wayne and I are having a ball going around to all the big hotels, but nobody has a record of a Ray Thorpe," she bubbled. "There's a Thomas P. Thorpe, but the clerk said he was tall and thin and ancient — around sixty. So it couldn't be him."

"Has Theo turned up anything?" Tracie asked.

"Oh, you know Theo," she rambled on. "He's been hanging around downtown a lot. But he did go to the Alexander Young, then he said he was going to check on the fleabag hotels, whatever they are. This morning he borrowed some money from Wayne, but he wouldn't say what it was for. Anyway, he didn't find out anything about Ray Thorpe either."

Aunt Jade came into the hall and silently stood before Tracie, who immediately picked up the hint. "Your mother wants to talk to you...hold on."

Aunt Jade took the phone wordlessly.

"I do not like your missing classes, Lili. Your friend Wayne and Theo can do these favors for your cousin. And remember, Wayne is a gentleman. Do not tempt him."

Tracie was surprised to hear her aunt have anything good to say about Wayne; she certainly hadn't expressed such an opinion while Tracie was dating him.

"Tell Theo that he's missed here at home," she continued in her typically cool manner. "Your uncle misses both of you. You should be here to help him. And tell Theo to behave himself..." She paused; obviously Lili was telling her about the borrowed money. A scowl crossed

Jade's face. "How much? He must tell Wayne that the money will be returned to him by the morning boat...where is he now? Tell him to stop sneaking around and come home. The *hukilau* is tonight. Both of you should be here for it."

Jade didn't say good-bye, simply handed the heavy black receiver to Tracie, who sent her love and hung up.

Usually Aunt Jade had little interest in Tracie's doings, but this time her curiosity got the best of her.

"I know why they're there...that they're looking for this former husband of Diane's. But why must my son borrow money from Wayne? Theo has money, and ten dollars is so small an amount."

"I really don't know, Aunt Jade," Tracie said apologetically. Could Theo have discovered something he was keeping from the others?

The two women had little time to puzzle it out. Jade, whose first concern was always the smooth running of the household, set about packing the bananas, guavas, mangoes and papayas for the evening's luau while Tracie went upstairs to see how her father was getting along.

She was just in time to witness the comical scene. Diane had opened the window and leaned out over the top of the orchid tree with what appeared to be Chin Loo's choice meat cleaver. Victor, who refused to stay in bed, was stretched out in an easy chair. He had been dozing off and awakened suddenly to find his wife hacking off the nearest branch of his beloved tree. The mauve blossoms had spread out in the recent tropic rains and were gently working their way into the room through the slatted windows.

Tracie was strictly on Diane's side in the battle that followed. "Dad, it's only a branch. The damned tree will take over the house pretty soon. Calm down and behave yourself."

"Thank you, Tracie," Diane gasped. "Thank you." But she stuck her head back inside the room and looked at the cleaver in a puzzled way, as if wondering what she had been doing with it.

Victor, feeling he was being ganged up on, shakily got to his feet.

"Don't give me orders in my own house. You're not the boss here quite yet. I suppose you thought I'd get sick enough so you women could run this place any way you wanted." He sat down suddenly, as if his legs had given away. Both Tracie and Diane ran to him in a panic. Sheepishly, he waved them away and grinned.

"Slipped, that's all. It's this sitting around

that's getting to me. Sorry, Dinah. Did I scare you with all this bellowing?" He reached for Diane's hand, but she still clutched the meat cleaver. Flustered, she handed it to Tracie, then knelt beside Victor's chair and tried to caress his fingers.

Tracie, feeling ill at ease, slipped out of the room unnoticed. She took the cleaver down to the kitchen, where Chin Loo was issuing orders to three women and a yard boy. After she handed the cleaver to Chin Loo he slammed it down so hard that it was buried in the cutting-board tabletop. Tracie found her patience wearing very thin with such temperamental displays and decided it was time she asserted a little authority.

"Send someone out to trim the orchid tree around Mr. Victor's window," she said, meeting his gaze.

"Mr. Victor does not like it—"

"Tell him Miss Tracie ordered it. Sooner or later, he and I are going to have a run-in and it may as well be sooner."

The servants gasped.

"But Mr. Victor's heart is not good," Kaahumanu reminded her, "the gentlemen from Honolulu, they said he must not be excited."

Tracie knew it was a losing battle and threw her hands up in the air. "All right, cater to his every whim. But you're only going to make him more impossible."

She left the kitchen in disgust, but not before overhearing Kaahumanu's young daughter say, "Maybe Miss Tracie doesn't care about her father's health."

They missed the point entirely, Tracie thought as she walked away, discouraged.

Diane brought her some small comfort when she met Tracie while on her way to get Victor's requested, though forbidden, dry martini.

"Tracie, I can't thank you enough for defending me about that tree. It just seems to hate me."

"I know. I sometimes think it hates me too." Tracie tried for a ray of humor in all the nonsense she and the others had conjured up about the tree. "Maybe it's lonely for Ilima."

Diane's stiff smile showed that she was not amused. "Anyway, if the phone would stop ringing for a while, maybe we could have a little peace and quiet."

Tracie offered to have all the calls routed through her office but Diane, after a quick glance over her shoulder, refused.

"He would never forgive me. He wants to be aware of what's going on." With that it seemed that Tracie wouldn't be needed by Victor or anyone else at the house, at least for the time being, and decided to walk down to the beach at South Harbor.

There she watched as Hawaiian workers from the pineapple fields dressed several fine, well-grown pigs inside and out with burning hot stones, then covered them with huge ti leaves and buried them. With the pigs were buried various Hawaiian delicacies including chicken and seaweed, small silvery fish, taro, sweet potatoes and other vegetables. A pair of field workers were preparing squid and mahi-mahi, the ubiquitous poi.

As usual when she visited the sugar-mill harbor, her appearance wasn't unnoticed. Standing on the shore, fascinated as always by the waves that rolled in, leaving a lacy edge along the wet sand, she felt two muscular arms tighten around her body, under her breasts. When she started to cry out in indignant protest, she had the further public embarrassment of being kissed. She couldn't mistake Bill Dempster's kiss for that of a casual friend's. It was applied square on the mouth, forcing her lips open to respond, and it achieved its purpose, exciting her.

"What the devil are you doing here?" she demanded when she'd freed herself and could speak. She knew she must look flustered; she might even have blushed.

Bill was perfectly aware of their interested audience and she felt sure his dashing impudence was deliberate, for the benefit of his newfound friends among the workers. His grin was infectious and when it disappeared as she spoke, she couldn't help wishing she hadn't been so tart.

"And what's this? Your Clark Gable imitation?"

His clasp tightened on her wrist but not with pleasure, and his response was casually sarcastic. "Anything to thaw out icy females. That's my specialty."

"So I've heard."

He laughed without humor and let her go. She wondered if it was contempt she read in his eyes or merely anger. She wished she knew when he was being sincere and when he was just leading her on, the better to victimize the Berensons with some new scheme.

She changed the subject quickly.

"You startled me, that's all. Anyway, I really am glad you're back. I gather your ankle is okay. And your arm looks as if it's definitely on the mend."

"Well, my stock seems to have gone up a point. I'd never have guessed it from my reception."

Nevertheless, she could see that she had revived his interest. "What happened?" he said, looking at her intently.

She took his hand, led him further out to the wet sand where there was no possibility of their being overheard. Here she told him about Ray Thorpe and her cousins' trip to Honolulu. He was fully as interested as she had thought he would be, but was also unexpectedly disapproving. "You shouldn't have let them go off on a chase like that. If this Thorpe is dangerous, he shouldn't be warned that someone is on his trail. Why didn't you call me? I was at the Parker Ranch on the Big Island. Anyone could have told you."

She wanted to tell him that, strictly speaking, it was none of his business, but he had already chosen to involve himself and she was grateful.

"I thought you might be able to check on the *Lorelei* and other ships in your company." He looked skeptical, but nodded. She added, "If he meant to sneak into the Territory, he might take another liner, the Japanese line or a freighter."

"I can check. Do you have a snapshot of this guy?"

"No. Diane tore them all up."

"She would. Not very farsighted." He frowned into the bright sunlight. "I'll check his whereabouts if I can."

"She says he's a gambler."

"I ought to be able to cover Reno. I was there last fall. May I use a phone at your house? There isn't very much privacy in the mill phone, and there aren't any phones in my palatial abode."

She laughed. "I'm not surprised. I've seen your palatial abode. Come along."

"Ah! I'm actually invited home with you. Anything can come of this." She smiled, took his arm and they walked back under the great cane flumes, then up across the lower slope of Mauna Pā-ele toward the Berenson house.

She left him alone in her office-study and went out onto the lanai to meet two of her father's overseers who came to report that their workers had left the fields early to prepare for the luau and the *hukilau*.

Huber wanted to know if the men's paychecks were to be penalized for the time missed. "They owe most of what they make anyway. And with all the agitation by outsiders, there's liable to be trouble. But it's up to Mr. Victor what we do."

Tracie wondered if Bill realized all the trouble he was causing. "Of course," she said. "I'm sure Mr. Victor wants you to let them go without penalty. And remind them that it's not some soulless corporation, but the Berensons who furnish the food and drink at the luau..."

"Just so, Miss Tracie," he agreed.

"But not too much okolehao, if it's available at all. We don't want the authorities coming down on us."

The men nodded, but she knew the oke would be flowing.

Diane came out to the lanai while Tracie was seeing the men off.

The young woman looked harassed and worn. Her makeup had been rubbed off, probably by her own nervous hands, which she couldn't keep still. "Theo is coming in on the inter-island late ferry. He said he would go directly to the *hukilau.*"

"Did he say he had found out anything? How did he sound?"

Diane looked guilty. "Very happy to see — us."

Knowing Theo's crush on his "Aunt Diane," Tracie was sure he had said he would be happy to see *her,* but she appreciated the awkwardness of Diane's position.

"I can imagine. He won't want to miss the *hukilau* either. No point in going to meet him if he heads directly for South Harbor. We'd probably miss him in the dark." After a short pause she added, "I don't suppose we're going to get anywhere until we have a picture of your ex-husband. I wish you could find at least one snapshot."

Diane bit a thumbnail, her forehead lined in a frown. "I might have one of our glee club in high school. He was a senior when I was a freshman but we were in glee club together and in the charleston class." She smiled softly at a memory. "He could charleston awfully well."

A snapshot of a boy of fifteen or sixteen would not be of great help in identifying a man in his late thirties, but, Tracie reasoned, it was better than nothing. She tried to show enthusiasm. "Do your best to find it. Anything would help."

Diane returned to her bedroom looking a little less worried.

When Bill and Tracie arrived at South Harbor around sunset Tracie was amused by his surprise at the big turnout. From every corner of the island, every plantation, truck farm or patch of fertile ground, the field workers had gathered on the long white beach, automatically dropping into place in parallel lines around the *Tapa* cloths on which the cold dishes and baskets of fruit had been set. Knives, forks and spoons were provided, but most of the diners, including the Caucasians, were proud to eat "sensibly with their fingers," as Tracie explained to Bill.

The Hawaiians and Orientals sat cross-legged, but this proved beyond the agility of most of the *haoles* present. Even Bill Dempster grunted as he dropped to the sand.

"Never mind," Tracie told him. "You can settle down Roman style, leaning on one elbow."

"I get the feeling you've classed me with the oldsters," he complained cheerfully. But he stretched out as she had suggested and she settled beside him.

Because Tracie expected to go swimming later in the evening, after the stars were out, she didn't wear a *holoku* or a *muu-muu* like most of the other women present. Her tailored white shorts concealed a black swimsuit. Bill obviously liked what he saw. He reached over, running his hand along one of her bare, tawny legs as he smiled at her appreciatively.

Again, the surge of pleasure she always felt at his touch...she didn't doubt that he enjoyed making love to her, that on some level he truly cared for her. If she could believe he loved her solely for herself she'd marry him tomorrow. But she knew better. Bill Dempster always had one eye on Orchid Tree Enterprises.

Their attention was diverted to the succulent, steaming pork which lay in its open ti-leaf covering. Hawaiian chefs expertly sliced meat while others piled plates high with fish and vegetables. The first plate was set before Lady Jade Wong Berenson.

Bill glanced over at the middle spread of *Tapa* cloth where Jade sat with legs carefully concealed by a dignified *holoku* and train. This subtly shaped gown merely accentuated her regal look. She remained her rigid self but she was surrounded by Chinese and even Japanese friends who seemed to be delighted by her presence. They spoke in several dialects, switching once to the more evenly pitched Japanese language.

Bill shook his head. "Incredible woman. I wonder what she knows about everything that's been going on. . . I'd swear she's always been in love with your father. You can see it in her eyes, the way they follow every step he takes. She must miss him tonight."

Tracie bristled. "Don't tell me you think *she's* responsible for this business with Ray Thorpe! Aunt Jade has too much class to be mixed up in something so sordid."

"She knows something," he insisted, and offered Tracie a square of succulent pork that she ate from his fingers, ignoring the argument between them. She pinched up a piece of squid and offered it to him. He ate it without hesitation, sensuously brushing his tongue over her two fingers afterward. The meal that followed left them satiated, but through it all Tracie was deeply aware of Bill Dempster's body close beside her.

Night came on so gradually that neither of them would have noticed the blue-dark or even the moonrise if the fishermen hadn't waded out with nets and torches along the beach away from the luau, some carrying spears, to demonstrate the *hukilau*. The burning of kukui nuts produced smoke puffs. The beach looked like an eerie desert dotted with little oases of smoke where the Hawaiians, holding the torches high and away from their bodies, stepped into the surf.

Along the shore three girls in ti-leaf skirts and wide-necked, revealing white blouses danced hulas to the music of the Sugar Mill Strings, a group made up of local mill workers.

Following their movements gracefully with her own hands, Tracie hummed the soft, beautiful ballads, "For You a Lei" and "Hawaiian Paradise." Bill appeared to watch the dancers, but his thoughts were elsewhere.

"You boasted once that you could do the hula," he challenged suddenly.

"Only in a small group."

"Sounds cowardly to me."

Tracie laughed. "Ask Theo or Lili. Lili usually performs a hula at the feast end of the party and Theo often wades out with the men. They kid him about it but they respect him for it. He ought to be here by now. He'd hate to miss this."

"I believe it . . . Your cousin has potential but his life has been too easy."

"Easy?" She reacted at once whenever he seemed to attack the family.

"He's clever but lazy, always out for the main chance." He felt her drawing away from him and he added slowly, "I don't think you can count on him as a tower of Berenson probity, but that doesn't come as a shock to you, surely."

"Certainly not. I'm only surprised you can say 'probity' after all that oke you've drunk." His abrupt laugh caused her to retract her quick agreement that Theo was inadequate in many ways. "Besides, Theo wasn't reared to run Orchid Tree."

"You were?"

She didn't hesitate to respond. "You bet I was! Though whether I'll keep the job is something else again." The instant she said it she wanted to cover her admission. Bill Dempster was the last person she wanted to know anything about her difficulties with her father.

But Bill showed no surprise. It was she who was astonished by his calm offer. "How about the same job with Dorado Star? Vice-president and managing director."

"You *are* drunk!"

"Suppose we throw in a percentage of the profits that accrue after you take over?"

She looked at him, still laughing. But from his expression she could tell that he was completely serious.

"Forget it," she said crisply, thinking she'd put him and his offer in their proper place.

Bill seemed to expect her answer and wasn't upset by it, though he persisted by adding, "The offer is on the level."

"So is the refusal." She grinned at him, then glanced at the fishermen. They were far along the beach, away from the crowd. She got up and made a dash for the water, hopping out of her shorts one leg at a time and dropping them on the sand just above the water line.

Not to be outdone by her, Bill removed his sandals, stripped down to his own swimsuit and waded in, splashing through the surf to dive into a cresting wave before she could show off her own modest skill. He rode the wave past her, then returned and groped for her under the first silver light of a quarter-moon. She panicked as he pulled her off her feet in the dark waters, but seconds later he lifted her high, dripping wet, and pulled her hard against him.

Their kiss tasted of salt and seaweed, and when they parted their eyes gleamed in the moonlight.

"You look ferocious!" Tracie cried and then coughed as a wave filled her mouth with water.

"Don't be too cocky!" he said, grinning. "You look like Medusa with those wet locks of yours."

She brought her palm down hard on the water, which should have showered him, but he'd turned suddenly to avoid the splash and stared at the beach where a gorgeous young blonde woman, a vision in white, strolled into the flaring light of the kukui torches. Within seconds she had attracted the attention of everyone on the beach and not a few of those swimming in the shallows above the breakers.

Although Jade was at the nearest *Tapa* cloth "table" and should have known the woman, she paid no attention. But others sitting around her recognized Marta Dempster and scrambled up to greet her.

Tracie asked Bill, "Did you know she was coming?"

"Last place I'd have expected to see her. She's not much for this kind of thing. Hollywood parties suit her better."

She wished she could read his expression. He sounded surprised and puzzled, but was he pleased to see her? Bill held out an arm to Tracie and took long, slow strides out of deep water into the shallows with Tracie high-stepping beside him.

Marta Dempster asked where she could find her "husband" just as he appeared, dripping wet, with Tracie right behind him. Tracie reached for the pile of hand towels in a basket beyond the nearest *emu* and tossed him several. While she rubbed herself down she watched for his reaction. He took his time in acknowledging his former wife's presence.

Marta was all gushing friendliness and cooing pleasure. She had never looked more dazzling or made Tracie feel more disheveled.

"Bill, I knew I'd find you. What a time it's been! A terribly nice Japanese man drove me here. Would you mind paying Mr. Nakazawa for me? There's a dear."

Bill automatically felt over his wet swimsuit, then remembered and reached for his slacks on the sand. He walked back up the beach to the coral jetty where Mr. Nakazawa waited, beaming and "most happy to oblige."

At the center of the growing crowd around her, Marta explained charmingly, "Theo told me so much about this native entertainment that I felt I just had to come and see it for myself."

The Hawaiians clearly didn't appreciate being referred to as natives, but the rest were turned to putty by her smile and the way she loved to touch everyone. Tracie thought her hands were much too busy, but it was clear that only the women shared her distaste.

Marta allowed herself to be fed a stick of pineapple, bite by bite, but daintily refused the squid, the salmon and the deep pink heart of a guava. The admiring crowd had spread out so much that one of the field hands almost stepped back on Lady Jade. It was Marta who made a fuss out of her apology, which was received by Jade with a cool smile.

Marta was undaunted. "I hoped to see my dear friend Victor here, but Theo says he's still confined to his room. Such a shame! I never knew a more active man. He even put *you* to shame, darling."

Those present were slightly surprised to hear the man who had divorced her addressed as "darling," but Bill was unperturbed. "I never was a match for Victor Berenson," he said, with a glance at Tracie, "though I'm working at it."

Jade asked abruptly, "You have seen my son?"

"Of course. He brought me on that — inter-island boat, I think is what he called it."

With admirable ease Jade got up from the

sand. "And so he is here?"

Everyone looked around for him. Marta seemed confused at their concern, and a little miffed when the interest wavered from her.

"No. Theo, the dear boy, will be here pretty soon. He said he had something to do in that tiny village. The one they call Akua City."

Jade nodded. "He does well. He has gone first to pay his respects to his uncle. He will come here later." She seemed restless and instead of sitting down again among her somewhat diminished group of friends, she started to walk along the beach toward the torch-fishermen.

Gradually, the crowd began to break up. There was still work to be done the next day among the plantation hands — hard, back-breaking work. As people started to gather their things for the walk home Jade approached Tracie and Bill, who stood near one of the fires. "Is the actress to stay with us tonight?" she asked Tracie in a low voice.

"I'm afraid so. Unless—" she looked at Bill, "you'd like to take her off our hands."

He quickly dismissed the idea. "Not me. It cost me enough to get rid of her the first time. I'm not getting involved again, Lady Jade. Sorry, but she's Theo's problem now. He brought her here."

"By the way," Tracie interrupted, "where is Theo?"

It was unlike him to miss one of his favorite events. His mother frowned, peered beyond the cane fields into the darkness across the ridge that separated Akua Sugar from the Berenson plantation house. Even if Theo was coming in this direction from Akua they could not see him among the scattered groups walking home.

"We're sure to meet him on the way back," Tracie suggested. "I just wonder how far the movie star will get in her high heels."

She needn't have been concerned. The young manager of the sugar mill won a battle with a pair of plantation overseers to drive Marta to the Berenson home in his 1923 Chandler.

Bill escorted the two Berenson ladies, showing off his Peking dialect to Lady Jade, who almost thawed under his charm.

They reached the house about one in the morning. Diane met them in the front hall, expressing in somewhat aggrieved tones the hope that they'd had a "lovely time." She whispered to Tracie, "He's been crabby all night. He did want so much to go, poor lamb. Thank heaven, he's asleep now." She turned to Aunt Jade, who was talking to Bill and said, "Is it all right if I put Marta Lang in the corner room downstairs?"

Tracie looked startled but she laughed. Jade seemed pleased at having been asked. "I have read that film stars have a great affection for orchids. She will have her fill tonight," she replied.

Bill Dempster made no objection. "I've slept there myself. She should love it." He bowed to Jade, then took Tracie by the shoulders and kissed her firmly. After a final good-bye to the others he left and for a moment her fears were swept aside...maybe, she thought, they would get together after all.

Feeling warmed by the enjoyable evening spent with Bill, she didn't even mind when Jade and Diane, who'd witnessed the scene, made remarks about their budding relationship as she stood in the doorway, watching him walk away.

"It is unfortunate that my son missed the *hukilau*," Jade said when Tracie turned back to the two women. "Was his uncle happy to see him?"

"He wasn't here at all," Diane said. "Maybe he thought it was too late. But Victor is so miserable these days, not able to do what he wants..."

Jade thought this over for a moment. "It is for the best, then. I will speak to him and find out why he didn't come to the beach."

"On the phone he said he had something to tell us," Diane reminded her. "Victor will be interested, I'm sure. He is bound to be in a better mood when he sees Theo."

"I am aware of Victor's moods," Jade said flatly, and the two women parted at the top of the stairs.

Tracie went to her room wondering why Theo hadn't bothered to see anyone when he returned...Or why hadn't he gone to South Harbor with Marta in Mr. Nakazawa's truck.

She dropped her wet swimsuit in a heap in the bathroom, took a quick bath to rinse the salt off and wearily dropped into bed. Her nagging little worry about Theo faded and she dropped off to sleep.

20

Tracie's dreams that night were confused. Nightmarish thoughts clung to the edges of sleep but she failed to understand why. Faces she had known all her life appeared as strangers to her, though they weren't threatening. Small sounds were magnified so that they reverberated in her head. In a state of half-sleep she reminded herself that it was because of all the oke she'd drunk.

It continued for an endless few minutes, punctuated by a voice calling her name. A low voice, quiet but authoritative.

She opened her eyes, lay quietly for a moment and suddenly realized it was her aunt's voice she heard calling her name. She tried the door. It was locked, which must have puzzled her. Tracie had started locking it — she wasn't sure why — after Ilima's death. The doorknob turned several times, then the knocking again.

Tracie sat up with a start, fully awake now.

Something was definitely wrong. Maybe her father had had another heart attack. She lurched out of bed and rushed across the room calling, "All right. I'm coming." She snapped on the nearest lamp, then unlocked the door.

Jade Wong stood in the doorway wearing one of her *paké*-styled quilted gowns. She was uncharacteristically tense. "He is not in his room," she blurted after a quick, frowning glance at the lock.

Tracie immediately knew whom her aunt was talking about. She looked over at her bedside clock but couldn't read it in the shadowy half of her bedroom.

"It is near dawn," Jade said. "Four o'clock."

Tracie thought of Theo's various girlfriends on the island. "Are you sure he hasn't just stayed over with someone in town?"

"In Akua? Has he ever done this?"

Tracie admitted that he hadn't. Theo's taste ran to women less easily won, like Diane or Marta Dempster.

"What about Marta Lang, could he be with her?"

Jade frowned. "I went first to that woman. She gave me cause for concern. She said she left him in front of Mr. Nakazawa's store. As they were driving away she looked back and saw my boy walking to the jetty again. But no one here in the house saw him come home."

Tracie knew there must be a dozen explanations for Theo's failure to show up, but at the moment she couldn't think what they might be. She wanted very much to return to bed and struggled to stifle a yawn. "What do you think we should do?" she said, wanting to show concern but unable to think clearly.

"I woke the Arguello boy. He will drive us to town."

"But if you have Rudi, why will you need—" she broke off when she saw the fear in her aunt's eyes.

"Give me five minutes. I'll meet you on the lanai."

Jade stood motionless for several seconds staring at the vine pattern on the wallpaper beside Tracie's door. Then she inclined her head and turned away.

Tracie crossed the room peeling off her nightgown. What the devil possessed Theo to pull this stunt on his mother? He was usually very careful not to upset her.

As promised, Tracie hurried down the back stairs five minutes later. She found Aunt Jade standing on the lanai beside the orchid tree and to her surprise, Marta Dempster was talking to her through the outer door to her room.

"Theo was acting a little strangely, I thought.

And he seemed very excited...Oh, hello, Tracie. Isn't it the weirdest thing? I can't imagine what could have happened to him."

"Where exactly did you leave him?" Tracie asked.

"Well, we walked to Mr. Nakazawa's store together and when I got in that funny old truck and it chugged away, I saw Theo had gone to the edge of the jetty again. He was looking down and watching the water, where that red boat is tied up. I think he waved to me but I'm not sure. He was in the shadow of an old grass shack up above the coral on the shore."

"There's a tool shed, and Albie Wimble's little shack," Tracie said while Jade nodded. "Who — or what — was he waiting for?"

"I asked him why he couldn't go to the beach with me. I thought he must be going directly home to see Victor but he just laughed and said, 'Later.' "

"He did not come home," Jade insisted.

Her certainty chilled Tracie. She was relieved when Rudi Arguello finally drove up in the Berenson Packard, yawning elaborately and wearing stained work pants with a purple-flowered cotton shirt. Before he could get out Tracie helped her aunt into the back seat and took her place beside him. Marta called after them, "And how sweet of you to give me all these lovely blossoms!"

Tracie stuck her head out the open window. "How is that?"

"Look here. These flowers floated right into my bedroom. I adore the darling things."

"There's no accounting for tastes," Tracie said dryly to her aunt.

But Jade was too deeply wrapped in worry to appreciate the remark.

They drove through the deep night of the jungle down to Akua harbor. The dawn light was hidden by the mountainous spine of the island, and the village remained shrouded in darkness.

From the beginning Tracie kept telling herself that a girl had to be behind Theo's disappearance, and half-expected to find that her cousin was in one of the fishermen's huts dotting the harbor. Still, she couldn't ignore her aunt's deep alarm and began to consider other possibilities, all of them unpleasant.

The water had never looked darker as it washed against the jetty and rocked Victor's beloved outrigger. "What now, Miss Tracie?" Rudi asked after the car was parked.

Tracie looked toward Aunt Jade, who had gotten out of the car and stood along the waterfront, which had never appeared more deserted. Only one light was on, a whale-oil lamp in the house of a fisherman that was well around the crescent-shaped harbor.

Rudi saw the lamplight and understood. "I will go see what Joe Kamalu and his wife know. He works part-time around Nakazawa's store. If anybody saw Mr. Theo, he or his wife did."

"Good idea," Tracie said, feeling more nervous by the minute. "And I'll talk to Mr. Nakazawa's daughter. I think she has a crush on Theo. She would have seen him if he was around here last night." She walked over to her aunt after Rudi left. "Would you like to talk to Mr. Nakazawa? I'll get hold of that old seadog who lives in the grass hut. Albie ought to have a good view just north of the jetty."

Jade moved stiffly toward the home of the Nakazawa's, which was behind their store. More uneasy over Jade's reaction than Theo's behavior, Tracie watched her, then climbed up over a coral outcropping to the hut made of weathered boards.

As she might have expected, the old man, once a deep-water sailor, was just coming out of a drunken sleep. She called to him and shook the door that was held closed by a length of unraveling hemp.

"Go 'way," he called out hoarsely.

"It's Tracie Berenson, Albie. Let me talk to you, please."

Bleary-eyed and unshaven Albie Wimble shuffled to the door after wrapping himself in an old blanket.

"It's my friend, Miss Tracie. All okay up *mauká*-way?"

She answered in her usual way with a smile. "All okay down *makai*-way?" But he could see even in the starlight that things weren't all right with her.

He tightened his shaky clasp on the blanket. "I guess you need help. I got hold of some choice dolphin late this afternoon. Real mahi-mahi. And there's liable to be something in my nets. I didn't get to 'em tonight. Kind of over-did the oke, as you might say."

"No, it's nothing like that. Did you see any-one on the jetty around the time the inter-island boat stopped by?"

He scratched his chin with the corner of his blanket.

"Tell you the truth, I wasn't in too good shape along about then. I rec'lect voices. And a mighty pretty girl. Lots of yellow hair."

That would certainly be Marta Dempster.

"And afterward? When she left?"

"Seems like your cousin, the young fella, he — it's kind of mixed-up."

"What do you mean? What did he do?"

Albie Wimble thought for a long time while

Tracie waited, frantic with impatience.

"Don't rec'lect. Waves make a lot of noise this side of the jetty." He brightened as if he'd had a new idea. "Say. Might've been something I caught in the net and the trap I set out. You know, shark meat's real good you fry it right."

"I know. Could you help us search the village? Maybe the Hawaiians and the others will talk easier to you."

Albie was proud to be of help. Next to Ma McCallister, the Berensons were his best friends — they never let him go hungry or, more important, thirsty.

"Sure. Soon's I get into my pants and empty my nets. You run along. I'll meet you on the jetty."

With some care Tracie climbed down off the sharp coral outcropping, aware of the sea close at hand, washing against Albie's complicated arrangement of nets and wire traps. After spotting thirteen-year-old Nara Nakazawa standing with her parents in the open doorway of their home, she hurried to join her aunt and question them.

They appeared polite as always to Lady Jade, with whom they conducted most of their everyday business, but tonight it was clear that her nervousness puzzled them. "You saw him when the inter-island boat came in, but after that?" Aunt Jade said, evidently repeating herself.

Mr. Nakazawa was doing his best to be helpful. "Mr. Theo is a very polite young man. He asked me to drive the *haole* with yellow hair. I had finished my evening meal, so I took the lady. Most pleasant. She talked very much. Very fast."

Tracie put in, "But you, Nara. And Mrs. Nakazawa, you didn't see my cousin afterward?"

The petite Mrs. Nakazawa bowed gracefully. "I'm afraid not. We were at the *hukilau* and saw no one on the way home."

Pretty Nara Nakazawa shook her head. "I didn't see anybody but Miss Lang, the movie star, and father."

Tracie thanked them and turned away, hoping for better luck with Rudi Arguello and his fisherman friend when she noticed Albie Wimble shakily walking down over the sharp coral barrier between his grass house and his nets in the basin behind the jetty. It took careful footing even by daylight. Now he had only the light at the far end of the jetty to judge his footing by. He was within a few steps of the wharf when he stumbled and began to slide over the edge into the tangled nets he had dropped in the basin between the jetty and the coral reef.

By now he had the attention of the entire group and Tracie broke out in a sprint, followed by Mr. Nakazawa, who hurried along in his padded *getas*. Tracie reached the wharf first and stretched over to grab Albie's arm. Luckily, Mr. Nakazawa caught him at the shoulder and saved Tracie from being pulled over as well. Together they pulled up Albie, who tottered on the brink between them, staring down into his nets, tangled with rope, cord and wire that was torn loose. As they looked down into the waters Tracie could see that Albie had caught something in his nets. As she stared down at them an idea flashed in her mind, too horrifying to dwell on. She glanced at Aunt Jade, who was walking along the unpaved harbor road toward Rudi Arguello and the fisherman. Willing herself to do what she knew she must, she made her way back to the Packard and turned its lights on. They were directed straight at the jetty, giving some illumination to Albie's nets. Albie peered down again in the added light.

"Caught me a big one," he said happily. "I can see the white of its belly."

Mr. Nakazawa shuffled to the edge and looked down. One glance at his face confirmed to Tracie her dreaded suspicion. She stumbled over the coral and rocks to join him, praying that he was wrong.

Theo's blue-white face, barely recognizable after being washed by tidal waters for hours, stared up at her from the tangle of nets, wires and wooden staves where a barrel-trap had been broken.

She closed her eyes, praying that this was an apparition, but the horror remained, even while in her mind she tried to convince herself it couldn't be true.

Albie dropped to his hands and knees for a closer look, gasped and reached toward the nets. When he couldn't quite reach them he looked up at Tracie, his mouth trembling. "He must've fell. He tripped and tumbled over in the dark."

Mr. Nakazawa, who was also peering over the jetty, nodded wordlessly.

"The jetty isn't that high," Tracie cried in panic, "he could have pulled himself out. For God's sake, help me get him out." She dropped to the ground and reached down but she too was unable to reach the body tangled in the nets. One of Theo's slim hands seemed to float just out of their reach. His jacket was torn and his upper arm had been washed bare by the force of the tide.

Nakazawa knelt with an effort, hampered by his kimono. He too failed. Tracie kept stretching and reaching into the water. Her body felt stiff, icy with the shock of their discovery, worse than all her imaginings. She knew Theo was dead. He must have been dead for hours; yet the insane idea clung to her that if they could rescue him, get him out of the water, they could revive him.

"He could not climb out if he became entangled," Mr. Nakazawa said gently. "It must be that. See over there? When he fell he must have broken the barrel-trap. Perhaps he struck his head when he fell." But his words fell on deaf ears as Tracie continued to try to pull the nets toward the jetty.

Suddenly she became aware of the soft patter of Mr. Nakazawa's *getas* over the ground and she roused herself to another critical matter. Since it was too late to help Theo, she must try to cushion the awful pain for Aunt Jade. She walked down the road, trying to appear calm. Running would only confirm her aunt's worst fears.

Arguello and the fisherman, Joe Kamalu, strode toward Tracie. As usual Jade walked beside them without being a part of the group. Although they clearly wanted to help her, she was still an outsider, never having allowed herself to be absorbed into the community. Now, when she would need friends, she remained alone, except for Liliha, and mother and daughter were hardly close.

Tracie reached for her aunt's concealed hands, drew them out between her own. Jade's eyes grew wider, her lips tightened. Without a word she questioned Tracie who nodded slowly, sharing her pain.

"Where?" Jade asked.

Tracie put an arm around her aunt but Jade's body stiffened, clearly rejecting this familiarity. Tracie adjusted her step to the gliding movements of her aunt. Strange, Tracie thought irrelevantly, how fast they reached the little tidepool.

Jade tore away from Tracie and looked down. Her hands flew to her face as she let out a high-pitched wail, like an unseen night bird, that made Tracie shiver.

Before anyone could stop her she dropped to her knees and let herself down into the water with its web of broken nets. Joe Kamalu climbed down after her, holding onto the high stone and coral edge of the jetty with one hand. Rudi and Tracie knelt to hold them up in the water. The pool was about eight feet deep but so clogged with barrel staves and debris that even Jade was able to keep her head above the water. Tracie lay flat on the wharf, stretching both hands to her aunt.

Jade had one arm around Theo, his head

cradled against her shoulder. She attempted to tread water while Joe Kamalu got his free hand behind Jade's shoulders. Tracie never knew how they managed it, but within minutes Theo's thin young body, water-soaked and dripping, rested on the jetty.

The men took turns trying to revive him by pressing hard and precisely under his breastbone. His mother knelt over him, calling to him, murmuring endearments in her own dialect, determined to restore him to life. Like Tracie, she could not conceive that the men's efforts were futile.

As Tracie watched she became aware of the tears streaming down her face and blinked, but even through this veil she couldn't help staring at her Aunt Jade as she had never seen her before, her smooth, high-piled black hair pulled loose about her face, the long strands dripping wet. The tight, long cheongsam she wore was saturated, clinging to her body.

Nothing was real about these terrible minutes that everyone but Jade slowly began to accept were useless. But these efforts were like an act of contrition which no one could stop.

The first morning light had rimmed the peak of Mauna Pā-ele when Mr. Nakazawa and his wife took Jade by the shoulders and gently eased her away from her son. Despising her own helplessness, Tracie joined them in urging her aunt to leave the wharf. The Nakazawas promised to see that Theo's body was brought to the little makeshift hospital belonging to the Akua Sugar Company.

"But why not home?" Tracie said, confused by the suggestion.

The men looked at each other. "They will want to know how it happened, Miss Tracie," Rudi Arguello explained.

But to Tracie it seemed self-evident. Theo was in high spirits and had become reckless. He must have tripped on the rough paved stone and coral of the jetty and fell. It was obvious, as Mr. Nakazawa had suggested, that his fall had broken the barrel-trap, hopelessly entangling him in net and wire. But for some reason the men felt an autopsy was necessary. What did they suspect?

She and Rudi helped Aunt Jade into the Packard. Aunt Jade's behavior continued to baffle Tracie. Though the tragedy had left her a broken woman, she did not look back once she sat down rigidly in the big car. Tracie got in beside her and tried to take her cold, damp hand. Jade withdrew it and looked straight ahead, seeing nothing. After Rudi started the car she said without expression, "I killed my boy."

Tracie protested as softly as she could. "Aunt

Jade, you did no such thing. It just happened."

Tracie knew her aunt was out of her mind with grief or she would never have said something so outlandish. Tracie wished she could offer some comfort, anything. If not a kiss or a warm touch, then surely a word of consolation, but there seemed to be no way to reach her.

Aunt Jade examined her long, elegant fingers. She seemed to be talking to herself or the strange gods she believed in. Tracie could scarcely hear her.

"They punish me through my innocent boy."

The hardest thing to bear was the sudden, high-pitched question she asked Tracie, with all her pain ragged in her voice:

"Is that fair?"

"It was an accident, Aunt Jade. It's nobody's fault. It just happened."

Long after they reached the plantation house Jade's strange self-accusations baffled Tracie. Whatever the injustice of Theo's death, his mother would have been the last person responsible.

Meanwhile, the sickening loss of the only young male in the family pervaded the household. Everyone went about in a daze, and Bill Dempster's arrival to pay his respects minutes after he heard the news only brought Tracie added tension.

In a corner of the entrance hall he patiently but persistently asked her questions. "Was he drunk?"

"We don't know."

"Have you ever known Theo to be that drunk? And whatever his moral sense, which I may question, I never knew anybody more sure-footed."

"Are you starting that again? First Ilima, now Theo." She tried to push past him but he put his arm out, barring her way.

"I'm sorry. I don't mean to imply anything against your family. But there is another possibility. You and I might have been killed the other day. Theo was killed — all right, he died — last night. Hasn't it occurred to you that this Ray Thorpe could be behind it?"

She couldn't believe that in the confusion of the last few hours she had forgotten about the man they'd all been searching for.

"Is it possible? Theo was acting as if he had a secret. Maybe it had something to do with Thorpe."

"Maybe," he agreed. "But in any case, he got a bad blow at the base of the skull. It may have happened when he fell. Or—"

"My God! Then who is next for this monster?" Her knees felt weak and she began to cry.

Bill's arms wrapped tightly around her were an enormous comfort.

21

Theo's death aroused the sympathy of the entire Territory. Many were personally familiar with the attractive, carefree youth. Others mourned as well, knowing the respected family from which he came.

Under the anxious eyes of Diane and Tracie, Victor stood up well enough through the funeral but looked as if he were on the verge of collapse. Theo was buried beside his father and his uncle's first wife in the small plot of hibiscus-bordered ground between the McCallister and Berenson spreads.

The funeral was attended by many prominent figures from Honolulu and Hilo, including the Territorial governor and the Croyde family, who accompanied Liliha home. Most of the working population of Akua appeared, and it was generally agreed among them that the Berensons must have angered some ancient Hawaiian god: first Ilima Mako's inexplicable suicide, then tough, irascible Mr. Victor was struck down by sickness. Now Theo, whom the Honolulu *Star-Bulletin* called "the flower of the Berenson youth and only male heir," had also died.

Through the service Victor insisted on supporting his sister-in-law. He remained by her throughout the day and was the only person she permitted to take her hand or put his arm around her. She had said no more about her own guilt in Theo's death, and everyone hoped she'd come to her senses even in the midst of her pain.

Knowing Bill Dempster's suspicions about Theo's accident, Tracie was troubled by the way he studied the Croydes. She had always thought they were friends, and could see no reason why Bill should regard them warily.

Liliha found more comfort in the tearful Diane than in her own mother, whose anguish was locked deep inside herself. Tracie too felt the loss of her bubbling, mischievous cousin in many ways and in every corner of the plantation house. She did her best to comfort Lili but Diane and Wayne Croyde seemed better able to sooth her. With Theo gone Tracie became aware of a score of questions being raised in the household about Orchid Tree Enterprises, which Victor was in no condition to handle. It was never remotely suggested that Theo would take over, which made the questions all the more odd.

Earlier in the day, hoping to take his mind off the approaching funeral and the many guests who had to be housed and given some sort of personal greeting, Tracie had tested her father's interest with the problem of the final payments on the unwanted pineapple cannery outside Honolulu, and the question of unionizing the Berenson plantation hands. She explained that these matters could wait but that he might want to think about them. Diane was near him as always, listening patiently.

He waved away all talk of unions. "The governor says there'll never be a union that gets a foothold on these islands."

Tracie knew the governor's view all too well. He had been wrong in the fall of 1935 and he was even more wrong in 1936. The International Longshoreman's Union was already there, unofficially, at least. Nothing had been agreed to, especially in the outer islands, but she had already seen the first signs of organizational power at the Akua sugar mill and in the cane fields. However much she might rail at Bill Dempster for opening this Pandora's box, she began to feel it was unavoidable. Victor and the other great plantation owners would have to look ahead, sooner or later. Had she explained this to her father he would have waved her away, but meanwhile the power he had spent his life accumulating was slowly slipping out of his hands.

"Do what you want," he said, obviously wanting to end the discussion. "You know what's best." During his illness he seemed to draw further from her, even when he surrendered more power. He added sulkily, "You always wanted to wear the pants in this family. Now's your chance."

"Dad, I never—"

Diane, who looked as if she had been crying before Tracie's interruption, cut in ineffectually. "Darling, you don't mean that."

"Sure, I do. This kid's getting so power-hungry I could write her out of my will tomorrow and in ten years she'd be queen of the whole damn shebang. Don't tell me, girl, that it hasn't occurred to you — with your cousin gone, there's more for your share."

Too hurt to reply, Tracie got up and left the room. Diane, who hadn't forgotten Tracie's support since she arrived in Akua, began to cry again, kneading her hands. "Surely you don't mean that, Victor. Tracie loved Theo."

"Don't tell me it never occurred to you either," he said, his voice harsh.

Now Diane was hurt and she ran from their bedroom, her sobs seeming to fill the entire second floor of the house.

On the June evening after the funeral, with a soft, welcome trade wind blowing, Victor insisted on driving over to South Harbor where a yacht was taking the governor's party on board for the trip back to Honolulu. Returning home Victor was silent. He sank down in the back seat between Jade and Liliha, looking smaller, shrunken.

Diane, in the front seat next to Tracie, who was driving, leaned over and whispered anxiously, "He needs peace and quiet."

Tracie did not mince words. "He needs a hospital."

"In Honolulu? But suppose Ray is still there?"

"He may possibly be here."

"Oh, dear God!"

From the back seat Victor started awake. "What? Anything wrong? You all right, Trace?"

Guiltily, Diane looked back and tried to touch his knee with her hand. Tracie wished he had mentioned his wife's name in that moment of awakening. "No, darling," Diane assured him. "It's nothing." She turned back to Tracie and said, "Things happened so fast, I didn't get a chance to tell you. I've found a picture."

She unfastened the clasp of her handbag and brought out a glossy picture of a dozen young people on the steps of a public building. Tracie had her eyes on the narrow road that had just cut its way between a poinciana tree and an entangled jungle of mango growth. She glanced at the photograph, but quickly looked back to the twisting road — the last thing they needed was another accident.

At the plantation house Victor and Jade sat in her room together, reminiscing about their early days on Akua. Tracie was relieved to see how much they counted on each other during this crisis. Meanwhile, Diane held out her picture for Tracie and Liliha to examine.

"What do you think?"

Lili said after one glance, "I could have gone for him then, but not now. Fat!"

Diane blushed faintly. "He was sweet in those days. He used to match coins and play poker for matches. That was the extent of it. Nothing like the later days when he'd gamble on anything."

Tracie considered the handsome boy in the back row of the dozen solemn young men and women, the girls in middies with dangling ties under their collars and pleated navy skirts. Diane was pretty even at fifteen or so, big-eyed, with a hesitant smile. Ray Thorpe stood behind her, tall and athletic, with curly hair and a wide, grinning mouth.

"Could he have followed you here with blackmail in mind?"

"I don't know," Diane said. "I still don't know what he wanted that day on the beach."

Lili looked at the photo blankly. She was trying hard to get her mind off her brother, but kept giving the staircase furtive looks, undoubtedly worried about her mother's iron self-control.

Tracie followed her glance. "Don't worry, Lili. Aunt Jade isn't the demonstrative type, but she loves you very much. And Wayne will be back any minute."

For once, Lili had lost interest in men. "But Wayne doesn't know. Nobody knows how it was with Theo and me. We had so much fun together. The jokes, the way we told each other all our secrets." She bit her lip, trying to hold back a new surge of tears. "Except the other day. He never told me why he was coming home. Maybe if he had told me, he wouldn't..."

Tracie squeezed her hand. Lili gave a small smile, but Tracie knew it would be a long time before she would recover from her brother's death. The sound of voices, Wayne Croyde and his parents along with Bill Dempster on their return from South Harbor, cheered her a little, and she looked around when they came into the long, cool living room.

"I'll go and tell Victor they're back," Diane said.

Tracie objected, her voice kind. "Leave them alone. They need a little peace. We can handle things."

But there was very little to handle; the Croydes took it upon themselves to care for the bereaved family, with Mrs. Croyde immediately heading for the rolling bar on the tea wagon to make drinks.

About this time Marta Dempster arrived unexpectedly, arousing Tracie's jealousy. But Marta had no interest in her ex-husband. She ran through a dozen excuses for going up to see and "console dear Victor." Between them, Mr. Croyde and Wayne convinced her that she wouldn't be at all comfortable talking to a sick man whose only interest in females at present was their nursing capacity.

Bill Dempster straddled a chair opposite Diane and Tracie, who sat on the old rattan couch. He looked at the women for a moment, and while Tracie didn't mind his attention, Diane was clearly made nervous by it. She smoothed her hair self-consciously and moistened her lips. Bill noticed the photo Diane was holding and asked to see it. She hesitated, then handed it to him.

"It's a picture of Diane's ex-husband," Tracie explained, leaning forward to point out Ray Thorpe. Bill sat quietly studying the photo of the grinning youth on the high school steps.

"He looks muscular enough. He could do it. And this fellow knocked Victor down?" He raised his eyes, giving Diane one of his hard stares. Tracie thought those piercing blue eyes were enough to scare anyone, and she wasn't surprised when Diane recoiled.

"I hardly recognized Ray at first. He was rude to us. Then he pushed Victor. Victor got to his feet and Mr. Croyde — I mean Wayne — came along." She looked over at Wayne, who heard this and put in, "I hit the guy once. He looked stunned but he walked away."

Bill said, "Neither of you saw him again? Anywhere?"

"What are you getting at?" Tracie asked abruptly.

Bill shrugged and waited until Wayne and the others went back across the room to freshen their drinks.

"There have been too many accidents here on Akua," he said in a low voice. "If these weren't accidents, then a murderer — a singularly nasty one — is somewhere around here, waiting to strike again."

"I knew it!" Diane started to rise but sank

down again. "He's here somewhere. I can feel it."

Tracie looked uneasily from her stepmother to Bill.

"What should we do? Can't we hire detectives, now that we know what he looks like?"

Bill gestured at the picture. "I'd like to borrow this to make some enlargements."

Diane almost stammered. "Do. Yes, anything. Do you think he's after me?"

"I wouldn't be surprised."

Diane looked so edgy that Tracie offered to walk her to Victor's room to rest. "It's time Aunt Jade gave some thought to Lili. All that talk about feeling guilty...she's guilty of ignoring her daughter, for one thing."

Bill gave her a quick, frowning look and she realized that her remark about Aunt Jade had interested him. She hoped he wasn't stupid enough to believe that Jade was responsible for the "accidents." She ignored his glance and went upstairs with Diane, who began to tremble again as they approached Victor's room.

"He's going to lose his temper and be mad at me. He hates being interrupted."

Surprising herself, Tracie said, "The hell with him! Somebody's got to make him realize there's a world out there and it doesn't always revolve around him."

She knocked and walked in. She found her father lying on his bed against the pillows, talking quietly. Aunt Jade sat in Diane's slipper chair that had been pulled up to the bed. She might have been a statue, motionless except for the ravaged look of her face as she stared at the door. For an instant her eyes showed a glimmer of hope, as if she expected to see her son. Then the light seemed to die out of them again.

Tracie and Diane were almost equally relieved when Victor, looking at his wife with affection, motioned to her. "I've been waiting for you, honey. How about keeping the old man company?"

Diane glanced at Jade, but the older woman did not appear offended. She got up and walked over to Tracie. "Is my girl in her room? I must go to her."

As they walked along the hall together Tracie agreed that Liliha had needed her but was all right now. Jade murmured, "I will do better. My Lili must have her chance. What she wants, she will have."

Tracie said gently, "I don't think either of your children ever wanted any material things they didn't get. But Lili certainly needs your affection."

Aunt Jade's scorn was palpable, even through

her ravaged face. "She has always had that. Everything I have done in my life has been for them."

They were stopped suddenly by Diane, who fluttered out of Victor's bedroom, calling to Tracie.

"He wants to talk to you. Quick."

Her alarm was contagious and Tracie rushed back to her father. His face looked pallid and old against the white pillowcases with their embroidered edges so carefully worked by his sister-in-law.

"Tracie-girl...Had another little twinge. Guess it's off to Honolulu for me. See to it, won't you?"

She assured him she would. From the hall phone she called the doctor at the sugar mill. He was far from a specialist or an expert, but Dr. Sam Chung had a reassuring bedside manner and Jade vouched for him. It was arranged that the family would travel to Honolulu on the next day's inter-island boat with the last of the funeral party.

When Tracie returned to their guests downstairs she was relieved to discover that most of the family had adjourned to the lanai. They crowded around Marta in the light of the Japanese lanterns that gave the lanai a golden glow. Only Bill stood to one side, waiting for

Tracie. Curious over the commotion, Tracie asked what it was about. Bill was indifferent.

"My beloved ex-spouse has decided to deck everyone out in orchids. She's at that tree by the south windows."

Tracie smiled, though the notion of such frivolity annoyed her. "For one thing, those aren't genuine orchids."

"Tell Marta. But I doubt if you'll convince her. Never mind that. Come here, I want to talk to you."

He put his arm around her waist and led her out into the front hall. She felt uncomfortable there in the perfumed darkness and would have reached for the light switch, but he pulled her arm down.

"No. This is just you and me. I've got to leave you for a few weeks and I want to be sure you'll be all right."

"Where are you going?" She had gotten used to having him near, where she could count on him. "I wish you wouldn't. I mean, right now." She didn't want him to think he was indispensable.

"I'll be back. But I've got to settle a few things. Can I trust you not to do anything stupid while I'm gone?"

She ignored the way he'd phrased the remark, knowing he was really concerned for her well-being. "I've got to get my father to a hospital, so I'll be on Oahu for a few days myself. Can I do something stupid in Honolulu?"

"Probably." Then he hesitated. When he spoke again he took her breath away with his proposition. "How about a word of business advice? Forget that pineapple cannery. It's skidding. Just buy into Dorado Star. Or I'll turn over payments for the cannery to Star, if you say so."

"You must be crazy." She tried to free herself but he had guessed her reaction and held her securely.

"I mean it. Orchid Tree is going downhill. It's not your fault. Or Victor's, for that matter. But he belongs to the old days of the Big Five. Their days are numbered."

"I don't believe it."

He shook her in a friendly way. "Oh, yes, you do. You know it. Take this and look it over in your spare time. Then sign it."

She felt a long envelope wedged into her hand. "What is it?"

"Three stock certificates. Two at ten thousand shares and one at five. Dorado Star will accept twenty-five thousand in Orchid Tree stock. Even trade."

She knew perfectly well that Orchid Tree couldn't be worth an even trade with Dorado

Star. In any case, Orchid was privately owned. It was an absurd deal by which Bill Dempster would stand to lose heavily.

"I'll have to think it over."

She thought he was going to admonish her again but suddenly she felt the warmth of his lips on hers and she surrendered common sense and suspicion for the moment.

Her arms went around his neck, locking behind his back with the envelope between her fingers. His offer meant little to her except another effort to buy into the Berenson properties. It did seem odd that he should choose this particular time when their worth was at a new low, thanks to Victor's illness and the fact that her discretionary power was entirely dependent on her father's whim.

He released her with a slightly breathless chuckle and drew her farther into the hall, away from the others in the warm, pikake-scented darkness.

"One or two other matters. These are crucial."

"I hear and I obey, mighty one."

"You'd better. I know how you Berensons are about family, even your household servants. Tracie," he said, after a moment's hesitation, "I don't want you to trust anyone. As far as you're concerned, everyone is suspect."

"What?"

"Everyone, Tracie. Even Rudi and Kaahu-manu, and the Croydes. Be wary of everything they say or do."

"But they're all nice people."

"Especially when they're nice." He paused and took a breath. She knew another blow was coming. "You said Lady Jade talked about being paid back for her guilt. Something to that effect."

"She said the gods destroyed Theo to punish her."

"Why?"

Confused, she asked, "You mean, why did the gods punish Theo?"

"Not exactly. What does Lady Jade feel she's guilty of? What has she done?"

Tracie didn't want to know. Ever since the discovery of Theo's body she had deliberately banished her first suspicion of the meaning behind Aunt Jade's lament.

"It could be a dozen things. A hundred. She was jealous of Ilima. She ignored her a lot. Treated her coldly. But that's Aunt Jade's way."

"Admit it, because I know you've thought about it...you think she had something to do with Ilima's death, even indirectly. The method, the subtlety, always struck me as her sort. Not Lili's. Not even Theo's. Or your father's."

"My father's!" This was all so pointless. Even

if Jade had planted ideas in Ilima's mind, she was suffering now. And Jade certainly wasn't responsible for what had happened in recent days. "It's Ray Thorpe," Tracie said firmly. "You mark my words. And if Theo was killed, it's because he was coming home to tell us what he found out. Lili and Diane both said he was being very secretive."

Bill slapped the round newel post of the staircase, startling Tracie.

"No question about it," he said. "That's why I believe Theo was murdered. He wanted to try a little polite blackmail first."

She would have liked to argue with him, but more importantly she wanted his assurance that no supernatural presence was around them now.

"Bill, do you smell that scented powder?"

This caught him totally off-guard, and to her surprise he was amused. "Why? You don't need it, my girl. You're quite enough for my libido without it."

"Don't be so conceited. Whom does it remind you of?"

Understanding from her voice that she was serious he sniffed the air thoughtfully.

"A lot of women. Could be anybody." He sniffed again. "What are you getting at? Not that business about some ghostly presence, I hope." Tracie didn't answer, only looked at him beseechingly. With obvious reluctance he added, "It makes me think of Ilima Mako, for some reason. I suppose you're going to tell me she haunts the place and is responsible for your cousin's death. If you think that, you didn't know Ilima."

"No, I don't think that. But she is here, in this hall. Now."

She had finally shaken his self-confidence. He turned away from her slowly, looked around as if he could see in the dark, then stood motionless for several seconds before he stepped over to the wall and felt for the light button. The hall and stairs looked harmless enough. He and Tracie were alone. But somewhat unexpectedly, he didn't make fun of her fantastic statement.

"It's possible, you know, that someone is deliberately contriving to make you think of ghosts rather than the real culprit."

"You never trust anybody. Not even a ghost."

"Always the best policy, honey. And I want you to promise me you'll do the same while I'm gone. For God's sake, be careful and don't trust anyone."

"Okay, I promise. Good Lord! You'll make me scared to go to bed at night."

"As long as you're alone, you'll be safe."

"Okay." Anything to get off the subject of her family's possible guilt. "But where are you going? How can I contact you in case I need you?"

"I'm flattered. You've never acknowledged that possibility before." But he didn't explain, except to say, "You can't. I've tried to look into a few things already but I've gotten nowhere with phone calls and cables, so it's better that I go myself."

"Cables? Are you going to the Coast?"

He pinched her nose. "Sure. China. I don't want it known that I'm out of the Territory." He studied the staircase and the hall around them, shook his head. "I don't believe in ghosts, even benign ghosts like Ilima."

Whatever was with them before had certainly been exorcised by his skepticism...*Maybe it's my imagination after all,* she thought...

"What I believe has happened in your family is certainly not Ilima Mako avenging herself. First of all, don't press your aunt into any explanations about her 'guilt.' Not yet." She nodded, aware of her cowardly relief. "And remember to be cautious, wherever you go. I'll contact you the minute I hear anything."

He kissed her, quickly this time, and gave her shoulders a firm squeeze. "Remember." Then he walked away along the moonlit road to South Harbor.

For the first time in her life she felt completely alone. Deep inside she knew he was right. She could trust no one in the house.

22

Bill's advice had affected Tracie in several ways. She was relieved when she learned that Aunt Jade and Lili would not be accompanying her and Diane when they took her father to the hospital in Honolulu. Somehow she felt more comfortable with as few family members around as possible. Bill's words didn't make her relationship with her father any easier, either.

Six days in the hospital proved to be the absolute limit of Victor's endurance, especially when he was told that his attack had been a light one and that he could live a normal life for years without another attack. Neither of the women believed it, but Victor pointed it out at every possible moment. Since he seemed to have an iron constitution and promised faithfully to take his medicines whenever the occasion warranted, he was released to recuperate in a Royal Hawaiian Hotel suite. He argued about this, as about everything else, insisting he preferred the Moana, which had been his idea of elegance since his first taste of Waikiki luxury shortly after the turn of the century.

Diane adored the lovely pink Royal with its look of a Moorish castle in Spain. "I can't get enough of it," she confessed to Tracie. "All those curved archways. And just standing at the long windows looking out at that incredible aquamarine surf — it's heaven. I don't know why Victor doesn't like it. I mean the room service and the gardenias and orchids they put on your trays...last night there were orchids on my pillow. And I believe I could almost get lost in all those grounds. Green grass and hibiscus and the big red blossom tree..."

Diane's enjoyment of her luxurious surroundings was one of the few good things that had come out of the last year. Tracie was warmed by her enthusiasm.

"Don't worry about my father. If he had been told not to stay at the Royal, you couldn't keep him away. What's his mood right now? I'd like to ask him a question or two about Orchid Tree investments."

Diane shivered. "That tree is a jinx. I know you'll think I'm crazy, but I believe that if that tree wasn't there, Victor and I would have a happy marriage."

Tracie found the idea so ridiculous that for

a moment she didn't know what to say. "Don't worry, things will be better when dad gets on his feet. He's a different man when he's well."

"But to treat his family. . . I don't understand. He and Mr. and Mrs. Croyde had a long conversation before lunch. They had a lovely time. But he treats you so differently, and after you've done so much to help his business. . ."

It was impossible for Tracie to explain to anyone that she regarded her father's business as a family enterprise and that she could overlook her father's moods. During the last three years she had worked as long and hard on it as her father ever had. But there was no doubt that since his illness he had become jealous and looked on everything she did as an effort to undermine his power. It was natural, given Victor Berenson's ruthless egotism. Since Tracie knew herself to be very like him, she understood his fear, but all the same, it hurt.

Diane went into Victor's bedroom in a hopeful mood, inspired perhaps by Tracie's confidence. She came out with a shaky smile.

"Maybe you'd better be very gentle. He does seem cross. It's all this confinement."

Tracie dismissed this advice with the impatience it deserved. "Rubbish. If there's one thing he hates above everything else, it's pussyfooting."

Diane stepped out of the way. Obviously, she didn't want to be in the line of fire. Tracie laughed at her cowardice and walked into the large room whose curtains were opened wide to catch the burning sunset on the Waikiki waters that turned the surf a dull red. Like dried blood, she thought, and was startled by the image.

Victor was stretched comfortably on the chaise longe fully dressed and reading a stack of Honolulu *Star-Bulletin*s that had accumulated over the last ten days. He scowled when he saw her.

"Come to gloat over the old ruin? Surprised you, didn't I? Need more than a little angina to knock me out of the ring."

She was delighted that she could be frank with him. "You look like a million, dad. I thought I'd leave something with you to look over when you have the time."

He glanced at the legal-sized envelope she dropped on the bed. His grin was satirical. "What's this? My latest will?"

She felt as if he had slapped her, but her shock quickly turned to indignation and anger. "Not your latest will," she snapped, "but an offer by Bill Dempster that's more than fair. He wants to give us a chance to buy into Dorado Star. He also gives us a way out of that useless cannery Marta Dempster talked you into."

"Sounds like the enemy has wormed his way in, all right. At least where my daughter is concerned."

She tried to laugh. "Dad, I'm not selling you out, as you well know. Anyway, I'll bring you the books for the last quarter whenever you say."

He rubbed his face, lingering over the eyes. "Sure. Easy enough to dope them up to satisfy the old man. Let me take a look at them. I can always get a CPA to check them."

The envelope dropped to the floor when he brushed it away with the back of one veined, freckled hand.

For one tense moment as she listened to his accusations she felt alone again, like the little girl whose beloved parent had been taken away from her...*I will not cry*, she swore to herself. To cover the hurt she knelt slowly and picked up the envelope. She knew the pain in her voice was evident, and hated its betrayal of her feelings.

"Father, would you be happier if I gave up my job?"

Victor Berenson sat quietly, staring into space, his eyes pale and watery. He struggled to speak, his voice hoarse as the words tumbled out.

"M-maybe...maybe it would be best, for a while. Just 'til we get things worked out."

"Sure, dad," she said stiffly. "I'll rustle around and see if someone else can use me."

"Right, you do that," he said, hesitating. "They're bound to need a girl at South Harbor. They always do. And you're a damned good stenographer."

"Damn good!" she said bitterly. She turned on her heel and left the room, brushing past Diane, who lingered in the hallway.

"What happened?" she whined. "Nobody ever tells me anything. You didn't make Victor angry, did you? You know how upset he gets when—"

"The hell with Victor!" Tracie spat out as she walked toward the exit.

She was in such turmoil that she crossed the spacious flower-scented grounds of the Royal Hawaiian and headed up Kalakaua Avenue before she remembered Bill's warning:

"Don't trust any of the family. Not even the Croydes."

The Croydes had visited Victor shortly before Tracie saw him. Strange that he had managed to be sociable with them. The Croydes had seemed eager to have either Tracie or, more recently, Liliha marry into their family. They had made a polite but prolonged fuss when Lili reluctantly decided to remain with her mother on Akua while her uncle recuperated in Honolulu. Could the Croydes need money? Tracie wondered. Stupid question – rich people always needed money.

She was passing the Moana Hotel when she decided it wouldn't hurt to do a little checking on them. Despite Bill's warning, she didn't believe that Wayne would be involved in any scheming of his parents...possibly he would unwittingly betray something about their plans and motives if she were to ask a few questions.

She went up the wide, old-fashioned steps into the hotel and put through a call to the elegant Croyde home up on the green heights overlooking Honolulu. The senior Croydes weren't home, but Wayne said he'd be glad to see her.

"You'll cheer me up," he said before they ended the conversation.

She suspected the root of his trouble. "How's the job-hunting coming along? Have you heard from any of the pros yet?"

"No. I can't believe they're dumb enough to be put off just because I got laid out during the New Year's game, but it looks like that's what happened. They've got me tabbed as injury-prone. No bids so far."

"How about other fields? Lili says you're

getting out of sports."

"Or it's getting out of me. Dad's advisers keep saying recovery is on the way but you wouldn't know it from the polite brush-offs I get." His laugh had an apologetic sound. "Know anybody who needs a dumb old halfback? I work cheap."

"Somebody must need a brilliant, hardworking halfback. In fact, we—" She broke off, remembering with a painful twist that she was no longer working for her father.

He insisted, "I want to pull my own weight, not be a drag on the market, or whatever they call it. It's specially important, what with my plans and all." He hesitated. "Couldn't you come to dinner tonight? The folks would love it. I know you're in mourning, but we can make it a family affair."

She had been hunting for such an invitation, hoping to find out if the Croydes had anything to do with Victor's new attitude toward her. "Well, I don't know. I suppose I shouldn't — Oh, the devil with it! Theo would have wanted me to. He was always so fond of your family."

"Wonderful! What's a good time for you? You name it, sweetheart."

His endearment made her wince. She had no intention of trying to cut out her cousin, who was far better suited to Wayne.

"I know your folks eat around eight. Suppose I show up a little after six?"

Wayne was delighted. She hung up and went out shopping for something to wear. She hadn't come to Honolulu expecting to do any socializing, but until today she hadn't suspected the Croydes of making trouble between her and her father. And if they went that far, could they — incredibly enough — be responsible for the tragedies that had recently struck the Berensons?

Tracie found a black silk dinner skirt with a long white surcoat. She hoped this, with her mother's diamond earrings, would impress the Croydes without making her look callous about her cousin's death. She wanted to throw the family off balance, let them wonder whether she was still interested in Wayne.

While dressing that evening she was surprised to receive a call from her stepmother, asking when they could expect her to join them in the hotel's elegant dining room.

"Victor gets so cross when he's kept waiting," Diane reminded her.

"Isn't that a pity," Tracie replied. The hurt was too deep. If her father wanted to make up, he would have to do better than that.

Diane was flustered as usual. "But he'll be upset if things don't go smoothly. He asked me particularly to say — I believe he wanted to go over some figures with you."

"Audit my books, in fact."

"He didn't say that. I know he couldn't mean anything like it. He meant — surely he meant some deal or other." She began to plead. "He's certain to blame me if you don't come."

Her constant worry and whining over Victor's bad disposition drove Tracie wild.

"All right, let him blame you. You're a big girl now. Just tell him to shut up."

Tracie heard an indignant gasp but was too upset to care. She knew perfectly well that she was behaving like Victor, but she finished quickly, "I've got an important appointment. I'll see you all later." At the last second she asked, "Have you seen your ex-husband on Oahu?"

She should have known better. Diane swallowed hard. "N-not yet. Have you?"

"No. I'll check with you later."

"Please do, Tracie. Stuck here like this, we never know what's going on."

Tracie said a brisk good-bye and hung up. She finished dressing, depressed and nervous. If she had it to do over again, she would have canceled the Croyde dinner and joined her father. To know peace and his good opinion again would be heaven, but with it had to come understanding and trust.

She had expected to use the car they'd rented for the drive up to the Heights and was made slightly uncomfortable when she received a call from Leopold Croyde, who was in the hotel lobby, just as she was leaving her suite.

"Your chauffeur awaits with pleasure, madame."

She pretended to find this amusing. The truth was, she hadn't planned on being alone with any of the family except for Wayne, and didn't look forward to any time spent alone with his father.

At the last minute she decided to leave a careful message at the front desk: "In case anyone should ask for me, I've gone to dinner with the Croydes. Leopold Croyde is picking me up." Feeling slightly foolish about the precaution she went outside to where Wayne's father waited.

With a great show of gallantry he took her arm, escorting her out along the drive to the tall, lean coco-palms that lined Kalakaua Avenue. There she found Arla Croyde in the big new black family Cadillac. While Leopold made a wide U-turn in the middle of the busy avenue, Arla, who insisted on sitting in the back seat with Tracie, felt it necessary to explain why they had no chauffeur. Leo had found them all inadequate and "It's been impossible to get good native help lately."

Tracie seldom pictured native Hawaiians as servants in livery, under a set schedule, and asked, "Why on earth must they be Hawaiian?" before she realized that economics rather than nationality was at the root of the problem. "It doesn't matter what nationality they are," she said frankly, "we Berensons still can't afford full-time chauffeurs right now."

She caught Leo's quick exchange of glances with his wife in the rearview mirror. Arla patted Tracie's knee.

"My dear, we're still in this wretched Depression. But just you wait. This November we'll get him out of the White House. A four-year term is long enough for any president — even Franklin D. Roosevelt. Personally, I've had to retrench like all our friends on the Heights. My Japanese hairdresser only comes once a week nowadays...but you say Orchid Tree is in trouble?"

"Not Orchid Tree itself. But I'll certainly have to retrench as well. Didn't my father tell you today when you visited him?"

Arla Croyde's voice held a tinge of suspense. "Tell us? About what?"

"Oh, I'm sorry. I thought he might have discussed it with you. We quarreled and my father and I agreed that I would leave the business."

This time she couldn't mistake the under-lying excitement that passed between them in their exchange of looks. They were glad, there was no question about it. But had they put Victor up to it? It made sense if they had, she reasoned. If Tracie and Victor remained alien-ated, Liliha remained the only substantial heir to what they conceived of as the Berenson fortune. And Liliha loved their son, at least for the moment.

Tracie reflected on the fact that she was the only stumbling block to Liliha inheriting the entire estate — something the Croydes had evidently thought of — and felt her flesh creep.

The subject of Tracie's argument with her father was quickly dropped as the Croydes be-gan to discuss how beautifully Wayne and Lili were getting along. For sheer devilment Tracie praised their son, hinting at a desire to resume her own relationship with him. It amused her cynical nature to see how desperately they now played down a connection they had formerly tried to advance.

But Tracie soon tired of this unpleasant game. Her mind wandered as she gazed out the window at the dark jungle growth as they passed Fort DeRussy. She thought of Ray Thorpe and the possibility that he might be stalking Diane or one of the Berensons, maybe even followed them to Honolulu. Could the Croydes know something about him? She hoped not, but there was only one way to find out.

"By the way, did Wayne ever find out anything more about the man on the beach? The one who knocked my father down?"

"A Mr. Thorpe or something like that?" Mrs. Croyde said vaguely. "Leo, how did that turn out?"

Leo shrugged. "I haven't heard any more about it. Except that business about Lili's brother making phone calls. Or was it cables?"

Tracie sat up straight. She remembered the curiously small amount of money Theo had borrowed from Wayne.

"Theo asked Wayne for some money. About ten dollars. Was it in coins?"

"As a matter of fact, it was," Arla Croyde said. "That's why Wayne thought he must have wanted it for pay phones or something. What else would he want a lot of change for? In the end, though, Theo behaved very oddly. Wouldn't tell Wayne a thing. He was quite secretive, in fact." Arla reconsidered. "Unless, of course, he intended to tell us all about it later."

They were heading toward Fort and King streets in the heart of Honolulu. As offices emptied and the many Oriental restaurants in the district filled up, the busy scene reminded

Leo Croyde of something else about Theo's last day in Honolulu.

"Lili's brother hung around several fleabag dumps in the red-light district before he came back to the Alexander Young Hotel."

Tracie sat forward impulsively. The Alexander Young was the best hotel downtown and it was possible that someone would remember Theo's visits.

"I wonder if I could ask an enormous favor of you. Would you make a brief stop there so that I might ask a question or two at the Alex?"

"Of course we'll stop, dear," Arla said.

"Sure thing," her husband echoed. He pulled up in the middle of the street. "I'll just drive around the block until I see you."

"I'll keep you company, dear." Arla pushed her way out of the car after Tracie. She suddenly wished she'd saved this visit for tomorrow, without the Croydes.

The women went into the hotel together and Tracie hesitated. If she gave Mrs. Croyde some innocuous assignment she could question the clerk at the front desk by herself.

"Mrs. Croyde, would you mind asking the cigar-stand people if they remember seeing Theo here ten days ago?"

The woman was delighted to oblige and quickly left.

449

But Tracie had outsmarted herself. The desk clerk had no recollections, one way or another. In fact, Tracie's self-esteem received something of a blow when he seemed never to have heard of any of the Berensons. Did that mean Theo hadn't stayed there? She turned away, feeling this had all been a waste of time, when she saw Arla Croyde waving to her frantically from the cigar stand.

The attractive young cigar-stand attendant, Jimmy Shibata, not only knew the Berensons but had personally known Theo. They had often exchanged gossip and the names of various *malahinis,* especially the pretty female tourists new to the beach at Waikiki. At least Tracie now knew Theo had been to the hotel, as he'd said.

"And you saw him the week before last?"

"That's right. He'd been all over town checking on some beachcomber...Miss Berenson, I was awfully sorry to hear about Theo. He and I had a lot of good times together. He was a great guy."

"Yes. We miss him terribly. The house seems deserted without him."

Jimmy Shibata nodded. He added, to her surprise, "I guess that ghost he talked about will miss him, too."

So Theo had believed in the presence after all!

450

How many things she hadn't known about her young cousin! The thought made her angry once more at the fate that destroyed him at twenty-four, with his whole life ahead of him.

Interestingly enough, Arla Croyde showed no surprise at the remark. "The ghost was a little joke," Tracie said, wanting to get back to Theo's activities in Honolulu. "Tell me, Mr. Shibata, do you know what he was doing here that day, before he left on the inter-island boat?"

Jimmy ran a hand through his thick black hair. "Funny thing. He said something I never figured out and he wouldn't explain. He said—" Jimmy paused for a moment, evidently trying to remember precisely what Theo had told him. "He said, 'I knew it all the time, but I didn't know I knew.'"

Arla Croyde and Tracie exchanged confused looks.

"Did he say anything else about it?" Tracie asked.

"Not exactly. He went on about how he'd been told the truth and hadn't paid any attention. I never did find out what it was about."

Tracie looked at Arla Croyde, whose forehead wrinkled in thought.

"What else do you remember?" Tracie said, coaxing him.

Jimmy stopped and sold a package of cigarettes to a portly Chinese businessman. When he came back to them he admitted he couldn't remember anything else about it.

"But he did use the cable office here in the hotel," Jimmy said.

Tracie looked around the lobby, saw that the cable office was closed. After thanking the young man she and Mrs. Croyde returned to the street.

"What on earth do you think that was all about?" Arla mused. "It sounds mysterious to me."

Tracie hoped to throw her off the track. She didn't need the Croydes hampering her investigation. "Who knows, but it couldn't be that important. Thank goodness, here comes Mr. Croyde. I could use a good dry martini."

Leopold Croyde rolled to a stop and picked them up. As Tracie got in after Arla Croyde she caught the woman's slight shrug in answer to her husband's raised eyebrows. Whatever they knew, they didn't know enough.

The picturesque drive cut straight into one of the many sharp green creases in the Koolau Range that served as a backdrop for Honolulu. When Tracie looked back, as she always did, the city itself was half-hidden by coco-palms, hibiscus, plumeria and a hundred tropical trees and plants that almost obliterated the twinkling city lights.

She found herself missing Bill Dempster more than ever, wanting to enjoy this scene with him. Curiously enough, it was no longer just the physical tie that bound them. She never tired of his company. He might annoy, anger or infuriate her, but the thought of him always set off sparks of excitement in her. She realized that she enjoyed the stimulation of conflict with him nearly as much as her memory of their lovemaking.

Leo Croyde drove up through almost impenetrable jungles of tangled trees, flowers, roots and carpets of eternally moist grass. Finally he pulled up and parked in the driveway of the big, two-story house whose lanai, on the cliffside, overlooked most of Honolulu far below. Wayne came loping out to meet them. He was so glad to see Tracie that she wondered uncomfortably if his affections had been rekindled.

It seemed unlikely, though. His attitude, while attentive, was more brotherly than romantic. Before cocktails he seated himself on the arm of her chair but patted her on the back in a comradely way when she ordered her usual dry martini.

"Tough as ever, our Tracie," he kidded her.

"She can hold her liquor, too."

"Not like dear little Lili," Mrs. Croyde purred. "She's so dainty. She doesn't have your strength and — force. But we adore her."

Leo Croyde handed his wife her thick, sweet brandy Alexander and settled down with his own martini, into which he carefully dropped a piece of chipped ice.

Tracie tried to maneuver them onto the subject of their visit with her father, but they appeared to know nothing beyond the fact that he was "a bit cross," probably because of his illness. Tracie then pressed Wayne for further details of the search he and Lili had made to find Ray Thorpe. Although it was clear that he knew nothing he hadn't told her, he seemed anxious to talk to her alone. Several times he mentioned that he would drive her back to the Royal Hawaiian. The third time was out on the lanai, where they ate dinner in the soft blue tropic night. The soft light dropping in little pools from Japanese lanterns strung at each corner of the lanai bathed their faces in gold light and shadow. Tracie was surprised and discomfited by the uneasiness this brought back to her; she felt a recurrence of the mistrust that troubled her earlier in the afternoon and remembered Bill's warning: *Don't trust anyone, not even the Croydes.*

She was relieved when the dinner ended and Wayne drove her down from the Heights shortly after eleven o'clock. The air was warm and thick with the scent of flowers along the roadside.

Wayne sniffed and grinned. "Kind of makes you drunk, doesn't it? Lili wears a perfume like that." He was in a strange mood, exultant but nervous. "Say, Trace, guess what?"

"What?"

He swung around toward the mountain pass instead of the *makai* direction, toward the sea, but her thoughts were elsewhere and she felt deeply depressed. She knew that her biggest problem, perhaps her greatest hurt, was the quarrel with her father. She wondered if they could ever mend it without leaving an irreparable break between them . . . The Croydes were interested in the news and though she couldn't be sure, they seemed to know nothing about it. Maybe the split had been inevitable, given Victor's character and her own.

Wayne's voice cut into her painful thoughts.

"I can't stand around waiting to be picked by the pros. That damned injury in front of sixty thousand fans blacklisted me. They think I'm a gimp, I guess."

"I'm sorry. It doesn't seem fair."

He slapped the wheel. "But it doesn't really

matter. I've got a job. An offer, anyway."

She was genuinely happy for him. "That's great. What is it?"

"Cruise director's office on Uncle Bill's steamship line. The *Lorelei* office called me just before closing. Maybe I'll be on the *Lorelei* itself if I can handle it. A lot of public relations. Bill's trans-Pacific manager thinks I'd be good at it."

"Wonderful! Then you didn't talk to Bill yourself?" If only she could have a long talk with Bill right now!

"No, he's wandering around somewhere on the Coast."

She looked out at their dark surroundings, aware for the first time that they were headed up the winding jungle-bordered road to the Nuuanu Pali. "What the devil?" She remembered their last trip up there, eight months ago. "Wayne, I hope we're not going to repeat out last scene up here."

He reached out to cover her hand with his. "Nope. Just wanted to be serious for a minute. I don't know any place where a guy can be more serious."

She was puzzled but his manner remained comradely and she decided not to worry that he would become obnoxious.

The pali was dark. Even the moonlight hadn't

yet illuminated the edges of the great, sheer cliff from which, long ago, King Kamehameha had sent the defending army of Oahu tumbling down to its death. Beyond the pali, the windward coast to the east and north lay dark and verdant, without a single man-made light to spoil the scene. Wayne pulled the car over and got out, leaving the engine running. She let herself out when he didn't come around to her side, and walked over to him.

"What's this all about?" she asked, more sharply than she had intended. He didn't look directly at her, but stood staring up at the stars.

"Honey, would you do me a big favor? It was right here I asked you to marry me the night you graduated. Remember? That was a great night."

"I remember. But it wasn't there. It was here." She walked closer to the edge, looking over and down at heavy growth that masked the face of the cliff.

It reminded her of Mauna Pā-ele.

The thought gave her a sudden chill. She turned to see Wayne standing there a few yards behind her, huge and hulking, his features faintly brushed by starlight.

"That's exactly the way it was," he said. His voice sounded hushed and reverent.

He couldn't mean her harm, she thought. Not Wayne.

She cleared her throat, spoke calmly. "I was here and you were there, Wayne. I was a lucky girl." Why did she imagine his eyes glittered? It was something completely foreign to his nature.

"Oh, I don't know about that. Anyway, you said you weren't sure." The matter-of-factness of it startled her. "But I had to be certain this time."

"Certain of what?" She told herself she was being very calm.

He started toward her with his long, loping stride.

"That it's over." His grin was definitely sane, and the starlight did wonders for that smile. "Honey, before I ask Lili to marry me, I have to be sure I'm over you." He clapped his hands. "And I am."

She didn't know whether to be relieved or insulted. While she recovered from the preposterous notion that Wayne might have meant to hurt her, he went on, his voice anxious. "I hope I didn't hurt your feelings, Tracie. But I don't think you and I would ever suit. Lili, on the other hand, is so — well." He brightened again. "She's Lili."

She took his hands and held them warmly. "I couldn't be happier. I just hope she appreciates you."

He protested that idea, insisting it was the other way around. As they walked back to the car, arm in arm, she couldn't get over the absurdity of her recent suspicions. *Talk about appreciating a man,* she thought. *I never appreciated Wayne enough. Or Bill, for that matter.* She resolved that now it would be different. Bill had certainly demonstrated, especially since Theo's death, that he genuinely cared for her — how many times had he cautioned her to be careful? — and he wasn't scheming to ruin her family's business in order to benefit his own. She only hoped it wasn't too late, that there was still a chance he would want her...

"Wayne, can we go right back to town, now that it's all settled about you and Lili?"

"Sure thing," he said. Tracie couldn't help noticing that dear, thoughtful Wayne sounded enormously relieved. "Then you won't object when I speak to your father about Lili?"

"Absolutely not. I'm behind the two of you all the way."

They drove back to town and then out to Waikiki, both in excellent spirits at the prospect of the marriage. As they talked about Wayne's plans Tracie found herself sharing in his excitement and almost forgot the bitterness between her father and herself.

23

Three days later Victor Berenson was on his way back to Akua.

The fact that an early season hurricane might be headed for the Territory had no cautionary effect on Victor. When informed of possible bad weather ahead, he reminded the Honolulu doctors that he had to be home to protect "my" island. No one bothered to remind him that Akua was an American territory and he didn't actually own it. He was simply an important landowner.

In listening to her father's conversation with the doctors, Tracie realized more and more that Bill Dempster had a point in his favor when he spoke of unions and the rights of those field and factory workers that she and Victor had taken for granted for as long as she could remember.

She went along in the Berenson steamer but found herself on the fringe of the group. She seemed more of an outsider even than Wayne Croyde, who made the voyage in order to propose officially to Lili. It was clear to Tracie that she was still out of her father's good graces. He avoided her whenever he could, spending most of his time with Wayne discussing football.

Diane, as usual, didn't know what to do. "If Theo were here, he could soothe Victor," she moaned.

"Well, he's not here and that's not true anyway. Wayne got along better with dad than Theo ever did. They have more in common... sports and all."

"Well, Theo was always ready to help me," Diane said as the two women watched the approaches of Akua from the upper deck of the steamer.

Diane waved her hands helplessly. "Somebody or something, I don't know what — is getting to him." She looked at the small island, her face etched with anxiety. "That house scares me, with the ghost of that woman and all."

Tracie was exasperated to hear her mention it again and made no attempt to hide her annoyance.

"And what about that rival of his, Bill Dempster?"

"What do you mean by *rival?*" Tracie said, though she well knew. It was a misreading of Bill's character that Tracie herself had encouraged for months.

"Well, friendly rival, I guess. I know how you feel about Mr. Dempster, that you like him. But I always thought maybe he wanted to cut Victor out on the Island." Tracie didn't respond, not quite sure what to say without betraying the extent of her feelings as well as her suspicions about the family, including Diane. They stood together watching the approaching shoreline, the first cliffs and then the crescent curve of Akua City's tiny harbor. There were no signs of the promised hurricane. The water was calm and only the excessive heat of the wind and the sultry air offered a promise of bad weather to come. Diane shivered as if she'd had a sudden chill.

"Tracie, the night Theo returned home he came this way, by this boat. Do you think there's something strange about Akua? Theo was fine until he reached here." She closed her eyes. "I know it's crazy. It's probably Ray after all, up to his old tricks."

"We just don't know," Tracie said, not wanting to commit herself one way or another. "After Wayne knocked him down at Waikiki he probably took the first ship back to the Coast."

Diane tried hard to throw off their morbid ideas. "Maybe you're right. We didn't see him this time in Honolulu. Not even once. And besides, he wouldn't know about Victor's pride and vanity. That's what his quarrel with you is all about. Just pride."

"You can blame dad's own ego. It's pure cussedness."

"Oh, don't say that! He isn't himself. That's all."

"Ha!"

Tracie wasn't about to let this young woman read her secret feelings. Her father's behavior cut her to the heart, but like Victor, she, too, had her pride.

A quarter of an hour later Victor went ashore, striding vigorously across the gangplank in an evident demonstration of his robust health. Though she pretended otherwise, Tracie couldn't help overhearing her father's references to Wayne as "my boy," blustering about how he would "fit in very well, kind of like the heir apparent." The remarks were biting and, as Tracie knew, for her sole benefit.

Wayne's reaction to it was offhand, a little confused. As they walked along the jetty to the Packard parked in front of Nakazawa's store he tried to head off Victor's effusive talk.

"This isn't my line of country, sir. Not for a

long time, anyway. I can make it on my own. You'll see . . . with Lili, I can do anything. She's such a precious little thing."

"Sure is," Victor said. "And plenty expensive, too. Just ask her mother. Not that Jade pays the bills. That's handled by my—" He glanced at Tracie, scowled and looked away, "—my bookkeepers." Having gotten in his final dig he waved expansively to Rudi Arguello, who greeted them as he walked down the slope to the jetty.

Lili had stopped to chat with the Nakazawas, but by the time Wayne reached the shore, only a step or two from the tide pool where Albie Wimble's fishnets, newly mended, had been weighted again, Lili was running down the dirt road to meet him. The sight of the powerful athlete lifting the petite, sloe-eyed beauty off the ground and welcoming her with a big kiss was enough to move even Victor. Tracie was happy for them, envious of the ease of their relationship, and Diane was predictably misty-eyed.

"If only her brother could have lived to see this," she murmured, fumbling for her handkerchief.

Tracie wasn't at all sure Diane's view of Theo's response was an accurate one. It sounded much too sentimental to Tracie, who had known him far better. Still, she was poignantly aware of something missing in this return to Akua. If Theo were home he would be on the jetty or on the hill beside the Nakazawas, waving cheerfully at the approaching steamer.

Victor put on a fair performance of sociability but Tracie thought he looked drawn and tired, despite his earlier show of exuberance. In Honolulu he had been living a more or less reclusive life, due in part to his doctors' instructions. He probably found it difficult to face all the family greetings and resultant confusion.

"Good to have you home, sir," Rudi said, shaking his hand. "It's been quiet as a tomb—" He stopped, correcting himself. "Awfully quiet." He turned to Tracie. "Very pleased to see you, Miss B. Orchid Tree missed you."

Victor looked away as Rudi greeted his daughter, seeming sad and puzzled as if he were momentarily lost. Tracie longed to cheer him up, revive his spirits the way she always had, and wished their feud could end. The moment was lost when Victor impatiently began to bark orders. "Well, let's go. What's the delay?"

He got into the back seat of the car, calling to the others. "Dinah, you coming? And you, Lili." He mimicked Rudi's greeting to Tracie in a low tone. " 'Orchid Tree missed you.' Missed *you,* as if *you* were Orchid Tree."

They had all heard Victor's mutterings and silently piled into the car, uncomfortable over what appeared to be an acceleration of Victor's feud with his daughter.

Everyone was grateful when Lili leaned forward and chattered away with Wayne, who shared the front seat with Tracie, breaking the tension. When they reached the house Jade stood on the west lanai to greet them. She welcomed Wayne with a frosty courtesy that must have unnerved him, and her attitude toward Tracie was curiously evasive. She didn't meet her niece's eyes, though she made no effort to draw back when Tracie hugged her. She looked very old, more than her fifty-five years. Her spirit seemed to be broken. She gave Victor a furtive side-glance, and when he kissed her briskly she spoke directly to him.

"Mr. Dempster cabled Tracie yesterday from his ship. I called the sugar mill. I asked them to send a cable to the *Lorelei* telling him Tracie was in Honolulu. I did not know then that you were returning so soon."

He scowled. "I see my family is still selling me out to Johnny-come-latelies."

Everyone looked at Tracie, which further angered her.

"If he's good enough to be your house guest and to make deals with us for useless pineapple factories, he can't be much of an enemy."

No one knew what to say to this, and the family broke up as they went their separate ways.

Diane walked with Tracie upstairs to their rooms. "I really can't figure out your father at all. What's wrong with him?"

"I don't know. Maybe his illness has gotten him further down than I thought. I suppose I'll have to keep it quiet when I send a message to Bill. If he's on the *Lorelei* it's due in at ten tomorrow morning. Too late to get the inter-island boat until the afternoon."

Diane looked worried. "Oh, is he coming here? That certainly will upset your father. But I really can't see why he's so bitter."

"Besides everything else, dad is going to hate sleeping on the ground floor...there are so many changes coming."

Diane had insisted that Victor should follow the doctor's orders and not use any stairs.

"I know," she said nervously. "For a while anyway he'll have to sleep in – her room."

"And you?" Tracie knew how Diane felt about the room, and couldn't imagine her staying there with him.

She clutched her bare shoulders, though the

air was as muggy as Kona weather. "I don't know. If I can just get to sleep at night, I'll be okay. Victor's medicine chest has some laudanum. I could take a drop or two now and then."

"For heaven's sake, throw it out!" Tracie said, admonishing her. "That must be very old. I remember they used to give it to my mother. It's illegal in some states now. Just get rid of it."

Diane didn't respond to this, but looked over her shoulder before she moved closer to Tracie and spoke again. "I wouldn't mind anything so much if only we could get rid of that awful tree."

"I couldn't agree more," Tracie said, though for different reasons. To her the tree was a nuisance. "If dad weren't so adamant, I'd have the damned thing cut down."

But Diane had other worries. "It was *her* tree. She's still here. Do you think she's trying to tell us something?"

Tracie knew she had to put Diane's fears to rest once and for all, and couldn't understand why she persisted in them. "Do you mean to say you think Ilima's ghost is acting through the orchid tree? Diane, don't you really see how silly that sounds?"

"I don't care," Diane persisted, her voice rising. "Maybe it's trying to warn us, make us see who was really responsible for her death. Maybe an heir, someone who didn't want her to marry your father."

"Don't be ridiculous," Tracie snapped angrily. "Ilima's suicide has nothing to do with what's going on now."

Victor's voice from the first floor cut through this preposterous yet disturbing conversation.

"Dinah! Where the hell did that boy put my stuff? What are you doing upstairs? You know that idiot doctor told me to stay down here. You want to get me killed?"

Diane started suddenly, then rushed past Tracie and hurried down the stairs.

No wonder Victor's relations with women were never entirely successful, Tracie thought with some contempt. They spoiled him rotten!

Tracie went to her own room and set about unpacking the sports clothes and the dinner outfit she had worn in Honolulu. Everything had to be done quickly before Aunt Jade sent Kaahumanu or one of the other women to hang her clothes all too neatly in the long closet. After such meticulous treatment it was always hard to find anything.

When she finished she went to the window, opening the slatted blinds to bring in more air. A faint, moist, muggy heat met her. She was about to close the shutters and rely on the overhead fan when she saw her aunt step off the east lanai below her windows and start toward the Mauna Pā-ele trail. The air moved among the flowering bushes. The hibiscus and plumeria turned as if their bright faces watched her somber form, leaner than ever in its black silk brocade.

What was Aunt Jade doing on that trail? She wasn't the adventurous type. She never hiked. Yet there she was, carrying something in one hand, a handful of sticks. Looking more closely Tracie saw that it wasn't sticks of wood, it was incense.

Tracie could think of nothing that Lady Jade Wong would use incense for. She had been married and her children baptized in the old Kawaiahao Church on Oahu, which was Christian, and presumably she did not practice any other religion, although her ancestors had been Buddhists. Perhaps she had reverted after Theo's death and was offering up prayers to those ancesters for the repose of her son.

But why on Mauna Pā-ele? Theo was buried in the family cemetery between the McCallister and Berenson fields.

Slowly it dawned on her...it was the suspicion Bill had planted that wouldn't go away, about the guilt Aunt Jade kept talking about after Theo's death. Tracie knew that eventually Jade would have to be confronted about it. Certainly her father wasn't up to the task — how could Tracie tell him about her suspicions when he wouldn't even speak to her? Her mind made up, Tracie went out quickly and raced down the stairs.

Her pace slowed when she reached the east lanai. She had no proof of anything — it was only a suspicion, based on her aunt's mysterious allusion to her own guilt. She might be feeling guilty about any number of things. Still, Tracie knew it was important to learn what troubled her so and she continued to walk carefully behind her aunt, hating every moment of the sly pursuit.

Tracie wondered how far Aunt Jade would go, climbing over and around the broken limbs and rotting greenery that had carpeted the trail since the persistent spring rains. She seemed to know the way and had evidently gone this route before. Was it a pilgrimage of conscience?

Jade moved rapidly without looking back. The hem of her surcoat was split up the sides, which helped her to move easily. Her pace was rapid and Tracie reasoned that, like herself, she must have been tired by the time she skirted the pool of Ribbon Falls, but she didn't stop.

Jade slipped on a pile of dead ferns just before she reached the point where Ilima had leaped to her death. To Tracie's horror Jade fell to one knee, but she quickly regained her balance, got up silently and went on. She seemed to be headed to the exact spot where Ilima had leaped to her death. A faint, warm breeze blew across the peak, carrying with it the mingled scent of fragrant flowers and the decaying undergrowth from the heart of the jungle that covered the mountain.

Having reached the spot where Ilima's body had been brought up, Jade sank to her knees again, carefully this time. She huddled over the incense sticks, protecting them from the wind until she'd finally succeeded in lighting one of them. She remained kneeling at the sheer face of the Mauna Pā-ele pali with her head bowed. Tracie supposed that she was praying, whether for the soul of the lost Ilima or for her own forgiveness, it was impossible to know. But the fact that she'd come to this place seemed to confirm Bill's suspicion that she'd had some part in Ilima's suicide.

Jade raised her arm, heaved one of the incense sticks over the edge while intoning something in her native language. She repeated the act with a second stick.

Tracie moved quietly to join her, touching her gently on the shoulder. Jade started at her touch, but looking up into Tracie's face she seemed resigned to having been found there. Her eyes looked dull, her body listless.

"It is not enough. Never enough," she said quietly, without expression.

Though on some level moved by her aunt's suffering, Tracie couldn't bring herself to sympathize. She could only remember Ilima's pain too well.

"I see her when I sleep," Jade said, avoiding Tracie's eyes. "I even see her each day when I go to my boy's grave." She leaned over and began to light another stick.

"No, Aunt Jade. This won't help. It won't bring her back." She spread her fingers over the incense, pushing it to the ground before she withdrew her hand. She took a deep breath, determined that now was the time to release all of her pent-up bitterness over her friend's senseless death. "Do you know how many of Ilima's bones were broken when Rudi found her?" Jade's lips worked nervously. "Can you imagine her last thoughts up here, her despair, just before she jumped?"

Jade raised her chin defiantly. "Yes, I can imagine," she said, her voice flat. "I know that despair since my boy died...and before. Yes. Even then."

Tracie knelt on the crushed grass, staring at

the older woman. For the first time in her life Tracie saw her aunt as a broken creature, helpless against the awful pain of her loss.

"You hounded an innocent woman to her death because you were afraid my father's wife would inherit Orchid Tree. Theo and Lili would get less. Isn't that it?"

Aunt Jade opened her tight mouth, gave an eerie cry that floated on the sultry air like a strange bird. A joss stick broke in her fingers.

"You think I did it for money? Property? You know me so little!"

Finally the awful truth was out.

"What then?"

"For him. Victor. Always it was the same." The ashes of the incense flared anew into life. "We were together all the years after your mother died." She waved the sticks. "Not physically, but what does that matter? Our spirits were one. We talked. Worked. Planned for Orchid Tree, the household. We were souls belonging together. Then this — this native woman came into the house. I was put aside. The old good times together were gone. This woman came along and took the place of all we were to each other."

"How did you find out about her father? Who betrayed her?"

She laughed abruptly. "She herself. The silly

creature, so worried because of a scurf upon her hands. There was a soap she used about then. Violets from France. It is most likely what caused her skin to break out. At first when I saw it, I am free to say, I told her it was ugly and Victor would despise it. I assured her of the truth. You know your father. He abhors sickness, weakness, ugliness."

"I know," Tracie said. He would hardly permit it even in himself.

"Well then, she cried, the poor, cringing thing! So like the one in the house now. She told me of her father, and I thought of the good years with Victor, the years without her. And I thought — these years can come again. All it needs is for this *hapa-haole* to be gone from here. One day, in the kitchen, she talked of dying...she would rather die than have Victor know...she would die before she would be sent to Kalaupapa. She had seen the way the lepers bound for Kalaupapa are kept on that lower deck of the boat. She knew they would never see their homes again, or those they loved. She thought of this. And she died."

"My God!" Tracie blurted, horrified.

This woman was a monster, and yet she was pitiful. Far more pitiful than poor, brave, suffering Ilima. Tracie knelt silently for a moment, struggling to comprehend what she was hearing. When she spoke her voice was heavy with irony. "And now are you happy, Aunt Jade? Do you think that when you get rid of Diane by frightening her to death with ghosts and whatnot, things will be the way they were before? Was it you who threw that sign into the ravine because you thought Diane was in the truck?"

Jade sat looking at her, shaking her head slowly. "But it was you who were hurt, not that one. You believe I could kill you? You are flesh of his flesh. I do not kill. Not even her."

"You killed Ilima Mako. And you seem to be just as effective in scaring Diane to death."

"I let the *hapa-haole* die. I would let this one die. But I would not kill her. If I did such a thing, maybe next time they would take from me my girl."

Jade was still afraid of her ancestral gods. Tracie believed that much was true. But was she responsible for the terrors the household had known since Victor announced his engagement to Diane Thorpe?

"Aunt Jade, what about that powdery perfume, the presence we feel in the house?"

Her aunt smiled grimly. "Now you talk a great deal of foolishness. Would I be here offering my prayers for the dead one if I made these things happen?"

Tracie got up, aching for the woman, for the dead Ilima and for what must come now. "I don't know. If you leave now, maybe we'll never know."

"If I leave?"

"You must."

Incredibly, Jade never seemed to have thought that she might be cast out of her home for her actions. She looked stricken, her pale skin drawn and haggard.

"I cannot go. My life is here. My child is to be married."

"She will be married wherever you go."

"I go? For how long?"

Forever, Tracie thought, but she couldn't say it aloud. Jade would never leave Akua willingly. "I don't know."

"For weeks? Months? How can I leave here? My life is here. My boy is buried here."

"At least for a little while," Tracie said. "We will see how things go." She helped the older woman to her feet, and for the first time in Tracie's memory her aunt didn't shrug off her assistance. When Tracie started to walk, Jade moved beside her like an automaton.

They had already passed the shallow pool at the top of Ribbon Falls when Jade spoke. "Victor will not want me to go. My husband was the first of the Berensons to settle on Akua.

Victor loved his brother. He will not forsake me."

Tracie fired herself to anger, forcing out all pity. Recent events for the family had been so traumatic that she could not afford to let Jade go on — who knew what extremes she was capable of? And what about Diane's safety? Clearly Jade had been filling the young woman's mind with talk of haunted trees and ghosts. Every time Tracie thought of what Jade had done to Ilima Mako and the devious manner in which she'd created an unbearable fear in Ilima's mind, she hardened against her. "Father must know what you did."

Aunt Jade pulled Tracie's sleeve. "No, never. Promise me."

"Only if you go."

Jade walked on, blindly unaware even when a fern frond snapped across her eyes. Tracie put her hand out, making a path for her aunt between the ferns, but she knew it didn't matter. Jade felt nothing. She was locked in the anguish of losing the house that was a part of her and the presence of the man she had loved for most of her life.

When they reached the plantation house Jade stopped before they stepped up on the lanai. She stared ahead, avoiding Tracie's eyes.

"I will go. I will visit Chin Loo's cousin in

Lahaina. She has asked me very often to come and see her."

The village of Lahaina, once a great whaling port, was just across the channel from Akua, but Tracie could not see how further exile could be explained without someone being forced to tell the truth. Aunt Jade's "visit" must simply be prolonged.

With a sudden, blustering confidence Jade said, "You are as hard as Victor. But you will need me. In a month, a week, you will ask me to come back."

The thought of Orchid Tree without Jade was a difficult one, but Tracie could not blot out the memory of this woman's subtle reign of terror, which had apparently gone on long after Ilima was dead.

Only Diane seemed to understand what was really happening when Jade explained her sudden voyage, saying that there was illness in Chin Loo's family and she was needed. The others assumed she would be returning in a matter of days.

"We want to be married in July," Lili insisted. "Don't forget, mother. That gives you less than two weeks."

"Or as soon as my job is official," Wayne added.

Victor and Diane sat on the lanai sipping

mai-tais while Jade was upstairs packing her things. She and Tracie had agreed that she would pack enough for a short trip so as not to cause suspicion; the rest of her things would be sent by boat later. Considering Diane's limited knowledge of the truth behind Jade's departure, Tracie thought her stepmother was most effusive in her farewell. Victor kissed Jade on the cheek, told her to be a good girl, and settled back into his chair.

Jade looked back only once, a long look as if to memorize every detail of the comfortable old house she had run for the last thirty years and the man she had loved as well.

Appropriately enough, she left on the Berenson cargo ship, *Akua Orchid,* the last of the privately owned ships with a commission from the Territorial Health Service to carry occasional patients to Kalaupapa.

There were three of them that afternoon on the lower deck, two men and a pretty, dark-eyed girl, all bound for the leper peninsula. The patients had already endured their farewells at the dock in Honolulu with hymns, prayers and forbidden embraces by their loved ones. The two men, not surprisingly, appeared a little the worse for liquor. Their swollen faces were partially hidden as they squatted on the deck close together, seeking a ghastly kind of brotherhood.

The girl had a strange, detached look as though she had already cut all ties with the life she knew. Swellings appeared across her forehead in a ridge, and on one of her hands. The bridge of her delicate nose was already attacked. She stared at the distant peak of Mauna Pā-ele and seemed beyond sadness, the lovely lower half of her face untouched as yet by the loathsome disease.

This "cargo" on the lower deck of the *Akua Orchid* was already considered dead in the eyes of the world.

Tracie could not bear to look at the girl. At times like this, she felt incredibly lucky just to be alive. She watched as Lili and Wayne hugged and kissed Aunt Jade, then added her own embrace, but the sight of the young woman going to Kalaupapa had reminded her again of her aunt's crime.

"Maybe I will go on to Honolulu," Jade said to Tracie in a low voice. "There is still trouble here. I could send help...maybe the Dempster man when his ship docks."

"No. We don't want you interfering," Tracie told her coldly. "The only evil in that house is leaving today."

Jade raised her head, turned and walked away.

Minutes later, while Jade stood on the upper

deck, staring up to where she knew Valley House lay, the ship pulled out.

Lili and Wayne walked back up from the jetty with Tracie. Lili puzzled over her mother's rapid departure, but Wayne kissed away her questions.

"Mother kept standing there on the deck, staring. It wasn't like her at all. She looked so sad."

"I'd be sad too, if I were saying good-bye to you, sweetheart," Wayne assured her.

Tracie stopped at the head of the hill above Nakazawa's store and watched the steamer turn in midstream and head for Molokai.

She felt a kind of relief knowing she wouldn't have to tell her father the truth about her aunt, but at the same time she knew it wouldn't be easy to carry the burden alone. In that moment she slowly realized she wasn't alone and never would be, even without her father's love and trust...now there was Bill, and with that comforting thought she hurried up the slope, anxious to send a message to his hotel in Honolulu. She wanted to tell him what she'd learned, and even more to feel the safety of his presence in the house. Aunt Jade's part in the recent tragedies was clear, but she had had nothing to do with Theo's death. Until they knew the whereabouts of Ray Thorpe, Tracie would be unable to rest easily. The unseasonal Kona weather gave the western sky a peculiar dusty glow and she felt briefly warmed, knowing that soon Bill would be there.

24

It was not until Diane was laying out Victor's bath towels, soap and pajamas that she realized a subtle change had come over the house with Jade's departure. Highly charged and excited, she called to Tracie who was, as she'd said, "battening down the hatches against the promised big blow."

"Come in here, Tracie. Quick."

In the rear cross-hall Tracie hesitated. Diane took her by the wrist. "Come inside. Now, sniff. What do you smell?"

Tracie obeyed. Not quite sure, she looked around Ilima Mako's room, which had been refurnished for Victor.

"I guess I smell that awful soap of dad's. I must say, a well-brought-up horse would kick up his heels at the idea of being scrubbed with that."

"No, no. Think. Her perfume is gone. See?"

Tracie moved slowly around the room. In

spite of the racket being made outside by the blowing orchid tree and the flowering bushes nearby, she thought that Diane was right. Whatever had been in the room had disappeared.

"I don't believe it," Tracie whispered. She felt stupid for having believed anything in the first place.

Was this all Ilima had wanted, just that the truth about her death be known?

"Frankly," Tracie said, "I was never completely convinced there was anything, but I'm glad you're not frightened anymore."

Diane sounded shocked. "There had to be. We all felt the same thing. But that's over now. I'm convinced of it. It's almost pleasant in here." She paused briefly, looked at Tracie and smiled. "I guess I won't be needing that laudanum now."

Tracie rolled her eyes. "I thought I told you to get rid of it."

Footsteps in the hall startled both women. Diane's euphoria carried over into her present mood. As they reached the door she laughed, talking loudly over the noise of the windblown bushes outside, "I will, but don't be silly. I'd never take laudanum. I know better than that."

Wayne Croyde looked at the two women. Arm in arm, he and Lili had come in to escape the hot night wind whipping across the lanai.

"Sure hope not, Mrs. Berenson. Mom knew an old lady that died that way."

"Heavens!" Diane cried. "What a horrid subject! I'm going to get Victor. It's time for his bath."

At least Diane had learned her lesson about sleep-inducing drugs. It was a relief to Tracie, who knew that the night was going to be noisy and might frighten the mainland woman who wasn't used to the lashing of tropic storms.

As the wind rose, preceding what they hoped was only the tail of a hurricane, the hot, muggy air rattled everything in the house that was not firmly protected behind heavy doors. The orchid tree tossed its flowery mane and showed signs of showering the area of the less-sturdy lanai with blooms. Wayne, Rudi and Sam Kahana went around barricading the fragile areas, staking the plants nearest the house and eyeing the gradually blackening sky uneasily. The tropic sky at this hour of the night was never quite black — always a faint ember of the day illuminated the westerly horizon, but this was curtained from them now by the approaching storm.

Tracie went out with Chin Loo and Kaahumanu to straighten the littered lanai, but they soon gave it up as useless. Tracie found herself being regarded strangely by the two servants she had known most of her life, and she realized that they blamed her for Aunt Jade's departure. Probably they thought she'd sent her away at Diane's behest. She longed for the sake of her own reputation among the servants to set them straight, but knew she couldn't.

The supervision of the estate at a time of danger was Victor's job. Though he did his best and stood for an hour giving orders, they were confused and contradictory. He finally weakened, yielding to Diane's insistence that he come inside.

Tracie heard him say to Diane, "She'll love this. She's finally running the place. Guess it's what she wanted all the time."

Wayne, who had overheard this, tried to reassure Tracie. "He's just feeling bad. He's afraid he isn't wanted."

"Sure, I know." But it hurt nonetheless.

She thought with longing of Bill Dempster's arrival the next night. She could tell Bill, and only Bill, all that had happened about Jade, about Victor's strange turning from her. Meanwhile, the noisy, roaring night and what she hoped would be the safer daylight hours lay ahead.

Tracie couldn't have told anyone, even Bill, why she still felt the awful, haunting sense of dread that awakened her in the hour before dawn. She sat up listening, then understood. The house was silent, so still that the silence itself had roused her. There were always rustlings of birds and small creatures outside her windows in the trees and on the grass close by. Now there was nothing but an unearthly silence. It was as if all the living creatures waited breathless for the big blow.

Although she couldn't see it from her windows on the east side of the house, she knew that the waters around the coastline must be in a ferment, no longer blue, now an eerie black, with reddish smears like blood in the trough of each wave.

She got up and dressed hurriedly. All her dresses were made in the current style, the straight skirts far too long to be serviceable. She wore her oldest pair of slacks and a cotton blouse that would protect her body in case of extreme heat. Above all, she would need her longest raincoat, with the yellow sou'wester rain hat.

She had barely finished dressing when the rain started. Wind-driven, it beat down in torrents only seconds after the first drops hit the slatted windows.

"We're in for it now," she said to Diane, who came running to her room in a panic. "But the house will survive. It always has."

Diane wrung her hands. "Why does it come from all directions? It's like being inside an egg beater."

They heard Lili's bright, high laughter in the hall. She, too, was up but with an enthusiasm Diane couldn't understand. She stuck her head into Tracie's room.

"That's what it is, Di. We're in this high valley surrounded on three sides by walls of jungle. What do you expect? Come out on the west lanai. You can see the Akua harbor. In a couple of hours it'll be a mess."

"I'd advise you to dress first," Tracie suggested. "Those satin pajamas aren't exactly regulation uniform in a hurricane."

Lili made a face at her. "No. But they are if you expect to run into your fiancé in these dark halls."

Her insouciance lightened the atmosphere inside the house, if not outside.

Few of the household slept after sunrise and soon everyone was up and dressing. The rain drove across the island in gusts, with sheets of water followed by a lull, and afterward winds so strong Rudi Arguello and a houseboy were knocked down in the south compound between the kitchen and the servants' cottages. It took the combined efforts of Wayne and Sam to drag them inside.

Although they weren't more than ten fee[t] from the house the group was lashed by wind and rain with such force that the men found themselves feeling bruised when they finally got back into the house.

Rudi had gotten a crack on the temple when he was blown against a coconut palm tree that stood guard over a corner of the stables. Luckily, Namu was safe at the far end of the stable, where no hurricane or big blow had ever harmed the tough Hawaiian wood that protected her.

But although retaining consciousness, Rudi had all the signs of having suffered a possible concussion. Tracie, backed by Victor, forced him to remain quiet in one of the bedrooms where he could be watched over by Kaahumanu.

From the broken shutter in the west room Tracie saw a cargo liner outside Akua harbor, bobbing and fighting the giant waves. She pitied the men aboard. They were in even greater danger than the islanders. They would have to dock at South Harbor around the jacaranda point of the island, unless the sugar mill area had also received the direct force of the blow.

With Rudi incapacitated, Victor used the opportunity to again assert his dominance. Tracie was proud of him, and genuinely welcomed these signs of his old, authoritative self. It was Diane who kept reminding her that she was risking her father's life in letting him march around the lower floor, giving orders about the piling of furniture and sand-filled burlap bags against the window slats.

Tracie watched happily as her father bellowed orders above the storm's roar and whine. He shouted to Wayne, "You, hero! Watch the drapes. They're going to fly out the damned window," and to Lili, "The hell with the rugs! I always slipped on 'em anyway. Pile 'em up. That's the girl." Then he turned to Diane. "Tell Jade—" He remembered. "Damn! Hope she's safe over in Lahaina. Dinah, any fruit and fish in the house? We'll need food."

"It will be cold fish, I'm afraid, dear. The lights are out. So is the phone. And there isn't much fresh water left."

Everyone laughed at that. Sam Kahana reminded her, "Plenty of fresh water outdoors."

Victor was still going strong. "Cold fish doesn't scare an islander."

During a moment's silence they all heard a distant whistling sound that grew in force until it seemed to cut through the house, shaking it on its foundation. Everyone reached for a wall. Lili fell against Wayne, who caught her neatly, but Diane, a native of the San Francisco area, produced the biggest scare when she screamed, "Earthquake!"

491

After a moment of stunned silence everyone tried to assure her that it was only the lashing tail of the hurricane, but she appeared to be unnerved by it. Victor, both irritable and worried, hovered over her. "Somebody get some water."

Both Tracie and Wayne started to move but Diane's fingers groped for Wayne's hand.

"Could you — just help me?" She dropped weakly into one of Jade's delicate ebony chairs.

Tracie went off to get a glass of water, accompanied by Sam Kahana, who headed outside to see if he could stake down some of the young trees outside the lanai. It was obvious to Tracie that they were being uprooted faster than they could be saved, and each tree trunk crashing down added to the din with the sound of lush foliage crackling and breaking. Even in the kitchen Tracie could hear the orchid tree beating at the side of the house in a kind of agony.

Peering out at the tree, Tracie's thoughts went to Aunt Jade. If the older woman wasn't to return to Akua, then they must send her the furniture that was rightfully hers. She wondered how Maui was taking the blow... *Please don't let Aunt Jade be hurt,* she prayed. *If she dies, I'll feel that I've killed her...*

The rain still whirled around the house, propelled by fierce gusts of wind pelting across the lanai floors, but as Tracie filled a glass of water and put in slivers of chipped ice from the icebox, she imagined the force of the storm lessening. She returned to the living room and gave Diane the glass.

Cupping the glass in both hands, Diane took a long sip and looked up. "Tracie, I wonder if you'd get my icebag. It's in our bedroom upstairs. In one of the dresser drawers. The bottom one on the left, I think. I'm sorry to be such a nuisance, but this storm has given me an awful headache."

"Me too," Lili echoed. She held her hand to her head. "Listen. Wouldn't you say it's slowing down?"

They all stopped whatever they were doing and stood frozen in various listening poses. Tracie glanced back at them, smiled at the sight, then proceeded upstairs.

Beyond the orchid tree at the south end of the lanai the dirt driveway was littered with broken hibiscus bushes, uprooted young trees and a palm tree that lay across the far end of the road to South Harbor.

She became aware that something peculiar was happening...her ears were no longer being assaulted by the roaring noise that wore on the nerves and lay deep underneath the many piercing shrieks and howls of the storm...

If Akua had been in the direct path of the hurricane it was possible Valley House might not be standing at the moment. Thank God it had blown out to sea! She hoped it hadn't hit Oahu and Honolulu's teeming population, or further north, Kauai or the privately run island of Niihau.

She forced open a slatted window and was hit by a shower from the roof and the swaying orchid tree. The trunk of the tree had split to a point only a few feet above the soggy ground. Sam Kahana and one of his men were trying to sink stakes into the ground around it. The upper half of the tree swayed precariously as its heavy top branches rattled.

With her head still out the window, she heard the chug of an old car motor. Looking up, she watched as half a dozen men from the sugar mill at South Harbor piled out of the old truck as it came to a halt on the far side of the fallen palm tree. Two people remained in the back of the truck. The men who got out wore rain gear and were unidentifiable under the spurts of rain that still misted over the area, but at least they were there to help; evidently the huge compound of South Harbor had been spared.

Incredibly enough, one of the men who re-

nained in the truck appeared to be wearing a
tetson hat. He had shaken the water off of it
nd now slapped the hat back on his head. He
vas no one she recognized from South Harbor,
nd thought it odd that a stranger would be
ere at a time like this. And why hadn't he
gotten out with the others? There was someone
else in the truck, someone smaller. A woman?

She would find out soon enough, Tracie reasoned. There was still Diane's icebag to be
found. Tracie searched until she finally located
it, not in the drawer Diane had indicated but
on the upper shelf of the closet, along with
two live beetles, driven in by the storm. She
chased them away, thinking that they probably
would have terrified Diane, who, unlike Tracie,
wasn't used to such common though distasteful
denizens of the Pacific island.

She suddenly heard a door slam on the upper
floor, reminding her that there were problems
to be tended to in the house. Her father's wife
was in a terrible state of nerves.

She returned down the back stairs to the
kitchen with the icebag and found it more difficult to recover bits and pieces of ice from the
mass that was already dissolving into water.

After filling the bag she walked over to the
hall door outside the living room. It had blown
shut during the violence of the storm, but the

double doors opposite the main hall staircase were still partly open. She reached the newel post where she and Bill had said good-bye two weeks earlier. She had never missed him more.

From the living room she heard her name bellowed suddenly and her heartbeat quickened at the harsh protest she heard in her father's voice. "Not Tracie! The rest she did, okay. It's possible. But my girl didn't do this."

Tracie moved to the partially open doors, listening. Without knowing the circumstances, she felt a jolt of terror.

Then Lili's voice: "Look at Diane, uncle. She's practically out on her feet. Wayne, don't let her go to sleep again."

Something serious must have happened. There was a flutter of activity, then her father's voice: "Walk, for Christ's sake! Walk it off. It's a mistake. Tracie wouldn't do this over a goddamned will!"

Tracie squeezed the icebag between tense fingers. Her stomach tightened as she listened to the inexplicable accusations being made. Worse, they were accusations made in her absence.

Wayne said hesitantly, "We all heard Mrs. Berenson say she never took laudanum. She said it last night when Tracie must have been urging it on her."

Tracie stiffened. Not Wayne, too! She recalled that conversation very well. Had it been maneuvered to appear as though she'd brought up the laudanum? Was this all Diane's doing?

Diane seemed to snap out of whatever ailed her and Tracie pushed the door open to hear more clearly. The woman's wispy voice had never been more shy, more embarrassed.

"She's been after me to take it so often. I didn't want to tell you, Victor. After she's nagged me so much about how she could do better than you at running the – oh, it's so horrible!"

Lili was unexpectedly sharp. "I don't believe it. Tracie is practically your image, uncle. Diane must have misunderstood her. We Berensons don't do that to each other, whatever we think of the rest of the world."

Bless you, Lili, whatever your reasoning!

"Maybe," Victor told her, "but what you don't know is that my own kid has walked right in and taken over from me. She even encouraged me to trade Orchid Tree stock for Dorado Star. That's stooping pretty low."

"Only Tracie would stoop so low." The voice was male and sounded lightly ironic. "Of course, Dorado Star is worth a bit more than Orchid at the present time. But that has nothing to do with what appears to be her present crime."

Tracie knew that one voice in a million — it was Bill Dempster and he had joined her enemies.

25

"Crime? That's a good one!" Lili jeered.

But Bill pursued the matter, his tone sounding horribly reassured and reasonable. "But can she deny Mrs. Berenson's evidence? Would Mrs. Berenson deliberately poison herself, only to blame someone else for it? What motive would Mrs. Berenson have for lying?"

Diane was moaning, "So drowsy...why did she do it?"

"If I had been here, I might have prevented it," Bill boasted. "I can assure you, I don't get my competitors out of the way with poison."

"I know that," Victor said roughly. "But Tracie was probably afraid Dinah would tell me what she's been up to. She didn't know this little girl has been loyal from the first. Told me everything every time my kid pulled some new shenanigans."

Wayne spoke up at once. "Honest, sir, nobody will ever persuade me Tracie would try to kill someone," he protested earnestly.

Diane perked up at this defense. "Oh, no. I don't believe it, either. She probably acted on the spur of the moment. She sees me as a threat, poor thing. Her dear father's will and all. But of course, I'm not. We signed an agreement. A...specified amount each year is to be set aside for me. Tracie is still his main beneficiary."

So that was why sweet little Diane had become desperate!

"Well, this changes all that," Victor said. "I'll — I don't know, I'll send her away. Do something, anyway."

"I'm sure I'll be safe once she's gone," Diane assured him.

Tracie braced herself and dropped the ice-bag. She had never known such fury. At this minute it exceeded her hurt and pain. She clenched her teeth, threw the door open wide and strolled in. Her long, graceful legs had never served her better. Diane began to shake, reached for her husband's arm. Wayne gasped and reddened, but Lili surprised them all by giggling hysterically.

Only Bill Dempster remained indifferent, standing at the door in his rain slicker. Ironic, Tracie thought, that he had been one of the men getting out of the sugar mill truck and she hadn't even recognized him. He barely glanced at her. Yet when Tracie passed him, his knuckles brushed against hers. He had the nerve to pretend they were still close. He would have squeezed her fingers but she pulled her hand away, avoiding any contact with him.

Victor greeted her with a kind of sadness that told Tracie more than his words. "I'm glad you were listening. Your friend Dempster here seems to have chartered a boat. Took his life in his hands, but they made it into South Harbor and here he is. I don't know why he thinks it's his business. Frankly, I think this whole thing would be better settled quickly among ourselves."

"I couldn't agree more. Let's hear it to my face." Tracie stopped before Diane's chair and stared down at her.

Diane cowered, her voice pleading. "Tracie, I know I owe you a lot. But I had to tell Victor. I couldn't let you go on usur-usurping his property. Even today you made him w-work when he should have been in bed. You made all those deals with Mr. Dempster—"

"Go on."

"And you know I warned you to throw out that laudanum your mother had. I told you it was dangerous. Wayne did, too. And you kept insisting I take a few drops. Was that what happened today? Did you feel I'd be better off...dead?"

Tracie had never heard such brazen effrontery. She looked around at the others, trying to control the rage that shook her. "You all believe this?"

"Don't be silly," Lili said.

Bill remained impassive, his attention now fixed on Diane.

But the other two men looked from Tracie to Diane and seemed doubtful. *Damn that insipid little creature with her whines and her sweetness and her innocent facade!*

"Speak up," Tracie ordered Diane. "Tell them what a vicious little liar you are."

Tears sparkled on Diane's long lashes. "Please don't keep this up. Your father will always love you. He understands your ambition. You just have to go away, make a new start. Mr. Dempster is your friend, and Victor will help you, darling?" She leaned forward in her chair, looking earnestly at Victor.

It was too much. Enraged, Tracie hauled off and slapped her hard across her sweet, porcelain face. "Liar!"

Bill stood watching the scene. Diane had cringed from the blow. It was Victor who forced Tracie away from his wife. "Stop it, Tracie! Don't think you can bluster your way

502

through anything this serious. Unfortunately, we have proof."

"Her word? The word of this conniving little hypocrite?"

Bill pressed the matter, and that hurt most.

"Diane seems to have been poisoned by the water you brought, Tracie. She admitted you always urged her to take some of your mother's laudanum."

"Oh, I see. Diane told you that."

"And," Bill went on, "it seems Mrs. Berenson says she never heard of laudanum before you spoke of it. That's about it, isn't it, Mrs. Berenson?"

Diane nodded. "None of us wanted to believe it was true. But then I grew so sleepy after drinking that water you gave...Victor sent Mr. Croyde upstairs and found the bottle. And Victor thinks he recognized the taste."

"So Wayne found the laudanum bottle. In mother's medicine chest."

Wayne admitted awkwardly, "No. In the back of your medicine chest. Pretty well hidden."

The old-fashioned little laudanum bottle with instructions written in black ink and a skull and crossbones in red was placed on a side table just out of reach. Tracie felt numb with shock, her legs weakened beneath her. Still, she wasn't going to collapse in front of this little monster.

"So that's your evidence. Did it ever occur to you that anyone could have put it there?"

Lili was disdainful. "I told them that. Ye gods! Anybody could see through it. I wouldn't put it past her." She caught her breath. They all stared at her as her dark eyes narrowed and she continued. "I wouldn't say anything was beyond her. Maybe she knows why Theo fell into the nets that night."

"But why, Lili?" Bill asked in a friendly, conversational tone. "Mrs. Berenson didn't have a motive, did you, Diane?" He looked at the others. "If she had a motive in — let's say — shutting Theo up, then it would have been a different matter."

"This discussion's...so unpleasant...Oh, please — will someone help me?" Diane drooped over Wayne's arm. One of her hands caressed her cheek, still red with the marks of Tracie's hand.

Victor, still torn between concern for and annoyance with his troublesome, sick wife, knelt over her.

Ignoring this, Bill persisted in questioning Diane. "If only somebody had seen Mrs. Berenson's ex-husband recently, we could blame him. You did say you saw him last on the beach at Waikiki three months ago, didn't you?"

She nodded, her face covered by her disheveled dark hair.

"You couldn't have been mistaken about his identity, could you? I mean, he hung around you causing all that trouble, so you couldn't be mistaken."

"N-no . . . Victor, I'm afraid I'm a little dizzy." She looked up at him as she fingered the red marks of Tracie's hand.

Victor patted her knee. "Sure. It'll never happen again. Trace won't—"

"No, she won't," Tracie said bitterly. "I wouldn't dream of touching that greedy, conniving liar."

Victor's mouth tightened as he attempted to lift Diane, trying to help her to her feet. "I don't see any point in discussing this further." Over his shoulder he gave his daughter final orders. "I won't have you tempted by my damned will. I'll have it changed, once and for all." His shoulders drooped and he avoided looking at her, but his voice was firm. "You'll get enough money to take care of you. But you'd better go off with your friend Dempster. You're his kind."

Victor had started across the room with one arm around Diane's waist, but Bill stood in his way.

"One more question, sir. Just so everyone

will be sure. Your wife never heard of laudanum before, I think she said."

Diane corrected him plaintively. "I've never seen laudanum before. But I may have heard of it. I believe it was commonly used in the past."

Something in Bill's attitude, the cool persistence of his questions confused Tracie. During the last few minutes she had begun to wonder what he was really up to . . . was it she who was his victim? Or her stepmother?

"Mrs. Berenson, I know you'll be happy to see an old friend of yours." Bill went to the double doors and pushed them wide open.

In the doorway stood the stocky, heavy-faced man Tracie had seen in the South Harbor truck. His stained and soggy Stetson was pulled forward over his eyes, making him look formidable.

The others were surprised while Victor was resentful at the intrusion. "What the devil?"

Seeing the man, Diane screamed. Almost at once she covered her mouth with a trembling hand. "I'm so sorry. The gentleman startled me."

The cowboy's heavy lips parted in a grin that didn't reach his hard eyes. He had a scarred leather briefcase under one arm. "Hi, Miz Thorpe. Like old times, wouldn't you say? You taking on, and laudanum all over the place.

Stuff you never heard of, I rec'lect you saying, and you didn't have no idea poor old Ray would do a thing like that."

"This is quite—" She wet her lips. "Quite different, Mr. Biddlecombe. I am the victim of a poisoning attempt."

No one said a word. Everyone except Bill Dempster was staring at the cowboy and then at Diane with open-mouthed wonder.

"Where are my manners?" Bill said with forced politeness. "I found my friend here in Dayton, Nevada. Mr. Biddlecombe is a deputy sheriff of Lyon County. Luckily, I found a pit boss in Reno who remembered Ray Thorpe. Seems he once came into a windfall over a blackjack game. That was before gambling was legal. So my pit-boss buddy sent me to Dayton."

Diane pulled herself together, focusing her tear-filled eyes on Victor and Wayne. "This man used to be after me all the time. He tried to—" She bit her lip and blushed rosily, "—to rape me once, but Ray saved me."

The deputy remained unruffled, though he took his hat off and bowed to the ladies.

"Hate to have my wife hear you say that, ma'am. She'd take and tan your hide, her being so fond of poor old Ray and all. That was Miz Thorpe's husband, you know," he explained to his rapt audience.

"Yes, I met him," Victor said gruffly. "He insulted my womenfolk and tried to knock me down."

"Oh?" Biddlecombe said, surprised. "When was this?"

"About three months ago."

Biddlecombe disagreed politely. "Couldn't quite be like that, sir. Ol' Ray was as nice a fella as you'd want to meet. Wouldn't do a thing like that. Many's the time we rode old Walker Range together before he settled down with his pretty missus here. He loved this lady ever since their high school days, but she was on the lookout for money. Then come the big haul he won in Reno and the little lady ups and marries him. But he never made another killin' and Miz Thorpe starts naggin'. She was the naggin'est woman!"

"He had no initiative. He wasn't like you, darling!" Diane burst out, giving Victor a beseeching gaze.

"The man was cruel and vicious," Victor said, picking up one of her wrists. "Look here. He tried to cut her wrists when she threatened to leave him."

"Not so's you'd notice." Biddlecombe spoke directly to Diane, who avoided his eyes. "Did you forget, ma'am? Your statement is in the records. When Ray got tired of your naggin'

508

and your public scenes, he threatened to leave; so you give that wrist a little swipe with a razor. Sheriff's got it all wrote down the way the folks in the Walker River Bar saw you do it."

Tracie heaved a big sigh and glanced at Bill. For the first time she saw him smile.

Wayne, however, was still confused. He reminded the deputy of Ray Thorpe's attack on Victor at Waikiki. "I know because I knocked the guy down," he insisted.

The deputy pulled a manila envelope out of his briefcase. "That'd be kind of hard to do, seeing as how this right here is a notarized copy of Ray Thorpe's death certificate. Dated June seventeenth, nineteen thirty-four, in Dayton, Lyon County, Nevada."

"What?" Victor's outburst made them all jump.

"Yep. Laudanum poisoning, it says."

They all turned to stare at Diane, who suddenly looked pale, her eyes enormous as she cowered from them. "Suicide. He took it himself. They agreed. The sheriff's report says so."

Biddlecombe agreed. "No proof otherwise. Ray's prints all over the bottle. Everybody knew he was what they call despondent. Wanted to leave this gal, but couldn't bring himself to. Had a job at Gantner's Hay, Grain and

Feed, but what with the Depression and all, they'd let him go that day. I guess this little lady made it so hard for him, he was glad to take the danged stuff."

"I loved him," she insisted tearfully.

"All the same, when you called the doctor Ray had been dead most of the night. You sure took your time, ma'am."

"I didn't know he was dead. He was sleeping on the couch in the front room."

Lili pushed Wayne aside, waving her fist in the deputy's face. Tracie had never seen her so angry, and with reason. Tracie, too, was beginning to wonder about a crime closer to home.

"That's all past. But she killed Theo. I'm sure of it." She bolted toward Diane, and Bill caught her firmly but with gentle assurance.

"We're getting to it. Mrs. Berenson, you must have decided from the first that only Tracie stood in your way, so you set out to separate her from Victor's trust. When that fellow on the beach caused trouble you made him the culprit in case you had to resort to violence in getting Victor's estate."

Tracie was slowly putting past events together. "You mean the man on the beach was just some obnoxious stranger?"

"That's the size of it. He certainly couldn't

have been Ray Thorpe."

She looked at Bill, the pieces suddenly fitting together. "Diane was at the head of the stairs that day when Rudi told me she had canceled her drive. But if Diane moved the danger sign she must have known it wasn't likely to kill me."

Bill's expression was grim, but he managed a smile. "Killing wasn't necessary. If you were laid up with a few broken bones, she might have seen that you never got back to your former relationship with your father."

"She damn near succeeded!" Victor barked, glaring at his wife.

"It isn't true," she insisted. "Why would I lie about Ray?"

"You did, though," Bill said. "He was to be the villain in your little melodrama if things didn't work out. But like most incurable liars, you never thought how easily you could be trapped if anyone ever found out about that little town in Nevada."

"You've always disliked me, Mr. Dempster, because I saw through your schemes to take over Orchid Tree."

Bill ignored this. "What happened? You and Theo were always together, always talking. Did you accidentally mention Dayton, Nevada, to him one day? You must have, because he remembered it while he was in Honolulu looking for the elusive Ray Thorpe. And he cabled Dayton, Nevada."

"You're making this all up to protect her. You still want to destroy Victor," Diane said, challenging him.

Biddlecombe grinned. "She's a sharp one, Mr. Dempster." He dug out a half-sheet with the copy of a cable from Hobart T. Spencer, sheriff of Lyon County, Nevada, to Theodore Berenson, in care of the Alexander Young Hotel, Honolulu, T.H. "Here goes: RE YOUR QUERY RAYMOND THORPE DECEASED JUNE 17 1934 STOP CORONER'S REPORT CAUSE OF DEATH LAUDANUM POISON-ING."

Bill added, "I think Theo tried a little black-mail on the happy new bride. Probably on the phone when he told Mrs. Berenson he would be home that night...Diane, tell us, did you meet him on the jetty after Marta had gone to the *hukilau?*"

"Never! Victor was ill. I was home with him."

For the first time Tracie saw the old fire in her father's eyes. "Now wait a minute. I felt okay. I intended to surprise everyone and go to the *hukilau*. I never made it. Dinah brought me a drink and I fell asleep right away. I re-member early the next morning I woke up with headache and a damned thick taste in my mouth."

"It was the brandy, darling."

Tracie had never seen more honest eyes, but they no longer moved her father. Thank God they had never moved Bill!

"Let me read your mind," Bill said. "If Theo told his uncle about your background, you'd be back on your uppers again. Did you coax Theo? Did you try everything else before you sent him tumbling into those nets?"

Lili began to weep, long, wrenching sobs broken by her desperate cries for her dead brother. Wayne comforted her while he scowled at Bill. "If you don't have that woman arrested, I will."

Bill tilted his head toward the door. Wayne nodded and gently urged Lili past the deputy and out into the hall. Bill moved to Tracie's side.

"Thank you," she whispered. "It's worse for Lili."

Diane, meanwhile, had gathered courage and said calmly, "There is nothing you can do." Almost as an afterthought, she added, "Because I am innocent. Victor, this whole thing is a frame-up between two people who want to ruin you."

Victor studied her for a long minute before

turning his back on her. The granite face and the weary, disillusioned eyes were not meant for Tracie. He reached for her hand, then dropped his arm as if it had lost all strength. He seemed to realize that his broken relationship with his daughter would take more than an apology to repair.

"Is it true?" he asked the deputy in a husky voice. "There are no charges against her?"

"Not in Nevada. You could, if you wanted, charge her with doping you the night your nephew died."

"I do."

"It won't stick unless you've got some evidence somewhere."

Diane made one more plea. "Victor, I admire you more than any man I've ever known. Don't throw me to the wolves."

Victor flung aside her groping hand. "You killed my nephew, I'll bet on it. I see it in your eyes. I remember how it was that night."

"Victor, please listen. You don't know the circumstances. You were sick. You weren't thinking straight."

He ignored her and turned toward his daughter. "Tracie, can you handle this? I want her things packed. I'm taking her to Oahu. Mr. Biddlecombe, we'll see if the Honolulu police can get evidence, even if we have to exhume

ny nephew's body. Can we count on your
help?"

"Sure thing, sir. I'm on vacation leave. Mr.
Dempster here, he got me passage on his boat.
I figured I owed it to my old buddy, Ray...
imagine, after what she put Ray through, she
finally marries money...Excuse me, sir."

"I'm afraid you're right," Victor admitted.
"Tracie, can you get her ready?"

Tracie said nothing. She was badly shaken
but had no pity whatever for Diane Thorpe.
She was convinced that the woman had murdered Theo. Her fingers closed hard around
Diane's arm and she shoved the woman ahead
of her. Diane moved along the hall but her
eyes were busy looking from side to side. Tracie
didn't doubt she was still scheming.

They reached the back hall that led to Ilima's
room when Sam Kahana came in from the west
lanai. "Got to get some strong hemp for those
stakes," he said. "Suppose there is some in the
kitchen?"

"I have no idea. Good luck finding it." Aunt
Jade could have found it in a minute but Tracie
had no notion where it would be.

When they were alone in Ilima's room Diane
swallowed a few tears. "I've got a right to nice
things. I earned them. Married to that weak,
worthless Ray, and now to an old man like your

515

father. I was a good wife." She gave Tracie malign glance. "But I knew it wouldn't last He seemed to get bored right after the honey moon. You had something to do with it, I'l bet."

"I had nothing to do with it. I wanted him to be happy."

"Sure. You always stood in my way. It wasn' until I showed him how you and your boyfrienc were conniving against him that he turned to me."

"And yet you drugged him the night of the *hukilau.*"

"That was to calm him," she snapped. "To keep him from exerting himself."

Her admission that she had drugged her father seemed to Tracie an admission that she had murdered Theo, but the woman was too crafty to be trapped. She looked around Ilima's room. "I wonder if it really was haunted. I never even knew the Mako woman, but she certainly had it in for me."

"You'd better pack."

Diane let out an hysterical laugh. "All I need to pack is the money I've saved. It's mine, all right! My allowance from your gracious father, and whatever I saved from shopping."

True to her word, she refused to take anything but her handbag and a tortoiseshell

anity case. She stood up and looked around
er with a twisted little smile.

"I always hated this room. And this whole
godforsaken island."

"Did you hate Theo?"

"Never," she said vehemently. "That was the
real horror. Knowing he—" She caught herself,
her eyes darting to Tracie and then away.
"Knowing he was dead...when they told me."

Could one commit a murder reluctantly?
Tracie wondered. If so, she believed this one
statement of Diane's, that she was sorry it had
been necessary to kill Theo.

Suddenly, Diane swung the vanity case at
Tracie and made a dash for the lanai door.
Tracie started after her, then decided to catch
up with her outside. Diane would have a tough
time getting down to one of the docks without
a vehicle of some kind.

As Tracie ran out of the room Diane slammed
the lanai door, then threw herself past the
wavering orchid tree, now held together with
thin sections of wire. Outside Tracie heard the
shriek of timber, the tearing away of the orchid
tree's broken upper half, followed by a high,
blood-chilling scream.

Tracie rushed around the lanai, aware that
whatever had happened was catastrophic. She
found Diane beneath the split trunk of the tree,

crushed under the top half of it with its wide spread branches, leaves and flowers. Tracie knelt beside her, trying to raise her head. Sam who was running toward them down the lanai said sharply, "No! Easy does it."

Diane stared up, and Tracie had the eerie feeling that those eyes saw nothing. Sam's big fingers felt delicately around Diane's head to the base of her skull while Tracie, moved to compassion at this sudden horror, murmured, "We'll get you out. Don't move. Sam will do it."

Diane's mouth worked, the lips rimmed with blood-streaked saliva. "He didn't suffer."

Tracie's heart thudded painfully. "What, Diane?"

Her lips went on moving, but no sound came out.

Her eyes remained open but when Tracie felt at the side of her throat for her pulse, there was no response. Sam shook his head.

"She shouldn't have come out here. I had it held together with wire temporarily. I was getting ready to stake the damned thing. It's terrible...terrible..."

Tracie felt for her pulse, but it seemed clear Diane was dead. She turned away, trying to control her own shock as the others came over from the front of the house to see what had happened.

At the end of the lanai, beyond the broken pile of branches a shadow moved. Tracie raised her head. Jade stood there, impassive as always, staring down at the dead woman. She must have been the woman in the truck, Tracie thought.

She had seen the entire accident a moment ago and said nothing in warning or in recrimination. Perhaps she always suspected who had murdered her son.

26

Wayne Croyde and Lili, with Jade between them, stood motionless on the jetty, watching as the coffin was loaded onto the *Akua Orchid.* Victor walked off the upper deck and onto the jetty. His step was unsure and Jade moved forward to join him. He rested one hand on her shoulder; neither of them spoke as they stood side by side on the jetty watching the cargo ship move out of the harbor. Diane Thorpe Berenson had begun the long voyage back to her birthplace in Oakland, California.

Earlier aboard the *Akua Orchid,* Tracie and Bill watched the coffin settled on the afterdeck under Deputy Biddlecombe's directions. "You don't have to do this," Tracie told Bill. "It's my fault she came to the Territory. If only I hadn't encouraged her that day in the store."

"I'll go halves on the blame. It took a hell of a lot of time getting to the Coast to nail the lady, so I'm partly responsible for what happened. Also, I thought we could trap or scare her into a confession, but she was too smart for us."

"Not too smart for the orchid tree."

"Now, now, none of that talk about ghosts or vindictive trees. It was ready to break apart and she gave it the last nudge."

Tracie shook her head. "You still aren't a true *kamaaina*. We islanders believe in nature's power. We have reason to."

But he remained unconverted and changed the subject.

"By the way, I never would have caught on to that town of Dayton if it hadn't been for my Reno pals. Little did I know that divorcing Marta would give me the contacts for this business."

She laughed. "So Marta was worth something to you, after all."

He ignored the remark and said, "I sent you two cables. But I sent them to Honolulu, where you were supposed to be." He grinned, looking deeply into her eyes. "Wasn't it lucky they didn't get through? You'd never have been obliged to marry me."

"Marry?"

"Might as well. I saved the day for Orchid Tree. I can't keep traveling back and forth to the Coast rescuing you from angelic stepmothers."

"With a little help from Aunt Jade. If she hadn't been waiting for you in Honolulu you might not have come over here in the middle of a Big Blow. It was bad enough for you to convince the deputy into coming through on that pineapple freighter you hired, but God knows how you got Aunt Jade on board."

"You don't know your redoubtable aunt. She insisted."

"Did you always suspect Diane?" It still seemed incredible when she remembered the young woman's shyness, her innocence and high respectability. And above all, that sweet sincerity.

"Lord, no! I'm not clairvoyant. Actually, I went to the Coast to nail Thorpe himself. I wanted to find out if he really had been prowling around here. But you remember, I warned you not to trust anyone. I had one eye on Lady Jade."

As they stood on the jetty she frowned into the distance, watching as her father and Jade walked silently back to the car, following Wayne and Liliha.

"I know Aunt Jade meant to help us all when she met you in Honolulu, but I can never live in the same house with her again. And I only hope no one else finds out what she did to Ilima."

"But can you live with your dear old dad again?"

The muscles around her high cheekbones tightened. It would be a long time before she could forget the absence of trust in her father's face and his voice during that awful time when she stood accused of poisoning his wife. She looked away, her eyes cast downward.

He pulled her closer. The afternoon breeze whipped around them, reminding Tracie of the disaster that had struck Akua three days ago. She looked out across the churning water at the jetty, which was still strewn with debris, coral, seaweed, broken nets and barrel staves from Albie's fish traps. Theo's red outrigger had been rammed against one coral outcropping near the shore. She closed her eyes, seeing too clearly the murderous Diane Thorpe pushing Theo into those nets or perhaps hitting him with a jagged piece of coral.

Not wanting to dwell on such morbid thoughts, she cast her gaze on other parts of the harbor. Several Hawaiian and Japanese fishermen were out along the shore mending nets and working on boats hauled up on the beach for repairs. At Jacaranda Point, the south barrier of the bay, trees had been mowed down in a direct line as though hacked away by a giant scythe where the tail of the hurricane had struck along the west coast of Akua. But a quarter of a mile inland the first jacaranda was still standing and the others were safe on the high, level ground beyond.

Bill saw her gazing at the area. "Looks a little better to you than it did a few months ago, wouldn't you say?"

Something in his tone, a faint huskiness, made her stare at him. She loved him and had loved him longer than she knew, but she had always assumed he was invulnerable. There was vulnerability now in his eyes with their still unasked question.

She looked from Bill to the south point of the bay again, remembered the day she had stood among the jacarandas and heard Bill joke about moving in and taking over Akua, building a house to rival her father's.

For the first time in her life she asked herself if her view and her father's view of Bill Dempster had been wildly off the mark. Bill was sincere when he had made that curious remark, asking her if she would live in a house built between the jacaranda trees. She started to ask him, was embarrassed, and ended by confessing with her warmest look, "I remember a few months ago somebody asked me if I would like to live there. If he asked me now—"

"Well?"

"I can't think of any place in the world where 'd rather spend my life. Only one request." He raised his eyebrows. She said quickly, "No orchid trees. Stick to jacarandas."

"That I can promise you. I proposed to you that day, but it didn't seem to register. I'll run it through again if I must." He bent his head to kiss her.

This time she had no difficulty understanding his proposal, and her lips, as well as her answer, were ready for him.

THORNDIKE PRESS HOPES you have enjoyed this Large Print book. All our Large Print titles are designed for the easiest reading, and all our books are made to last. Other Thorndike Press Large Print books are available at your library, through selected bookstores, or directly from the publisher. For more information about current and upcoming titles, please call us, toll free, at 1-800-223-6121, or mail your name and address to:

THORNDIKE PRESS
P. O. BOX 159
THORNDIKE, MAINE 04986

There is no obligation, of course.

F   17.95
COFF   THORNDIKE
COFFMAN   LARGE PRINT
(THE) ORCHID TREE

MAR 27 1997

AUG 28 1990

APR 6 1991   DEC 04 1997
AUG 5 1992   JAN 12 1998

APR 2 1993   MAY 30 2000
JUN 13 1995   JUL 03 2000
                   JUN 18 2002
OCT 13 1995   SEP 25 2003
DEC 09 1996   MAY 22 2004
JAN 28 1997   JUN 10 2004
                   JUL 12 2004
                   OCT 14 2005

3

TEACHER'S RESOURCE BOOK

SCHOLASTIC
LITERACY
PLACE®

ESL/ELD

Grade 4

AUTHORS

IRMA N. GUADARRAMA, PH.D.
Associate Professor
University of Houston

MICHELE HEWLETT-GÓMEZ, PH.D.
Associate Professor
Sam Houston State University

HILDA MEDRANO, PH.D.
Dean, College of Education
University of Texas Pan American

TABLE OF CONTENTS

NOTE
*Numbers in bold type refer to page numbers.
 Numbers in roman type refer to Activity Masters.

Introduction

Why were these materials created?

The recent and ongoing waves of immigration into the United States are producing profound changes in the American educational system. More and more today, students who speak a language other than English are being integrated into mainstream language arts classrooms. These students must face the challenge of struggling with new material in a new language.

The reading selections in *Literacy Place 2000* may present a challenge to the English Language Learner, whether it be complex new sentence structures, idioms, and vocabulary, or subtleties of plot and character. Without extra help, the English Language Learner may be overwhelmed, and give up in frustration. The *ESL/ELD Teacher Resource Books* were created as a means for these students to benefit from the stories, through activities limited to the basic elements of each story. They offer story and language support for *Literacy Place 2000* through the use of activity masters, accompanied by teacher instruction pages, as well as a set of posters that can be used to further English language development. The books are not intended as a stand-alone ESL program. Rather, the lessons offer a way for English Language Learners (ELLs) to better comprehend the stories, and to practice related sentence structure and vocabulary.

Additional support is offered to the English Language Learner in the *Literacy Place 2000* Teacher Edition in the form of numerous ESL teaching tips, as well as an audio tape that enables students to listen to the stories they will be reading and discussing in class.

How do these materials conform to ESL standards?

Over the past few years, a number of states, as well as the international professional organization TESOL (Teachers of English to Speakers of Other Languages), have created standards in ESL instruction as a way of quantifying the acquisition of language skills by ESL students. While the standards vary somewhat from state to state, there is much overlap, and the overall goals are the same. We have incorporated these standards into the *ESL/ELD Teacher Resource Books*, in the form of *Essential Knowledge and Skills*, which can be found as the focus of the second activity master in each lesson.

About the Books

What skills are practiced in the ESL/ELD Teacher Resource Books?

Each of the three activity masters focuses on a particular skill. These skills are: language, conceptualization, and comprehension. The *Multi-Level Instruction* includes suggestions for adapting each activity to learners' needs, since ESL students are at different levels of language proficiency. These activities are indicated by up and down arrows.

The three lessons can be done in any order, though the information contained in the first two activity masters (*Focus on Language* and *Essential Knowledge and Skills*) usually helps lead the students to the third activity master, *Focus on Comprehension*. There is a *Take It Home* feature for each story, which helps to reinforce the lesson at home with the family. Whenever possible, the vocabulary in the lessons is based on the theme of the story, and can be used across the curriculum.

Who are these activities for?

These activities are designed for English Language Learners or any student who needs language enhancement, and are appropriate for all students in your class. Although students may not know enough English to understand the reading selections in *Literacy Place 2000*, these worksheets will allow them to participate in the activities with native speakers, using their current language skills.

Be aware that English Language Learners may come from different language backgrounds, and the amount of English they have been exposed to may be minimal. However, it is not necessary to know your students' native language in order to teach them English.

The activities in the *ESL/ELD Teacher Resource Books* are geared towards the pre-intermediate level, but come with suggestions for simple ways to adapt the activities for both higher and lower level students. Some of the adaptations involve simple variations in the activity, while others involve changing the sentence structures used.

It is important to understand that there is not necessarily a correlation between a student's grade level and language level. In *Literacy Place 2000*, the complexity of the language as well as the content increases with the grade level. The activity masters, however, provide age-appropriate activities while keeping reading level and vocabulary controlled for easy accessibility. The language level is consistent, while the content is tailored to the grade level.

What is the goal of the worksheets?

The average English Language Learner may find some of the selections in *Literacy Place 2000* difficult in terms of vocabulary, grammar, and idioms. Asking learners to struggle with the mainstream activities will only add to their frustration. The goal of *ESL/ELD Teacher Resource Book* is to give students an entry into the story. The activities are designed to help students understand the basic elements of the plot, setting, and/or characters, and to learn related vocabulary and sentence structure. It is important for both the teacher and the students to keep in mind that they can follow the main events and ideas in the stories without understanding every word. The students should be encouraged to use context clues and illustrations to guess and predict.

The goal **IS**:

- to help students grasp the main idea of the story.
- to help students learn some related vocabulary.
- to allow students to practice model sentence structures and build upon them.

The goal **IS** **NOT**:

- to make students understand every word in the stories.
- to make students understand every detail of plot and character.
- to teach specific grammar rules and terminology.
- to serve as a complete language course.

What types of activities are included in the worksheets?

Activities include cut and paste, finger and stick puppets, mazes, sentence completion, matching, coloring, graphic organizers, and sequencing. These activities are to be used as tools to guide students toward the goal of using the language in a model sentence at the end of the activity. The model sentences are excellent jumping-off points for real dialogue, where students can elaborate on what they have learned. Grammar patterns are taught and reinforced by using the language in context. The teacher notes also include set-up activities that precede the work on the activity sheet.

How do the worksheets fit into my overall lesson?

The worksheets offer great flexibility. You may use them individually, in small groups, or with the whole class. Students may work independently, or be teacher-directed. These worksheets are best used before or after reading. If your school has an ESL program, you may wish to share them with the ESL teacher.

You will find that many of these activities are appropriate for use with the whole class. They are the same kinds of activities that are used with mainstream students. It is important that the English Language Learners not feel separated or isolated from the rest of the class. Involving the whole class in the same activity is a valuable way to help the English Language Learners feel a part of the group, and for the mainstream students to understand that they can work and play with the English Language Learners despite any language barriers.

How can I extend the lessons beyond the classroom?

Each story has a lesson that includes a *Take It Home* activity. It offers a way for the students to share what they do in the classroom with their families, thus extending the language learning process to the home. In addition, the activities the student does at home with the family can provide a springboard for discussion and sharing in the classroom. Inviting parents and caretakers to visit your classroom is a good way to bring students and their families together in the language learning process.

How can I use the posters?

The posters offer additional language support and can be used in a variety of ways. Activities for the posters can be tailored to suit your students' levels of language ability. You may use the posters for small or large-group instruction or in learning centers for independent study. Students at the beginning stages of language acquisition do well with activities that involve visual comprehension. Ask these students questions related directly to the elements depicted on the poster. Use basic vocabulary and simple sentence structures.

At the intermediate level, students are able to express their personal interpretations of what is shown. Ask them questions designed to elicit their opinions about what is pictured.

Fluent students may be ready to be creative. Ask questions that require them to use their imagination. For example, ask them to invent a "history" for the story characters, or to imagine being a television newscaster and give a live report.

The following list offers suggestions for activities that may be adapted for multi-level groups.

- Brainstorm vocabulary in pairs or small groups. Each student contributes at his or her own level.

- Ask and answer *who, what, why, where, when,* and *how* questions about the poster.

- Play *I Spy.*

- Have students find objects in the poster that fit a specific category, i.e., that are red, start with B, are round, you can eat, etc.

- Use as a springboard for guided writing or discussion.

- Have students write captions for the poster.

- Practice prepositions, adjectives, etc. by describing the elements of the poster.

- Have students count and compare things and identify colors and shapes.

- Play a memory game: Have students study the poster for one minute. Then, hide the poster and ask questions that focus on visual recall.

How can I use the *Literacy Place 2000* audiocassettes?

The audiocassettes may be used before or after reading, either for independent listening, or in a group. These cassettes will help students grow accustomed to the rhythms and intonation patterns of spoken English. They can also be used to have students listen for specific information. For example, you could ask students to raise their hands each time they hear a certain vocabulary word.

What techniques can I use to teach vocabulary?

Since vocabulary development is a major goal of the activity masters, we have mentioned a variety of techniques in the teacher pages. Following is a more detailed description of some of these techniques that facilitate vocabulary acquisition by English Language Learners. Whenever possible, use language in natural contexts. Remember: It is more important to use the language through demonstration than to talk about it!

Word Bank/Phrase Bank Throughout the activity masters, students will encounter lists of vocabulary words (or phrases) around a theme or category related to the lesson. They are grouped in a box called a Word Bank or Phrase Bank that students will refer to when they are asked to choose the correct word in an activity. You can expand the Word or Phrase Banks by adding other words. You can do this before and after students complete the activity, but make sure to keep within the theme of the story. Provide additional words yourself or elicit more examples from students.

Realia Realia is any prop or object that is used in a lesson. In teaching vocabulary, it is easier to show an object than to define it, and this eliminates the need to translate into the student's native language. You don't need to bring in elaborate props—simple classroom objects can provide a treasure trove of language learning opportunities.

Total Physical Response This technique, often called TPR, is based on the concept that at early stages of language acquisition, learners can respond physically to a series of commands before they are able to respond verbally. For example, if you tell a student to walk to the window and open it, he or she can follow the directions in English without being able to say *I am opening the window.* Young children of any language background can follow their parents' and caregivers' directions long before they can speak. (*Come to Mommy/Drink your juice/Pick up your toy*) You can practice this principle with your ESL students by asking them to respond to a series of directions and commands based on the lesson at hand. Although they do not give a verbal response, they show understanding by performing the action. In combination with realia, TPR is a very effective technique for teaching vocabulary. Possible commands are:

- *Point to the _____.*
- *Pick up the _____.*
- *Show me the _____.*
- *Give the _____ to _____.*

Some of these same commands can also be used successfully with the posters. (For additional vocabulary teaching tips, please refer to the previous section on using posters.)

Beyond the Books

What is the difference between ESL and native language instruction?

ELLs learn in much the same ways as mainstream students; however, they are burdened with learning new subject matter and new language at the same time. ESL breaks information into smaller, more manageable chunks. Directions are also broken down into their discrete steps. Remember that ESL instruction emphasizes all four language skills: listening, speaking, reading, and writing. The four skills are not treated separately; ESL activities may incorporate all of these skills as much as possible.

What is the relationship between the four language skills?

It is important to remember that fluency in speaking and fluency in reading and writing often do not go hand in hand. Normally, comprehension precedes production. Some students pick up spoken language quickly, while their reading and writing skills lag far behind. This is especially true if they do not read and write well in their first language. You can facilitate students' development in the four communication skills of listening, speaking, reading, and writing by integrating them in your lessons. For instance, engage students in reading activities that will give them the opportunity to develop their listening and speaking skills and extend their reading comprehension by giving them writing activities.

How do the activities conform to second language methodology?

Some teachers and even some students expect language learning to progress quickly and smoothly, and think that errors are unacceptable. However, second language acquisitions theorists know that these are unreasonable expectations. They realize that language learning is a process that takes place along a continuum; from pre-production to full, native-like fluency. Second language methods focus more on helping the student move along the continuum, rather than reaching a certain point. We set attainable goals along the way, and are happy with the small steps the students make towards those goals.

Because learning does take place on a continuum, it is likely that no two language learners in a given group will be at the same stage. For this reason, the writers of this book have tried to accommodate learners at various stages. Each lesson is meant to be modified to suit the needs of individual learners.

Language learning takes place in the context of human interaction. Being exposed to natural language, rather than performing rote grammar drills, gives learners models to follow when they begin producing language on their own. For this reason, these activities focus on natural language.

Effective learning cannot take place when a student is afraid to make mistakes. Second language methodology allows room for growth via risk taking, and accepts errors as a natural part of the language learning process. It is important to accept those errors, model correct language, make sure meaning takes precedence over form, and feel confident that with time the errors will begin to disappear. When students are involved in meaning-making, language learning is more likely to occur.

Young Arthur

Ⓐ FOCUS ON LANGUAGE

SEE ACTIVITY MASTER 1

USE STORY VOCABULARY Read aloud and discuss the meanings of the words in the Word Bank. Use illustrations in the story or synonyms to clarify meanings. Then ask students to sort the words into one of the lists, based on their meanings. Have the students use the words to orally complete the sentences.

Ⓑ ESSENTIAL KNOWLEDGE AND SKILLS

SEE ACTIVITY MASTER 2

USE ACCESSIBLE LANGUAGE AND LEARN NEW AND ESSENTIAL LANGUAGE IN THE PROCESS Discuss the words *brave, truthful,* and *kind.* Give examples of classroom behavior that demonstrate these concepts and have students act out the examples. For example, for the word *kind,* have one student give another a compliment for a job well done. Ask students to name other words that describe Arthur. For example, *wise, strong, gentle, good,* and *just.* Have students complete the activity master.

Ⓒ FOCUS ON COMPREHENSION

SEE ACTIVITY MASTER 3

SHOW ORDER OF STORY EVENTS Use stick figure sketches or the illustrations in the story to clarify the sentences. Explain to students that the order of the sentences is incorrect. Ask students to draw pictures for the sentences. Then, have them number the pictures to show the order in which they occured. Finally, have them label their pictures with the words *beginning, middle,* and *end.*

MULTI-LEVEL Instruction

FOCUS ON LANGUAGE

⬇ Have students name other words from the story they did not understand. Discuss the meaning for each word and write it on the chalkboard. Then write short sentences on the chalkboard, leaving blanks where these words might be used, and have students volunteer to fill in the blanks.

⬆ Ask students to write or say original sentences using each of the words in the Word Bank.

ESSENTIAL KNOWLEDGE AND SKILLS

⬇ Help students find illustrations or passages in the story that demonstrate how Arthur was *brave, truthful,* and *kind.*

⬆ Challenge students to extend the sentences using examples in the story.

FOCUS ON COMPREHENSION

⬇ Have pairs or groups of students assume the roles of the characters and act out the events described in the sentences, using as much dialogue as fluency permits. Before students label their pictures, show them the *beginning, middle,* and *end* of the book.

⬆ Have students use the ordered pictures to help them retell the story.

MULTI-LEVEL Instruction

FOCUS ON LANGUAGE

On the chalkboard, draw a rough sketch of a forest, a valley, a rolling field, and a pasture. Help students label your sketches.

Ask students to add and label four more items in their pictures that are not in the Word Bank. For example, *trees*.

ESSENTIAL KNOWLEDGE AND SKILLS

Have a volunteer ask you the questions in the second section of the activity master. With partners, have children take turns asking and answering the questions.

Have students ask questions 5–8 of a classmate. Have them record the answers.

FOCUS ON COMPREHENSION

To strengthen concepts, have students pantomime eating crawdads, reading a book, and doing a stomp dance.

Have students look through the pictures in the story and describe people or things they see. For example, they might say *The crawdad looks hot and delicious.*

Cherokee Summer

Ⓐ FOCUS ON LANGUAGE

SEE ACTIVITY MASTER 4

ILLUSTRATE NOUNS FROM THE STORY SETTING Use pictures from books and magazines that show places named in the Word Bank to demonstrate the meanings of the words. Ask students to draw and label their pictures. Say the sentence on the activity master and have students complete it using one of the words in the Word Bank.

Ⓑ ESSENTIAL KNOWLEDGE AND SKILLS

SEE ACTIVITY MASTER 5

ASK AND GIVE INFORMATION SUCH AS DIRECTIONS AND ADDRESS, AS WELL AS NAME, AGE, AND NATIONALITY Discuss the meanings of the words in the Word Bank. Ask the questions in the first section, and have students respond by saying or pointing to a word in the Word Bank. Then have them complete the sentences. Finally, help students answer the questions about themselves.

Ⓒ FOCUS ON COMPREHENSION

SEE ACTIVITY MASTER 6

IDENTIFYING STORY DETAILS Discuss the meanings of the words in the Word Bank by having students find examples in the illustrations. Ask them to think of a synonym for the word *legend* (story). Have students complete the sentences.

Growing Up with Jerry Spinelli

Ⓐ FOCUS ON LANGUAGE

SEE ACTIVITY MASTER 7

DEVELOP VOCABULARY ABOUT CREATURES Discuss the meanings of the words in the Word Bank. Have students point to the creatures in the picture. Have them label the picture and add more creatures such as: *a turtle, a bird, a salamander,* or *an animal drinking from the creek.* Write the names of the creatures drawn by students on the chalkboard and model pronunciation. Have students complete the sentences.

FOCUS ON LANGUAGE

⬇ Ask students to point to the animals in their pictures as you talk about each one. Say the words in the Word Bank and have students repeat after you.

⬆ Ask students to talk about what is happening at the creek using complete sentences. For example, *The fish is swimming in the water. The snake is looking for food. The lizard is resting in the sun.*

Ⓑ ESSENTIAL KNOWLEDGE AND SKILLS

SEE ACTIVITY MASTER 8

DESCRIBE HOW ILLUSTRATIONS SUPPORT WRITTEN TEXTS OR TELL A STORY Cut out the strip of speech bubbles at the bottom of the page. Hold them up and have students identify each person shown in the pictures. Have them try to guess what is being said before gluing each bubble to its picture.

ESSENTIAL KNOWLEDGE AND SKILLS

⬇ Have students point to people and things they see in the pictures, as you say commands, like *Show me the father.*

⬆ Have students write a response for the second character in each picture.

Ⓒ FOCUS ON COMPREHENSION

SEE ACTIVITY MASTER 9

IDENTIFY STORY DETAILS Go over the sentences with students to ensure comprehension. Then instruct students to write the words *true* or *false* for each sentence. If the sentence is false, have students tell what really happened. Have them find text or illustrations in the story to support their answers. Have them invent a sentence about Jerry or Roger, then ask another classmate whether it is *true* or *false.*

FOCUS ON COMPREHENSION

⬇ Have students look through the story to match each true statement to the related picture.

⬆ After students have completed the activity, read each true sentence and ask students to say what happened as a result and why.

MULTI-LEVEL
Instruction

Mufaro's Beautiful Daughters

FOCUS ON LANGUAGE

Say each word aloud and discuss its meaning. Have students point out examples from the story which demonstrate the words in the Word Bank.

Have students think of other antonyms that describe Nyasha and Manyara, such as the words *polite* and *rude*. Encourage them to use the story for help.

ⓐ FOCUS ON LANGUAGE

SEE ACTIVITY MASTER 10

IDENTIFY ANTONYMS Discuss with students the concept of opposites. Provide pictures for students that illustrate the words *up/down, big/little,* and *black/white.* Have students match each picture with its opposite. Then have students point to a picture in the story. Be sure students understand the word pairs on the activity master. Then guide them in writing the correct words under the characters' names.

ESSENTIAL KNOWLEDGE AND SKILLS

Make sure students don't confuse the daughters' names. Ask the questions aloud and have students point to the answers in the chart.

Ask students to write two original sentences about each daughter.

ⓑ ESSENTIAL KNOWLEDGE AND SKILLS

SEE ACTIVITY MASTER 11

DEVELOP AND EXPAND REPERTOIRE OF LEARNING STRATEGIES SUCH AS REASONING INDUCTIVELY OR DEDUCTIVELY, LOOKING FOR PATTERNS IN LANGUAGE Discuss the words in the Phrase Bank. Also review the words *garden, forest,* and *city.* Have students complete the chart. Ask the questions aloud and encourage students to volunteer answers aloud before having them complete the sentences.

FOCUS ON COMPREHENSION

Have students point to the pictures as you identify them.

Have students write a sentence about the story using a rebus-style picture of their own.

ⓒ FOCUS ON COMPREHENSION

SEE ACTIVITY MASTER 12

IDENTIFY STORY DETAILS Have students identify the three pictures of the *snake, yam,* and *sunflower seeds.* Write the words on the chalkboard. Help students read the sentences, and then have them cut out the picture boxes and paste them into the sentences. Have them read their completed sentences aloud.

A Piece of String
Is a Wonderful Thing

Ⓐ FOCUS ON LANGUAGE

SEE ACTIVITY MASTER 13

USE NOUNS FROM THE STORY Provide actual examples or pictures of the words in the activity master. Clarify meanings of verbs in the sentences and have students fill in the blanks. Provide old magazines for students to cut out other objects that use string.

FOCUS ON LANGUAGE

⬇ Read each sentence aloud, pausing to allow students to say the word that completes the sentence.

⬆ Have students draw, label, and write a sentence for additional items that use string.

Ⓑ ESSENTIAL KNOWLEDGE AND SKILLS

SEE ACTIVITY MASTER 14

DESCRIBE HOW ILLUSTRATIONS SUPPORT WRITTEN TEXTS OR TELL A STORY Ask students to look at the illustrations in the story. Point out that the illustrations give information. Ask students to find examples of *spinning thread*, *weaving cloth*, and *knitting wool* in the reading selection. Then have them point to the items in the activity master as you read aloud the excerpt on the page.

ESSENTIAL KNOWLEDGE AND SKILLS

⬇ Have students work with a partner to make picture flash cards. Have them draw a picture of an object that uses string on one side and write the word on the other side.

⬆ Ask students to list other examples of objects that use string in the story.

Ⓒ FOCUS ON COMPREHENSION

SEE ACTIVITY MASTER 15

ORGANIZE FACTUAL INFORMATION Go over the words in the Phrase Bank. Guide students to discover that *rope* and *thread* are kinds of string. Then go over the examples from the Phrase Bank and discuss how each is related to string. Have students complete the graphic organizer, and then orally complete the sentence for each use of string.

FOCUS ON COMPREHENSION

⬇ Make rough sketches on the chalkboard of the uses listed in the Phrase Bank. Read the completed sentence aloud for each use of string, and have students point to the appropriate picture.

⬆ Have students expand their graphic organizers to include other kinds of string named in the story such as *yarn* or *rope*.

MULTI-LEVEL Instruction

FOCUS ON LANGUAGE

⬇ Bring in pictures of all kinds of sneakers and ask students to describe them with adjectives such as *big*, *little*, *ugly*, or *pretty*.

⬆ Ask students to make an additional Word Web for the word *rubber*.

ESSENTIAL KNOWLEDGE AND SKILLS

⬇ Have students use the caption for the tennis player as a model for their caption for the basketball player.

⬆ Ask students to write a second caption for each picture. Cut out and display a picture from a magazine. Have students write a caption for it.

FOCUS ON COMPREHENSION

⬇ Read each sentence and have students point to the corresponding picture, while repeating the sentence.

⬆ Have students draw a picture to reflect another event from the story and write an original sentence about it.

The Invention of Sneakers

Ⓐ FOCUS ON LANGUAGE

SEE ACTIVITY MASTER 16

MAKE A WORD WEB Discuss the meanings of the words in the Word Bank. Wear or bring a pair of sneakers and use pantomime, when possible, to convey the meanings. Then say a word and have the students pantomime. Give definitions for the words that cannnot be demonstrated easily. Have them put the words on their Word Webs and use each word to complete the sentence.

Ⓑ ESSENTIAL KNOWLEDGE AND SKILLS

SEE ACTIVITY MASTER 17

DESCRIBE HOW ILLUSTRATIONS SUPPORT WRITTEN TEXTS OR TELL A STORY Discuss the pictures with students, asking them to describe what they see in each one. Tell them to write their own caption for the last picture. Divide students into groups and have them discuss their captions.

Ⓒ FOCUS ON COMPREHENSION

SEE ACTIVITY MASTER 18

RECOGNIZE STORY DETAILS Have students discuss what they see in each picture. Discuss the words in the chart. Have students complete the sentences, matching them to the correct pictures. Ask students about things they *made, wore,* or *collected*. Write some example sentences on the chalkboard and turn them into present tense. For example, if a student says *I made a cake,* change this statement to *(Student Name) is making a cake.* Ask students to point out the *beginning, middle,* and *end* of each new sentence.

The Doughnuts

Ⓐ FOCUS ON LANGUAGE

SEE ACTIVITY MASTER 19

DEMONSTRATE KNOWLEDGE OF PREPOSITIONS OF PLACE Ask students to study the picture carefully before they complete the sentences. Review with students the meanings of each word and phrase in the Phrase Bank. Ask volunteers to stand up and help you demonstrate meanings. Have students complete the activity master.

Ⓑ ESSENTIAL KNOWLEDGE AND SKILLS

SEE ACTIVITY MASTER 20

DESCRIBE HOW ILLUSTRATIONS SUPPORT WRITTEN TEXTS OR TELL A STORY Discuss the meanings of the words *bracelet, stop,* and *fixes.* Review the sentences with students and have them draw pictures to illustrate the sentences. Have them use the pictures to retell the story to partners.

Ⓒ FOCUS ON COMPREHENSION

SEE ACTIVITY MASTER 21

RETELL EVENTS Discuss the chart with students. Review the sentences, using pantomime, where possible, and story illustrations to ensure comprehension. Have students complete the chart. Then, read the beginning of the first sentence and ask students to complete it orally. Write the completed sentence on the chalkboard.

MULTI-LEVEL Instruction

FOCUS ON LANGUAGE

⬇ Discuss the meanings of the words *sitting, standing, stool,* and *counter.* Point to the part of the picture described in each sentence as you read the sentence aloud. Say the sentence and let students complete it orally.

⬆ Have students add to the picture to show the meanings of the words *in, over, under,* and *against.* Then have them write sentences about what they drew.

ESSENTIAL KNOWLEDGE AND SKILLS

⬇ Say each sentence and have students repeat it, while showing the appropriate drawing. Have students retell the story, using pantomime, where possible.

⬆ Have students include additional details from the story as they retell it.

FOCUS ON COMPREHENSION

⬇ Have students say the sentence then point to the corresponding illustration in the story.

⬆ On a separate sheet of paper, ask students to make a column for Mr. Gabby. Have them write two things about Mr. Gabby in the new column.

MULTI-LEVEL Instruction

Wings

FOCUS ON LANGUAGE

⬇ Say a simple sentence using each of the labels, such as *Ariadne's thread helped them find their way out of the maze.* Make sure students understand the meaning of the sentence and the vocabulary used.

⬆ Have students write a sentence to go with each picture.

ESSENTIAL KNOWLEDGE AND SKILLS

⬇ Before completing the activity master, have students circle the parts of the two original sentences that are the same and underline the parts that are different. Make sure students understand the vocabulary.

⬆ Have students write two sentences for a partner to combine.

FOCUS ON COMPREHENSION

⬇ Use story illustrations to make sure students understand the sentences. Then, help students match the characters' names to the sentences.

⬆ Ask students to explain, either verbally or in writing, who their favorite and least favorite characters are and why.

Ⓐ FOCUS ON LANGUAGE

SEE ACTIVITY MASTER 22

IDENTIFY IMPORTANT OBJECTS FROM THE STORY Help students identify the story objects on the activity master. Read the labels together and have them find the illustrations in the story. Then, have them complete the activity.

Ⓑ ESSENTIAL KNOWLEDGE AND SKILLS

SEE ACTIVITY MASTER 23

COMBINE MULTIPLE SENTENCES INTO UNIFIED SENTENCES Read aloud the first pair of sentences. Say the combined sentence and write it on the chalkboard. Then explain to students that the new sentence contains the same information as the first two sentences. Have students underline the key words used in each new sentence.

Ⓒ FOCUS ON COMPREHENSION

SEE ACTIVITY MASTER 24

IDENTIFY CHARACTERS' ACTIONS Review information about the characters. Have students find pictures of each character in the story or have them provide a word or two about the character's actions in the story. Have students use the words from the Word Bank to complete the sentences on the activity master and draw pictures to illustrate them.

The Best New Thing

A FOCUS ON LANGUAGE

SEE ACTIVITY MASTER 25

USE *I CAN/I CAN'T* WITH VERBS FROM THE STORY
Review the phrases in the first column of the chart. Talk about the phrases with students and give them examples of each. Make sure students understand what the phrases *on Earth* and *in space* mean. Ask students *Can you (verb phrase) on Earth?* Have them respond with the words *I can* or *I can't*. After they complete the chart, have students finish the sentences using the phrases in the action column.

FOCUS ON LANGUAGE

Say each verb phrase and have students repeat after you.

Have students draw a picture to illustrate things they can do in space, and label each action with the sentence *I can (verb phrase).*

B ESSENTIAL KNOWLEDGE AND SKILLS

SEE ACTIVITY MASTER 26

USE GRAPHIC ORGANIZERS AS PRE-WRITING ACTIVITY TO DEMONSTRATE PRIOR KNOWLEDGE, TO ADD NEW INFORMATION, AND TO PREPARE TO WRITE Use pictures and pantomime to clarify meanings of words and phrases in the Phrase Bank. Ask students *Do the children see a black sky on Earth? Do the children see grass in Rada and Jonny's world?* Demonstrate putting the phrase *the sun* in the center section of the diagram. Repeat with another phrase, and then have the students complete the diagram. Model completing the sentences, then have students write two answers of their own.

ESSENTIAL KNOWLEDGE AND SKILLS

Instead of the Venn diagram, have students write the words and phrases under three columns on the chalkboard.

Have students think of other things Rada and Jonny might see in the two worlds.

C FOCUS ON COMPREHENSION

SEE ACTIVITY MASTER 27

RECOGNIZE REASONS FOR STORY EVENTS Have students work with a partner to match the sentence parts. To clarify meanings of sentences, ask volunteers to pantomime, where possible, what is happening in each sentence. If necessary, use illustrations from the story to help. Have students draw and color a picture to illustrate one of the sentences.

FOCUS ON COMPREHENSION

Create sample illustrations for the sentences, using stick figure drawings or photos. Discuss the pictures before matching the sentences.

Have students cut out their pictures and use them to make new sentences. One student says a phrase from column A, while another displays his/her picture.

MULTI-LEVEL Instruction

The Desert Beneath the Sea

FOCUS ON LANGUAGE

Ask students to point to the items you indicate. Ask them simple questions. For example, point to a fish and say: *Is it a big fish or a little fish? What is the fish doing?*

Have students draw and label additional sea creatures and other objects from the ocean.

ESSENTIAL KNOWLEDGE AND SKILLS

Help students identify the objects in the pictures, such as *mound* and *bag*, before they do the activity master.

Have students write the sentences in a paragraph form, using the words *then, next,* and *finally.*

FOCUS ON COMPREHENSION

Find illustrations in the story that relate to the words and phrases in the Phrase Bank. Read the sentences and have students complete them orally.

Have students expand the Word Web. Ask other questions, such as *What do you need to study tilefish?* Have students add ovals to the Word Web and fill them in with more information from the story.

Ⓐ FOCUS ON LANGUAGE

SEE ACTIVITY MASTER 28

VOCABULARY IN CONTEXT Have students label the objects in the picture, reviewing as necessary the phrases in the Phrase Bank. Review with students the terms *top, middle,* and *bottom,* and have them complete the sentences.

Ⓑ ESSENTIAL KNOWLEDGE AND SKILLS

SEE ACTIVITY MASTER 29

READ AUTHENTIC LITERATURE TO DEVELOP VOCABULARY, STRUCTURES, AND BACKGROUND KNOWLEDGE NEEDED TO COMPREHEND INCREASINGLY CHALLENGING LANGUAGE Review the passages in the story that describe *how to study a tilefish mound.* Clarify vocabulary in the sentences and help students identify the objects in the pictures. Have them complete the activity master.

Ⓒ FOCUS ON COMPREHENSION

SEE ACTIVITY MASTER 30

IDENTIFY STORY DETAILS Read aloud the questions from the Word Web and use picture examples from the story to explain the words in the Phrase Bank. Explain to students that the Word Web can be filled in with the words and phrases in the Phrase Bank. They should write each phrase under the question that it answers. Have students fill in the web and complete the sentences.

The Lost Lake

A FOCUS ON LANGUAGE

SEE ACTIVITY MASTER 31

RECOGNIZE STORY PLACE NAMES Show students pictures of places from magazines or books, depicting the scenery words in the Word Bank. Display them one by one, and say *This is a (place name)*. Have students find the picture on their activity master that is similar to the picture you are displaying, and repeat the name of the place. Then have them label the pictures on the activity master.

FOCUS ON LANGUAGE

Say the words in the Word Bank and have students repeat after you.

Have students think of things they can do in each of the settings.

B ESSENTIAL KNOWLEDGE AND SKILLS

SEE ACTIVITY MASTER 32

CONSTRUCT CORRECT SENTENCES, INCLUDING A VARIETY OF SENTENCE TYPES AND STYLES Read the chart with students. Say the names of the items pictured in the chart and have students repeat them. Discuss the activities named and encourage students to brainstorm other things you need for each activity. Do the first sentence orally and write it on the chalkboard. Show how all the parts of the sentence are found in the chart. Have students complete the activity.

ESSENTIAL KNOWLEDGE AND SKILLS

Have students complete the sentences orally berfore writing the words in the blanks. For more practice, show pictures of other things you need for these activities. Say the word for each new picture and have students substitute them in the sentences.

Have students pick another activity and write a sentence about it. Have them follow the same pattern as the one in the activity master.

C FOCUS ON COMPREHENSION

SEE ACTIVITY MASTER 33

DESCRIBE CHARACTERS' FEELINGS AND MOTIVATIONS Have volunteers name the words that go with the pictures. Discuss any new vocabulary words that appear in the sentences. Make sure students understand the tenses in each sentence. For example, the action in the first sentence (*has read*) is already finished. Have students complete the activity master.

FOCUS ON COMPREHENSION

Use the pictures to clarify the words in the Word Bank. Read each sentence and have students point to the picture. Say the words and have students repeat them as they are gluing the pictures in the boxes.

Ask students to write two original sentences that tell why Luke's father wanted to go camping. For example, *He sees the pictures on Luke's wall.*

Sarah, Plain and Tall

FOCUS ON LANGUAGE

Show students pictures of the seaside and the prairie and help them find each item from the Word Bank in the pictures before doing the activity.

Ask students to sort the words in the Word Bank into another category, such as *Things I Have Seen*.

Ⓐ FOCUS ON LANGUAGE

SEE ACTIVITY MASTER 34

CATEGORIZE NOUNS FROM THE STORY Review the words in the Word Bank and have students find picture examples for the words in the story. You may want to show students some pictures from a book or magazine to convey the meaning of the words. Talk about which words are things that can be found on the prairie and which words are things that can be found at the sea. Then have students list the words in the appropriate column.

ESSENTIAL KNOWLEDGE AND SKILLS

Read each phrase that is true for Sarah, and have students point to it. Make sure students understand the meaning of each phrase. Then have them copy the phrases onto the Word Web.

Have students work with a partner to ask and answer questions about Sarah, such as *Does Sarah have a dog? No, she has a cat.*

Ⓑ ESSENTIAL KNOWLEDGE AND SKILLS

SEE ACTIVITY MASTER 35

ARRANGE PHRASES, CLAUSES, AND SENTENCES INTO CORRECT AND MEANINGFUL PATTERNS Read aloud passages in the story that relate to the phrases in the box, and then ask questions about them. For example, read lines from the passage in the story where Sarah swims in the pond, and then ask students *Does Sarah like to swim?* Have students complete the Word Web. Instruct students to choose only three of the phrases to complete the sentence. Give an example of the completed sentence.

FOCUS ON COMPREHENSION

Work with students to complete the chart. Show pictures and read sections from the story that describe Sarah talking about or doing these things on the prairie.

Have students write two sentences that tell what they would do at the sea, and on the prairie.

Ⓒ FOCUS ON COMPREHENSION

SEE ACTIVITY MASTER 36

RECOGNIZE STORY DETAILS Discuss meanings for the phrases in the box. Ask students which phrases relate to the sea and which relate to the prairie. Point out that Sarah now lives on the prairie, so she can't do some of these things, but she talks to the children about the things she did at the sea. Have students complete the chart and then use one of the phrases from the chart to complete each sentence. Encourage students to talk about their favorite places and have them draw a picture of an activity they would like to do.

Yours Truly, Goldilocks

Ⓐ FOCUS ON LANGUAGE

SEE ACTIVITY MASTER 37

RECOGNIZE AND DESCRIBE FOODS Have students name the vegetables on the activity master and write their names under each picture. Ask *What is your favorite vegetable?* Have students draw their favorites. Discuss words that might be new *(Dear, tiny, crunchy, fresh, salad)*. Have students cut out the pictures and complete the letter. Then have them practice reading the letter with a partner.

Ⓑ ESSENTIAL KNOWLEDGE AND SKILLS

SEE ACTIVITY MASTER 38

DEMONSTRATE KNOWLEDGE OF PARTS OF SPEECH Ask students to name words that describe things you can do and offer a few examples, such as the words *play, read,* and *walk.* Point out that these words are verbs. Say the words in the Word Bank, and have students point to the picture that describes each verb. Have students complete the activity master, then practice reading the sentences with partners.

Ⓒ FOCUS ON COMPREHENSION

SEE ACTIVITY MASTER 39

USE OPPOSITES TO DESCRIBE CHARACTERS IN THE STORY Show pictures of some examples of opposites, such as the words *black/white, happy/sad,* and *day/night.* Encourage students to name other examples. Say the words printed on the house and invite volunteers to name opposites for them. Then ask students to use a word to describe each character from the Word Bank. Have them complete the activity master.

MULTI-LEVEL
Instruction

FOCUS ON LANGUAGE

⬇ Encourage students to brainstorm names of their favorite vegetables. Have them work in groups to complete the letter. Then have volunteers read it aloud.

⬆ Have students write an original letter from Mrs. Rabbit to Goldilocks, asking for different vegetables from the garden. Help them get started by writing a salutation and first sentence on the chalkboard.

ESSENTIAL KNOWLEDGE AND SKILLS

⬇ Ask volunteers to identify the verbs in the Word Bank. Write these verbs on the chalkboard and pantomime them to clarify meanings.

⬆ Have students find other verbs in the story and use them in sentences.

FOCUS ON COMPREHENSION

⬇ Write opposites on the chalkboard and give corresponding pictures to students. Have them match the pictures to the words.

⬆ Have students brainstorm words that describe other characters from the story *(fast rabbit, busy Goldilocks, scary wolves)*. Have students use the description words in sentences.

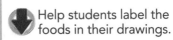
MULTI-LEVEL
Instruction

The Hoboken Chicken Emergency

FOCUS ON LANGUAGE

⬇ Help students label the foods in their drawings.

⬆ Have students ask each other *What do you want to eat for Thanksgiving?*

ESSENTIAL KNOWLEDGE AND SKILLS

⬇ Ask a question from the *Effects* column, such as *Why is Momma surprised?* Read aloud the choices from the *Causes* column to help students match the *Causes* with the *Effects*.

⬆ Have students find and list additional *Causes* and *Effects* in the story.

FOCUS ON COMPREHENSION

⬇ Have students pick out other events in the story and act them out.

⬆ Have students add other events to the sequence. Then, have them write the events in a paragraph on a separate sheet of paper.

Ⓐ FOCUS ON LANGUAGE

SEE ACTIVITY MASTER 40

USE FOOD WORDS FROM STORY Discuss and show pictures of a Thanksgiving dinner. Point out the date on a calendar. Talk about what foods you would like to eat at Thanksgiving, and then ask students what they would like to eat. Help them write the names of the foods they mention. Then have them draw pictures of two of the foods they like on the plate in the activity master. Have them fill in the sentence using one of the words from the Word Bank or their own word.

Ⓑ ESSENTIAL KNOWLEDGE AND SKILLS

SEE ACTIVITY MASTER 41

USE BASIC CAPITALIZATION AND PUNCTUATION CORRECTLY SUCH AS CAPITALIZING NAMES AND FIRST LETTERS IN SENTENCES AND USING PERIODS, QUESTION MARKS, AND EXCLAMATION POINTS Guide students to identify *Cause* and *Effect* by demonstrating a simple *Cause/Effect* situation, such as pushing a pencil off a desk. Say *The pencil fell on the floor because I pushed it.* Point out that a cause is something that makes another thing happen; the effect is the thing that happens. Help students connect the causes and effects in the first part. For the last part, review the story to help them understand which phrase is the *Cause* and which phrase is the *Effect*.

Ⓒ FOCUS ON COMPREHENSION

SEE ACTIVITY MASTER 42

SHOW ORDER OF STORY EVENTS After students have put the events in order, read aloud the scenes, and let students take turns acting out the text. Students can make and use props. Discuss why they put the events in this particular order and explain to them why the order makes sense.

Fifteen Minutes

Ⓐ FOCUS ON LANGUAGE

SEE ACTIVITY MASTER 43

ANALYZE COMPOUND WORDS Explain to students that some words are made up of two smaller words that have been joined. Write the word *dollhouse* on the chalkboard. Draw a line between *doll* and *house*. Show students actual or illustrated examples for each word. Work with students to write a simple definition for *dollhouse*, such as a *house for dolls*. Then help students write definitions for each compound word.

FOCUS ON LANGUAGE

⬇ Write the compound words from the activity master on strips of paper. Then cut each word into two smaller words. Shuffle the words and have students work with partners to reconnect the compound words.

⬆ Write other compound words on the chalkboard and have students identify and circle the two words that make up the compound word.

Ⓑ ESSENTIAL KNOWLEDGE AND SKILLS

SEE ACTIVITY MASTER 44

LEARN SOUND/SYMBOL RELATIONSHIPS AS THEY APPLY TO THE PHONOLOGICAL SYSTEM OF ENGLISH; PRODUCE PHONOLOGICAL ELEMENTS OF NEWLY ACQUIRED VOCABULARY SUCH AS LONG VOWELS AND SILENT LETTERS Write the words *right, might,* and *bright* on the chalkboard. Emphasize the pronunciation of the words while drawing a circle around the letters *-igh* in each. Have students repeat the words after you. Explain that the letters *-igh* together, usually stand for the *long -i* sound. Have students read the words *night, fight,* and *light*. Show examples of each sentence, if possible, then have them complete the activity master.

ESSENTIAL KNOWLEDGE AND SKILLS

⬇ Write the letters *-ight* on the chalkboard. Then write letters *(s, t)* and blends *(fl, fr)* or others, on separate index cards. Distribute the cards and have students take turns placing them in front of the letters *-ight* and pronouncing the new words.

⬆ Have students find examples of other words that have the letters *-ight*.

Ⓒ FOCUS ON COMPREHENSION

SEE ACTIVITY MASTER 45

DISTINGUISH FACT FROM OPINION Discuss the difference between a fact and an opinion. Provide students with examples, such as *Toothbrushes come in many colors* (fact). *Blue is the best color for a toothbrush* (opinion). Review the story, and then direct students to label each sentence on the activity master as fact or opinion.

FOCUS ON COMPREHENSION

⬇ Help students distinguish between facts and opinions by prefacing the statements with the words *I think* or *I know*.

⬆ Have students write one statement of opinion and one statement of fact about the selection for a classmate to mark with the letters F or O.

MULTI-LEVEL Instruction

Sally Ann Thunder Ann Whirlwind

FOCUS ON LANGUAGE

⬇ Read the completed sentences and have students fill in the blanks.

⬆ Have students act out and write a sentence using another adjective from the story, such as the word *shy* or *dizzy*.

Ⓐ FOCUS ON LANGUAGE

SEE ACTIVITY MASTER 46

USE ADJECTIVES Review the words in column 1 and have students name things in the classroom that are *tall* or *open*. Pantomime the words *sleepy* and *scared*. Use each word in a sentence, then have students give examples of their own. Next, have them match the pictures to the words and complete the sentences on the activity master.

ESSENTIAL KNOWLEDGE AND SKILLS

⬇ Have students find the story illustrations that describe the sentences on the activity master before they answer the questions.

⬆ Have students expand the responses by adding explanations or *because* clauses. For example, students may add *Sally uses the snakes to help Davy.*

Ⓑ ESSENTIAL KNOWLEDGE AND SKILLS

SEE ACTIVITY MASTER 47

DEVELOP AND EXPAND REPERTOIRE OF LEARNING STRATEGIES SUCH AS LOOKING FOR PATTERNS IN LANGUAGE Review the story to discover what Sally does. Read each of the questions on the activity master aloud, and have students respond with the sentence *Yes, she does* or *No, she doesn't*. Ask students other questions like *Why does Sally fight?* or *Why doesn't Sally read?* Continue down the list until they have answered each question. Encourage students to point out things in the illustrations and text that help them to support their answers. Then have students write the responses to each question and draw the pictures for each *Yes, she does* answer.

FOCUS ON COMPREHENSION

⬇ Help students find story illustrations to match the first three questions on the activity master.

⬆ Have students combine each question and answer into a single sentence, such as *When Mike Fink tries to scare her, she hits him.*

Ⓒ FOCUS ON COMPREHENSION

SEE ACTIVITY MASTER 48

IDENTIFY STORY DETAILS Review the story and have students identify the characters and vocabulary in the sentences. After they complete the activity master, have them use the questions and answers to help them retell the story to a partner. As students retell the story, encourage them to ask each other questions like *What happens after Sally hits Mike Fink?*

Ali Baba Hunts for a Bear

Ⓐ FOCUS ON LANGUAGE

SEE ACTIVITY MASTER 49

IDENTIFY ANIMAL NAMES Let students look at animal picture books, nature magazines, dictionaries, or beginning encyclopedias. Have students work with partners to match the animal names with the pictures on the activity master. Then help students determine which animals Ali Baba saw. Ask them *Did Ali Baba see a deer?* Repeat this question for each animal.

FOCUS ON LANGUAGE

⬇ Have students point to the corresponding pictures as you name the animals listed in the Word Bank.

⬆ Expand the activity by asking students if they see other animals in the story that were not mentioned on the activity master.

Ⓑ ESSENTIAL KNOWLEDGE AND SKILLS

SEE ACTIVITY MASTER 50

READ AUTHENTIC LITERATURE TO DEVELOP VOCABULARY NEEDED TO COMPREHEND INCREASINGLY CHALLENGING LANGUAGE Point to each illustration in the story and ask students to supply words, phrases, or complete sentences to describe the action. Have them match the actions to the corresponding phrases in the Phrase Bank. Help them write the phrases from the Phrase Bank on the Web. Ask them what they would like to do in the park, and have them respond using the sentence frame on the activity master.

ESSENTIAL KNOWLEDGE AND SKILLS

⬇ Ask students to draw pictures to illustrate each of the phrases.

⬆ Challenge students to add more phrases to the Word Web.

Ⓒ FOCUS ON COMPREHENSION

SEE ACTIVITY MASTER 51

DISTINGUISH BETWEEN TRUE AND FALSE STATEMENTS Review the story events. Have students work in small groups to discuss whether each statement is *true* or *false*. Suggest that they refer to the story to check any statements of which they are unsure. Have partners work together to rewrite the *false* sentences to make them true. Then have them read their sentences to each other.

FOCUS ON COMPREHENSION

⬇ Summarize the story orally for the students, making sure to include the true statements from the activity master. Have students mark the statements *true* or *false* as you summarize.

⬆ Have students write a true sentence and a false sentence about the story for a classmate to mark with the letter *T* or *F*.

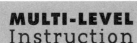

MULTI-LEVEL Instruction

FOCUS ON LANGUAGE

⬇ Have students draw pictures to illustrate the seasons.

⬆ Have students brainstorm additional words to add to the chart.

ESSENTIAL KNOWLEDGE AND SKILLS

⬇ Read aloud sentences 1-3, using gestures or pantomime to convey the meanings of the underlined words.

⬆ Have students write original sentences in which they use the underlined words in sentences 1-3.

FOCUS ON COMPREHENSION

⬇ Help students label the following items in the pictures: *coyote, buds, leaves,* and *strawberries.*

⬆ Challenge students to draw pictures showing one of the nine other moons in the story, such as the *Baby Bear Moon.*

Thirteen Moons on Turtle's Back

Ⓐ FOCUS ON LANGUAGE

SEE ACTIVITY MASTER 52

CLASSIFY SEASON WORDS Discuss the three seasons in the chart and the meanings of the words and phrases in the Word Bank. Ask students questions about the seasons, such as *Is it cold in the winter? Is there snow in the winter?* Have them sort the words into the correct columns. Complete the first sentence for them, and have them continue with the rest on their own. Ask students to describe the weather that accompanies each of these seasons. Ask them to describe things people can do in the winter, spring, and autumn.

Ⓑ ESSENTIAL KNOWLEDGE AND SKILLS

SEE ACTIVITY MASTER 53

USE PRIOR KNOWLEDGE AND EXPERIENCES TO UNDERSTAND MEANINGS IN ENGLISH Extend the activity master by asking questions like: *What places have you entered today?* (the school, a classroom) *Where can you use a canoe?* (on a river, on a lake) *What do animals shed?* (fur, skin)

Review the story events and have students complete the sentences. After students have completed the sentences, continue discussion by asking them why these different events occurred.

Ⓒ FOCUS ON COMPREHENSION

SEE ACTIVITY MASTER 54

IDENTIFY MAIN IDEAS AND DETAILS Review the vocabulary words in the sentences. Have students identify the picture elements, and then match the sentences and pictures.

Divide the class into four groups, with each group representing one of the seasons. Tell each group to draw a picture of its season. Put the drawings on the wall to make a year-round mural.

Swimming with Sea Lions

Ⓐ FOCUS ON LANGUAGE

SEE ACTIVITY MASTER 55

IDENTIFY ACTION VERBS Have students pantomime the words in the Word Bank. Ask students which actions can be done on land and in the water. Have them complete the Word Webs.

Let students make sea lion finger puppets out of construction paper and craft sticks or hand puppets out of socks. Encourage them to use their puppets to act out the action verbs in the Word Bank.

FOCUS ON LANGUAGE

⬇ Make tagboard seals to illustrate each of the verbs in the Word Bank. Label each seal with a verb. Then ask students to draw pictures of the sea with land near it. Tell them to place the seals in the land or in the water.

⬆ Help students make Venn diagrams to compare themselves to seals.

Ⓑ ESSENTIAL KNOWLEDGE AND SKILLS

SEE ACTIVITY MASTER 56

PRODUCE VISUALS FOR HIS/HER OWN MESSAGES; USE PRIOR KNOWLEDGE AND EXPERIENCES TO UNDERSTAND MEANINGS IN ENGLISH Point out to students that the story is a diary or writing that records events or feelings. Have them use the sentences in the activity master to write their own diary entry about a sunset. Students may draw their pictures before or after they complete the sentences. Encourage them to continue writing diary entries. Have them write a sentence every day and draw a picture to describe what they wrote.

ESSENTIAL KNOWLEDGE AND SKILLS

⬇ Draw a sunset on the chalkboard. Have students say words in the Word Bank that describe it.

⬆ Have students extend their journal entry by writing about what they were doing when they saw the sunset.

Ⓒ FOCUS ON COMPREHENSION

SEE ACTIVITY MASTER 57

RECALL STORY DETAILS Lead students in a discussion about the facts they learned about the Galápagos tortoise. Use yes/no, either/or, or short-answer formats as students' level of fluency permits. Assist students in reading the sentences on the activity master. Ask them whether each sentence is true. If students are unsure, help them locate and reread small sections of the story to find the answer.

FOCUS ON COMPREHENSION

⬇ Tell students that there are two sentences that are not true. Read through each sentence with them. Help them sort the sentences into categories of *true* or *false*.

⬆ Encourage students to arrange the sentences in an order that tells a story.

FOCUS ON LANGUAGE

Have students orally complete the following simplified sentence frame: *In a rain forest, I can find _____s, _____s, and _____s.*

Encourage students to describe the plants and animals on the activity master.

ESSENTIAL KNOWLEDGE AND SKILLS

Help students read each sentence. Help them write their own sentence about the rain forest.

Encourage students to write a complex sentence about the rain forest. Model the pattern of an *if/then* or *because* statement.

FOCUS ON COMPREHENSION

Have students draw pictures to represent each part of the story. Have them talk about their drawings with a partner.

Encourage students to expand on the paragraph. Have them add the word *because* and extend each sentence.

The Great Kapok Tree

Ⓐ FOCUS ON LANGUAGE

SEE ACTIVITY MASTER 58

IDENTIFY PLANTS AND ANIMALS OF THE RAIN FOREST Display pictures of a rain forest. Help students identify plants and animals of the rain forest, using illustrations from the story if necessary. Have students label the illustration on the activity master.

Point out that the first sentence refers to plants, and the second to animals. Have students classify the words in the Word Bank as either plants or animals, and then complete the sentences.

Ⓑ ESSENTIAL KNOWLEDGE AND SKILLS

SEE ACTIVITY MASTER 59

USE ACCESSIBLE LANGUAGE AND LEARN NEW AND ESSENTIAL LANGUAGE IN THE PROCESS Help students summarize why saving rain forests is important to life on Earth. You may want to reread sections of the text in which the animals are whispering to the man. Help students identify the picture clues in each sentence and match the clues to the words in the Word Bank. Encourage students to supply their own reasons for saving the rain forests.

Ⓒ FOCUS ON COMPREHENSION

SEE ACTIVITY MASTER 60

DESCRIBE CHANGE IN A STORY CHARACTER; SUMMARIZE STORY EVENTS Ask students whether the man behaved in the same ways at the beginning and at the end of the story. Have them describe the differences. Encourage them to discuss why they think the man changed, then have them complete the diagram and fill in the blanks to finish the paragraph.

Dinner at Aunt Connie's House

Ⓐ FOCUS ON LANGUAGE

SEE ACTIVITY MASTER 61

USE JOB NAMES IN CONTEXT Lead students in a discussion about various jobs, using photos or illustrations as available. Have students pantomime an activity related to each job. Then help students identify the illustrations on the activity master and the corresponding words from the Word Bank.

Encourage a volunteer to read the sentences. Point out the clue to the occupation in each sentence, for example *sing* in sentence 5, and have students circle it.

FOCUS ON LANGUAGE

▼ Have students write each word from the Word Bank on an index card and draw a picture clue for themselves on the back of it. Have them use these cards to help them complete each sentence.

▲ Have students think of real people who do the jobs listed in the Word Bank. Have them write a sentence for each word.

Ⓑ ESSENTIAL KNOWLEDGE AND SKILLS

SEE ACTIVITY MASTER 62

IDENTIFY PEOPLE, PLACES, OBJECTS, EVENTS, AND BASIC CONCEPTS Write the words *big house, attic,* and *dining room* on the chalkboard. Point to each illustration in the story and ask, *What place is this?* Have students say what happened in each place in the story. Have them brainstorm a list of other things people can do in these places. Ask students what kinds of objects they might find in each place.

ESSENTIAL KNOWLEDGE AND SKILLS

▼ Tell students where each event occurred, and have them draw a line from the Event column to the Setting column.

▲ Ask students to choose their favorite place in the story—*big house, attic,* or *dining room*—and tell why.

Ⓒ FOCUS ON COMPREHENSION

SEE ACTIVITY MASTER 63

DISTINGUISH BETWEEN REAL AND FANTASTIC STORY EVENTS Recite a few statements of possible and impossible events, such as *A fish can live in the water; A person can live in the water.* Have students respond with the sentence: *It can happen* or *It can't happen.* Show students how to make the impossible statements true by changing *can* to *can't.* Have them complete the activity master.

FOCUS ON COMPREHENSION

▼ Have students draw pictures to match each sentence in the *It can happen* column.

▲ Encourage students to go to the library to find another fantasy storybook. Ask them to talk about things that happened in the story and tell what can happen and what can't happen in real life.

Rain Player

FOCUS ON LANGUAGE

⬇ Help students learn the words in the Word Bank. Read each sentence with the word in parentheses, and have students pantomime the action.

⬆ Have students write a sentence using a word in the Word Bank and underline the word they used. Have a partner read the sentence, replacing the underlined word with a word from the list.

ESSENTIAL KNOWLEDGE AND SKILLS

⬇ Ask students to draw a picture of a basketball game and a picture of a *pok-a-tok* game.

⬆ Have students write brief sentences explaining which game they would rather play—basketball or *pok-a-tok* and why.

FOCUS ON COMPREHENSION

⬇ Put the story events in order for students. Then have them fill in the sequence of events chain.

⬆ Ask students to explain the reason why Pik and Chac played the game.

Ⓐ FOCUS ON LANGUAGE

SEE ACTIVITY MASTER 64

IDENTIFY SYNONYMS FOR ACTION WORDS Ask a student to pantomime an action word, such as *jump*. Have students identify the action. Together, brainstorm and list words that mean almost the same thing, such as the words *hop, bounce,* and *leap*. Repeat the activity for each word in the Word Bank.

Read each sentence aloud using the clue words. Have students go back and supply a word from the list that means almost the same as the clue word.

Ⓑ ESSENTIAL KNOWLEDGE AND SKILLS

SEE ACTIVITY MASTER 65

MAKE CONNECTIONS ACROSS CONTENT AREAS AND USE AND REUSE LANGUAGE AND CONCEPTS IN DIFFERENT WAYS If possible, allow students to watch or play a basketball game. Emphasize the actions of playing with a ball, passing the ball, using a net and a hoop, and dribbling. Look at the story illustrations of the game and discuss with students the similarities and differences between basketball and *pok-a-tok*.

Ⓒ FOCUS ON COMPREHENSION

SEE ACTIVITY MASTER 66

RETELL ORDER OF EVENTS Orally summarize the story for students. Have students volunteer story events as you write them on the chalkboard. Then read aloud each event in the activity master list. Have students write each event listed in a box to complete the story event chain.

The Rag Coat

A FOCUS ON LANGUAGE

SEE ACTIVITY MASTER 67

DESCRIBE USING COLOR AND SHAPE WORDS Draw a square, a circle, and a triangle on the board and help students identify them. Have students point to the word in the Word Bank that identifies each shape. Hold up crayons or markers and have them point to the color in the Word Bank. Have them complete the sentences on the activity master and read them to a partner.

B ESSENTIAL KNOWLEDGE AND SKILLS

SEE ACTIVITY MASTER 68

USE ACCESSIBLE LANGUAGE AND LEARN NEW AND ESSENTIAL LANGUAGE IN THE PROCESS Help students identify the words in the Word Bank. Ask them questions about each word, such as *When do you wear a coat? When do you play with your friends? When do you eat?* Have them use the words in the Word Bank to complete the sentences.

Help students read the beginning of the sentence in Column A. Then have students draw lines to match the beginning of the sentence to its ending in Column B.

C FOCUS ON COMPREHENSION

SEE ACTIVITY MASTER 69

RETELL THE ORDER OF EVENTS Demonstrate the meanings of the words *first, then,* and *finally* by discussing the sequencing of an activity students are familiar with. Help them interpret and sequentially order the phrases. Have students complete the first paragraph on the activity master. Point out the use of the comma.

Help students identify the pictures and read the phrases. Have them label the pictures with the words *first, then,* and *finally* to show order. Have them complete the paragraph using the same structure as the paragraph in the beginning of the activity master.

MULTI-LEVEL Instruction

FOCUS ON LANGUAGE

⬇ Have students write the words from the Word Bank on another sheet of paper. Ask them to circle the color words with corresponding crayons or markers and draw the shapes around the shape words.

⬆ Have students use additional colors and shapes to complete the sentences.

ESSENTIAL KNOWLEDGE AND SKILLS

⬇ Demonstrate the sentence pattern in columns A and B by saying and acting out a sentence, such as *If I have a pencil, I can write.*

⬆ Have students create additional sentences about Minna, using the structure in Columns A and B.

FOCUS ON COMPREHENSION

⬇ Have students point to pictures you name.

⬆ Have students expand on the paragraph by adding details. For example, *First, you collect the rags. They can be from clothes or blankets.*

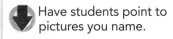

MULTI-LEVEL
Instruction

Teammates

MULTI-LEVEL Instruction

FOCUS ON LANGUAGE

⬇ Read the completed sentences aloud. Have them circle the -ly word on the activity master and then write it on the line.

⬆ Give students more base words. Tell them to add -ly to the words. Write a sentence using the base word, and let students write a corresponding sentence using the new -ly word.

ESSENTIAL KNOWLEDGE AND SKILLS

⬇ Talk about the phrases in the box with students. Ask them to point out illustrations in the story that match the phrases.

⬆ Have students extend the sentences about each League with a *because* clause.

FOCUS ON COMPREHENSION

⬇ Have students brainstorm single words and short phrases to describe *Jackie Robinson, Pee Wee Reese,* and the *fans.*

⬆ Have students write a *true* and a *false* sentence about the story for a classmate to mark with the letters *T* or *F*.

Ⓐ FOCUS ON LANGUAGE

SEE ACTIVITY MASTER 70

ADD THE SUFFIX -LY Read each word on the activity master aloud, first without the -ly ending, and then with it. Have students repeat the words after you. Then ask them to find examples of words ending in -ly in the story. Explain that -ly can be added to an adjective and that the new word is used to describe an action.

Ⓑ ESSENTIAL KNOWLEDGE AND SKILLS

SEE ACTIVITY MASTER 71

READ AUTHENTIC LITERATURE TO DEVELOP VOCABULARY, STRUCTURES, AND BACKGROUND KNOWLEDGE NEEDED TO COMPREHEND INCREASINGLY CHALLENGING LANGUAGE Reread the parts of the story that describe the conditions in the two leagues. Lead them to conclude that the conditions for the Major League players were much better. Have the students read the phrases in the box, and work in pairs to write them in the correct column on the chart.

Ⓒ FOCUS ON COMPREHENSION

SEE ACTIVITY MASTER 72

IDENTIFY STORY DETAILS Review the story events. Have students work in small groups to discuss whether each statement is *true* or *false*. Suggest that they refer to the story to check any statements of which they are unsure. Review the words *cruel, nice, afraid, brave,* and *hero.* Have students circle the word that completes the sentence. Have them check their work against a classmate's and discuss any differences in their answers.

Name

Young Arthur

Fill in the chart with words from the Word Bank. Use words from the chart to complete the sentences.

Words About Battles	Words About Kings

The soldier will fight the enemy in a battle for the _____.

The king wears a _____.

Young Arthur

The words below describe Arthur. Can you think of other words that describe him? Write them below.

brave   kind

truthful

_____

_____

_____

_____

Use the words above or words you know to write sentences about Arthur.

Arthur was _____.

Arthur was _____.

Arthur was _____.

Arthur was _____.

TAKE IT HOME
Ask a family member to tell you about a time when he or she was brave, truthful, or kind. Then tell the class about it.

Young Arthur

The sentences tell the story of Young Arthur.
Draw pictures to go with the sentences. Number the
pictures from 1 to 4 to put them in the correct order.

Arthur is crowned king.	Merlin takes the baby from the castle.	King Arthur wins the battle at Caerleon.	Arthur pulls the sword from the stone.

Tell where in the story these events happened. Write the words *beginning*, *middle*, or *end* below each picture.

Cherokee Summer

Draw a picture of the countryside where Bridget lives. Include the places named in the Word Bank. Then label your drawing, using the words in the Word Bank.

WORD BANK

forests   pastures
hay fields   valleys

Complete the sentence using one of the words from the Word Bank.

I see _____ in Bridget's countryside.

Name

Cherokee Summer

Use the words in the Word Bank to answer the questions about Bridget.

WORD BANK	
Oklahoma	Cherokee
English	northeastern
Cherokee Indian	crawdads

1. Where does Bridget live?

   Bridget lives in _____.

   It is in the _____ part of the state.

2. What is her nationality?

   Bridget is a _____ _____.

3. What does she like to eat?

   Bridget likes to eat _____.

4. Which languages does she speak?

   Bridget speaks _____ and _____.

Now answer these questions about yourself.

5. Where do you live?

   I live in _____.

6. What is your nationality?

   I am _____.

7. What do you like to eat?

   I like to eat _____.

8. Which languages do you speak?

   I speak _____ and _____.

Cherokee Summer

Complete the sentences below using the words from the Word Bank. Then draw a picture showing what is happening in each sentence.

WORD BANK

stomp dance

crawdad

legend

He is eating a _____ .

She is reading a Cherokee _____ .

They are doing a Cherokee _____ .

 TAKE IT HOME
Ask family members to help you make a list of a special food, a special story, and a special dance or song from your culture.

Growing Up with Jerry Spinelli

WORD BANK

fish	snake
frog	lizard

Use the words in the Word Bank to help you label the creatures that live near creeks. Can you think of other creatures that live in or near creeks? Draw pictures of them.

Write sentences about the creatures.

There's a _____ at the creek.

There's a _____ at the creek.

_____.

Growing Up with Jerry Spinelli

Cut out the speech bubbles at the bottom of the page. Glue them into the pictures to show what each person is saying.

Oh, no! You broke the window!

Do you want to share my tent?

I don't like boys.

Name

Growing Up with Jerry Spinelli

Write the word TRUE next to each sentence that describes something that happened in the story. Write the word FALSE next to each sentence that describes something that did not happen in the story.

1. _____ Jerry's father breaks the neighbor's window.

2. _____ Jerry breaks the neighbor's window.

3. _____ Jerry and Roger stay in the tent all night.

4. _____ Jerry is afraid to sleep in the tent.

5. _____ Jerry gets leeches on his legs.

6. _____ Jerry sees a snake in the creek.

TAKE IT HOME
Ask a family member to tell you about something funny that happened when he or she was young. Tell the story to the rest of the class.

Name

Mufaro's Beautiful Daughters

Look at the paired words in the Word Bank.
They are opposites. Write the words describing
each daughter under the correct daughter's name.

_____ Nyasha _____ Manyara _____

Now finish the sentences with the words you wrote.

1. Manyara is _____, _____, and
   _____ .

2. Nyasha is _____, _____, and
   _____ .

Mufaro's Beautiful Daughters

**Read the words and phrases in the Phrase Bank.
Complete the chart by writing what Nyasha saw
on the left side and writing what Manyara saw
on the right side.**

Nyasha saw	Manyara saw

**Use the chart and the story to help you complete the answers
to the questions below.**

What did Nyasha see?

Nyasha saw _____ in the garden.

Nyasha saw _____ in the city.

What did Manyara see?

Manyara saw _____ in the forest.

Manyara saw _____ in the city.

TAKE IT HOME
Ask a family member to think of a trip you have taken together.
Write two sentences about what you saw.

Mufaro's Beautiful Daughters

Cut apart the pictures. Paste them into the correct sentences.

1. Nyasha sang to the ⬚ .

2. Nyasha gave a ⬚ to a hungry boy.

3. Nyasha gave ⬚ to the old woman.

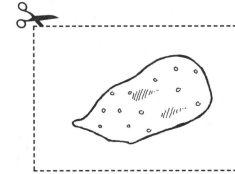

A Piece of String Is a Wonderful Thing

Make a picture dictionary for string. Draw a picture of a thing with strings for each of the words.

kite	**guitar**	**necklace**

ribbon	**boat**

Use the words to complete the sentences.

1. I can wear a _____ .

2. I can play a _____ .

3. I can fly a _____ .

4. I can sail a _____ .

5. I can tie a _____ .

TAKE IT HOME
Make a list of possible uses for string that you find in your home. Bring your list to class.

A Piece of String Is a Wonderful Thing

Look at the picture. Find each thing named in the box below. Circle each thing you find.

a fishing line	a thing for anchoring a boat
a thing for holding a kite	a place for your wet socks
a thing for tying up packages	a thing for fastening gates

A Piece of String Is a Wonderful Thing

Complete the chart using information from the story about two kinds of string. Use the words in the Phrase Bank.

PHRASE BANK

anchor a boat
make blankets
sew clothes
pull heavy things
rope
thread

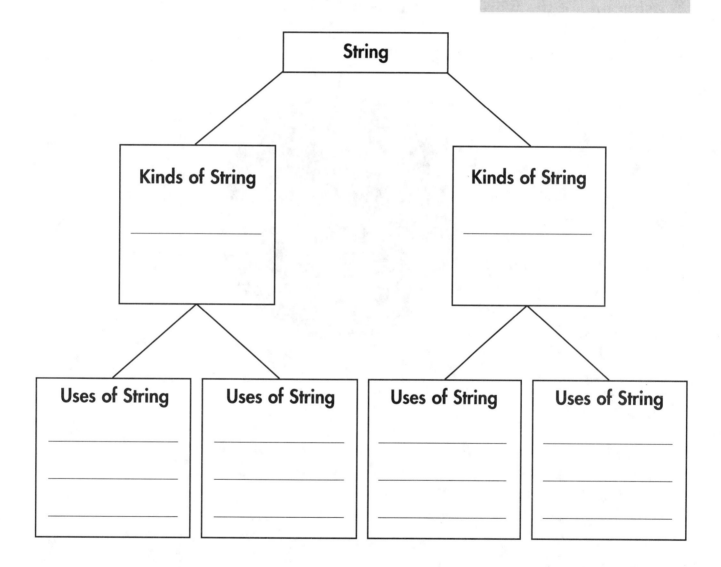

String

Kinds of String
_____

Kinds of String
_____

Uses of String
_____
_____
_____

Uses of String
_____
_____
_____

Uses of String
_____
_____
_____

Uses of String
_____
_____
_____

Complete the sentence aloud using words from the chart.

You use _____ to _____ .

The Invention of Sneakers

Find the words in the Word Bank that describe sneakers. Use them to complete the Word Web. Then complete the sentence below using one of the words from the Word Web.

WORD BANK

popular	light
comfortable	noisy
heavy	non-slip
quiet	

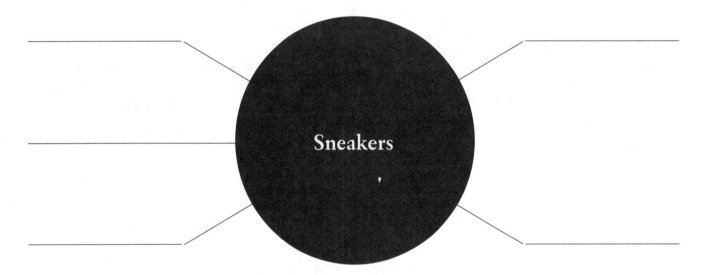

Sneakers

Sneakers are _____.

TAKE IT HOME
Use the words on the Word Web to ask your family members about the shoes they are wearing. For example, ask them *Are your shoes comfortable?*

Name

The Invention of Sneakers

Cut out the captions below. Glue each caption underneath the picture it describes. Write a caption for the last picture.

This shoe is made of canvas and rubber.

This woman is playing tennis.

This man is making rubber.

The Invention of Sneakers

Use the words from the chart to write a sentence about each picture.

Beginning	Middle	End
He	is making	vulcanized rubber.
She	is wearing	sneakers.
They	are collecting	rubber.

_____ _____ _____
Beginning   Middle   End

_____ _____ _____
Beginning   Middle   End

_____ _____ _____
Beginning   Middle   End

 TAKE IT HOME
Find out how many pairs of sneakers there are in your home.
Write down the number and who they belong to.

Name

The Doughnuts

Look at the picture. Use the words in the Phrase Bank to help you complete the sentences describing the people in the picture.

PHRASE BANK

next to	in front of
behind	on

The boy is sitting _____ the stool.

The woman is standing _____ the boy.

The man is standing _____ the counter.

The woman is standing _____ the counter.

TAKE IT HOME

Draw a picture of you and your family at home. Write two sentences about where the people are in your picture in relation to each other.

The Doughnuts

Draw a picture for each sentence.

Homer fixes the doughnut machine.

The lady makes the doughnut batter.

The doughnut machine won't stop
making doughnuts.

Rupert Black finds the bracelet.

Use your pictures to help you retell the story to a classmate.

Name

The Doughnuts

Read the chart. Fill in the characters' names at the top of the chart to match what happened in the story. Use the words in the Word Bank to help you.

_____	_____
fixed the doughnut machine.	made the batter.
called Uncle Ulysses.	lost her bracelet.

Use the chart to complete the sentences.

The lady _____.

Homer _____.

Homer _____.

The lady _____.

Name

Wings

Look at the pictures. Each picture shows something belonging to a story character. Cut out each label below and paste the label under the correct picture.

1.

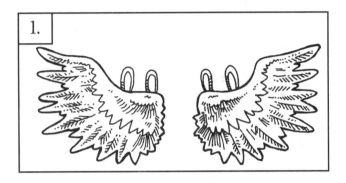

2.

3.

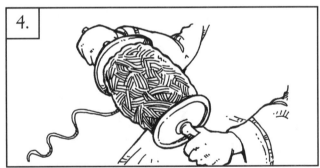
4.

✂

| Ariadne's thread | King Minos' prison tower |
| Daedalus' wings | The Minotaur's maze |

Name

Wings

Combine each of the two sentences into one new sentence. Write the words to complete each new sentence. The first one is done for you.

1. Daedalus was clever.

   Daedalus was proud.

   Daedalus was <u>clever</u> and <u>proud</u>.

2. Daedalus made statues.

   Daedalus made mazes.

   Daedalus made _____ and _____.

3. Icarus flew over strange lands.

   Icarus flew over strange seas.

   Icarus flew over _____ and _____.

4. Daedalus made wings of wax.

   Daedalus made wings of feathers.

   Daedalus made wings of _____ and _____.

Name

Wings

Complete the sentences with the names from the Word Bank. Draw a picture to go with each sentence.

_____ built clever mazes.

_____ killed the Minotaur.

_____ sent Icarus and Daedalus to the tower.

_____ flew too close to the sun.

 TAKE IT HOME
Draw a maze for a member of your family to solve. Then ask him or her to draw a maze for you.

The Best New Thing

Rada and Jonny can do things in space that we
can't do on Earth. Read each action in the list.
Can you do it in space? Can you do it on Earth?
Circle *I can* or *I can't* in both cases.

Action	In Space	On Earth
walk on walls	I can. I can't.	I can. I can't.
roll down hills	I can. I can't.	I can. I can't.
breathe air	I can. I can't.	I can. I can't.
jump higher than a man	I can. I can't.	I can. I can't.
hear a bird sing	I can. I can't.	I can. I can't.

Now complete the sentences using phrases from the action column.

On Earth, I can _____ .

In space, I can _____ .

The Best New Thing

Read the phrases in the Phrase Bank. Complete the diagram by writing words or phrases describing things Jonny and Rada see only on Earth on the left. Write the words for things Jonny and Rada see only on their world on the right. Write the words or phrases for things they see both on Earth and on their world in the middle.

PHRASE BANK

a blue sky

floating milk

grass

a black sky

the sun

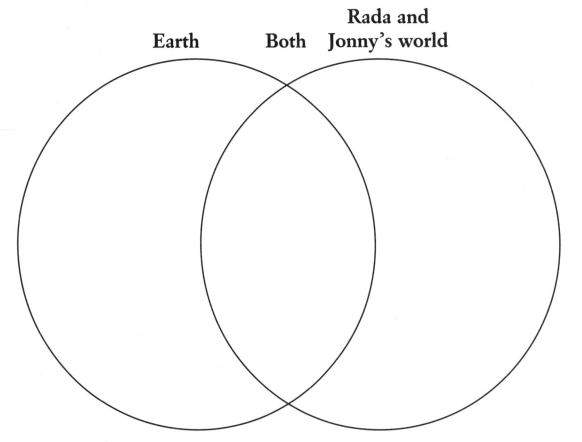

Earth   Both   Rada and
                         Jonny's world

Now complete the sentences describing the two worlds.

1. On Earth, the children see _____.

2. On Rada and Jonny's world, the children see _____.

TAKE IT HOME
What would you like to see in Rada and Jonny's world? Make a list and draw a picture with a family member. Bring your picture to class.

The Best New Thing

Complete each sentence by drawing a line from its beginning in Column A to its end in Column B. Then draw and color a picture to illustrate one of the sentences.

Column A	Column B
1. Rada jumps up high	to hug her father.
2. Rada walks up the wall	to go to Earth.
3. They pull on springs	to see new things.
4. They want to go to Earth	to see her father.
5. They get on the spaceship	to roll down.
6. They climb the hill	to get strong.

The Desert Beneath the Sea

Label the picture with the words or phrases in the Phrase Bank. Use them to complete the sentences.

PHRASE BANK

a boat

a fish

sand

a scuba diver

a tilefish home

1. There is _____ at the top of the picture.

2. There is _____ in the middle of the picture.

3. There is _____ at the bottom of the picture.

Name

The Desert Beneath the Sea

The pictures and sentences tell how to study a tilefish burrow. Cut out the pictures and glue them under the sentences.

1. Divide the mound into four parts.

2. Put the coral pieces in a bag.

3. Weigh the pieces.

4. Take pictures of the pieces.

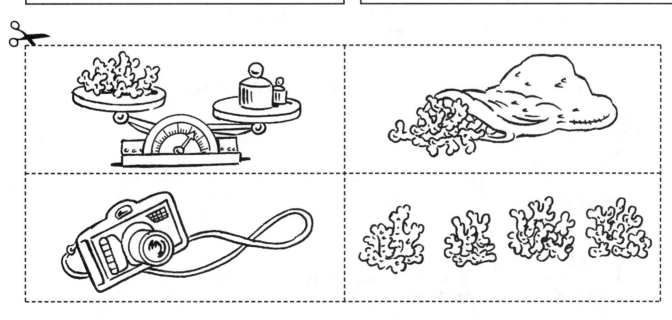

The Desert Beneath the Sea

Fill in the Word Web about the tilefish. Use the Phrase Bank for ideas.

PHRASE BANK

builds its home

coral rubble

lives in burrows

lives in the Caribbean Sea

uses its mouth to pick things up

trash

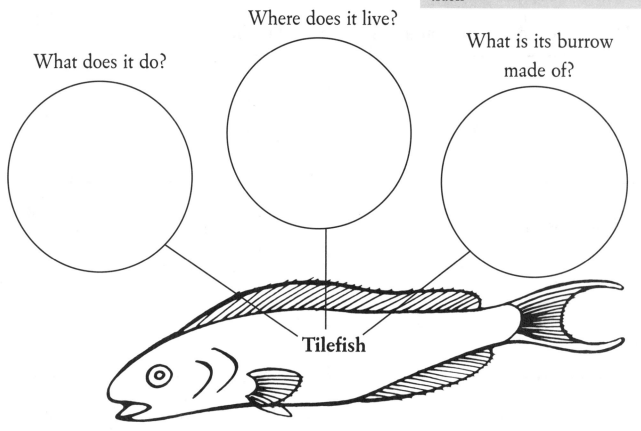

What does it do?

Where does it live?

What is its burrow made of?

Tilefish

Now use the information in the diagram to complete the sentences.

The tile fish _____ .

It lives in _____ .

Its burrow is made of _____ .

TAKE IT HOME
Work with a family member to make a diagram like this one for an animal that you know something about. Bring the diagram to class.

The Lost Lake

Use the words in the Word Bank to label each picture.

WORD BANK

trail	creek
hills	lake
mountains	forest
apartment	

_____

_____

_____

_____

_____

_____

_____

The Lost Lake

Read the chart. Circle the thing that you need for each activity. The first one is done for you.

Activity	You Need	
To go camping	a bicycle	a tent
To go camping	a sleeping bag	a bowling ball
To go hiking	a rod and reel	boots
To go swimming	skates	a swimsuit

Use the chart to help you complete the sentences.

To go camping, you need _____ and _____.

To go hiking, you need _____.

To go swimming, you need _____.

 TAKE IT HOME
Ask a family member if he or she goes camping. Write two sentences about the things he or she takes camping.

The Lost Lake

Use the words in the Word Bank to label the pictures below. Cut out the pictures and paste each one in the correct sentence.

Luke has read all his _____ .

Luke is tired of watching _____ .

He cuts out pictures of _____ .

He wants to go _____ .

Sarah, Plain and Tall

Write the words from the Word Bank that tell about the prairie in the first column. Write the words that tell about the sea in the second column. Then draw a picture of your favorite thing from the chart in the box below.

The Prairie	The Sea

Sarah, Plain and Tall

Read the phrases in the Phrase Bank. Write the
phrases that are about Sarah on the Word Web.
Then use three of the phrases to write a
sentence about Sarah.

PHRASE BANK

is from Maine

likes to sing

has a dog

takes care of the children

likes to swim

hates flowers

cooks

tells stories

goes back to Maine

has a cat

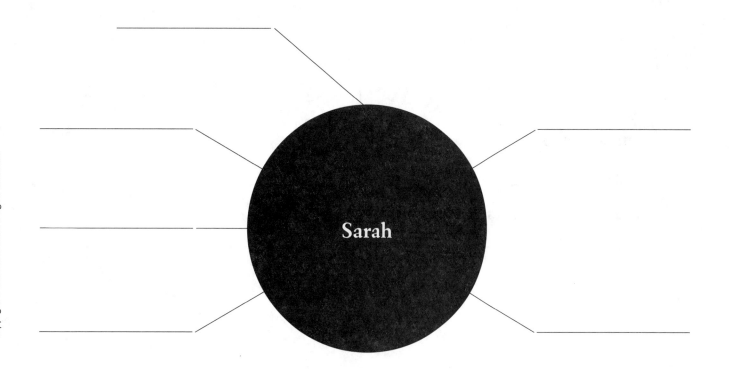

Sarah

Sarah _____ , _____ , and _____ .

TAKE IT HOME
Work with family member to make a Word Web like the one on this
page describing a character in a story you both know. Bring your web
to class.

Sarah, Plain and Tall

The following is a list of things that Sarah talks about or does in the story. Write each one in its correct column on the chart. Use the chart to complete the sentences about Sarah.

playing on the sand dunes	petting the seals
petting the sheep	swimming in the sea
swimming in the pond	playing on the hay

Things Sarah Talks About	Things Sarah Does

1. Sarah talks about _____ .

2. Sarah is _____ .

Draw a picture of something you would like to do.

Yours Truly, Goldilocks

WORD BANK

carrots   peas

lettuce   spinach

Write the names of the vegetables below the pictures at the bottom of the page. Use the words in the Word Bank. Draw a picture of your favorite vegetable in the last box and write its name. Color and cut out the pictures. Now read the letter and glue the pictures where they belong.

Dear Mrs. Rabbit:

Thank you for the vegetables. The [ ] are orange and crunchy.

The [ ] are tiny and fresh. The [ ] and the

[ ] are yummy in my salad. I like the [ ] best of all.

Your friend,

Mrs. Bear

Yours Truly, Goldilocks

Verbs are words that name things you can do. Choose a verb from the Word Bank that tells what each character is doing. Write the word on the line below the picture. Draw lines through the words in the Word Bank that are not verbs.

_____ _____ _____ _____

Use the verbs to complete the sentences.

She is _____ on the path.

He is _____ the vegetables.

The rabbit is _____ the carrot.

The old woman is _____ a letter.

Name

Yours Truly, Goldilocks

Opposites are two things that are completely different from one another. Read the words on the three pigs' house. Use the words in the Word Bank to help you write an opposite for each word.

mean

big · · · old

friend

Read the sentences on the left. Write the opposites of the underlined words to complete the sentences on the right. Use the words on the house if you need help.

Baby Bear is the three pigs' <u>friend</u>.

The wolf is the three pigs' _____ .

Peter Rabbit is <u>little</u>.

Mother Bear is _____ .

Little Red Riding Hood is <u>young</u>.

Grandmother is _____ .

Goldilocks is <u>nice</u>.

The wolves are _____ .

TAKE IT HOME

Use words that are opposites to describe people in your family or things in your house. Make a list and share it with your classmates.

The Hoboken Chicken Emergency

Plan your Thanksgiving dinner. Draw a picture on the plate. You may wish to use the words in the Word Bank for suggestions. Then complete the sentence.

For Thanksgiving, I want to eat _____ .

TAKE IT HOME
Make a grocery shopping list for a meal you might eat at home.
Share it with your classmates.

Name

The Hoboken Chicken Emergency

Draw lines to match the causes on the left with the effects on the right.

Causes	Effects
Henrietta jumps on the bed.	Arthur tries to buy a turkey.
The professor says the chicken will be good to eat.	Momma is surprised.
	The chicken is afraid.
Poppa gives Arthur twenty dollars.	The bed breaks.
Momma sees the chicken.	

Now use the chart to complete the paragraph.

The chicken is afraid because _____.

_____ because she sees the chicken.

Finally, the bed breaks because _____.

Use the phrases in the Phrase Bank to write a complete sentence.

_____.

The Hoboken Chicken Emergency

Write the sentences in the boxes to tell the correct order of the story events.

Arthur buys a chicken from the Professor.
Poppa tells Arthur to buy a turkey for Thanksgiving.
Poppa is angry, but he says Arthur can keep the chicken.
Arthur meets the Professor.

Name

Fifteen Minutes

Read each compound word in the list below.
Write the two smaller words that, together,
make each compound word.

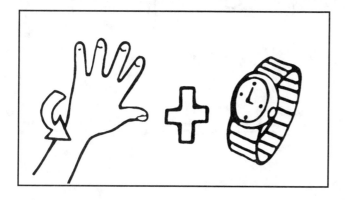

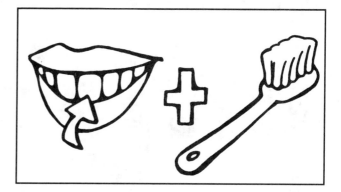

1. wristwatch _____ _____

2. toothbrush _____ _____

3. eyelid _____ _____

4. toothpaste _____ _____

5. bathroom _____ _____

**Use the words in the list above to help you write a definition
for each compound word. The first one is done for you.**

6. wristwatch: _____ *a watch you wear on your wrist* _____

7. toothbrush: _____

8. eyelid: _____

9. toothpaste: _____

10. bathroom: _____

TAKE IT HOME

Work with a family member to find more compound words in a
book, a newspaper, or a magazine. Write the words on a sheet of
paper, then write the two smaller words that make up the larger
word. Bring your words to class.

Fifteen Minutes

Complete each sentence with a word from the box.

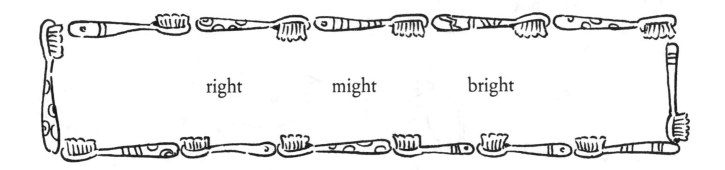

right   might   bright

1. Violet Deever _____ want the green toothbrush.

2. Pat likes red because it is a _____ color.

3. Which is the _____ color for a toothbrush?

Below are more words that end in -ight. Draw a line to match each sentence with the word that completes the sentence, then write the word on the line.

Column A	Column B
4. The color green can be dark	night
or _____ .	
5. Pat brushes his teeth each morning	fight
and _____ .	
6. Violet and Pat should not	light
_____ over the toothbrushes.	

Fifteen Minutes

**Write the letter F on the line if the sentence is a fact,
or the letter O if the sentence is an opinion.**

_____ 1. Pat's mother bought two new toothbrushes.

_____ 2. Green is the best color of all.

_____ 3. Red is a lucky color.

_____ 4. Pat chose the red toothbrush.

_____ 5. Grass is green.

_____ 6. Red is a beautiful color.

**Complete the following sentence. Write the color of the
toothbrush you would choose and explain why.**

I would choose the _____ toothbrush

because _____ .

Sally Ann Thunder Ann Whirlwind

Draw a line to match each word with its picture.

Column 1	Column 2

tall

sleepy

scared

open

Complete each sentence with a word from above.

1. Davy was _____ so he fell asleep under a tree.

2. Sally was as _____ as a tree.

3. The door swung _____ and the bear came in.

4. Sally's heart was thumping because she was _____ of the bear.

TAKE IT HOME
Use the words in Column 1 to make up sentences with your family.
Bring your sentences to class.

Sally Ann Thunder Ann Whirlwind

Answer the questions by writing _Yes, she does_ **or** _No, she doesn't._

1. Does Sally fight? _____

2. Does Sally read? _____

3. Does Sally dance? _____

4. Does Sally cry? _____

5. Does Sally have snakes? _____

6. Does Sally make butter? _____

Draw a picture in the boxes for each question you answered _Yes, she does._

Name

Sally Ann Thunder Ann Whirlwind

Answer the questions by gluing the sentences in the boxes.

1. What does Sally do when Davy's head is stuck in the tree?

2. What does Sally do when the bear wants to eat her?

3. What does Sally do when Mike Fink tries to scare her?

4. What does Sally do when Davy asks her to marry him?

✂

She hits him.	She asks the bear to dance with her.
She says yes.	She pulls the tree apart.

Name

Ali Baba Hunts for a Bear

Write the correct animal name from the Word Bank under each animal picture.

WORD BANK	
squirrel	beaver
gopher	coyote
bear	deer
buffalo	horse
moose	

1.

_____

2.

_____

3.

_____

4.

_____

5.

_____

6.

_____

7.

_____

8.

_____

9.

_____

Ali Baba Hunts for a Bear

What does Ali Baba do at Grand Teton National Park? Use the Phrase Bank to help you.

PHRASE BANK

stay in a log cabin

play in the sandbox

ride a horse

see animals

go to school

ride on a rubber raft

take pictures

Things Ali Baba does at Grand Teton National Park

Complete the sentence with one of the above phrases.

I would like to _____ at the park.

Name

Ali Baba Hunts for a Bear

Write the letter T next to each statement that is true. Write the letter F next to each statement that is false.

_____ 1. In the story, Ali Baba is 10 years old.

_____ 2. Ali Baba is from Minnesota.

_____ 3. People from all over the world visit Grand Teton National Park.

_____ 4. Ali Baba does not see a bear.

_____ 5. Greg is Ali Baba's brother.

_____ 6. Ali Baba learns a lesson about how stories grow and change.

For each sentence that you marked with the letter F, rewrite the sentence to make it true.

_____

_____

_____

_____

TAKE IT HOME
Work with someone at home to write some true and false sentences about your family. Give them to another family member to mark with the letter T for true or the letter F for false. Bring your sentences to class.

Thirteen Moons on Turtle's Back

Read the words in the Word Bank that describe the seasons. Sort the words into three groups: winter, spring, and autumn. Write the words in the correct columns. Do a drawing on another sheet of paper that shows one of the seasons.

Winter	Spring	Autumn

Now use the words to complete the sentences.

In winter, there is _____ and _____.

In spring, there are _____ and _____.

In autumn, there are _____ and _____.

TAKE IT HOME
Work with a family member to think of things to add to the columns. Share what you added with your classmates.

Name

ACTIVITY MASTER 53
ESSENTIAL KNOWLEDGE
AND SKILLS

Thirteen Moons on Turtle's Back

Circle the best meaning for the <u>underlined</u> word or words in each sentence.

1. He <u>entered</u> the house.

   a. went into   b. went out of   c. built

2. The boy went down the river in a <u>canoe</u>.

   a. power   b. house   c. boat

3. The children <u>shed</u> their winter coats in the warm room.

   a. took off   b. kept   c. grow

Complete the sentences using the underlined words above.

4. The Little People gave the boy a magic _____ and strawberries.

5. Ju-ske-ha _____ the lodge of Old Man Winter and sat down

   by the fire.

6. Cedar trees and pine trees stay green all year. The other trees

   _____ their leaves.

Thirteen Moons on Turtle's Back

Grandfather tells Sozap about the 13 moons.
What does he tell Sozap about each moon?
Under each picture, write the correct sentence from below.

Moon of Popping Trees

Budding Moon

Strawberry Moon

Moon of Falling Leaves

The trees turn green with new buds.

The cottonwoods have frost, and the coyotes sing.

The leaves of the sleeping trees fall.

He gave them red strawberries.

Swimming with Sea Lions

What do sea lions do on land? What do sea lions do in the water? Complete the Word Webs, using the words in the Word Bank.

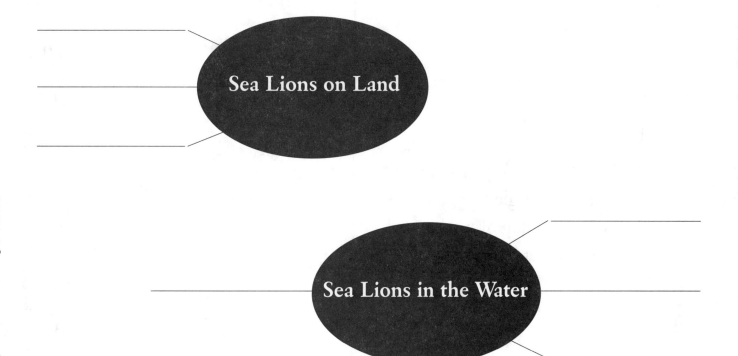

Complete the sentences using words from the Word Bank.

1. Sea lions like to _____ on land.

2. Sea lions like to _____ in the water.

Swimming with Sea Lions

Think about sunsets you have seen. Complete the sentences. You may use words from the Word Bank to help you. Then draw a picture of your sunset on another sheet of paper.

WORD BANK

colorful	purple
lovely	pink
orange	glowing
red	bright

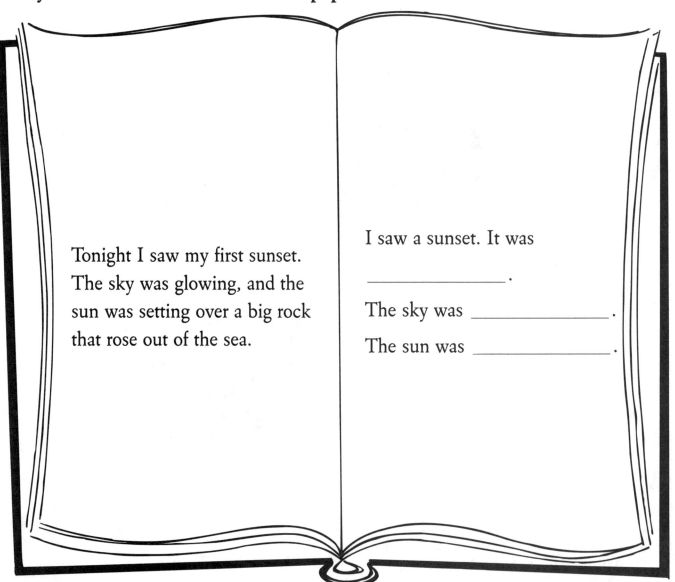

Tonight I saw my first sunset. The sky was glowing, and the sun was setting over a big rock that rose out of the sea.

I saw a sunset. It was

_____ .

The sky was _____ .

The sun was _____ .

 TAKE IT HOME
Go outside and look at the sunset with a family member. Describe it. Tell a classmate about the sunset.

Swimming With Sea Lions

Cut out the sentences. Paste each _true_ sentence on the tortoise.

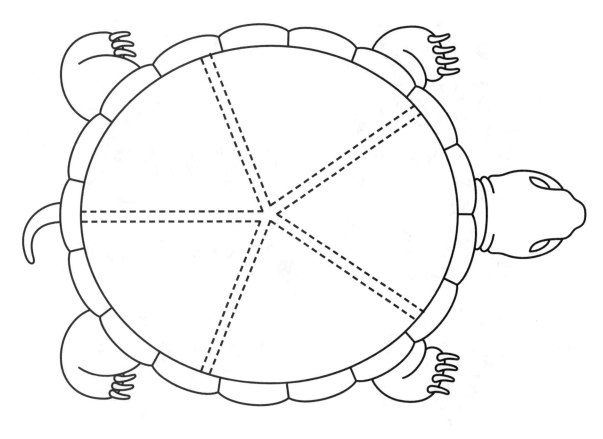

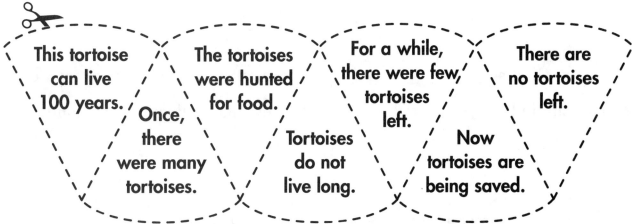

This tortoise can live 100 years.

Once, there were many tortoises.

The tortoises were hunted for food.

Tortoises do not live long.

For a while, there were few tortoises left.

Now tortoises are being saved.

There are no tortoises left.

The Great Kapok Tree

Label the animals and plants found in the rain forest. Use the words from the Word Bank. Then use the words to finish the sentences.

1. _____
2. _____
3. _____
6. _____
5. _____
4. _____
7. _____

1. You can find a _____ and other plants growing in the rain forest.

2. You can find a _____ and other animals living in the rain forest.

TAKE IT HOME
Plan an imaginary trip to a rain forest with someone in your family. Talk about things you would need to take. Talk about things you might see and do in the rain forest. Tell the class about your plans.

The Great Kapok Tree

**Tell people about rain forests. Use words from the
Word Bank to complete the sentences.**

WORD BANK	
plants	rain forests
animals	trees

1. Save the _____ .

2. Many _____ live there.

3. Many _____ grow there.

4. Many _____ grow there.

5. _____ help the earth.

Now write your own sentence about rain forests.

_____

Name

The Great Kapok Tree

Write a sentence in each section of the diagram
to tell how the man changed.

Turning Point

Man at Beginning of Story	What Caused the Change	Man at End of Story

Use the words in the Word Bank to complete the paragraph.

At first, the man started to _____ the tree down. Then he

_____ asleep. The animals _____ to the man.

They _____ him why the rain forest is important. At the end,

the man _____ his ax and walked away.

Dinner at Aunt Connie's House

WORD BANK

singer	writer
teacher	artist

Read the definitions. Write the word from the Word Bank for each definition.

1.   a person who teaches   _____

2.   a person who creates art   _____

3.   a person who sings   _____

4.   a person who writes stories or books   _____

Use your answers above to complete the sentences.

5. My mom likes to sing. She is a good _____ .

6. Who made this painting? The person is a good _____ .

7. Mr. Nelson teaches math. He is a good _____ .

8. Did you write this? You are a good _____ .

TAKE IT HOME
Talk about jobs with a family member. Write a sentence about what he or she does at work. Write another sentence about what you would like to be when you are older. Share the sentences with your classmates.

Dinner at Aunt Connie's House

What happened in each setting? Draw lines to match the events to the settings. Then use one of the settings and one of the events to complete the sentence below.

Event	Setting

found paintings

played hide-and-seek

Attic

ate dinner

listened to paintings

Dining Room

helped hang paintings

toasted Lonnie

Big House

At Aunt Connie's, we _____ in the _____ .

Name

Dinner at Aunt Connie's House

Cut out the sentences and glue them in the correct columns.

It can happen.	It can't happen.

Rewrite the sentences you glued in the column headed *It can't happen.*

1. _____

2. _____

A painting can talk.	Children can be friends.
A family can eat dinner together.	A painting can be a dinner guest.
A woman can paint a picture.	A woman can be president.

Rain Player

**Read each word. Write the word from the
Word Bank that means almost the same thing.**

1. jump   =   _____

2. throw =   _____

3. grab   =   _____

4. fly   =   _____

**Use the words you wrote above to complete the sentences about
how people play the game *pok-a-tok*.**

5. They _____ as high as they can.
            (jump)

6. Then they _____ the ball through the ring.
            (throw)

7. They make the ball _____ through the air.
            (fly)

8. When the ball comes down, they _____ it and begin again.
            (grab)

 TAKE IT HOME
Have someone at home help you make a list of several action
words. Act out the words for your family. Bring your list to class.

Rain Player

Compare the game *pok-a-tok* to the game of basketball. Tell how the games are alike and different. Use the words in the Word Bank.

WORD BANK

play with a ball

pass the ball

ask animals for help

use a net

use a hoop or a ring

dribble the ball

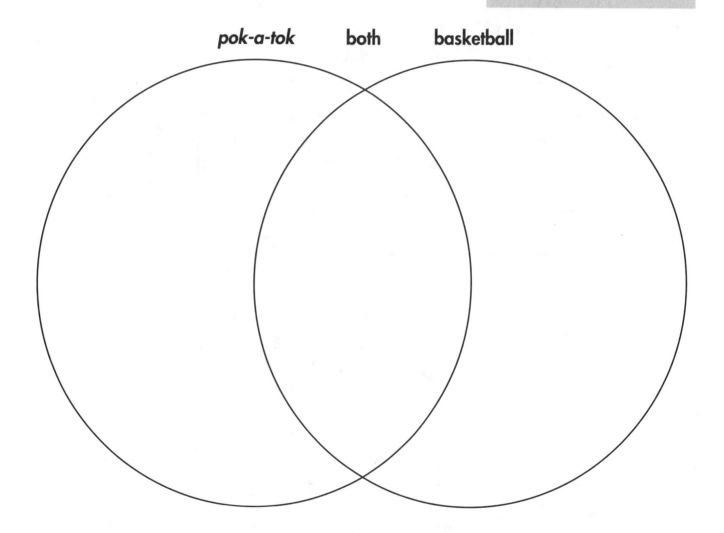

pok-a-tok   both   basketball

In *pok-a-tok*, players _____.

In basketball, players _____.

In both *pok-a-tok* and basketball, players _____.

Rain Player

Read the story events in the box. They are out of order.
Write them in the other boxes to show the correct order.

> Pik asked special friends for help.
> Pik won the game and got rain for his people.
> Pik and Chac played the game.
> Pik asked Chac to play *pok-a-tok*.

The Rag Coat

Add details to the coat. Draw shapes on the coat.
Color the coat. Use at least three colors.

WORD BANK	
orange	big
pink	small
green	square
red	circle
yellow	triangle
blue	

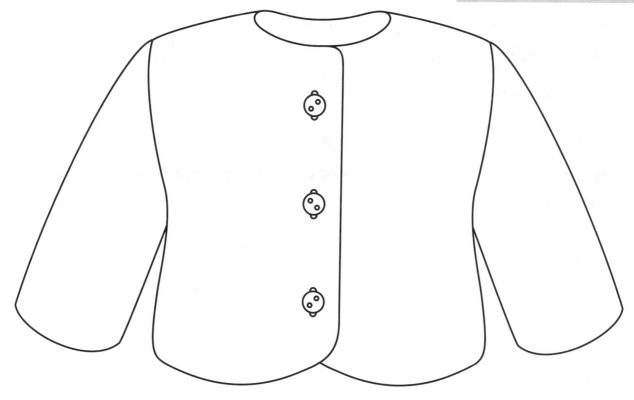

**Complete the sentences. Use words from the Word Bank
to help you or use other words you think of.**

The coat has _____ shapes.

The coat is _____ .

TAKE IT HOME
Use the words in the list to describe a family member's coat, shirt, or
dress. Write about it. Tell a classmate about the coat, shirt, or dress.

The Rag Coat

Complete each sentence using a word from the Word Bank.

WORD BANK

coat   food

friends

What does Minna need?

1. Minna is cold. She needs a _____.

2. Minna is hungry. She needs _____.

3. Minna is lonely. She needs _____.

Draw lines to match the beginning of each sentence in Column A with its ending in Column B.

What can Minna do?

Column A   **Column B**

4. If Minna has a coat, she can   play.

5. If Minna has food, she can   go to school.

6. If Minna has friends, she can   eat.

TAKE IT HOME
Ask your family to name three things they need. Then write a sentence about what they named. Share your sentences with classmates.

The Rag Coat

Retell the story by writing the sentences on the lines.

Minna went to school   Minna didn't have a coat
the women made a rag coat for Minna

First, _____. Then, _____.

Finally, _____.

Write the words *first*, *then*, and *finally* on the lines above the pictures. Then complete the paragraph, using the words you wrote and the caption.

_____   _____   _____

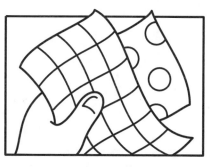 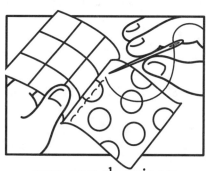 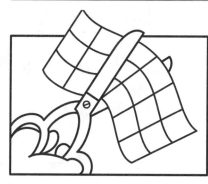

you collect the rags   you sew the pieces   you cut the pieces

How do you make a rag coat?

This is how to make a rag coat. _____,

you collect the rags.   , _____, _____.

Finally, _____. Now you have a rag coat!

 TAKE IT HOME
Retell the story *The Rag Coat* to someone in your family using the words *first*, *then*, and *finally*. Tell the story to your classmates.

Teammates

The ending -ly has been added to each word below.
Look at the new words.

cruel + ly = cruelly

successful + ly = successfully

different + ly = differently

equal + ly = equally

broad + ly = broadly

rare + ly = rarely

Use the new words to complete the sentences. Follow the first example,
which has been done for you.

The players were <u>cruel</u> to Jackie. They treated him <u>cruelly</u>.

1. Pee Wee had a <u>broad</u> smile. He smiled _____.

2. Jackie Robinson was <u>successful</u> in competing. He competed

   _____.

3. It was <u>rare</u> for Pee Wee to see a black person. He _____ saw a

   black person.

4. Jackie wanted <u>equal</u> treatment. He wanted to be treated _____.

Teammates

Read the phrases in the box. Which league does each
phrase describe? Write them under the correct column
headings. Then use one of the phrases from each column to
complete the sentences.

ate in fine restaurants	slept in good hotels
slept in their cars	ate meals they could carry with them
didn't make much money	made lots of money

Negro League	Major League

In the Negro League, players _____.

In the Major League, players _____.

Name

Teammates

Circle the sentences that are true.

1. Jackie was not the first black player in major league baseball.

2. Jackie was the first black player in major league baseball.

3. The fans were glad that Jackie was on the team.

4. The fans were angry that Jackie was on the team.

5. Jackie and Pee Wee played on different teams.

6. Jackie and Pee Wee were teammates.

7. Pee Wee wanted Jackie on the team.

8. Pee Wee wanted Jackie to leave the team.

Circle the word that makes the sentence true. The write the word on the line.

9. Many fans yelled _____ things at Jackie.   **cruel   nice**

10. Jackie is a hero because he was _____ .   **afraid   brave**

TAKE IT HOME
Use the true sentences to tell a family member about Jackie
Robinson.

Young Arthur

Activity Master 1

Words about Battles	Words about Kings
attack	kingdom
slay	castle
wound	crown
fight	throne

The soldier will fight the enemy in a battle for the *kingdom*. The king wears a *crown*.

Activity Master 2
Written responses will vary.

Activity Master 3
Students should illustrate the sentences. The pictures should be numbered 3, 1, 4, 2. Sentences should be labeled *middle, beginning, end, middle*.

Cherokee Summer

Activity Master 4
Students will accurately label their picture.
Written responses will vary.

Activity Master 5
1. Bridget lives in Oklahoma. It is in the northeastern part of the state.
2. Bridget is a Cherokee Indian.
3. Bridget likes to eat crawdads.
4. Bridget speaks English and Cherokee.
5–8. Answers will vary.

Activity Master 6
He is eating a crawdad.
She is reading a Cherokee legend
They are doing a Cherokee stomp dance.
Pictures will vary.

Growing Up with Jerry Spinelli

Activity Master 7
Students should label the frog, lizard, fish, snake, and whatever creatures they have added to the picture. Students may complete the sentences with names of any animals they have drawn, or the following:
There's a frog at the creek.
There's a lizard at the creek.
There's a snake at the creek.
There's a fish at the creek.

Activity Master 8
Picture 1: Do you want to share my tent?
Picture 2: I don't like boys.
Picture 3: Oh no! You broke the window!

Activity Master 9
1. false
2. true
3. false
4. true
5. true
6. false

Mufaro's Beautiful Daughters

Activity Master 10

Nyasha	Manyara
kind	unkind
happy	unhappy
sweet-tempered	bad-tempered

1. Manyara is unkind, unhappy, and bad-tempered. She becomes a servant.
2. Nyasha is kind, happy, and sweet-tempered. She becomes a queen.

Activity Master 11

Nyasha saw	Manyara saw
Nyoka	a monster
the king	laughing trees

Nyasha saw Nyoka in the garden.
Nyasha saw the king in the city. (*Nyasha saw Nyoka in the city* would also be correct.)
Manyara saw laughing trees in the forest.
Manyara saw a monster in the city.

Activity Master 12
1. Nyasha sang to the snake.
2. Nyasha gave a yam to a hungry boy.
3. Nyasha gave sunflower seeds to the old woman.

A Piece of String Is a Wonderful Thing

Activity Master 13
Students will draw pictures that illustrate each word.
1. I can wear a necklace/ribbon.
2. I can play a guitar.
3. I can fly a kite.
4. I can sail a boat.
5. I can tie a ribbon.

Activity Master 14
Students will circle the named items appropriately.

Activity Master 15
Kinds of String: rope, thread
Uses of String:
  Rope: anchor a boat, pull heavy things
  Thread: make blankets, sew clothes
You use (*rope; thread*) to (*anchor a boat, pull heavy things; make blankets, sew clothes*).

The Invention of Sneakers

Activity Master 16
Students should put the following words in the word web:
popular, comfortable, quiet, light, non-slip.
Written responses will vary.

Activity Master 17
Students should paste the captions in the following order:
Picture 1: This shoe is made of canvas and rubber.
Picture 2: This woman is playing tennis.
Picture 3: This man is making rubber.
Picture 4: Accept all reasonable answers.

Activity Master 18
Students should write the sentences in the following order:
Picture 1: They are collecting rubber.
Picture 2: He is making vulcanized rubber.
Picture 3: She is wearing sneakers.

The Doughnuts

Activity Master 19
The boy is sitting <u>on</u> the stool.
The woman is standing <u>next to</u> the boy.
The man is standing <u>behind</u> the counter.
The woman is standing <u>in front of</u> (or next to) the counter.

Activity Master 20
Students should draw pictures to illustrate the sentences, then use their pictures in retelling the story to a classmate.

Activity Master 21
First column head: Homer; second column head: The lady
The lady made the batter.
Homer fixed the doughnut machine.
Homer called Uncle Ulysses.
The lady lost her bracelet.

Wings

Activity Master 22
Students should paste labels in the following order:
Picture 1: Daedalus' wings
Picture 2: King Minos' tower
Picture 3: The Minotaur's maze
Picture 4: Ariadne's thread

Activity Master 23
1. Daedalus was clever and proud.
2. Daedalus made statues and mazes.
3. Icarus flew over strange lands and strange seas.
4. Daedalus made wings of wax and feathers.

Activity Master 24
1. Daedalus built clever mazes.
2. Theseus killed the Minotaur.
3. King Minos sent Icarus and Daedalus to the tower.
4. Icarus flew too close to the sun.

The Best New Thing

Activity Master 25

Action	In Space	On Earth
walk on walls	I can	I can't
roll down hills	I can't	I can
breathe air	I can't	I can
jump higher than a man	I can	I can't
hear a bird sing	I can't	I can

Written responses will vary.

Activity Master 26

<u>Earth</u>	<u>Both</u>	<u>Rada and Jonny's world</u>
grass	the sun	floating milk
a blue sky		a black sky

Written responses will vary.

Activity Master 27
Students should match the following sentences:
1. Rada jumps up high to see her father.
2. Rada walks up the wall to hug her father.
3. They pull on springs to get strong.
4. They want to go to Earth to see new things.
5. They get on the spaceship to go to Earth.
6. They climb the hill to roll down.
Students should draw a picture to illustrate one of the above sentences.

3R's   DTP   Proofreading   Production   Edit   Edit Sup   Copyedit   A&D

The Desert Beneath the Sea

Activity Master 28
1. There is (*a boat*) at the top of the picture.
2. There is (*a fish, a scuba diver*) in the middle of the picture.
3. There is (*sand, a tilefish home*) at the bottom of the picture.

Activity Master 29
Students should match sentences and pictures in the following order:
1. Divide the mound into four parts. [Picture 4]
2. Put the pieces in a bag. [Picture 2]
3. Weigh the pieces. [Picture 1]
4. Take pictures of the pieces. [Picture 3]

Activity Master 30
What does it do?
uses its mouth to pick things up
builds its home
Where does it live?
lives in burrows
lives in the Carribean Sea
What is its burrow made of?
trash
coral rubble
Written responses will vary.

The Lost Lake

Activity Master 31
Students should match each word with the correct picture in the following order: trail; hills; apartment; mountains; lake; creek; forest.

Activity Master 32
Row 2: circle *a sleeping bag*
Row 3: circle *boots*
Row 4: circle *a swimsuit*
To go camping, you need a tent and a sleeping bag.
You need boots to go hiking.
To go swimming, you need a suit.

Activity Master 33
Pictures: camping, books, television, mountains
Luke has read all his books.
Luke is tired of watching television.
He cuts out pictures of mountains.
He wants to go camping.

Sarah, Plain and Tall

Activity Master 34

The Prairie	The Sea
field	dune
hay	sea shell
pond	

Pictures will vary.

Activity Master 35
1. Sarah is from Maine; Sarah likes to sing; Sarah takes care of the children; Sarah likes to swim; Sarah cooks; Sarah tells stories; Sarah has a cat
Students should complete the sentence, using information from any three of the above.

Activity Master 36

Things Sarah Talks About	Things Sarah Does
playing on the sand dunes	petting the sheep
petting the seals	swimming in the pond
swimming in the sea	playing on the hay

Sarah talks about (*playing on the sand dunes, swimming in the sea,* or *petting the seals*).
Sarah is (*petting the sheep, swimming in the pond, playing on the hay*).
Students should draw a picture of their chosen activity taken from the list.

Yours Truly, Goldilocks

Activity Master 37
Students should label, color, cut out, and glue vegetable pictures into the body of the letter in the following order: carrots, peas, spinach, lettuce (these last two may be in reverse order), and the student's favorite vegetable.

Activity Master 38
Students will match the words to the pictures.
Forest, house, pigs and, *why* should be crossed out.

She is walking on the path.
He is watering the vegetables.
The rabbit is eating the carrot.
The old woman is reading a letter.

Activity Master 39
mean/nice
big/little
old/young
friend/enemy

The wolf is the three pigs' enemy.
Mother Bear is big.
Grandmother is old.
The wolves are mean.

The Hoboken Chicken Emergency

Activity Master 40
Drawings should include correctly labeled pictures of food and drink.

Accept reasonable answers.

Activity Master 41
1. Henrietta jumps on the bed.—The bed breaks.
2. The professor says the chicken will be good to eat.—The chicken is afraid.
3. Poppa gives Arthur twenty dollars.—Arthur tries to buy a turkey.
4. Momma sees the chicken.—Momma is surprised.

The chicken is afraid because the professor says the chicken will be good to eat. Momma is surprised because she sees the chicken. Finally, the bed breaks because Henrietta jumps on the bed.

Poppa is angry because Arthur didn't buy a turkey.

Activity Master 42
Poppa tells Arthur to buy a turkey for Thanksgiving.
Arthur meets the Professor.
Arthur buys a chicken from the Professor.
Poppa is angry, but he says Arthur can keep the chicken.

Fifteen Minutes

Activity Master 43
1. wrist   watch
2. tooth   brush
3. eye   lid
4. tooth   paste
5. bath   room
6. a watch you wear on your wrist
7. a brush for teeth
8. the lid or cover of the eye
9. paste for cleaning teeth
10. a room with a bathtub

Activity Master 44
1. Violet Deever might want the green toothbrush.
2. Pat likes red because it is a bright color.
3. Which is the right color for a toothbrush?
4. The color green can be dark or light.
5. Pat brushes his teeth each morning and night.
6. Violet and Pat should not fight over the toothbrushes.

Activity Master 45
1. fact
2. opinion
3. opinion
4. fact
5. fact
6. opinion
Answers will vary.

Sally Ann Thunder Ann Whirlwind

Activity Master 46
Students will match words in Column 1 with pictures in Column 2.
1. sleepy
2. tall
3. open
4. scared

Activity Master 47
1. Yes, she does.
2. No, she doesn't.
3. Yes, she does.
4. No, she doesn't.
5. Yes, she does.
6. Yes, she does.
Students will draw their own pictures for numbers 1, 3, 5, and 6.

Activity Master 48
1. She pulls the tree apart.
2. She asks the bear to dance with her.
3. She hits him.
4. She says yes.

Ali Baba Hunts for a Bear

Activity Master 49
1. deer
2. squirrel
3. horse
4. coyote
5. bear
6. gopher
7. beaver
8. moose
9. buffalo

Activity Master 50
stay in a log cabin
ride a horse
see animals
ride on a rubber raft
take pictures

Responses will vary.

Activity Master 51
1. T
2. F
3. T
4. T
5. F
6. T
Possible responses:
Ali Baba is from New York.
Greg is not Ali Baba's brother.

Thirteen Moons on Turtle's Back

Activity Master 52
Winter words: snow, frost
Spring words: strawberries, new buds
Autumn words: falling leaves, colored leaves
In winter, there is snow and frost.
In spring, there are strawberries and new buds.
In autumn, there are falling leaves and colored leaves.

Activity Master 53
1. a. went into
2. c. boat
3. a. took off
4. canoe
5. entered
6. shed

Activity Master 54
Moon of Popping Trees: The cottonwoods have frost, and the coyotes sing.
Budding Moon: The trees turn green with new buds.
Strawberry Moon: He gave them red strawberries.
Moon of Falling Leaves: The leaves of the sleeping trees fall.

Swimming with Sea Lions

Activity Master 55
Sea lions on land like to doze, bark, cough.
Sea lions in the water like to dive, somersault, blow bubbles, flip.
Answers will vary.

Activity Master 56
Answers will vary.

Activity Master 57
Once there were many tortoises.
The tortoises were hunted for food.
For a while, there were few tortoises left.
Now tortoises are being saved.
The tortoise can live over 100 years.

The Great Kapok Tree

Activity Master 58
Students will label picture

1. vine, tree, flower
2. snake, monkey, frog, bird

Activity Master 59
1. rain forests
2. animals
3. plants
4. trees
5. rain forests

Students' own sentences will vary.

Activity Master 60
Sentences will vary, but should relate to the story.
Words will be written in paragraph in this order: chop, fell, whispered, told, dropped

Dinner at Aunt Connie's House

Activity Master 61
1. teacher
2. artist
3. singer
4. writer
5. singer
6. painter
7. teacher
8. writer

Activity Master 62
found paintings: Attic
played hide and seek: Big house
ate dinner: Dining Room
listened to paintings: Attic
helped hang paintings: Dining Room
toasted Lonnie: Dining Room

Final sentence will vary, but should include one of the above pairs.

Activity Master 63

It can happen.	It can't happen.
A family can eat dinner together. A woman can paint a picture. Children can be friends. A woman can be president.	A painting can talk. A painting can be a dinner guest.

A painting can't talk.
A painting can't be a dinner guest.

Rain Player

Activity Master 64
1. leap
2. toss
3. seize
4. soar
5. leap
6. toss
7. soar
8. seize

Activity Master 65
In pok-a-tok, players ask animals for help/use a hoop or a ring.
In basketball, players use a net/dribble the ball.
In both pok-a-tok and basketball/players play with a ball/pass the ball.

Activity Master 66
1. Pik asked Chac to play pok-a-tok.
2. Pik asked his special friends for help.
3. Pik and Chac played the game.
4. Pik won the game and rain for his people.

The Rag Coat

Activity Master 67
Answers will vary, but should include words from the Word Bank.

Activity Master 68
1. a coat
2. food
3. friends
4. go to school
5. eat
6. play

Activity Master 69
First, Minna didn't have a coat.
Then, the women made a rag coat for Minna.
Finally, Minna went to school.

first–you collect the rags
then–you cut the pieces
finally–you sew the pieces

This is how you make a rag coat. First, you collect the rags. Then, you cut the pieces. Finally, you sew the pieces. Now you have a rag coat!

Teammates

Activity Master 70
1. broadly
2. successfully
3. rarely
4. equally

Activity Master 71
Negro League: slept in their cars, didn't make much money, ate meals they could carry with them
Major League: ate in fine restaurants, slept in good hotels, made lots of money

The sentences should reflect the appropriate phrases written in the chart.

Activity Master 72
2. true
4. true
6. true
7. true
9. cruel
10. brave

Literacy Place ESL/ELD Activity Masters	Texas Essential Knowledge and Skills English as a Second Language
Young Arthur	
Activity Master 1: Focus on Language	4.26E, 4.26G, 4.28F, 4.30F, 4.31A
Activity Master 2: Essential Knowledge and Skills	4.26G, 4.27F, 4.28F, 4.31A
Activity Master 3: Focus on Comprehension	4.26D, 4.26E, 4.29K
Cherokee Summer	
Activity Master 4: Focus on Language	4.26D, 4.26G, 4.28A
Activity Master 5: Essential Knowledge and Skills	4.26B, 4.28A, 4.28C
Activity Master 6: Focus on Comprehension	4.26E, 4.27F, 4.28D, 4.28E, 4.29K, 4.31A
Growing Up with Jerry Spinelli	
Activity Master 7: Focus on Language	4.26B, 4.26G, 4.27A, 4.28A, 4.28F
Activity Master 8: Essential Knowledge and Skills	4.26A, 4.28A
Activity Master 9: Focus on Comprehension	4.26D, 4.26E, 4.27A, 4.28A
Mufaro's Beautiful Daughters	
Activity Master 10: Focus on Language	4.26A, 4.26D, 4.26E, 4.26G, 4.27F, 4.28A, 4.28E, 4.29E, 4.31A
Activity Master 11: Essential Knowledge and Skills	4.26A, 4.26D, 4.27A, 4.28A, 4.29K, 4.30F
Activity Master 12: Focus on Comprehension	4.26A, 4.26D, 4.28A, 4.28F, 4.31A
A Piece of String Is a Wonderful Thing	
Activity Master 13: Focus on Language	4.27A, 4.28A, 4.30C, 4.30E(iii), 4.30F, 4.31A
Activity Master 14: Essential Knowledge and Skills	4.26D, 4.27A, 4.28A, 4.31A
Activity Master 15: Focus on Comprehension	4.26B, 4.26G, 4.27A, 4.28A, 4.28F, 4.29I, 4.30B
The Invention of Sneakers	
Activity Master 16: Focus on Language	4.26E, 4.26G, 4.27F, 4.28A
Activity Master 17: Essential Knowledge and Skills	4.28D, 4.30F, 4.31A
Activity Master 18: Focus on Comprehension	4.26D, 4.28A, 4.28D, 4.28F, 4.29I, 4.31A, 4.31E
The Doughnuts	
Activity Master 19: Focus on Language	4.26D, 4.28A, 4.28F, 4.29J, 4.31A, 4.31E
Activity Master 20: Essential Knowledge and Skills	4.26D, 4.26E, 4.27A, 4.28A, 4.29J, 4.29K, 4.31A
Activity Master 21: Focus on Comprehension	4.28A, 4.28F, 4.29I, 4.29J, 4.29K, 4.30B
Wings	
Activity Master 22: Focus on Language	4.26D, 4.27E, 4.28A, 4.29D, 4.30F, 4.31A
Activity Master 23: Essential Knowledge and Skills	4.30F, 4.30G
Activity Master 24: Focus on Comprehension	4.26D, 4.28A, 4.28E, 4.29K, 4.31A
The Best New Thing	
Activity Master 25: Focus on Language	4.28A, 4.28F, 4.29I, 4.30E(iv), 4.30F, 4.31AE
Activity Master 26: Essential Knowledge and Skills	4.26A, 4.26D, 4.26E, 4.26G, 4.27A, 4.27D, 4.28F, 4.29I, 4.30B
Activity Master 27: Focus on Comprehension	4.28D, 4.29J, 4.31A
The Desert Beneath the Sea	
Activity Master 28: Focus on Language	4.26B, 4.26D, 4.26G, 4.27A, 4.28A
Activity Master 29: Essential Knowledge and Skills	4.26D, 4.28A, 4.28B, 4.29C, 4.30H
Activity Master 30: Focus on Comprehension	4.26D, 4.26E, 4.26G, 4.27A, 4.27B, 4.27F, 4.28A, 4.28F, 4.29C, 4.29I, 4.29J, 4.31A
The Lost Lake	
Activity Master 31: Focus on Language	4.26D, 4.28A, 4.28D, 4.28E, 4.28F, 4.29E
Activity Master 32: Essential Knowledge and Skills	4.26G, 4.28A, 4.28D, 4.28F, 4.29I
Activity Master 33: Focus on Comprehension	4.26A, 4.26D, 4.26E, 4.28A, 4.30F
Sarah, Plain and Tall	
Activity Master 34: Focus on Language	4.26D, 4.28A, 4.28D, 4.29I
Activity Master 35: Essential Knowledge and Skills	4.27A, 4.28F, 4.29I
Activity Master 36: Focus on Comprehension	4.26D, 4.28F, 4.29I, 4.31A

Literacy Place ESL/ELD Activity Masters	Texas Essential Knowledge and Skills English as a Second Language
Yours Truly, Goldilocks	
Activity Master 37: Focus on Language	4.26B, 4.26D, 4.26G, 4.28A, 4.28D, 4.28G, 4.30H
Activity Master 38: Essential Knowledge and Skills	4.28A, 4.29E, 4.29J
Activity Master 39: Focus on Comprehension	4.26A, 4.26D, 4.26G, 4.28A, 4.28F
The Hoboken Chicken Emergency	
Activity Master 40: Focus on Language	4.26G, 4.27B, 4.28D, 4.29I, 4.31E
Activity Master 41: Essential Knowledge and Skills	4.26A, 4.26B, 4.26D, 4.28D, 4.29I, 4.30A
Activity Master 42: Focus on Comprehension	4.28F, 4.29J, 4.31A
Fifteen Minutes	
Activity Master 43: Focus on Language	4.26G, 4.28A, 4.28F, 4.29E
Activity Master 44: Essential Knowledge and Skills	4.26G, 4.28G, 4.29F, 4.29I, 4.29J
Activity Master 45: Focus on Comprehension	4.26B, 4.28D, 4.28E, 4.30F
Sally Ann Thunder Ann Whirlwind	
Activity Master 46: Focus on Language	4.26D, 4.28A, 4.29I, 4.29J
Activity Master 47: Essential Knowledge and Skills	4.26A, 4.26D, 4.27A, 4.28D, 4.31A
Activity Master 48: Focus on Comprehension	4.28A, 4.29K, 4.30H, 4.31A
Ali Baba Hunts for a Bear	
Activity Master 49: Focus on Language	4.26B, 4.26G, 4.27A, 4.27B, 4.28A
Activity Master 50: Essential Knowledge and Skills	4.28D, 4.28E, 4.28F, 4.29C, 4.31A, 4.31E
Activity Master 51: Focus on Comprehension	4.27A, 4.28D, 4.29C, 4.30F
Thirteen Moons on Turtle's Back	
Activity Master 52: Focus on Language	4.26D, 4.27A, 4.28A, 4.29I
Activity Master 53: Essential Knowledge and Skills	4.26B, 4.26E, 4.27A, 4.27F, 4.30F
Activity Master 54: Focus on Comprehension	4.28A, 4.31A, 4.31E
Swimming with Sea Lions	
Activity Master 55: Focus on Language	4.26B, 4.26E, 4.28A, 4.29I
Activity Master 56: Essential Knowledge and Skills	4.26B, 4.31A
Activity Master 57: Focus on Comprehension	4.26B, 4.27A, 4.28D, 4.28F, 4.29C
The Great Kapok Tree	
Activity Master 58: Focus on Language	4.28A, 4.28E, 4.28F, 4.31A
Activity Master 59: Essential Knowledge and Skills	4.28E, 4.29C, 4.29D, 4.31A
Activity Master 60: Focus on Comprehension	4.26E, 4.27F, 4.28D, 4.28E, 4.29I, 4.30H
Dinner at Aunt Connie's House	
Activity Master 61: Focus on Language	4.26D, 4.26E, 4.27F, 4.28A, 4.28D, 4.29J, 4.30F
Activity Master 62: Essential Knowledge and Skills	4.26B, 4.28A, 4.28D, 4.28E
Activity Master 63: Focus on Comprehension	4.26D, 4.29I, 4.30E(iv), 4.31C
Rain Player	
Activity Master 64: Focus on Language	4.26C, 4.27F, 4.28A, 4.28D, 4.29E, 4.30F
Activity Master 65: Essential Knowledge and Skills	4.26B, 4.28D, 4.28E, 4.30F, 4.31A, 4.31E
Activity Master 66: Focus on Comprehension	4.26B, 4.27A, 4.28E, 4.28F
The Rag Coat	
Activity Master 67: Focus on Language	4.26G, 4.28A, 4.29E
Activity Master 68: Essential Knowledge and Skills	4.26E, 4.27A, 4.27F, 4.28A, 4.29E, 4.29I, 4.30F
Activity Master 69: Focus on Comprehension	4.26B, 4.28A, 4.28F, 4.30A, 4.30F
Teammates	
Activity Master 70: Focus on Language	4.26A, 4.26E, 4.28G, 4.29A, 4.30E(iii)
Activity Master 71: Essential Knowledge and Skills	4.26A, 4.27F, 4.28F, 4.29C, 4.29I, 4.30G
Activity Master 72: Focus on Comprehension	4.26E, 4.28A, 4.28D, 4.28E, 4.28F, 4.30F